# VENEZUELAN GOLD

## The CIA, a Colombian Cartel, and the Communist Chinese Clash for Oil in the Jungles of Venezuela

by
M. Albert Collins

*Other Books by M. Albert Collins*
Prelude to Pearl, 2014
Brazoria Sunrise, 2015
Race to War's End, 2018

Venezuelan Gold
Copyright 2012 M. Albert Collins
Copyright 2018, M. Albert Collins

ISBN-13 978-1-936539-90-1
ISBN-10 1-936539-90-X

*Venezuelan Gold* is a work of fiction, set in the geographic, economic, and political framework of the 1990s. Characters are either the creation of the author or fictitious portrayals of real persons, living or dead.

Venezuelan Gold (2018) revises the original Venezuelan Gold (2012). This revision, besides correcting typographical and grammatical errors, includes maps, updated historical references, and an expanded Epilogue.

Originally published in 2012 under the title of Venezuelan Gold
Revised 2018

Cover Illustration: Shutterstock_115189144, April 24, 2018
Interior Illustrations: Prologue Maps
North & South American Map:
     Modified by author from
     Wikipedia commons – http//commons.wikimedia.org/ commons
Northern Venezuela Base Map:
     Modified by the author from
     http://www.clipartbest.com/cliparts/9TR/Rxr/9TRRxr4ac.gif;

To
My wife, "Sam"

# PROLOGUE

Oil is discovered in Lake Maracaibo in western Venezuela in 1914, capturing international interest. Exploration and development—and financial investment—by foreign oil companies begin to transform the mostly rural and poor agrarian Venezuelan economy to an economy—and life—based on oil.

Extensive exploration of the Orinoco Hydrocarbon Belt—a rich, heavy crude oil-bearing formation in eastern Venezuela stretching from the Orinoco River on the Venezuelan-Brazilian border northeastward nearly 400 miles to the Atlantic Ocean—begins in the mid-1930s. Oil seeps along the coastal mountain range between the Caribbean Sea and Maturin, the capital city of the eastern state of Monagas, fuel the discovery of massive oil fields in the Maturin Sub-Basin north of the Orinoco Belt. Experts speculate that the hydrocarbon accumulations of eastern Venezuela could exceed those of the Lake Maracaibo fields to the west.

Venezuela becomes a significant source of oil for the Allied war effort during World War II. The years after World War II see widespread growth of political parties, labor unions, and a socially conscious-middle class. In 1960, hoping to push oil prices higher, Venezuela becomes a founding member of the Organization of Petroleum Exporting Companies—OPEC.

Domestic and foreign oil companies in Venezuela are nationalized on January 1, 1976. The Republic of Venezuela establishes a national oil company, naming it *Petróleo de Venezuela SA*—PDVSA. PDVSA is to manage and operate every facet of oil exploration and development in Venezuela. Foreign investment plummets.

Over the next decade, the hoped-for benefits of nationalization of the oil industry fail to materialize. By the mid-1980s, PDSVA is reconsidering its policies. It initiates the *aperturea*—oil opening— program to encourage foreign reinvestment in oil exploration and development by promoting competitively awarded Operating Service

Agreements. Under the auspices of a service agreement with a private—and usually international—oil company or consortium, PDVSA becomes the nominal operator of a specific oil exploration and development area, commonly termed a development "block," with the oil company providing PDVSA exploration and development services for the block. Recovered oil is the property of PDVSA and is sold on the open market. But PDVSA pays fees to the service company, with the net result that the oil service company commonly receives nearly two-thirds of all the revenues generated from the recovered oil. After years of decline, Venezuelan oil production begins to rise in 1985. By 1997, oil production has risen from 1.6 to 3.5 million barrels per day; imports to the United States more than triple during this same period.

— ~ —

In 1917, the U.S. Navy establishes a training center and submarine base at San Pedro, California. The facility expands into the adjacent city of Long Beach. By 1939, major facility development is underway, setting the stage for the facility to serve critical naval needs in World War II. After World War II, the base becomes one of the nation's premier naval shipyards. But in the early 1990s, downsizing of the base begins. The Port of Long Beach, already one of the nation's leading commercial shipping terminals, takes ownership of many of the Navy's former facilities.

In 1995, the Chinese state-run China Ocean Shipping Company—COSCO, a tenant at the Port of Long Beach since 1981—begins negotiating with the port for additional terminal space. The COSCO proposal to lease lands of the former Long Beach Naval Shipyard is endorsed by then President Clinton.

But on April 15, 1997, a United States Congressman from California announces bi-partisan opposition to the COSCO proposal, and Congress halts the negotiation of the 20-year lease sought by COSCO.

— ~ —

In February 1992, Hugo Rafael Chávez Friás, a career military officer, leads a failed coup d'état to depose the repressive Venezuelan government. Chávez is sent to prison but is pardoned two years later. Immediately upon his release, Chávez begins reorganization of his political supporters under the banner of the leftist *Movimiento Quinta República*—MVR—the Fifth Republic Movement. The unpredictable and, as some say, egotistical Chávez appeals to the Venezuelan masses—the poor and the working class—for their support as president. On December 6, 1998, Chávez wins the national election. Chávez rapidly initiates programs of road building, housing construction, and mass vaccination. Less noticed, he also begins to revamp a lax and, some say, corrupt tax collection and auditing system, focusing mainly on alleged abuses by major foreign corporations providing services to PDVSA.

— ~ —

After an absence of 38 years of Category 4 hurricanes striking the Texas coast, Hurricane Bret roars across Padre Island and Matagorda Bay along the southern coast of Texas on August 22, 1999. Because of the location of the hurricane's landfall, damages are limited. But there are repercussions for the lives of some ....

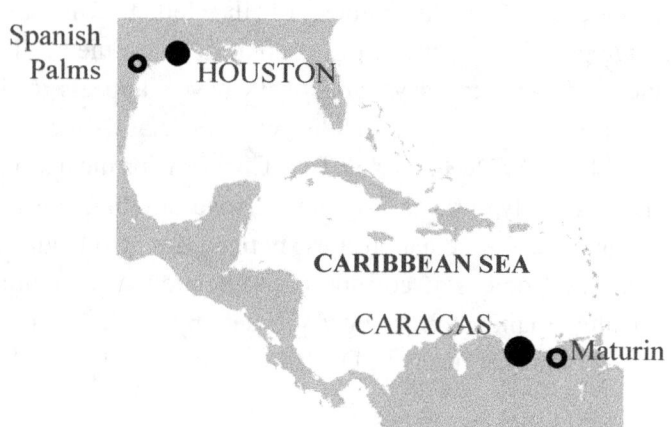

# I
# VOICES FROM THE PAST

## 1

"Why are you calling me, Grover?" growled Kelley Castellano, like a bear awakened from hibernation. "You know I'm off tonight."

He turned on the bedside lamp, pushed the sheet aside, and pulled his large, firm, but aging frame to a sitting position. He looked at his watch in the dim light of the lamp—almost 2:30 a.m. *Damn him.*

"Sorry, but we got a problem down here, Chief," Grover answered. "Thought you should know—right away."

"So, what's the damn problem?" Kelley ran his long fingers through his thinning black hair to bring some order to the tousled mass.

"A body washed up on the beach near Goldie's pier—a bunch of kids screwing around on the beach found it."

"A body—you mean we got another boat turned over again? Jesus H. Christ. When are those damn shrimpers goin' to learn not to go out in bad weather?" The western Gulf had been kicking up quite a bit the last several days because of a late August hurricane—Hurricane Bret—that had passed over the southern tip of Texas two days earlier.

"Hell, you handle it." Kelley looked at the woman lying beside him, the upper half of her naked body exposed by the twisted sheet. "I got more important things to take care of."

"More than that, Chief. The guy's head is bashed in."

*Damn, what shit has hit the fan now?* "Be there in a few minutes." Kelley stood and began tugging on his jeans. "Sorry, *dulcinea,*" he said to the woman, "Have to go."

"*Despuès*?" she invited.

"Yeah, later ... maybe," Kelley answered without much conviction. The woman's smile turned into a disgusted smirk. She rolled over and yanked a pillow over her head.

— ~ —

Ten minutes later, Kelley pulled into the gravel parking lot near the pier at Goldie's place, next to the two squad cars already there. Their still-flashing lights poked into the night, periodically illuminating a worn-out Volkswagen van. It had "Goldie's Beer, Shrimp, and Bait" hand-painted in large gold letters on its side.

Kelley wondered how many more years Goldie would continue to use the van—*it had to be at least twenty years old*—before turning it into a monument. Goldie's was an institution around Spanish Palms and the southern Texas coast. Goldie's father had built the pier, with its accompanying bait shop and bar, after he came back from Southeast Asia a few years after the American pullout—bugout was what Kelley called it. Some of the old-timers told Kelley, when they got a little drunk, that Goldie's father had used drug money to build the place.

Back then, Spanish Palms was little more than a hole in the wall for a bunch of shrimpers who spent as much time in Mexico as they did in Texas. But over the years, Spanish Palms had grown into an often used, easily accessed port for shrimpers to sell their high quality, succulent shrimp to willing buyers. And Goldie and her father, and then Goldie after her father died, not only ran the bar and pier but also became very savvy buyers and wholesalers of the shrimp unloaded at their dock.

It was different now, of course. The economic resurgence after Reagan's election had changed things. Spanish Palms had grown into a vacation community for people who couldn't afford Rockport up the Texas coast. Shrimping had become almost a sideline and was as much a tourist attraction as anything.

Kelley got out of the car. He looked up at the sky—it was really looking mean now, after the sky-clearing rain shower earlier in the day. Long, stringy clouds were filling the dark sky, blocking most of the light from the quarter moon. And the few lights strung along the edge of the pier gave only a tinge of color to the dirty beach sands near the pier.

Kelley walked to the edge of the parking lot, skirting some of the still remaining pools of muddy water. He saw a beam of light sprouting into the dark from what had to be the water's edge about a hundred yards away. He clicked on his own flashlight as he started angling his way across the wide beach toward a cluster of people. Kelley soon saw Grover jogging toward him.

"All right, Grover, what's the story?"

"I got the call from Reynaldo that some kids—they're over there," Grover said as he pointed a bobbing flashlight toward a small group of teenagers standing off to the side, as if seeking isolation from the several other people gathered about Reynaldo—and a dark mass lying in the sand at Reynaldo's feet. "They called in and said they found a body down here. I came right over. Goldie was waiting for me when I rolled up. Two of the kids said they was walking," Grover gave a smirk, "on the beach, and they found it—saw it in the sand. They said they ran to the bar and got Goldie to call the station. About that time, Reynaldo rolled up. We both went down to where the kids said it was and started to look at the body. That's when we saw the back of the guy's head—all bloody."

By this time Kelley had reached the body. Reynaldo shined his flashlight on it. It was half submerged in the sand. Small wavelets splashed across the sand to within a few feet of the body before they rolled back. Apparently, it had washed up on the rising tide. Kelley looked at his watch, noting the time and mentally estimating when the body would have likely gotten stuck in the sand on the in-coming tide—probably about ten or maybe as late as eleven—somewhere in that range.

Kelley swung his flashlight around to scan the beach along the water's edge—nothing unusual there. The beach was strewn with small logs and larger pieces of wooden planking, seaweed, bottles and cans, a few dead fish, their rotting smell already permeating the air, an old canvas tennis shoe, and a few other bits of unidentifiable debris from the stormy weather. This particular section of beach, because of its position opposite the inlet to the landside bay and the swirling currents that rising tides created there, was always a final resting place for current-carried flotsam during rough weather.

Kelley switched off his flashlight and turned back to look at the people gathered about the body. At one side of the group stood Goldie, her flaming—and dyed—golden blonde hair easily seen even in the limited moonlight, and, next to her, some guy Kelley didn't know.

A few steps away from Goldie stood Claudio, the old, grumpy Greek shrimp boat captain who worked out of Spanish Palms and regularly supplied fresh shrimp to Goldie for shipment north to restaurants in Chicago and other Midwest cities. Though she didn't say much about it—it really didn't fit the image she tried to paint for tourists coming to her bar—Kelley had a pretty good idea that Goldie made a hung of money buying and selling shrimp.

The group of kids stood some distance away, wanting to look at the body but apparently afraid to get too close. Another couple stood much farther back, as if not wanting to be near anyone. Kelley recognized them—the Weedens. They were a well-to-do retired couple from Chicago who came to Spanish Palms off and on during the year to spend a few weeks or so vacationing.

Turning on his flashlight again, Kelley finally turned to look at the body.

The body was face down. The wet clothes didn't look, as best Kelley could tell with the sand covering much of the body, out of the ordinary. They were like the ragtag clothes any shrimper might wear, except that the upper back of the man's shirt was covered with what looked like crusted blood. And on the backside of his head, at least what was left of it, was a massive, bloody, and pulpy looking gash— like something big and hard had been swung at the head of the man, found the target, and ruptured his skull.

Kelley bent down to examine the body more closely. "Grover, pull up the shoulder a little so I can get at the front side of the body," Kelley ordered.

Grover put his hand into the wet sand, pushing it under the shoulder of the body, and lifted upward. The sand gave off a sickening sucking sound as the body pulled free.

"Pull it up a little more so I can see better."

Reynaldo put his hand beside Grover's and lifted the man's shoulder higher.

Kelley shined his flashlight on the man's face—he gave a gasp and then coughed to cover his surprise.

"You ever see him before, Chief," Grover asked.

*Shit! What is Carrillo doing here—dead, and after all these years?* "No, no. I thought for a moment I did, but I haven't." Kelley pretended to study the face more.

Kelley reached into the large pocket on the dead man's shirt, hoping to find something, perhaps even a wallet. But, instead, Kelley felt a strange coldness coming from the body—a cold clamminess that was more than evaporation of wet clothes would cause. Finding nothing inside the shirt pocket, Kelley moved his hands down to Carrillo's pants' pockets. He didn't find anything in them either. Kelley pulled his hands away. "Okay, put it back down."

Grover and Reynaldo let go of the shoulder; the body fell with a small splash of water.

Kelley moved his hands to Carrillo's back pants' pockets, feeling for a wallet—again nothing, except for the strange coldness of the body. "Grover, you didn't pull a wallet off him before I got here, did you?"

"No sir, Chief," Grover answered.

"Reynaldo, what about you?"

"No, Chief, we didn't take nothing from the body," Reynaldo answered.

Kelley stood, still shaken by seeing the dead Carrillo. *What the hell is going on? No identification and dressed like a shrimper. Unless Carrillo changed his line of work from what we both used to do, he is—or was—not a shrimper.*

"Goldie, you're my witness. There was no wallet or identification on him when we first examined him. Got that? I don't want somebody saying we stole his money," Kelley said, still looking at Carrillo.

"Right, Chief," Goldie answered.

Kelley lifted his head and took a step toward Goldie. "All right,

Goldie, tell me what you know," Kelley ordered.

"I don't know nothin', Chief. The two kids over there, the girl with the big tits and the boy with the shorts," Goldie said as she pointed to the group of teenagers, "they started banging on my door up at the bar just as I was turning off the lights. They was yelling about this body and wanted to call the police. Me and Vic here came back down here to look, just to be sure they wasn't just shitting us. And it was like they said it was, so we went back up to the bar and called. Just waited there until Grover got here—we didn't touch nothin'."

"You sure you didn't touch anything?"

"Damn sure. I didn't want to touch nothin'," Goldie said.

"You Vic?" Kelley asked, looking at the man he didn't know standing beside Goldie. He was dressed like a typical weekend fisherman, although his large mustache looked out of place on him.

"Yeah, Vic Valdes—friend of Goldie's. We was going into town, maybe over to her place for a while as soon as she finished shutting down. We were doing that when the kids came up yelling," Valdes said with a slight Spanish accent.

Kelley could not remember seeing Valdes before—and Kelley was good at remembering names and faces, a skill he had learned long ago, one that had kept him out trouble quite a few times. "You're not from around here, are you?"

"No, I live in Houston," Valdes answered.

"How long have you known Goldie?"

"Well, ah ... quite a while ... so to speak."

"Dammit, you had better tell me the truth," Kelly said quickly/.

"Okay, okay. I know Goldie from some years back when I started fishing off and on around here. Came out to do some fishing down the coast a little—thought the weather would have died down by now. But it was still pretty lousy, at least for fishing. Decided to have a few cold ones in her place tonight. Didn't have to rush back to Houston tomorrow, so I thought we might just sort of ... ah ... well, you know," Valdes said.

Kelley knew. Goldie was easy to get along with, and she got along with a lot of men who came to the coast to fish and then didn't hurry home to their wives.

"Okay, I get the picture. So, what happened?"

"Just like Goldie said. The kids come banging on the door, and we went down to the beach and saw the body. When we did, we came back up to the bar and called."

"Touch the body?" Kelley asked.

"No—I only got close enough just to be sure it was a body," Valdes answered.

"Is your car around here?"

"No, it's at the motel down the street."

"Grover, you get this guy's name and address—check his driver's license to make sure he gives you the right address—and make sure he gives you his room number at the motel," Kelley ordered.

Grover opened his notebook and stuck his flashlight under his arm as Valdes pulled his wallet from his back pocket.

"Claudio," Kelley said as he turned to look at the old man, "what are you doing up here?"

"Can't shrimp now—weather too bad. I come to talk to Goldie about getting more money for the shrimp I sell to her," Claudio said.

"Did you?" Kelley asked, a smile coming to his face.

"No, she too hard to bargain with. I think about maybe selling my shrimp somewhere else."

"You won't get a better deal than I can give you, Claudio," Goldie said, unasked.

"Pipe down, Goldie," Kelley said, not wanting the two to get into a shouting match, something that Claudio, with his temper, often did when somebody didn't agree with him.

"Awfully late to be up here, isn't it, Claudio?" Kelley asked.

"I come early to talk to Goldie. Rain start, and I stay late to drink beer—no place else to go, so why not drink beer," Claudio said with a shrug of his shoulders. "Weather maybe better tomorrow, then I go get the shrimp."

Kelley looked at Claudio. "Okay, you give your name and address to Grover, just for the record."

Then turning to look at Goldie and both the men, he said, "When you all finish with Grover, you can leave, but I want you at the station by ten in the morning—no excuses. And that includes you, Claudio.

No shrimpin' tomorrow until you give a formal statement down at the station. When Mary gets in, you write out your statement, and she will type it up. Then you sign it. And Goldie, in the meantime, don't start blabbing all over town about this, okay?"

"Sure, Chief. I won't talk about it."

*Like hell you won't,* Kelley said to himself, knowing the body would be the hot topic all day when Goldie opened up. *But maybe I can do what I have to do before the news gets around too much.*

"Reynaldo, stay here by the body. I am going to talk to the Weedens," Kelley said.

"They didn't get here until after I did, Chief," Reynaldo volunteered.

"Okay, but I want to hear it from them." Kelley turned to walk toward the Weedens.

"Hello, Mr. Weeden, Mrs. Weeden. A little late for you to be up and about, isn't it?" Kelley asked as neared the couple.

"We flew into Houston—thought we might enjoy the car ride down here, but it was a bit more tedious than we thought it would be. By the time we got here, it was pretty late. We thought the walk along the beach would relax us after the ride," Weeden answered.

"Did it?"

"It was beginning to—we were just walking along, watching the moonlight on the waves and the café lights shining on the water. As we got about there," Weeden said pointing toward the edge of the beach near the parking lot, "when Officer Reynaldo drove up. He said there was a dead man on the beach."

"Did you see anybody around the body, anybody acting strange, besides the people standing out here right now?"

"No, we didn't, Chief. I wish we could help you, but we didn't see anything out of the ordinary," Weeden said.

"Okay. Would you both, for the record, please give your full name and address to Officer Grover over there? Then you can go home."

"Certainly, Chief," Weeden answered.

"Thank you, Chief," Mrs. Weeden said with a sigh.

Kelley walked back to the teenagers; there were eight of them. "Which of you found the body?"

"We did," a boy in shorts said as he waved his hand at himself and a girl in a halter top that didn't hide much.

"What were all of you doing here this time of night?" Kelley asked as he smelled the faint but pungent aroma of pot emanating from the group.

"We were just having a party—down the beach there," another boy answered as he pointed down the beach.

Kelley looked down the beach and could see what appeared to be the remnants of a small fire still glowing in the dark.

"So how did you two find the body if your party was way down the beach?" Kelley asked.

"We thought we'd walk up this way, maybe get some more ... cokes from Goldie's before she closed up," the boy in shorts answered.

*Dammit. Goldie is selling beer to kids on the beach again. I'm going to have to get on to her about that.*

"We got about here and saw something big at the edge of the water. When we got close to it, we saw it was a body. We ran up the beach to Goldie's and told Goldie—she and that guy with the mustache went right down to the beach," the girl in the halter top answered.

"Yeah, I don't think they believed us," the boy added.

*Surprise, surprise,* Kelley said to himself.

"That's right, but they did after they went down to the beach. She called you right away when she got back," the girl added.

"Did you see anybody else around, on the beach?"

"No, nobody. Only Goldie and that man, when we ran up to the bar," the boy in shorts answered.

"Anyone else see anything or anybody touch the body?" Kelley asked of the eight teenagers. Nobody said anything.

"All right. I want each of you to give your name and address to Officer Grover over there—he's the thin guy. Then you can go—but give the goddamn joints you have left in your pockets to Officer Grover before you leave," Kelley said casually.

"Pot ... Chief, we don't' have any—"

"Don't give me a hard time. The only reason I'm not running all of you in is because these two here called in when they found the body," Kelley said as he pointed to the boy in shorts and the girl in the halter top. "Next time I find you smoking pot down here, I'll bust you—got it?"

Grover walked over to Kelley. "Got everybody's name and address, Chief. What next?"

Kelley pursed his lips, thinking about what had been said by everybody. Something didn't seem to fit quite right, but he couldn't put his finger on it. Maybe it would come to him later.

"You get the names and addresses of all these kids—make sure you note which two found the body." Kelley turned to look at the group of teenagers. "You two that found the body come down to the station in the morning and give a formal statement."

Kelley turned his back to the teenagers, walked a few steps, and motioned for Grover to follow him. Then Kelley said in a low voice, "When you finish getting their names and addresses, get the pot they have on them. Make sure they give you all the joints they're carrying—check their pockets. Then send them home," Kelley said.

"What do I do about the pot?"

"Book it as crime scene evidence. Just say you found it on the beach," Kelley answered, thinking, *that's pretty close to the truth.*

"Crime scene? You think we got a murder on our hands, Chief?" Grover asked with almost palpable excitement.

"I don't know yet—could have been a fishing accident, but for the moment we treat it as a possible murder," Kelley answered, but thinking, *I know damn well this was murder.*

Kelley went back to his squad car and called into the station on the radio. "Sophie," Kelley said to the woman who manned the radio during the night shift, "you call Doc Henshaw and tell him to get down to the beach by Goldie's. I want him to look at a body before we move it. Tell him to bring that big camera of his, too. And get a hospital ambulance to come over from the med center. Tell them it's county business, and we need to take a body down to the county medical examiner's office. And do it damn quick. It won't be long before the tide starts back in—and it looks like another storm is brewing."

# 2

Kelley felt drained. He had followed the ambulance to the county seat to fill out the necessary papers at the medical examiner's office for an autopsy—on a John Doe found on the shores of Spanish Palms. During the drive, he remembered the times that he and Carrillo had spent in Nicaragua—and in the years before that, Venezuela. After the botched job in Nicaragua, he and Carrillo had never seen each other again. But that's what it was often like in their line of work—people moved in and out of each other's lives, like cogs in the machine of world politics. That was one of the reasons why he finally got out— too damn much behind the scenes, backstabbing politics.

The medical examiner came out of the examination room and approached Kelley sitting on the bench. Kelley stood, stretching his arms and legs.

"Well, it pretty much confirms what you thought. The man was dead before he hit the water. There wasn't any water in his lungs— seawater or fresh. The blow to his head is what killed him for sure. Whether it was a loose boom on some boat which swung into him and knocked him overboard or someone hitting him on purpose to kill him, I don't know."

*Well, it sure wasn't some damn accident*, Kelley said to himself.

"Another thing, his organs—strange," the doctor said with a professorial tone.

"Why's that, Doc?"

"Some of his organs, even some of his blood, were nearly frozen. His whole body—well, it looks like he had been in cold storage for some time, like a piece of meat. That's the only way that I can describe it," the doctor answered. "And I don't think the Gulf waters are that cold, so being in the water wouldn't explain his body temperature being so low."

Kelley remembered the coldness of Carrillo's body on the beach. "But being in a cold storage hole on a shrimper or a fishing boat for a long time—that could explain it ... right?" Kelley asked.

"Yes, that could be it, in a ship's fish hole filled with ice. Yes, that would explain the near freezing condition of the body."

"So, Doc, it could be that the body was stored in a ship's cold storage locker before it ended up in the water—"

"Yes, that is very possible," the doctor interrupted. "And if that's the case, he could have died almost anywhere. And that certainly suggests that things were not accidental unless someone went to a great deal of trouble to hide an accident."

"Not likely, Doc. But I'll tell you what. You need to keep the autopsy report under wraps. If it was murder, I don't want to tip my hand that we know it was—at least for the time being. Can you keep things quiet for a while, Doc?" Kelley asked.

"Umm," the medical examiner said as his face became stern and he pursed his lips. "Well—I can slow my filing of the report, get more red tape into the process, and keep it from getting into the public files for maybe several days—will that help some?"

"Anything will help, Doc." Kelley paused a moment. "I suppose, because he was in the condition he was, that you can't fix the time of death?"

"No, not really," the doctor replied. "It would have taken probably a day for him to get to the condition he was in, except that warming by the Gulf waters and the drive over here from the coast messes up any calculation based upon temperature, particularly if he was in the water a fairly long time. So, I can't give you any really good estimate. Sorry."

"Well, thanks anyway, Doc. I appreciate your help about the autopsy. I will be in contact with you about the formal filing of the autopsy report—and let you know when I can about the disposition of the body," Kelley said as he stuck his hand out to shake the doctor's hand.

"Chief, before you go, there is one other thing ... it is something I think you need to see. It's not what killed him, but it is something I've never seen before. Come back to the examination room with me, will you?" the medical examiner said as he turned and started walking down the hallway.

"What is it?"

"I think you had better see it," the doctor answered over his shoulder.

Kelley followed the doctor through the swinging doors of the examination room. A body—Carrillo—was lying on a gurney next to a table of instruments, a sink, and a door to a morgue. A pile of wet clothes was inside a large, clear plastic bag on the table. Except for its feet, the body was covered by a sheet. A tag dangled from one toe of the right foot. The doctor's assistant stood near the gurney.

The doctor approached the gurney—and the body. He removed the sheet, revealing Carrillo's naked body. The doctor instructed the assistant to lift the side of the body. "Take a look at his back," the doctor directed.

Kelley looked at Carrillo's back. Crisscrossing Carrillo's back were long-healed but large, ugly welt-like scars. Kelley was shocked by what he saw, but not because it was something he had never seen before. He was just shocked to see them on Carrillo.

"Are those what I think they are, Chief?" the doctor asked.

Kelley answered with a flat voice. "Yes. They're scars from being whipped."

"Who whips people like that in today's world?"

"Just about anybody who wants information bad enough, Doc," Kelley said without trying to hide his anger.

"And there is one other thing, Chief," the doctor said.

"What's that?" Kelley asked.

"When I cut his underwear off," the doctor said as pointed to the plastic bag of clothes on the table, "there was a card—like a business card—rolled up and stuck right under the fold of cloth across the crotch in his underwear—like it was being hidden."

"Card? Where is it?"

"Right over here," the doctor said as he picked up another plastic bag and gingerly removed a small, wet, rolled up piece of cardstock. It was obviously a business card, but not readable in its rolled-up condition. "I haven't tried to unroll it yet—afraid it might fall apart."

"Let me try, Doc. Give me some tweezers and some of those larger specimen plates by your microscope," Kelley said.

For the next several minutes Kelley carefully peeled back the edges of the rolled paper with the tweezers, laying the edge of the unrolled paper down on one of the glass specimen plates as he did, and using the other plate to gently squeeze the water from the card. When he had finished, he placed the second plate over the first, gently pushing downward to press out more water.

Kelley looked at the card through the glass of the specimen plate. It was printed in Spanish. It was still in good enough shape for Kelley to read: "Antonio's Night Club and House of Pleasure. Pleasant Ladies 24 Hours a Day. No. 5058 Avenida Bolivar, Maturin." A telephone number was followed by, "We provide taxi service." Kelley read the words to the doctor. Beneath the telephone number was the handwritten name, "Bettina."

"Maturin?" the doctor asked. "Where's that?"

Kelley paused as old memories came flooding back. "Venezuela, Doc ... Venezuela."

"Does that mean this guy is from Venezuela?" the doctor asked.

"I'm not sure what it means, Doc," Kelley answered slowly.

— ~ —

Four hours later Kelley was back in the Spanish Palms police office. The afternoon newspaper was spread out on the counter. It was already open to the news story on the drowning. The story was long on speculation and short on accuracy: An apparently Mexican national or illegal immigrant had been found on the beach at Spanish Palms, near a widely known eating establishment named Goldie's, after being washed overboard from an unidentified shrimp boat believed to be out of Mexico. Witnesses said that the man had been struck in the head by a boom before being sweep overboard during the hurricane that passed inland two days ago. The police were still investigating, according to Officer Reynaldo of the Spanish Palms police force. The police chief, the story went on, was unavailable for comment, apparently unwilling to disclose information about what may have been foul play. The rest of the article talked about previous drownings along the Texas coast, and how many of the victims were Mexican nationals working onboard fishing boats. *Jesus Christ*, Kelley thought, *what a bunch of bullshit.*

"Do you give out all this crap, Reynaldo," Kelley asked angrily as he looked at Reynaldo sitting at his desk behind the counter.

"Well, this reporter called from Corpus. I don't know how he found out about the drowning, but I didn't tell him much of anything," Reynaldo said.

"Well, apparently you—and probably Goldie—told him just enough so that he could fill in between the lines and get everything screwed up," Kelley said.

The phone rang. Reynaldo picked it up. A loud voice immediately began to come from the phone. "Yes, Mr. Mayor, yes, sir. There was a body found on the beach last night," Reynaldo answered in a few moments. More noise from the phone followed.

"Chief Castellano?" Reynaldo said as he looked at Kelley with questioning eyes, raising his eyebrows. Kelley shook his head. "Well, he's not here right now .... Yes, sir, I sure will. I'll tell him as soon as I see him." Another burst of noise followed. "Yes, sir, right away, sir, I sure will, sir," Reynaldo said as he finally hung up the phone.

"Well?" Kelley asked.

"Shit, he's mad—something about bad publicity making the town look bad. He said, quote, you tell him to get his ass up to my office right away, unquote."

"Well, I have got something to do first," Kelley said as he went into his office and shut the door.

Kelley picked up the phone and punched in a number he had hoped he would never have to call again. In a moment a voice came on the line. "Central Intelligence Agency. Give your identification and reason for calling."

# 3

The phone rang loudly in the Langley, Virginia, Central Intelligence Agency office of Assistant Deputy for South American Operations-Northern Hemisphere, Admiral Francis Marian. He kept it at high volume all the time now, ever since his hearing had started deteriorating a few years ago. His age was finally beginning to really catch up with him. He wondered how many more years they would let him sneak past the standard retirement age. He picked up the receiver and pressed it against his better ear.

"Marian here."

"Admiral, this is Samuelson. I have bad news. Carrillo has apparently been murdered."

"What!"

"We got a call about an hour ago from a sheriff—a chief of police, actually—down on the Texas coast. He said Carrillo washed up on the beach late last night, apparently murdered. He called one of our monitoring stations here at the Agency about an hour ago to notify us," Samuelson said.

"Carrillo! Damn. Are we sure it was murder?"

"Pretty likely. The cop said Carrillo had been struck on the head and then apparently thrown overboard from a boat somewhere out in the Gulf of Mexico. Carrillo sure wasn't out in the Gulf on a vacation," Samuelson answered.

"But how did the cop know to call one of our monitoring stations? Carrillo wouldn't have anything on him that would tie him to the Agency ... unless—"

"That's right, Admiral. I ran the cop's name through our computer. He is, or at least was until a few years ago, one of ours."

"Who?" the admiral asked.

"A guy named Kelley Castellano."

"Kelley Castellano! I'll be damned. All right, you shut down everything tight on this until we find out more. What's the name of the place down there where Castellano is?"

"Spanish Palms. It's on the Texas Gulf coast—somewhere between Galveston and Brownsville," Samuelson said with an uncertain voice.

"Well, I think it's about time I took a trip to Texas. You contact Kelley; tell him to keep a tight lid on this until I get there in the morning," the admiral ordered.

— ~ —

The admiral saw Kelley standing at the side of a police car near the end of the short runway as the plane taxied toward the tarmac in front of the administration building. As the plane jerked to a halt, the plane's two propellers slowed, but never stopped their rotation. The plane continued to wobble slightly.

Inside the plane, a bushy-haired Navy pilot opened the cockpit door and yelled, "Okay, sir," as the copilot got up and went back to the cabin doorway.

The admiral undid his seat belt, slowly got up, and moved cautiously to the doorway. As the door was opened by the young lieutenant, steps unfolded and linked the plane to the ground. The admiral climbed down and looked toward the parked car. Kelley had already started walking to the plane.

The admiral put out his hand. Behind him, the officer put the admiral's small travel bag on the ground.

"Well, aren't you a sight for sore eyes, Admiral. When I got your message that you were coming, I didn't believe it. I thought you were probably retired by now. But except for those civvies you're wearing, you look about the same, sir—maybe just a little more gray in the hair, maybe a few more wrinkles," Kelley said with a smile.

"Well, you're looking good, too, Kelley—except you have a bigger gut than the last time I saw you." Kelley laughed.

The admiral bent down and picked up his bag, waving away Kelley's offer of help, saying, "I'm not dead yet."

Kelley and the admiral got into the police car. The Navy plane taxied away. As the police cruiser turned onto the main roadway along the airport, the plane was already winging its way toward the naval air station at Corpus Christi.

"Well, Kelley, I was wondering where you ended up. When we finished down there in Nicaragua, you sort of went off like it was the end of the world. I was wondering how you were going to get things straightened out," the admiral said.

"Yes sir, it took awhile. Had to let the wounds heal, so to speak. I bummed around for a while trying to find something not too hard to do but something I was sort of cut out for. Tried getting back into the oil patch again—but shit, I found out pretty quick I was getting too old for that—I'm not a young buck teenager anymore. Then I heard about this job opening down here for police chief—my uncle Raphael put me on to it. My police days in El Paso turned the trick,

I suppose—and I think my uncle called in a few chits with some people he knows in law enforcement. And for the way I was feeling, it looked like a pretty good deal."

The admiral frowned.

"No ... no, I didn't tell anyone what I was really doing in El Paso—I just gave my cover story," Kelley said with a reassuring smile. "But it was, sort of, police work anyway—and I am a licensed peace officer here in Texas, so it's all legal. It's okay work, and it gives me plenty of time to fish. Best combination you could have. Hell, they even give me a place to live—nothing fancy but okay."

The admiral looked at Kelley with a tilt of his head. "So, everything is going okay—and you're okay?"

"Sure am. This is great down here," Kelley lied.

The admiral looked at Kelley and smiled.

— ~ —

The sun had passed its zenith when Kelley stopped the car down the road a short distance from Goldie's pier. Kelley and the admiral walked out to the beach.

"The kids found the body about here. This beach faces right out onto the channel to the Gulf so the body could have been dumped way out somewhere, particularly since the currents were probably pretty strong about that time. We have been having a lot of stormy weather in the last several days because of the hurricane down south. The autopsy was finished by the county M.E. yesterday. He faxed over a preliminary write-up of his report to me this morning," Kelley said as he withdrew three pieces of paper from his shirt pocket, unfolded them, and handed them to the admiral.

The admiral read the first sheet. "I see the medical examiner says death by a blow to the head. But he doesn't say whether it was accidental or not. Any doubt in your mind that it was murder?" the admiral asked.

"Hell, no."

"So, what do you think happened?"

"The M.E. said there wasn't seawater in the lungs, so he was dead when he was thrown into the water."

"Anything else?" the admiral asked.

"Damn straight there is," Kelley said as he pointed to a paragraph on the second sheet of paper in the admiral's hand. "It looks like he had been kept in cold storage quite a while before he was dumped into the sea."

The admiral studied the paragraph to which Kelley had pointed. "Well, it looks like that could be the case. So, he might have been held captive somewhere, somewhere cold ... a meat locker maybe, and then brought near here, somewhere along the coast and then dumped into the Gulf."

"Could be," Kelley responded. "Or, more likely I figure, he was killed and shoved into an ice-filled fish hole on the boat he was on—most good-sized fishing boats have them—and kept there a pretty long time before he was dumped overboard."

"So, does that mean the boat was not from around here—that it came from a long distance?" the admiral asked.

"Maybe, maybe not," Kelley said as he shrugged his shoulders. "The way I see it, they knocked Carrillo in the head and put him in cold storage on a boat until they—whoever 'they' are—got ready to really get rid of him in a safe place. Try to make it look like he was killed wherever he would be found."

"Sounds like somebody didn't want anyone to know where Carrillo really was when he was grabbed and murdered," the admiral said as he stroked his chin.

"Probably so. It looks like they went to a lot of trouble to do that. Maybe whoever wanted him killed thought by dumping him into the ocean the sharks would get him and leave nothing, or if something was left, not enough to make it look anything but like an accident. But the sharks didn't get him. He came ashore too soon for that—which makes me think that either he was killed by a bunch of amateurs, or they were in a rush. Something happened, and they didn't have time to think it all out."

"Which would be consistent with not being far offshore when he was thrown into the water—for some reason they ran out of time, got scared by something—and had to get Carrillo off their boat as quickly as possible," the admiral said.

"Yes, maybe, but by what?" Kelley asked.

"Another boat? Maybe a boat that might discover Carrillo's body onboard if they didn't get rid of it right away," the admiral said as he again stroked his chin as he thought through what he had just said.

"A cutter—a Coast Guard cutter," Kelley said with deliberation. "It might have been a Coast Guard cutter."

"That could be it. When I get back to Langley, I will have a check run on all cutters operating in the last several days in the area and get a report on their operations. They might just have run across something," the admiral said. "What time did he wash up on shore?"

"Given the location of the body and tide conditions the night before last, I would say it was somewhere in the range of ten to eleven."

"I'll have our oceanography people back at Langley see if they can backtrack where he might have come from based on when you found him and the tide conditions."

"Good luck. The currents were probably pretty screwed up by the hurricane—but maybe they can figure out something."

"What did you find on him?" the admiral asked.

"He had nothing on him, except shrimper work clothes. No identification, no wallet—except for one thing."

The admiral looked expectantly at Kelley. "What?"

Kelley told the admiral about the rolled-up card that had been found in Carrillo's undershorts—and what it said.

"Maturin? Well, that might be the connection. Carrillo was working in Venezuela."

"Doing what?"

"You know I can't tell you that, Kelley," the admiral said firmly.

"Okay, none of my business," Kelley responded. "But there is one other thing, Admiral. Carrillo's back—it was covered with old whipping scars. He went through a real torture session sometime back. Did you know about that?" Kelley asked.

The admiral shifted his eyes to watch the surf roll in for several long moments. Then he turned to look at Kelley. "Yes, I did."

"Well?" Kelley asked.

"I don't think you really need to know, Kelley."

"The hell I don't. Carrillo was a friend of mine—he saved my life a couple of times," Kelley said.

"You're not on the Agency payroll anymore, Kelley. You don't have a need to know. And it doesn't have anything to do with his murder, so forget it," the admiral said firmly.

— ~ —

It was early in the morning of the next day. Kelley and the admiral were at the landing strip again, waiting for a plane to arrive. All the details that Kelley had found or he and the admiral had been able to deduce had been discussed, and a cover story for Carrillo's body had been created.

In two days, the FBI would call Kelley and the county medical examiner's office to inform them that a fingerprint match had been made for the prints the medical examiner had forwarded to Washington—something the medical examiner would do at Kelley's request when he called him later in the day. Carrillo would be identified as a veteran who had physiological problems and for a number of years been wandering about the country doing odd jobs. Carrillo's father, actually a CIA agent, would come to Texas a few days after that to claim the body. Shortly after that, the investigation would be taken over by the FBI, under the guise that Carrillo was probably killed in far offshore waters under federal jurisdiction, not the jurisdiction of the State of Texas—and Kelley wouldn't object. With the takeover of the investigation by the FBI, Spanish Palms could forget about the body on the beach and return to its sleepy, quiet, normal self.

The admiral turned his eyes to look up at the morning sky. "Kelley, I want your help in finding out what happened to Carrillo—and why. And because I want your help, I am going to tell you what Carrillo was doing," the admiral said as he clasped his hands behind his back.

"Admiral, Carrillo and I were friends—good friends—but I've done all that I can. It's up to you and the Agency to figure out the rest. I left the Agency, and don't intend to go back," Kelley said firmly, thinking, *I left it, dammit, and I had enough of it—its endless back-stabbing conniving, its constant bending to gutless politicians, and the loss of good people, like Carrillo.* Kelly wasn't about to succumb to the admiral's arm twisting.

"Just hear me out, Kelley," the admiral said.

Kelley sighed. "All right, go ahead, but I am not going to get involved with the Company again."

"Carrillo was investigating drug trafficking out of Colombia and Venezuela. W know that a lot of drugs move through the Lake Maracaibo area in western Venezuela and then north to the U.S. We were—and still are for that matter—hunting one particular cartel: the Metillo cartel operating out of the Puesto Asis area in central Colombia. They are using the oil business to move their stuff. Some of the oil field operations in the Maracaibo area are less than one hundred miles from the Colombian border," the admiral said.

"The coca paste is smuggled out, we believe, as part of the oil business traffic—on tankers or cargo ships from the oil fields bound for Panama, the U.S. or Mexico—something like that. Somehow the drugs are smuggled ashore along the Gulf coast, maybe unloaded before the ship gets into port, or maybe after it docks—we don't know," the admiral said with a disgusted shrug. "Carrillo had been working for me on this investigation for almost a year. We think he was getting close to figuring out what was going on."

"But, Admiral, I thought drug smuggling was not in the Agency's area of responsibility—isn't that State and DEA's responsibility? I would have thought the Agency would know better than to stick its nose into areas it doesn't belong."

"Normally, I would agree with you, but on this one, Kelley, we are not stepping outside of our authority," the admiral said. "We think several Colombian drug cartels, under the leadership of the Metillo cartel, may be trying to use the oil business in a much more insidious way than ever before to move massive amounts of drugs into the U.S."

"What makes this different from what they have always have been trying to do—or should I say, what's so different now that makes the Agency take an interest? Hell, Admiral, those drug cartels have been bribing people right and left for years down there," Kelley said with a smirk. "What's happening to make things different now?"

"Your right, Kelley. Something has changed—or might be going to change if we don't stop it. That change is why the Agency is taking such an interest."

The admiral sighed. "The Colombian cartels have been trying to stir up trouble in Venezuela in the last couple of years, just to distract government drug interdiction so the cartels could move their stuff up Lake Maracaibo and into Gulf ports more easily," the admiral said.

Then, lowering his voice, the admiral continued, "But here's what's really different. From the bits and pieces that we have been getting and from what Carrillo was beginning to find out, we think the cartels are trying to weasel their way into much higher levels of government—not just bribing border inspectors or police, but controlling actual government officials in the national oil business so that they can manipulate oil shipments to move their drugs: Set the timing on shipments, or maybe redirect them to places where they know they would have less inspection—somehow make it easier to get the drugs on or off a ship or be less likely to be found on a ship."

Kelley nodded in agreement. "Something like that—you're right. It might cause some real problems for us,"

"Might—hell, there's no might about it," the admiral said. "If they were to start manipulating how oil is shipped out of Venezuela, it would affect everything we are trying to do down there, not just what the DEA is doing. Haggling over oil shipments would wreak havoc in our relations with Venezuela. All DEA's joint efforts with the Venezuelan government to stop drug movement through their country would probably just go down the drain."

Kelley began to think through the enormity of what the admiral had said. "But to make something like that work, wouldn't a cartel have to have the cooperation of the oil company the cartel was directing to change its shipping patterns? The DEA would know pretty quick exactly which oil company was cooperating with the cartels if a company went along with a cartel in fixing schedules for transporting crude back to the U.S. And if an oil company was doing the bidding of a cartel, then they could be dealt with directly by U.S. law. The oil company could be hauled into court here in the U.S., even if the cartel couldn't be touched," Kelley reasoned as he stroked his cheeks.

"And, if the company could be hauled into a U.S. court so easily—

so to speak—why would the company want to become involved?" Kelley asked rhetorically.

After a pause, Kelley answered his own question. "The big oil outfits wouldn't—they would have too much to lose if they were exposed. But small companies, particularly those that are closely-held corporations already skirting the law to make big profits—at least while they can—they might just be drawn into such a deal, either to hide something else going on or to make under-the-table profits."

"That exactly what we figure, Kelley."

"Damn, if a cartel can get some deal like that setup—controlling oil shipments to the U.S. with the help of some oil companies— a double whammy. The volume of the drug shipments would go up, and we wouldn't even know what was going on."

"And there's more than that, Kelley, and this is the scary part. If the cartels start disrupting the export of oil to the U.S., or anywhere else for that matter—that affects our whole economy. We could have gas lines again like we had back in the Carter administration."

"Well, from what I see in the newspapers, with Chávez's election last year, our relations may not be so hot with Venezuela right now anyway. I guarantee you, Chávez is just another power-hungry commie-in-disguise like Castro," Kelley said with cynicism.

"Well, maybe, but he isn't purposely trying to screw things up—at least not yet. We may not have the best relations, but they would get a hell of a lot worse if some Colombian cartels get to the point of controlling oil exportation from Venezuela. And if they were to do that—or just try to do it—we are moving from simple drug trafficking to international subversion of a government—and that *is* Agency business," the admiral said with conviction.

"Okay, you convinced me. But it's still your business. And I'm out of your business," Kelley said firmly.

"I really think you are the best man for this job, Kelley. You worked down there before—and you know the oil patch. More importantly, you know how Carrillo's thinks—or did think. I want you to pick up where Carrillo left off. Find out who killed your friend and why. Find out what's going on and how we can stop it."

"Shit, Admiral, I came here to get away from things like that. I don't need to get back into that line of work again. Hell, I'm out of shape for it anyway," Kelley protested.

"The hell you say. I don't need you for how fast you can run a mile. I need somebody who knows Latin America—knows Venezuela—and who can dig out information like you can. You know more about what happened to Carrillo than anybody, except the guy who did it. I need you, Kelley," the admiral said with no equivocation, but with no hint of begging.

Kelley clinched his teeth, saying nothing.

The admiral looked Kelley in the eyes and then spoke as if the weight of the world were on his shoulders. "I need someone I can trust, Kelley—really trust. Something smells very bad about this whole thing. I'm afraid maybe someone on our side has gone across the line and started working for the bad guys."

"Like I said, Admiral, I'm out of the Agency," Kelley said as he slowly shook his head.

The admiral looked silently at Kelley for a long time, then sighed. "I am going to tell you something, Kelley—about Carrillo—something you don't know but maybe, now, you should."

Kelley looked at the admiral with questioning eyes, wrinkles coming to his forehead.

"You remember the last several days of that fiasco in Nicaragua—before we could extract you and your team?" the admiral asked.

"Of course, I do. If the government's army goons had found out where we were going for the pickup, a bunch of people, including me, wouldn't be alive today. But Carrillo wasn't on my team, so what does he have to do with that."

The admiral looked at Kelley with unblinking eyes. "Well, that's not quite right. Carrillo was with a second team, a backup team, which for security reasons we didn't tell you and your team about. If things started falling apart—which they did—Carrillo's team was to move in and help get things straightened out and—"

"Whose fucking, stupid idea was that?" Kelley asked incredulously.

"Someone at the director's level—or higher," the admiral answered.

"Shit. Fucking politicians again," Kelley said with disgust.

"I don't disagree with your sentiments, Kelley, I don't disagree. But that's the way it was. But, unfortunately, Carrillo's team didn't get a chance to help you out. He was caught because, we later found out, one of his team had sold out. But we did learn about his capture before you and your team were to be picked up—that's why we shifted the pickup location at the last moment."

"I always wondered about that," Kelley said.

"But Carrillo didn't know about the change. So, when the Nicaraguan security people tried to get the location for the pickup out of Carrillo, he did his damnedest not to break and tell them. But he did break, but only after being tortured so badly—his back is testimony to that—that his torturers couldn't believe that he wasn't telling them anything but the truth. And Carrillo thought it was the truth. That's why you and your team weren't wiped out at the pickup site—that's why you are alive today," the admiral said. "As for Carrillo—we were able to arrange a hush-hush agent swap later to get him back."

— ~ —

A solitary, moaning buzzing sound came from the sky as a two-engine plane began to sink toward the runway. A few minutes later, it rose upward with its single, aging passenger.

# 4

Kelly sat in his usual place by the window eating a late lunch and drinking a beer. The few people in the cafe knew him and wouldn't mind. Besides, he needed to relax—and think. It had been two days since the admiral had left and he was still troubled—no, not troubled, More than that: guilty about what the admiral had told him about Carrillo.

He was halfway through a chicken-fried steak when the phone behind the counter rang. "Yeah, he's here," the cook said. A few moments of silence followed. "Okay, I tell him." The cook hung up the phone.

"Hey, Kelley," the cook called to Kelley, "Mayor Cranston's secretary just called. The mayor wants you to come to his office, pronto."

"Aw, shit. Did she say what he wanted? Did it sound like an emergency?"

"I don't think so. She just said get over to his office," the cook answered.

Kelley debated with himself awhile. *Crap.* Kelley threw down his napkin. He wasn't finished with lunch, and he had hoped to have some of the pecan pie that was sitting under the glass cover on the counter.

*That damn Cranston. Ever since that guy was elected last year, he has been a pain in the butt. And he is just looking for a reason to fire me. Cranston's brother is a lowly sergeant on the Galveston police force looking for some job somewhere as a chief—like my job.* And from what Kelley knew about him, Kelly figured Cranston's brother was probably on the take—like some of the mid-rank officers there in Galveston who were just "good old boys."

Kelley decided he had better go. "Put it on the tab," Kelley said to the cook as he sighed and stood up.

"Sure thing, Chief," the cook said with a wave of his hand.

— ~ —

"You wanted to see me, Mayor?" Kelley said as he entered the mayor's office at the small bank building which also had offices that served as the city hall.

"Yes, I did. What are you doing about that murder down on the beach? Have you figured out what happened? How long is it going to be before you find out who did it? We are getting bad publicity about that thing—and that is not helping our tourist trade here. You are just taking too long to figure out who did the murder. The newspapers won't let it go—even the *Houston Chronicle* is still carrying the story in its back pages. And I can't say that I blame them. You seem to be pretty inept at finding out anything."

Kelley was finally able to get a word in. "It's a difficult case. Besides, we don't have clear evidence yet that it was a murder—it could have been an accident—"

"What? You don't even know if it was an accident or a murder! What the hell have you been doing the last few days?" the mayor fumed.

"Mr. Mayor, the man was not even from around here. We haven't got conclusive evidence one way or the other. But the man's fingerprints have been sent to the FBI in Washington, and they are running a check to see if they have him in their files." Kelley didn't want to say more. The next step in the admiral's plan called for Kelley to wait for a call from the FBI, which was scheduled to come later in the day.

"So, you still don't know who he really is yet, do you?" Cranston's voice was getting louder.

"No, but I am checking it out," Kelley said quietly.

"I don't think you have any idea what to do. I think you need help—I know you need help. I've put in a call to the Galveston Police, to get some assistance from them," Cranston said.

"You what!" Now he knew why Cranston had summoned him.

"What the hell do you think you're doing? This is not a Galveston police case—Galveston is not even in the same damn county. And I suppose you just happened to request some help from," Kelley was getting angry, "that sleazy brother of yours."

"Sleazy! That is insubordination. He will be here tomorrow. He is very good at what he does," Cranston shot back.

"Yeah, I bet he's very good—at getting money on the side to look the other way," Kelley said with flat finality.

"That's it. I am bringing you up before the council next week. We are going to have a vote as to whether we need to keep you around here anymore. Now, get out of here!" Cranston shouted.

"Don't worry, Mayor. You can have this job and shove it. You'll have my resignation in the morning," Kelley said with contempt.

A smirk came to Cranston's face as Kelley turned and walked out.

— ~ —

The phone rang only twice before it was answered.

"Marian here."

"Admiral, this is Kelley."

"Hello, Kelley. How are things progressing?"

"Right on schedule, Admiral. I got the official call from the FBI a little while ago. I have got things set up so the transfer of jurisdiction will be made without any hitches as soon as they arrive."

"So ... got anything else on your mind?" the admiral asked.

"Yes, sir. That offer you made ... for me to help. Is it still open?"

"Damn right, Kelley. Have a change of heart?"

"I guess so," Kelley said meekly.

"Well, I was wondering how long it would take you to change your mind. How soon can you get on a plane and get up here to Langley so we can talk about details?"

"Damn soon."

# II
# THE LATIN
# CONNECTION

## 5

Sitting in his office in the Government House of the State of Monagas in the capital city of Maturin in northeastern Venezuela some 400 kilometers east of Caracas, the governor of Monagas State, Juan Francisco Uriarte y Esquivel, read again the new policy that was to be formally announced tomorrow by the *Ministro de Minas y Hidrocarburos*. Its title was impressive: "Policy for Equitable Lease and Use of Mineral and Petroleum Resources of Venezuela for the Benefit of the People of Venezuela." In essence, it said that award of future mining and oil development leases in the various states of Venezuela would be made with due regard to not only economic considerations—which in practical terms meant the size of the bid made for a service agreement with PDVSA—but also the welfare of the people of the state in which the development block in question was located.

Uriarte smiled to himself. The power-hungry Chávez was finally making good on his promises to repay the very sizeable political favors that Uriarte had exhausted on Chávez's behalf to help Chavez win the presidency in the last national election. Uriarte knew that after Chavez's failed coup—which many still believed laughable—of nearly seven years ago, Chavez would have never gained the presidency had it not been for Uriarte's help.

Now, as repayment, Chávez's had guided the behind-the-scenes maneuvering of Julio Munguia, one of his chief political henchmen, to assure that the new "equitable lease" policy would be proclaimed by the Ministry of Mines and Hydrocarbons and endorsed by the powerful Board of Review of the National Assembly.

Uriarte knew much of the policy was purely bureaucratic nonsense, merely things to expand the need for people in the government to review and monitor petroleum development activities, things that increased the need for more people in the government's employ—and more people beholden to Chávez. But hidden far down in the policy was the requirement that was at the core of why Uriarte had so often subtly, and sometimes not so subtly, reminded Munguia of the political debt Chávez owned to him.

The new policy required that for a service agreement bid to be valid, the governor of the state in question had to provide to the ministry a certification—a certificate of benefit—that the welfare of the people of the state was being adequately addressed by any bid that might be made for a petroleum development block in that state. The governor, in turn, was to reach his decision about such certification with the advice and counsel of representatives of the people in the state. And who was to select those representatives? Why, the governor, of course.

Uriarte clenched his fist. He knew potential service agreement bidders, the large—and wealthy—American and British oil corporations, would quickly realize the importance of the new policy and, in particular, the importance of the certification that would have to be provided by Uriarte.

Uriarte knew he now had the power to make or break the viability of a service agreement bid. And he fully intended to use that power to assure that the welfare of the people of Monagas would not be shortchanged.

*Of course, the well-being of the people of Monagas is clearly tied to the strength of the PHC—Partido del Hombre Común—the Party of the Common Man, of which I, Juan Francisco Uriarte y Esquivel, am chairman. Strengthening the PHC can do nothing but improve the lot of the citizens of Monagas.*

It was the political support of the PHC that Uriarte was able to bring, as national leader of the PHC, to the '98 election that had assured the victory of Chávez—and Chávez knew it. Chávez could not carry the national vote with only the Caracas region supporting him—there were just not enough people living there. He needed a strong vote from the petroleum-rich states around Lake Maracaibo in the west and the state of Monagas in the east, an area where the PHC was strong. And when the national election came, Uriarte had delivered his party's vote to Chávez as he said he would.

Uriarte turned to look at his appointments secretary Eulogio Marulanda, his political aide and confidant of many years, who had been sitting quietly after bringing Uriarte the document announcing the new policy.

"Eulogio, you realize the importance of this policy to our party?" Uriarte said excitedly. He continued without waiting for an answer. "Our party stands for the common man. Contributions to the party, which you and I can gladly receive on its behalf, from potential service agreement bidders can help enormously in filling our party coffers."

"*Si*, it is good news," Eulogio replied. "The money we have had to expend to assure continued support for Chávez has put a severe strain on our resources. Your efforts to have this policy adopted have finally born fruit—and now we can begin harvesting that fruit."

As treasurer of the PHC, Eulogio Marulanda was intimately aware of how many of the PHC's political resources—not only substantial pecuniary inducements but also personal favors long held in reserve—had been exhausted on behalf of Chávez. To win the election, Chávez had to appear to have a growing groundswell of widespread political support by members of the PHC, not only in Monagas but in Anzoátegui and the less affluent but adjacent states of Sucre and Delta Macuro, where the PHC strength was limited but where Uriarte wanted PHC power to grow. That was why Eulogio had devised the concept of such a policy and subtly suggested it to Uriarte more than two years ago as a means to rebuild their party's coffers.

"This policy," Eulogio predicted, "will allow us to fill the void created by our support of Chávez and his election as president—if we are careful in how development blocks are carved out in the future. Block sizes must be kept small so that the potential bidders will be many."

"So true, Eulogio," Uriarte said as he nodded his head. "As always, you recognized the importance of details. This will continue to be an important responsibility for you—working with the ministry and PDVSA in Caracas, as you have done so effectively in the past on other matters, to assure the appropriate delineation of blocks and the qualification of many bidders. I want to you build an even stronger personal relation with Minister Bonilla—and assure that he understands our needs. But do it carefully—you must not evoke the ire of Chávez. You and I both know the distrust they have of each other."

"I fully understand, but if I were to have to take sides—"

"Don't take sides," Uriarte broke in. "But if you must, let it be the side of Chávez. Ultimately, he has and will continue to have, with our support, the final power. But without our support, he has nothing—and he knows it. He does not have enough support, within his own party, to run this country. There is only so much he can do without our support and agreement. He likes to think he is in complete charge—that he is all-powerful, even if we know better. We must court him as if he were an emperor, as you and I know he seeks to be. But as his power grows, so will ours. So, we must support Chávez—or so it must seem to him and that sycophant Munguia when in truth it is for our benefit. As for Bonilla, if it were not for Bonilla's wealth and power in the country's elite circles, I have no doubt but that Chávez would replace Bonilla."

"That is likely true," Marulanda responded.

"More than likely—it is for certain! But, that is with what you must deal at the moment. I," Uriarte paused with an air of importance, "will look to our future. As our party coffers are replenished, we must build a stronger party, one that can span, someday, the entire country, and one that will have not to sell its votes to others, like the MVR party. Someday our party will be stronger than Chávez's MVR, and who knows what we might be able to accomplish then, Eulogio—perhaps even the presidency."

Then Uriarte gave a small laugh. "But, of course, Eulogio, that possibility is something that you and I need only know—I do not think our president is prepared to relinquish his position just yet."

# 6

Arturo Benavides y Metillo looked intently at the man in front of him standing on the patio of the palatial hacienda about a hundred kilometers from the Colombian city of Puesto Asis in the southeastern Colombian state of Putumayo. The cool breeze from the mountain ridges marking the edge of the Andes not far to the west was strong enough to give a slight ruffle to the shirts of the two men. It was a welcome respite to the midmorning humidity that always clothed the hacienda because of the nearby jungle forests.

"This is a very bad situation, Alexis," Benavides said. "Killing some American drug officer here in Colombia is one thing—something with which we could easily deal. The Americans expect that type of thing to occur here in Colombia—they believe we are a lawless country. But to kill such a man in the United States, or let it even appear that is where he was killed—that can cause us much difficulty. Killing an American agent on American soil makes the Americans think that the cartels are invading their homeland; they could become unpredictable and truly dangerous. We will have to redouble our efforts to overcome what has happened."

"I know," Alexis responded. "But Valdes says the newspapers seem to be treating it as an accidental drowning of a fisherman along the American Texas coast. It has been more than a week now, and Valdes has reported nothing to indicate otherwise. The police in the town where the body washed ashore have no suspicion—they do not even know the man's name."

"Impossible! I don't care what the newspapers say—or what Valdes says," Benavides exploded. "You and I know—and Valdes should have known earlier than he did—what the man was. Valdes should not have had to be told that he was an American DEA agent; there could be no other reason why he was snooping around."

Benavides' face became contorted. "The American DEA will soon know, if they do not already, of the man's murder. They are not going to announce to the newspapers what they know. Valdes is just trying to pretend that his operations are still safe so that we will continue to use him—and not blame him for what happened. But he should know better than to pretend all is well."

"So, Arturo, what should we do?" Alexis asked.

"We have already done some of what we must do. We have taken some drastic action, but it was necessary. Getting rid of Huerta was the first step. If he had been arrested, the consequences would have been dire. You handled that in an excellent fashion—including the woman. Our Maturin contact was helpful in dealing with her?"

"*Si*, quite helpful," Alexis confirmed.

"Good. Do not forget his usefulness to us—we may have to use him again," Benavides ordered.

"*Si, si.* His efforts have been rewarded."

"So, even if the police were to suspect some foul play, there is no path for the police to follow. They can do nothing," Benavides said as a smile came to his face.

Alexis returned the smile, happy that Benavides was pleased with what Alexis had arranged—and particularly glad that Benavides was placing all the blame for the foul-ups on Valdes.

"If only Valdes had gotten rid of that DEA agent like he had been told, things would be perfect," Benavides said with a shake of his head.

"Do we stop shipping with Valdes?" Alexis asked.

"No. Valdes' market and connections to the north are our most lucrative—right into the heart of the *gringos*' land without the middlemen as we have on the west coast. No. We do not stop working with Valdes, at least for now. We just must reach him by a different route—a very different and much safer route—one for which it will take many years for the American DEA to uncover, or at least stop its use," Benavides said confidently.

"Do you not intend to expand our routes through Barcelona, like the cartel has discussed before—as we had once planned to do?"

"No, more than that, Alexis, much more than that. Valdes' Barcelona route is just a small group of insignificant fishing trawlers. Even if we could add more trawlers, it is a minuscule operation—

*insignificante*—when compared to what I now plan. And the Barcelona operation has too many people, too many boat transfers—that the American DEA agent was able to infiltrate himself into the operation demonstrated that. No, we are going to move ahead with our original plan, despite the killing of the American. We will not draw back in fear as the cartel wants. We will move forward, but on a different, more secure path—and on a more grand scale."

"You mean the Maturin route in eastern Venezuela—we will still try to open it—as you have talked about before?" Alexis asked with surprise.

"Yes, Alexis, yes, despite the bungling of Huerta." Benavides looked intently at Alexis. "It is time to take matters into our own hands. We cannot wait for the others in the cartel to make up their mind about what to do. I did not approve of giving Huerta the responsibility that he was, but I was outvoted," Benavides said with disgust.

"Huerta should have never put himself in such a precarious position—where he might become arrested by the Venezuelan police. If he had used an intermediary as I wanted, Huerta might be alive now. Our friend in the governor's office would have been an excellent intermediary, but, no, Huerta knew better than we—better than me. And his clumsy attempt to bribe Bonilla: it just proves his ineptness."

"Yes, it does. And because of it, your plan to have someone in the highest levels of the Venezuelan government assisting us has been bungled," Alexis said in a disheartened voice.

"Yes, our plan to bring Bonilla into our web and what it meant for our ability to reduce cargo inspection—yes, that plan has been disrupted. But if we have the courage, we can do something better," Benavides said with conviction.

"Do you feel that is wise, Arturo? The cartel—"

"Yes, Alexis, yes," Benavides interrupted angrily. "The others in the cartel are the ones that let that idiot Huerta try to take the initial steps in expanding our routes through Barcelona. All he could do was get himself tangled up with Casares and, except for your intervention, almost get arrested in Venezuela," Benavides said without trying to hide his anger.

"But, Arturo, if this DEA agent uncovered information about Huerta's intent, might not others know what we intend to do?"

"Well, that is perhaps the only thing that has gone right in this mess. His death in America, despite the clumsy way it was handled, got the agent out of Venezuela so that no one would connect him with our current operations through Barcelona. Our actions may have prevented the Americans from becoming aware of our trawler operations, but it has also surely raised the suspicion, and anger, of the DEA to a new level. And Valdes should have recognized that possibility when he was getting rid of the body so ineptly."

"I agree, Arturo. Huerta and Valdes made a terrible mess of things," Alexis said, nodding his head.

"Yes, and that is why you and I, Alexis, must work together to overcome their stupid mistakes," Benavides said conspiratorially. "The DEA agent's death only makes the need for more secure routes more imperative—that means we must forget about using Barcelona as soon as possible and begin using new routes that Maturin can provide us. We must move rapidly, or some others in the cartel will try to gain control of the new routes. And I am not going to let that happen. No one else is going to control those routes."

"Yes, I suppose using a new route through Maturin would be a good thing to do, but it will take considerable effort to get it well organized," Alexis said without enthusiasm. "And will it really be worth the effort?"

"Yes, the Maturin route will be much better—worth every bit of effort to make it work," Benavides said with a satisfied air. "The Maturin route will be so different, so much better, than what we do now—even better than what it would have been even if Huerta had been successful with Bonilla and what we proposed for Barcelona. It will enable us to ship product—directly and safely—not only to our existing distribution points along the American coast but many new points as well."

"But how do we establish such a new route? And why will it be different than what we already do now—what we do through the Barcelona route?" Alexis asked.

"It will be different, Alexis, because you and I will make it different, far more effective, far more lucrative than the cartel could even begin to imagine!" Benavides said with excitement.

A questioning look appeared on Alexis's face.

"What is it, Alexis, that Americans need more than anything else from South America?" Benavides asked retrospectively.

Wrinkles came to Alexis's brow.

"Oil, Alexis, oil! And where do they get that oil? Venezuela, Alexis, Venezuela," Benavides said as he answered his own question, his eyes aglow.

"But, Arturo, we make use of the Lake Maracaibo oil operations now to help move our goods," Alexis said. "And what we proposed for Bonilla was intended to capitalize on his influence on oil operations. So, what would change?" Alexis asked.

"Change, Alexis, change? I will tell you what we can change, Alexis. Do you think we really make effective use of the power that the oil gives us? No!" Benavides said as he slammed a clenched fist onto the table, making coffee jump from his cup to the white linen tablecloth.

"We use the Venezuelan ships and people—because they go north—but we don't really use the power of oil. And our plan for Bonilla did not really use that power—it did not have the grandeur, the greatness of what I plan to do now."

"But, Arturo, how would things be different? The route will be different, but that will only mean we will have to bribe different officials—officials which Bonilla knows and with whom he could help us. What would change from how we operate our Maracaibo routes now?"

"It will be different because we will use control of oil to strangle America, and force them—the Americans, Alexis, the Americans— to close their eyes to our shipments! Search and inspection will come to a halt; nothing will impede the movement of our product directly into the United States. We will use new routes the Americans do not know and for which no inspection will be done, even if they were to know about them. Is that not a grand scheme, Alexis?"

"It is, Arturo—but the Americans, to close their eyes—how, Arturo?" Alexis asked.

"We will restrict the flow of oil to America. Where now they get one-fourth of their oil from Venezuela; they will get nothing unless they agree to Venezuelan demands to reduce their inspection and control of not only oil shipments but all Venezuelan goods into the United States! While the American public will not know, the American government will know that if Venezuelan demands are not met, the flow of oil will dwindle to a trickle," Benavides explained.

"But how can we get Venezuela to do that—to do that would require decisions at the highest levels in the Venezuelan government—at the ministerial level, or perhaps even by Chávez himself. Decisions would have to be far different than merely reducing inspection of cargo in Venezuelan ports," Alexis said with skepticism.

"You are absolutely correct, Alexis. And that is why I intend to have a special friend to us become the next minister of mines and hydrocarbons. A friend in such a high place can bring the Americans to their knees—and assure us virtually unlimited entry of our product into the United States," Benavides said with satisfaction.

"But how can we do that unless Chávez replaces the oil minister— and I don't see how Chávez can do that. Minister Bonilla is a powerful, and rich, man. He is not beholden to Chávez. Chávez may detest Bonilla, but with Bonilla's power, his influence—and Huerta's crass attempt at simply bribing him may have only alerted Bonilla to what the cartel was thinking of doing," Alexis said.

"You are correct, Alexis. But if the current minister were to become unavailable—permanently—to perform his duties … well … a new minister would have to be appointed, and Bonilla … well, he would no longer be a concern," Benavides said with a smile.

"But how—" Alexis started to ask. Then he stopped, his voice turning cautious, "Do you think it wise, Arturo, to involve us so directly in Venezuelan affairs—eliminating a Venezuelan minister?"

"I see no real problems if it is done so one will suspect—and the rewards will be enormous. And it will cut the link between Huerta and Bonilla; get rid of the one remaining loose end that Huerta's bumbling created. We might have had Bonilla in our pocket if Huerta had handled it right. But even if Bonilla were in our pocket, we still would have no assurance that Bonilla would have agreed with what we now plan—and certainly, the prospect of doing that appears unlikely now. I have already started considering how a convenient and unsuspecting accident, which you can so conveniently arrange, might occur to the minister when he is without his bodyguards. I have already instructed our contacts in Caracas to provide reports on the minister's activities and interests. I am sure his bodyguards cannot watch his every moment. The opportunity is there. We merely must find it," Benavides said with assurance.

Alexis let out a deep sigh. "I hope you are right, Arturo."

"I know I am. But to make the whole thing work, we must have someone in the right position to be appointed by Chávez as a replacement for the departed minister, someone we can trust—and control—and whom Chávez will appoint because of his considerable indebtedness to us."

"But do you really think Chávez will go along with what we want?"

"Of course; he has no other choice. Chávez knows that without our support he cannot remain in control of his MVR party. Chávez will appoint him because we shall tell Chávez he must appoint him. But, of course, we will present our desires to him only as a suggestion—we must protect his ego—but let him realize our continued financial support of his MVR party might be affected if he does not concur with our suggestion. Our Caracas contacts in the MVR party will be able to get our message to him—they maintain important contact with Chávez's lieutenant, Munguia. And Munguia does not have to know why we want this person as a replacement; it is enough only that we want it. Chávez will have no more than an inkling of what we are really going to do until it is done. By then, our power will be unbreakable. Can you imagine the power we will have!"

"No, I cannot, but who, Arturo, would that replacement be?"

"I think our friend in Maturin is the perfect choice. Make a call to him tonight and ask him to join us here as soon as possible for some important discussion," Benavides said with a confident smile.

# 7

"... and damn, Kevin, if it wasn't for the support that all you independents gave me during my election—well, you can be damn sure that I won't forget you when Cronin and his crowd try to change that exploration set-aside—damn sure," Senator Roland Beal said as he looked out the large window of his spacious River Oaks home in northwest Houston to watch the limbs of the trees being whipped back and forth by the wind of an early, howling September rainstorm

"Well, Roland, I ... we ... will all appreciate that. The Coalition was proud to be able to give you its support." *Coalition—ha! What I did, mostly*, Kevin Matthew thought. The independent producers in Texas, Oklahoma, and New Mexico, a large number of which were members of the Coalition, weren't really that keen on Roland Beal for United States senator. It was a more a matter of alternatives. Roland Beal had gained only marginal support from the oil producers in Texas after a lackluster, so far as most oilmen were concerned, three terms as a congressman.

But when the office of junior senator from Texas came up for grabs, Beal seemed to be the only realistic choice for those whose livelihood depended directly on oil development in Texas and other states of the Southwest. And, fortunately for Beal, during his last year as a congressman, just before he made the decision to run for senator, Beal had successfully sponsored a little-noticed—at least by the majority of voting congressmen—amendment to the president's economic stimulus bill. The amendment created significant rewards for what were described as "small" oil exploration and development companies.

The bill allowed oil companies, like Kevin's Trans-Texas Petroleum Development and Field Services Company—"Trans-Texas Oil" as everybody in the business called it—and other exploration and development firms doing business in no more than three states—international business activity was conveniently not included in the limitations—to make nontaxable set-asides for exploration equipment needs. The set-asides could be made using profits from good years to pay for equipment—so broadly defined as to mean virtually anything—which would be needed for the lean years when profits were small—sort of a rainy-day fund, or so Congressman Beal had, with his mellifluous tones, described the amendment during the short discussion on the floor. The limits on the nontaxable set-asides were generous, and the tax implications for firms like Trans-Texas Oil were considerable—and lucrative. That, along with Kevin's hidden support, had pleased the Coalition and—after the election—continued to be a base of support for, now, Senator Beal.

Kevin had been a consistent, if not highly visible, supporter—which meant giving lots of money—over the years to Beal's campaigns, as far back as Beal's early years in the Texas legislature—or the "Animal House" as Beal had referred to it on more than one occasion. When Beal decided to run for Congress, Kevin was not about to lose the influence and behind-the-scenes power he had gained by latching onto the coattails of Roland Beal ever since their college years when Kevin had helped Roland become senior class president. So, Kevin formed a coalition of independent oil producers—The Coalition for a Strong Texas Economy—to generate what appeared to be broad-based support for Roland's run for Congress.

In reality, much of the Coalition's support was provided through Trans-Texas Oil. Trans-Texas Oil had actually put up most of the Coalition money—considerably more than the law allowed—by some conveniently arranged subcontracts to many of the members of the Coalition. The subcontracts were for providing almost nonexistent services to Trans-Texas Oil at a very high price—a price that generated excess profits for Coalition members that just happen to end up in Roland Beal's campaign fund. And it had worked. Roland Beal had been elected with a sizable majority.

"But you and I both know that the first job of an elected official is to make sure he gets elected again. That's the only way to survive and be around long enough to really help your constituents. You start getting ready for the next election the day after you get elected," Beal said.

*Getting ready—yeah.* Kevin knew what that meant: more money. *Well, first, I need to start recouping some of the money I shelled out for this last election.*

"I certainly know that, Roland. And that's really sort of the reason I'm wanted to talk to you today before you head back to D.C. I know that we need to start developing support for your re-election. And I have some specific ideas that might contribute quite a bit to that over the next couple of years," Kevin said.

"Really? What do you have in mind?"

"The board of Trans-Texas Oil has decided, at my urging, that we expand our operations in Venezuela. You and I both know that's where the real action will be for the next several decades. Promises to be a whale of a money machine down there—if we can get things set up right," Kevin said enthusiastically.

"Venezuela! Are you sure Trans-Texas Oil is ready for that, Kevin?" Beal asked.

"Damn right I'm sure. Trans-Texas has been supplying drilling services and equipment for the majors down there for almost five years—whenever they run out of people or equipment they call us. With all the customs delays and red tape for moving exploration equipment and supplies into and of the country, they need us to handle the work that they can't do—and that they are obligated to do under their contracts with PDVSA," Kevin said with firm confidence.

"PDVSA? Oh—yes, *Petróleo de Venezuela*, the national oil company," Beal said with a sudden look of understanding.

"Right. And we've made good use of the experience we gained. Now Trans-Texas is ready to get out on its own down there. Instead of just getting the leftovers, we can sit down at the table and eat the main course," Kevin said, hoping to infect Beal with his enthusiasm.

"I didn't realize things were going so well, Kevin," Beal said with surprise.

"Sure are," Kevin said, wondering just how long things could go on in Venezuela without some significant new influx of money into Trans-Texas. He was locked into things, and they could blow up in his face if he didn't make things pan out—and soon.

"The country opened up the oil business to private out-of-country firms in the late '80s. Maybe PDVSA theoretically holds a monopoly on oil development, but their service agreements are just a sham—international companies are the ones who really run the oil business down there. But you know a lot about that, already, I guess—what with your chairmanship on that subcommittee on commerce and trade."

"Ah ... yes ... I'm generally knowledgeable of the situation down there, though not intimately aware of the details," Beal said.

Kevin continued, knowing that Beal, as usual, was covering his ass with his "generally knowledgeable, but not intimately aware" phrase to which he often resorted. "I know Chávez doesn't appear to be too concerned about democratic ideas, but that's no big deal for oil exploration—in fact, it maybe helps. It can eliminate a lot of the red tape in getting things moving," *or*, Kevin thought, *provide a better opportunity for payoffs to make things happen quicker.*

"Chávez? Oh, yes, he does seem to be perhaps moving the country toward socialism, doesn't he?" Beal said.

Kevin gave a smirk. "Chávez is not going to upset the apple cart; he's got too good a thing going. He knows how his bread is buttered. The real power lies with the oil ministry."

"You are probably quite correct about that, Kevin," Beal said with attempted authority.

"The oil ministry—Ministry for Mines and Hydrocarbons, that is—has already gone through several rounds of bidding for oil development tracts," Kevin continued. "The last round was almost two years ago, and the word is out that they are probably going to formally start another round of bidding soon, probably around the first of the New Year. Now is the perfect time to get in on that round—if you get yourself positioned right. And I have already started getting positioned. I have formed a new subsidiary: *Tejas Petróleo de Venezuela.* It's already licensed to do work in Venezuela. If Tejas can get a good exploration block for the right price, I—the company—can make some real money. And, of course, Roland," Kevin paused to make sure that Beal would catch the significance of his next words,

"*Tejas Petróleo* could work with the Coalition to establish an international arm—in a completely legal setup, of course—that could be very supportive of your campaign, even more than the Coalition has ever been able to do in the past."

"But how can you be so sure that you can get the right block for an acceptable price—the majors can put up a hell of a lot more money than Trans-Texas—uh, Tejas. If you don't win the right lease, then you've got nothing—isn't that right?" Beal asked.

"That's where you come in, Roland. As chairman of the subcommittee on Latin American Commerce and Trade, you just might have some ideas for legislation that could promote greater hemispheric trade for small businesses. Maybe there could be some type of set-aside, or maybe even a special government loan fund for appropriately qualified small companies to promote greater international economic cooperation in critical business sectors—like oil," Kevin said.

"Well ... I suppose ... it might be a possibility," Beal said. "Of course, you know," Beal continued as he looked at Kevin with an appropriately serious look on his face, "there would have to be hearings—to examine the issues. But, since such a bill would be for small business—and everybody knows the pressures facing small business—they might be rather perfunctory. Couched in the proper language, and given proper rationale and justification, and written so that one entity does not seem to be singled out, it might be pretty easy going. Can't guarantee anything, of course, but there is a good chance such a bill might be readily tacked on to some other more general legislation and move pretty quickly through the Senate and onto the House. If necessary, an amendment might be tacked on during joint conference committee hearings that will most certainly be set up to resolve the differences on the President's foreign trade bill," Beal concluded.

"Right! Once potential backers, from the Coalition and others that I am talking to about Tejas, see that the right legislation was going through, even if it would take a while for it to be become official— well, investors will be clamoring to get in on the ground floor. Money would be no problem then," Kevin said confidently.

"You think that contributions to my campaign would be helped by the legislation we are talking about—benefits for small business always seem to have widespread support?" Beal asked almost rhetorically.

"Damn sure they would, Roland. Your legislation could be a win-win situation for everyone. With the right legislation, the people with the money will be fighting to open their pockets for your reelection," Kevin said enthusiastically.

"I'll talk to my chief of staff in the morning and get him started on laying out the verbiage for an amendment to the new trade bill. That bill is likely the best vehicle for tacking on what we are talking about. We can use the same language, more or less, that we used for that legislation back when I was in the House—before I ran for the Senate. And I think we could schedule some hearings by mid-October—plan to have them right after Cinzia and I get back from her birthday celebration in Venezuela," Beal said.

"That sounds really good, Roland."

"Yes, I think by the end of October we should be really able to be quite confident about the amendment being accepted. Do you think the timing will be adequate for working with your prospective investors in Tejas?"

"I believe that will work out fine," Kevin answered as he winced to himself. The timing was going to be tight; he would have preferred to start the hearings before Beal went off to Venezuela, but there was little he could do without showing Beal how flimsy the whole scheme really was. If Beal, or his wife Cinzia for that matter, got a whiff of his concerns, Beal might just get a case of stage fright and back out of the whole deal.

"One thing, Kevin. You are going to be relying a lot on, I suppose, how you can work with the necessary people in Venezuela. You know how unpredictable those people are down there, don't you?" Beal asked with a hint of concern.

"Sure, I do. And I plan to care of that—with your help again, help that the Coalition wouldn't forget. To make sure that we get the right reception by the Venezuelan oil ministry, perhaps your wife's brother, Jorge, might like to sit on the board of directors of Tejas—he could help put in some good words for us at the right time down there," Kevin suggested.

"Jorge? But why?"

"Isn't the sister of Jorge's wife—your sister-in-law—married to some guy in the Venezuelan government down in one of those states of eastern Venezuela—Monagas or something like that?" asked Kevin, as if he didn't know many details.

Beal paused a moment, trying to think through the convoluted family relations that his marriage to Cinzia Maria Valentina y Cappadoro had produced. "Yes ... that's right. Eulogio ... Marulanda, I believe his name is. He's the chief aide to the governor of Monagas ... apparently a longtime confidant to the governor, and, I think, some type of important political party official. I've been there to Monagas several times—went with Cinzia for some big family get-togethers. Marulanda introduced me to the governor of Monagas—even had dinner with him. He might only have been running for governor when I first meet him ... I'm not sure. This governor ... the name sounds like urine or urinate ... something like that."

Beal laughed; Kevin laughed with him. "At least that's the way I remember it. He heads up some offshoot political party—big enough, though, to get him elected several years ago. That Monagas place, at least what I saw of it around the capital—I think it's called Matdor ... Metindor ... no, Maturin ... that's it, Maturin—is like a third world country filled with ranchers, oil field workers, farmers, and people thinking the government should take care of them, mixed in with a lot of swamps, palm oil plantations, cell phones, TVs, beggars, and people trying to get a handout from the U.S."

"Marulanda, you say—aid to the governor; that's interesting," Kevin asked in mock surprise.

"Yes, very tight with him, as best I remember. He probably could be quite helpful in getting in to see the right people and all—if you could get in to see him. But, I guess that's where Jorge could probably be a big help," Beal said with a questioning voice.

"Yeah, you're probably right about that, Roland. Jorge could probably help out quite a bit."

*At least I damn well hope so*, Kevin thought.

"About Jorge ... wouldn't he have to be a major stockholder in Tejas to be on the board?" Beal asked.

"Well, that would be no problem. Tejas shares will be going at a very low cost, at least initially—being a new company and all, and before the word gets around about your proposed bill in Congress. Probably less than a few pennies a share. But when Jorge's connection to the governor becomes known and your bill is on its way to passage—well, who knows? The share price might just skyrocket, and there will be plenty of money for making a solid—and guaranteed to win—bid," Kevin said with a satisfied smile.

# 8

Eulogio looked down at the coastline as the airplane made its final turn toward the Simón Bolívar International Airport at Maiquetia on the seaside edge of the mountains separating Caracas from the Caribbean Sea. Less than two weeks had passed since the announcement of the equitable lease policy, and already feelers were already being put out by the foreign oil companies doing business in Venezuela.

In telephone discussions with the Ministry of Mines and Hydrocarbons, Governor Uriarte had been told that major oil companies from the United States, the United Kingdom, the Netherlands, and even the Chinese had been calling the ministry about the new policy.

When Eulogio suggested that he go to Caracas and make some discrete contacts with the oil companies, Uriarte thought it an excellent idea. Eulogio officially represented only the PHC, not the government, so, there could be no accusation of impropriety. But, just to avoid any such possibility, Eulogio would maintain a low profile, not contacting any senior ministry officials of his presence in Caracas—unless it seemed really necessary. But not having to inform anyone of his arrival in Caracas also served another useful purpose. Since no one was expecting him, he could make an important side trip.

As the plane landed and Eulogio exited it at the eastern end of the in-country terminal, Eulogio quickly picked up his bag and took a taxi into Caracas. After checking into his hotel, he hung his clothes in the closet and ruffled the bed, as if it had been slept in. Leaving the room, he hung the *No Molestar* sign on the door and went down the stairs and out the back door of the hotel.

Eulogio walked two blocks down the hill from the hotel and then flagged a taxi. "Aeropuerto," he directed the taxi driver.

Returning to the airport he had left less than five hours ago, he bought a ticket for Bogotá, Colombia. Five hours later he arrived in Bogotá. After a fitful night of sleep, he arose early the next morning and rented a car. By nightfall, he had reached the city of Puesto Asis.

Eulogio checked into a hotel and took a shower. After dressing in the same clothes in which he had arrived, he went down to the street—and to a public telephone in the square a block from the hotel. Stepping to the phone, he pulled his phone card from his wallet and inserted it into the card slot. In a moment the phone emitted a buzz, and he punched in a number.

After several clicks interspersed with silence, a voice answered, "*Hola.*"

Eulogio thought he recognized the voice. "*Hola.* Alexis, is that you?"

"Yes. Is that you, Eulogio?" Alexis asked.

"Yes, it is I, Eulogio. I am here in Puesto Asis. Could you send a car for me—in the morning?"

"Certainly. I will pick you up at the usual place by the square—at ten. I will be driving a black SUV."

— ~ —

Benavides greeted Eulogio warmly as Eulogio and Alexis got out of the SUV. "It is a welcome sight to see you, Eulogio. Please come into the house—it is much cooler there."

"It is a pleasure to see you again, Arturo," Eulogio said.

As Benavides led the two men into the large living room of Benavides' hacienda, he spoke again. "A drink, my friend. What would you like?"

Eulogio answered. "Just a Polar—it is too hot for anything else."

"Fine," Benavides said. "Alexis, did you have any problems in town—no one took any particular notice of you did they?"

"I do not think so, Arturo," Alexis answered.

"And your luggage, Eulogio?" Benavides asked.

"I left it at the hotel in Caracas—as far as anyone knows, I am still there."

"Good. Now, my friend, Eulogio, as to why I was so anxious for you to come and talk with me: It is about a plan, a very important plan that I have for expanding my operations, and something that will be very important to you—personally. But, it will take time to describe, so I think you should rest before dinner—take a bath, put on fresh clothes. All the clothes in the closet should be your size. We can discuss the details of my plan after dinner."

"*Gracias,* Arturo. I would like that," Eulogio answered.

"Juanita," Benavides called out as he turned his head toward the back of the room. A slim, attractive teenage girl entered the room. "Please take *Señor* Marulanda to the guest room. Help him select his clothes—and help him with his bath, if he desires," Benavides ordered.

"*Si, Señor* Benavides," the girl answered with downcast eyes.

"I shall see you at dinner, my dear Eulogio. Relax and enjoy yourself until then. Juanita will be available for your pleasure during your stay here," Benavides said as he turned back to Eulogio with a smile on his face.

# 9

The three men sipped their wine from their lead crystal glasses. The dinner plates had been cleared and the servants ordered to leave the house and return to their quarters. The men were alone.

"And now, Eulogio, let me explain why I have asked you here," Benavides said as he put his glass down. "As you know, with the cartel's contribution to the PHC's coffers in the Maracaibo area, your party has not only been able to prosper and grow, it has also allowed us to carry out our activities with very little interference from military and police forces. In only eight years—only eight years," Benavides said as Eulogio nodded, "the shipments of our product to Panama and across the Gulf to the north have multiplied by more than four times. The cartel is now the major supplier to Texas and several states of the American Midwest. Times have been good to us, have they not, Alexis?" Benavides said as he tilted his head toward Alexis.

"Yes, very, Arturo. Times have been very good to us," Alexis answered.

"Let me ask you, Eulogio, why do you think things have gone so well in the last several years?"

"Well, the demand has increased, of course, and, I would say, our payments to more senior officers and government officials have increased," Eulogio answered, wondering, *what is Benavides leading up to?*

"Yes, that is correct, Eulogio—particularly the payments to the right government officials. We used to bribe only the customs officers—but now we go to their bosses and their bosses' bosses. The higher the government officials we bring into our fold, the more successful we have become. And you and the PHC have prospered—have they not? Have you ever regretted our relationship, Eulogio?" Benavides asked, watching Eulogio closely.

"Of course not, Arturo. I value it enormously," Eulogio answered, knowing only one answer was acceptable, but in fact telling the truth.

"That is what I hoped you would say, Eulogio, because I have a plan to make us both richer and more powerful," Benavides said. Taking a sip of wine, Benavides' eyes seemed to glow.

Eulogio wondered what Benavides had in mind.

"I and others of the cartel have decided to expand our routes through eastern Venezuela. We wish to initiate new—and very major—routes through Maturin, and I want your help in doing that."

*New routes through Maturin—interesting, but dangerous,* Eulogio thought. "Why are new routes necessary; what is wrong with the current routes? It would seem that going through Maturin will only lengthen the route, Arturo—and make it more dangerous. Your contacts must be well established along your existing routes."

"That is just the problem, Eulogio. They are probably getting too established. We are reaching the point that, despite the money we pay for government inspectors and the military to look the other way, our routes may be becoming unsafe—too easy for the American DEA agents to find them and arrange to intercept our shipments," Benavides said as he refilled Eulogio's wine glass.

"So, you wish to ship through Maturin—"

"And perhaps through Barcelona as well—at least by means other than we currently use," Benavides interjected.

"Oh, Maturin and Barcelona. I suppose we will have to begin to identify appropriate police and customs officials in Barcelona and Maturin. It may take a while for everything to get set up. But, dear Arturo, you said these routes would make us richer and more powerful. How will these routes accomplish more than what our Maracaibo routes have done?" Eulogio asked.

"Because we will use them in a totally different way, Eulogio," Benavides said. "I want to make our shipments using American oil companies—doing work in eastern Venezuela. But to assure that use of the oil companies will be successful, we are going to do something more, much more, Eulogio. I want American inspection of the oil company shipments to stop—so there is virtually no chance of our product being discovered!" Benavides said with a clenched fist. "And," Benavides beamed, "make them stop inspection of other goods, as well!"

Eulogio was incredulous. *How could Benavides believe the Americans would stop their inspections?* "Arturo, how can that happen? We may be able to bribe some of the American customs people, but to have the customs people just stop inspection—I just don't see how that is possible," Eulogio said.

"Oh, I know it won't happen overnight. It will take time, but it will happen. And I will make it happen—with you, Eulogio," Benavides said as he stood and reached across the table to shake Eulogio's shoulders as if in congratulations.

"With me? What do you mean, Arturo?"

"You will be the Minister of Mines and Hydrocarbons, Eulogio! With you as the minister, you can cut the flow of oil to the Americans to a trickle—unless the inspection stops. Of course, it is not something that would be admitted in public, but we will let the

Americans know what we want their customs officials to do—or more precisely, not do—if they want their oil shipments to begin again," Benavides said.

*What an outrageous plan—so outrageous that it just might work!* Eulogio speculated. "But, Arturo, I am not the minister—and there is no reason for a new minister to be appointed by Chávez—he would have to have an extreme reason to demand resignation," Eulogio hoped Arturo would not become angered by his apparent resistance to his plan.

"Ah, but, Eulogio, if Minister Bonillo were to suffer some unfortunate accident—an accident leading to his death, a new minister would have to be appointed," Benavides said, as he sat in his chair with a confident, reassuring smile.

*My God*, Eulogio thought, *Benavides wants to kill the Minister of Mines and Hydrocarbons! I can't get mixed up in that—but still, to become the next minister, next to the president, one of the most important men in Venezuela.* The idea was intoxicating—and had the added benefit that he could become free of Uriarte. His only reservation was how to assure that he could not become linked with Benavides' dirty work.

"Arturo, it would be very dangerous for me to be put in a position of even suggesting that I might have something to do with the ... demise ... of the minister. I just could not get ... personally involved."

"I do not expect you to become personally involved, Eulogio—not at all. I just want you to be prepared to come to the aid of your country when the president must appoint a new minister—his honorable Minister Eulogio Marulanda. Has a nice ring to it, does it not, Eulogio? And the President will turn to you, the one man who can revitalize, re-invigorated the support of the PHC party for him, a re-invigoration that our support of your party can make possible. He, with the encouragement of some of our well-placed friends in the MVR, will fully recognize how important the support of the PHC party—and you—are. We can make it happen, Eulogio. Within weeks, we can make it all happen," Benavides said with a fierce look of determination as he raised his wine glass.

"Yes—yes. I believe we can, Arturo, I believe we can," Eulogio said, as thoughts of the power he could have danced in his head.

"All you need to do, Eulogio, besides being prepared to become the new minister when the opportunity arises, is to help us identify an appropriate oil company that can assist us in establishing and using our new routes—a company which can provide the transport we need from Venezuela to the American coast," Benavides said.

"An appropriate company—I am not sure what you mean, Arturo?"

"We need to bring under our control an oil company that ships oil or oil-related equipment regularly from and to eastern Venezuela to the American coast, preferably to the Houston area. We need to identify a company that would be receptive to allowing us to use its shipments—to include additional goods, so to speak—among the things they ship," Benavides explained as he twisted his glass with his fingers and watched the sparkle of the dark red fluid.

"Receptive? You mean, I presume, some company that we can force to cooperate with us," Eulogio said.

"Yes, to put it bluntly. We need a company on which we can get a stranglehold and gain the cooperation of the proper people in it— basically by blackmailing them—get them to do what we want and not tell the American authorities. There must be companies, particularly smaller ones, Eulogio, that we can identify that would be susceptible to some pressure—if we can merely find the right pressure point."

"And how do we find the right company ... the right pressure point?" Eulogio asked.

"Simply step by step, Eulogio. First, we find possible companies and the people in them. And that, Eulogio, is where your assistance will be so valuable. And we will speak of the details of that tomorrow before you return to Caracas. For now, I think it is time to retire. I believe Juanita awaits you," Benavides said with a smile.

# 10

Two days later, Marulanda was back in Caracas, where he announced his presence to the office of the Assistant Minister of Mines and Hydrocarbons, saying he was in Caracas on behalf of the governor of Monagas investigating issues regarding international oil development in the State of Monagas.

"But, *Señor* Marulanda," the assistant minister had objected, "the records of which you speak are normally confidential. Service agreement bidder qualification information often—almost always—contains sensitive financial information about a company's operations."

"Yes, Minister, I am well aware of that. But that is precisely why I must review that information. The governor is concerned that any company that might seek to operate an oil exploration block in Monagas be sufficiently sound to assure that it can meet its obligations under the new equitable lease policy."

"Yes, I understand your concern, but still ...." the assistant minister said hesitatingly.

"Perhaps if I were to have Governor Uriarte call the minister—perhaps even President Chávez—to inform him that your assistance is desired?" Eulogio said with gracious politeness, knowing full well the man in front of him understood the threat, irrespectively of how politely it might be made.

"I don't believe that will be necessary. You represent Governor Uriarte—and of course, I am sure the governor fully understands and respects, as will you, his representative, the confidential nature and sensitivity of the information that you wish to see," the assistant minister said, clearly washing his hands of what he was about to do.

"Most assuredly," Eulogio responded.

The assistant minister lifted his phone and requested an extension. In a moment, he was directing that a temporary office be made available to a representative of the governor of Monagas for some records review and that the representative be allowed to review the qualification statements of the international companies seeking service agreements with PDVSA.

— ~ —

After some additional bureaucratic delay—completing a series of formal records inspection documents at the Ministry records office—Eulogio was finally able, by the afternoon of the next day, to have the necessary files brought to the small temporary office that the assistant minister had arranged for his use. Nearly forty consortiums had filed papers of financial responsibility as part of the qualifications requirements for potential bidding on the latest round of leases that had occurred two years ago and might occur again with the next.

Eulogio slowly reviewed the files. He gradually worked his way through the considerable body of financial data until he was able to finally distinguish the truly financial sound companies from those whose financial strength was built upon mostly smoke and mirrors—companies that were trying to make a fast killing in the oil-rich lands of eastern Venezuela before they lost their shirts.

After three days of tiring examination, Eulogio had narrowed his search to eleven companies. Each was, when one really read between the lines of the information presented in the qualifications package, struggling. These consortiums would be those which would potentially be more susceptible to cooperating in the shipment of special goods back to the United States—consortiums that might be more willing to establish arrangements within their companies to which they could close their eyes in return for special considerations in the bidder selection process that the new equitable lease policy so conveniently made possible. Eulogio took careful notes on the names of the officers of the eleven companies as well as their addresses in the United States.

But of the eleven consortiums, four consortiums, actually single companies, seemed particularly suitable to Eulogio. Each of the four companies was small, at least from an international oil business perspective, and, of the total senior officers in each of these four promising companies, fifteen men were located in the American city of Houston in Texas. Houston was the place where Benavides said it would be most useful that the company whom they would use be located.

As he finally concluded his investigations at the ministry offices, Eulogio sighed with satisfaction, thinking, *tonight, after the toil of the last several days, I deserve to reward myself. I will go to my favorite Caracas club—the one in the Santa Rosa district—and find a companion with whom I can have dinner and spend an enjoyable evening—and night.*

Then tomorrow, he would begin meeting with representatives for some of the larger multi-national oil companies, whom he had often met before, and discuss with them the need for a continuing demonstration of their support—their financial support—for the future campaign of Governor Uriarte, particularly in view of the new equitable lease policy.

# 11

Alexis saw Valdes sitting at the table at the side of the patio, near the large windows looking out across the one runway of the *Aeródromo Francisco De Mirando* near the national park in Caracas. The early morning drone of private jets and military airplanes taking off could be heard. After Alexis told the hovering waiter what he would have for breakfast, he and Valdes exchanged cordialities until their meals were brought to their table and the waiter finally left them alone.

"Well, Alexis, what was so important that I had to come to Caracas to speak to you," Valdes asked.

"You should know, Victor, that Benavides is not happy about what happened to the DEA agent," Alexis said calmly.

"I already told you—and him. Nothing is being made of it."

"We find that hard to believe," Alexis said as he raised his hand to stop Valdes from interrupting with a denial. "You may know nothing about it, but don't believe it is nothing. We find it hard to believe that the disposal of the body was handled so poorly."

"It was out of my control. The man had to be killed. Something had to be done—after what the agent apparently found out. If we only had had more time—but we didn't. You—Benavides—should be thankful that we were watching the man, knowing what he was finding out so I could do something about him before he was able to tell things to his American DEA superiors," Valdes said with only slightly hidden anger.

"And so, Arturo is. That is why he has decided to overlook what you allowed to happen," Alexis said with faint politeness.

Valdes looked at Alexis and realized the thinly-veiled threat in Alexis's words. Valdes was silent for a long moment; then with a shake of his head, he said, "So, we just go about our business—be glad, at least, nothing about our operation got beyond the agent."

"Benavides doesn't think we should 'just go about our business.' He is concerned about what may have been compromised, whether we know it or not. And he wants to give you an opportunity to redeem yourself."

"Redeem myself—what do you mean? I don't have to redeem myself," Valdes said defensively.

"Victor, my friend, let's not argue about semantics. Irrespective of what you want to think, the fact is, Benavides is not happy about what happened and wants you to do something for him—and he considers it essential that you do it if we are to continue our business together. And, of course, as you know, Benavides speaks for the full cartel. Any reluctance on your part would not be well received by many," Alexis said.

"I ... I am not ... objecting to ... u h ... helping ... it's just that you have to realize ... it wasn't my ... fault." Valdes objected. "But what can I do? What does Benavides want?"

Alexis smiled and withdrew a file folder from a slim briefcase resting on the chair beside him. He opened the folder and handed a sheet of paper to Valdes. "I have here a list of companies—small American oil companies doing business here in Venezuela. It has come to our attention that they may be able to assist us in moving our product in the future."

Valdes looked at the list. "So, what am I to do with this list?" Then as he looked more at the list, he said. "Wait a minute—these addresses you have for them. They're all located in Houston—any reason for that?"

"Yes, very much so. Here," Alexis said as handed Valdes another three sheets of paper, "are the names and addresses of the officers of the companies. Most of the officers are located in Houston or other cities in the American state of Texas. You should have no difficulty, therefore, in finding out information about them. In particular, we want you to find one of them who may be susceptible to pressure from us. Surely some of them have things they don't want people to know about—women, unusual sexual preferences, gambling debts, perhaps even a drug habit. You have the contacts with your people in Houston. Use them to find out about these people—soon. Find out what these people may do that would cause them to be agreeable to arrangements we would like to make with them."

"What arrangements?" Valdes said.

"When you find a person we can use, then Benavides will specify the appropriate arrangements—and then we will tell you what they are and what we will expect from our new business associate. In the meantime, return to the United States and find the information we need—quickly," Alexis ordered.

Alexis lifted his arm and waved the waiter to bring their checks. "Please allow me to pay for your breakfast, Victor. It has been, I hope, a productive morning for both of us," Alexis said as he signed his room number to both the checks.

In a few moments, Alexis and Valdes stood, shook hands, and exited the restaurant.

# III

# VORTEX

## 12

Kevin walked into his Williams tower office, a broad smile on his face. Only a few days had passed since Roland Beal had returned to Washington to wrap up Senate business before the autumn politicking for the state office primaries in the spring was to start—activities for which the junior senator from Texas was expected to be home in Texas to assume an essential role in supporting the Party's preferred nominees.

Beal, so he had said on the phone to Kevin, was already beginning to confer with his colleagues and the chairman of the Senate Committee on Small Business and Entrepreneurship about a need for Roland, as chairman of the new Subcommittee on Western Hemispheric Commerce and Trade for American Small Business, to hold hearings well before the Thanksgiving holidays on improving trade with Latin America using small businesses—a perfect time for the hearings to occur.

In the hustle and bustle of Congress' maneuvering to tie down legislation before the holidays so that each Senator could extol at hometown pre-Christmas gatherings the things he was doing for his constituents, there would be little concern about some minor subcommittee hearings requested by a new Senate subcommittee chairman. Kevin gave a contented smirk. *Over the years, I have learned how to manipulate Beal rather well.*

Kevin looked at the young receptionist as he approached her desk. Her breasts strained against her blouse—one of the reasons he had hired her, along with the fact that during her interview she had made a point of seductively crossing and uncrossing her shapely legs several times. It was about time he started taking her to lunch—now that he didn't have to worry about that damn detective Barbara had hired to follow him during their separation before the divorce. "Hi, Rebecca. Any messages?" Kevin asked.

"Only three—one from your broker, Mr. Falcon, another from Larry at Rig 3—he said it wasn't urgent—and one from a Mr. Frankie. Mr. Frankie didn't say much, just that you should call him, that you knew his number."

*Frankie,* Kevin thought. *What the hell is he doing calling me? I told him that everything would be taken care of, that he wouldn't have to worry.*

"Do you want me to get any of them on the phone, Mr. Matthew?"

"Uh ... no, no ... not immediately. I'll call myself when I'm ready. Thank you," Kevin said as the smile faded from his face. He walked quickly along the short hallway to his office.

Kevin absentmindedly nodded to Jessica as he passed her open office door. She had been hired at Barbara's urging—actually insistence—to be a personnel officer for the company. Barbara was an outspoken—at least for the Houston community—activist. That had really been the root cause of the divorce—Barbara's activism didn't stop when she entered the bedroom. Kevin's sexual preferences were more satisfied by women who didn't feel they had to prove their importance in the bedroom. With the divorce finalized, Jessica probably knew her days were numbered with Trans-Texas Oil.

Kevin closed his office door and sat heavily in his chair. *What did Frankie want?* Well—Kevin really knew what Frankie wanted: the money. *Frankie has always been accommodating in the past. God, with the number of bets that I have placed with Frankie over the years, Frankie can well afford to be accommodating. What the fuck does he think he is doing calling here, goddamn him. Well, by damn, I'll just get him straightened out.*

Kevin picked up the phone and quickly dialed the number he knew so well.

"He'lo," came a squeaky voice over the phone.

"Frankie, is that you?" Kevin asked.

"Well, howdy, Mr. Matthew. I'm glad you returned my call."

"What the hell are you calling me for? I thought we understood each other. You know I'll get the money to you as soon as I can—I've always paid up, haven't I? You don't need to be calling me, dammit."

"Hold on, Mr. Matthew. I know you're an okay guy—that you're good for the money. But I got a little problem here."

"Problem?" Kevin asked with surprise.

"Well, Mr. Matthew, it seems like I've come across some hard times of late—"

"Well, that's not my problem," Kevin said quickly.

"Oh, I know that, Mr. Matthew, I know that. But, you see, I needed some cash, right away so to speak, so I sold some of my markers to a friend—"

"Sold your markers—you mean I own the money to someone else now?" *Jesus Christ, what will that mean?* Kevin wondered with apprehension.

"'Fraid so, Mr. Matthew. I just wanted to let you know—so you wouldn't be surprised when he contacted you. His name is Boutrand, Floyd Boutrand. And one thing, Mr. Matthew, Mr. Boutrand don't like to give no long-term credit. I think maybe it's a good idea that you get some cash together—real soon."

— ~ —

Kevin bit his lip, the compulsive habit that surfaced whenever he got worried about money. Kevin's return call to his broker had confirmed his fears. Kevin's margin account was in a precarious situation. If things happened to take even only a modest dip in the coming weeks, Kevin would have to come up with additional margin money, a lot—or liquidate some sizable holdings and come up with almost nothing. *Diversification—that's what the damn broker had told me I needed to do. So, I got into precious metals, and now the goddamn market in gold and silver is like shit.* Even if Kevin fired his broker, he still had a lot of money at risk. And most of the good stocks, the things that were soaring now, had been taken by Barbara. *Damn her—damn the situation!*

The phone gave a soft warble, some young engineer's idea of a pleasant interruption that had been built into the office telephone system. "Yes, Rebecca?"

"A Mr. Boutrand wishes to speak to you."

*God, when it rains, it pours.* "Put him through." There was a click as the connection was made.

"Mr. Matthew, my name is Floyd Boutrand. I believe we have a mutual friend by the name of Frankie."

"Yes, yes. He called earlier today," Kevin said with an air of arrogance.

"Then you probably understand why I am calling—"

"Well, as I told Frankie, the debt will be paid shortly," Kevin said sharply—and with unmistakable condensation. "It will be taken care of as—"

"Let's get two things straight, Mr. Matthew. I don't like being interrupted, and I don't give long-term credit. Got that?" Boutrand asked.

Kevin paused. "Yes."

"Okay. So, let me see if I have got the situation straight. Right now, you owe—me—twenty-eight thousand, five-hundred, twenty-eight dollars. Next week this time, with my interest rate—very reasonable, all things considered—it will be thirty thousand, eight hundred, and ten," Boutrand said.

"Thirty—Jesus Christ! What the fuck do you think you're doing?" Kevin asked with astonishment.

"Mr. Matthew, what I am doing is running a business. I expect to be paid that amount, in cash, by this time next week. I will come to your office to pick it up and give you a receipt." A loud click followed as Boutrand cut the connection.

# 13

The week had passed, and Kevin was at his wit's end. All he could raise in cash was a little over eighteen thousand dollars—unless he went directly into Trans-Texas Oil money. And that was out of the question. With the auditing going on as part of the Tejas stock offering, he couldn't pull any extra cash out of Trans-Texas Oil until all the i's had been dotted and the t's had been crossed, and the offering could go on the market. *Well, Boutrand will just have to be satisfied for the time being with the eighteen thousand. That is all there is to it. Boutrand will just have to understand.*

The phone gave its soft warble. Kevin picked the phone up as if were red hot. "Yes, Rebecca?"

"There is a Mr. Boutrand and ... his associate here to see you. He says they have an appointment, but I don't have them on your calendar."

Kevin took a deep breath. He began biting his lip. "Send them in, please."

In a moment Boutrand entered. He looked like an ordinary businessman, dressed very conservatively—and expensively. The man with him did not have Bertrand's refined air. The man was big, black, and looked mean as hell. Kevin could even see tattoos on his upper chest and neck above his open, pale pink shirt collar.

"Good afternoon, Mr. Matthew. You know why I am here." Boutrand's words were not spoken as a question but as a statement of fact.

"Yes. As I said to you last week, I have full intentions to pay you, with your interest," Kevin said.

"You mean you don't have the money now?"

"I have most of it—eighteen thousand. The other amount will be provided in a few weeks, at most. You just have to understand that running a business like I do, there are ups and downs in our cash flow. The company is limited in available cash at the moment—and since Trans-Texas Oil means me, of course, my funds are likewise limited at the moment. But that will be rectified soon," Kevin said.

"You mean you don't have *all* the money—only eighteen thousand?" Boutrand asked.

"As I just told you. The cash flow situation is a little tight right now—"

Boutrand looked at the black man. The man nodded his head and began to take off his sports coat. His muscles and tattoos bristled. Kevin couldn't believe Boutrand would try anything like that.

The black man reached into his pants' pocket, pulled out a small zip-lock bag filled with white powder, and approached the glass top desk at which Kevin was sitting. He pushed aside some papers and slowly poured out the contents of the packet onto the glass in front of Kevin—the contents made a small mound. Kevin recognized what it was. On the street, based on the times he had gotten some—when he wanted a relaxing evening when Barbara was out of town—the little mound might have been worth about five-thousand dollars. The black man walked around the table to Kevin's chair and grabbed the back of Kevin's head with his huge hand.

"What are you doing—," Kevin started to protest.

The black man pushed Kevin's face down to the desk, slamming Kevin's mouth into the little mound of coke. A trickle of blood oozed from Kevin's mouth, staining the coke.

"I understand, Mr. Matthew, you like to occasionally indulge. Well, here, have a feast. Start licking it up—all of it," Boutrand ordered.

"That'll kill me—I can't do that. Listen—"

"Then we will just have to force feed you. Right, Thomas?" Boutrand said.

The black man smiled, reached into his pocket again, and pulled out a baby spoon. He handed it to Boutrand.

Then Thomas pulled Kevin's head back, forcing it against the back of the chair and holding it there. Boutrand filled the spoon with coke and brought it to Kevin's face. The black man used his hand to force open Kevin's jaw.

Kevin struggled, but the black man was far too much for him. "Wait, wait ... can ... I'll do," Kevin sputtered as he tried to force his tongue to move and mouth words. "I'll do anything ... anything."

"Anything? Did I hear 'anything,' Mr. Matthew?" Boutrand said with satisfaction. He nodded to the black man.

The black man released Kevin's head and mouth. Kevin slumped in his chair, more frightened that he had ever been in his life. Blood continued to ooze from his mouth. Drops of blood fell onto Kevin's shirt, creating a small circular pattern.

"Did you say anything, Mr. Matthew? Did I hear you correctly?" Boutrand asked.

"Yes ... yes. I'll do whatever I can to get your money back to you—right away," Kevin said.

Boutrand smiled. "That's very commendable, Mr. Matthew. But, as I see it, you can't get the cash. Isn't that what you told me?" Boutrand smiled and then continued without waiting for Kevin to answer. "But you seem like a resourceful man. Maybe you can do something else— any ideas?"

Kevin was afraid to say anything.

"No? Maybe I have one. Yeah. I've got an idea. Maybe we could work something out. Would you like to hear it, Mr. Matthew?"

Kevin nodded his head, still frightened by the man standing in front of him.

"Good, Mr. Matthew, good. Here's what I have in mind. I want you to meet someone—have a little discussion. He needs some assistance—something I am sure you can readily provide, being a big oilman like you are, with all your international connections. It is correct that Trans-Texas Oil is planning to expand its business in Venezuela, isn't it?"

Kevin looked at Boutrand in shock. *How in the hell does Boutrand know about that?*

"Now wait, Trans-Texas Oil is a company, you can't—"

"Now, Mr. Matthew, let's not have to continue what we just stopped. Besides, as you said before, you are Trans-Texas Oil."

Kevin looked at Boutrand, not knowing what to do.

"What I want you to do, Mr. Matthew—what you are going to do—is meet with an associate of mine, a Mr. Valdes. Have a friendly little discussion about some things you and Trans-Texas Oil can help him in. Meet him at six this Wednesday at *Ernesto's Nuevo Sudamerica Café* on Richmond," Boutrand said.

"How will I know him?" Kevin asked.

"You don't need to. He knows what you look like."

*Jesus,* Kevin thought, *what have I gotten into?*

"You don't need to show us out, Mr. Matthew. By the way, you can keep that stuff that's on your desk—I don't deal in used merchandise.

We'll just add it to your bill. You'll be able to work it off as you help Mr. Valdes."

Kevin watched Boutrand and the black man exit his office, trying to stem the oozing blood with his handkerchief and wondering what he was going to do with the white mound on his desk. He didn't see Boutrand drop a thick envelope into Jessica's inbox as he passed her office.

# 14

Kevin looked across the room of tables as he entered *Ernesto's Nuevo Sudamerica*, an upscale cafe—the term used along the Richmond strip for restaurants with big bars and mini-menus—a few minutes after six. As he approached the young girl taking names in the nearly filled room, he wondered whether Valdes was already there. As the girl, in an outfit that was supposed to evoke exotic thoughts of South America, asked whether he was alone, he saw a man with a thick mustache get down from a bar stool and walk toward him, waving his hand in a friendly fashion.

"Well, Mr. Matthew, I see you have arrived—though a little late. But, of course, lateness is the way of things south of the border, is it not?" Kevin could detect an accent in the man's words.

"Mr. Valdez?" Kevin asked.

"But of course. Who else?" Valdes answered.

Valdez turned to the girl. "I'll take my table now—the one I picked earlier."

As the girl brought them to a table in a less crowded area in the back of the cafe, Valdez handed a $20 bill to her. "Thank you for holding my table, *Señorita*." The two men sat down.

"We should be able to talk undisturbed here, Mr. Matthew. Mr. Boutrand informs me that you can provide some assistance to me, as a means to reduce the debt that you apparently own him," Valdes said politely.

"Well, I don't know about that, Valdes. I may or may not be able to help. It all—"

"All right, my friend, I thought we could behave as gentlemen here, but that is apparently not to be. Any lack of cooperation will force Mr. Boutrand and his associate Thomas to return to your office to not only stuff that coke down your throat but, I can absolutely assure you, cut off your balls right then and there. And if you should somehow happen to survive all that, you can be assured that your little buys of coke from time to time will be appropriately documented for the auditors and legal counsel working on the Tejas stock offering—as well as their being publicized to potential buyers of Tejas stock," Valdes said with a gravelly, threatening voice.

Kevin was overwhelmed with helplessness.

"It is not as bad as you think it is, Mr. Matthew. You may, in fact, be able to turn a sizable profit in this arrangement as well," Valdes said.

*Profit? What's going on here?*

Kevin gathered the courage to speak. "What is it that you want me to do? I don't understand."

Valdes smiled. "I am pleased you are so willing to help," Valdes said as his voice returned to its former politeness. "I, and the people I represent, merely want you and your Trans-Texas company to begin to provide some services to us as part of your already ongoing oil field services you currently provide to the oil companies in eastern Venezuela—site investigations, geological testing, equipment replacement, and the like. And, as the activities of your company grow, as we think they may if your Tejas subsidiary is successful as we think it might be, we would like your assurances that we could increasingly use your services."

"Services?"

"Trans-Texas currently moves equipment and supplies into and out of the country on a regular basis via Caripito north of Maturin—is that not correct?"

"Caripito ... yes," Kevin answered, thinking, *shit, why does Valdes even ask? He seems to know everything about Trans-Texas and me already.* "Most of our shipments for the Maturin area are done out of Caripito. It and Barcelona are the standard points-of-entry."

"Yes, shipment of industrial equipment and supplies coming into eastern Venezuela, as I understand it," Valdes continued. "And, as well

I would imagine, used equipment and supplies, as well as samples for testing, will have to be returned to Houston for repair and refurbishing?" Valdes said as he tilted his head for a sign of confirmation from Kevin.

Kevin gave a tight smile as he nodded his head.

"*Si*, as I expected. Oil is king in Venezuela—you know that. If there is one thing that customs will allow to pass rapidly with little inspection, it is equipment for the oil field. So, we merely want you to allow, from time to time, some relatively small items, appropriately and discreetly packaged, to be included in your Trans-Texas, and perhaps later Tejas, shipments back here to Houston. They would, of course, be expected to arrive in an unopened state," Valdes said.

*Damn, fucking, damn! What that I was afraid of—smuggling drugs into the U.S. How had things gotten to this? But was there a way out?*

"Well, these ... packages. How would they be delivered to me—that is, Trans-Texas or Tejas. How would I include them in equipment shipments back to the U.S.?" Kevin asked.

"That is straightforward," Valdes assured Kevin. "A package would come to your field office in Maturin by ordinary business courier. You have a local office there already, so I understand."

Kevin nodded in resigned agreement.

"It would be labeled as test samples and would be merely included in other materials in the larger shipments of equipment and samples going back to the U.S. Some of the sample containers would contain materials other than soil; our product, before its final processing, has a remarkable resemblance to the soil that one finds several meters below the surface. So, should a package be opened it is highly unlikely that inspection, even if it were ever to occur, would even reveal what is in those oily-looking soil containers at the bottom of the stack of other containers of oily soils."

"You mean I would never even have to open and really know what was in the package? I mean, it could be delivered like it came from a drilling site—sent by someone there? I would merely have to be sure it got put on an appropriate shipment of equipment going back to the U.S. without being opened?" Kevin asked.

"*Si*, that is all. And we believe the interest in your shipments will only decrease with time. Of course, upon receipt here in the U.S., the packaged sample would be picked up, according to the instructions on the label, by an appropriate representative of the laboratory."

*Damn*, Kevin thought, *nobody but the receiving lab ever looks at soil samples sent in for analysis from the field sites—nobody!* And, Kevin speculated, that with the drugs looking like oily soil samples, nobody would ever find them—and probably no dog would be able to smell them either. Kevin began to think this could be a deal made in heaven—if it were handled right.

"Mr. Valdes," Kevin said with pretended courtesy, "you said that I might be able to profit from this arrangement. Just how might that occur?" Kevin asked.

"You would be paid—with deposits to some account or location you specify—at a rate of four-thousand dollars per package that is picked up by our messenger in Houston. If there is more than one package per shipment, you will receive a payment for each. The initial payments, of course, will be directed to Mr. Boutrand for payment of debts owed to him by you. After that, by which time the process should be flowing smoothly, the payments will be made to you," Valdes said.

"Just how many packages are we talking about, say on a monthly basis—typical?" Kevin asked.

"At first no more than five. Later, perhaps as many as ten or twenty—we will have to know how much you can arrange to handle," Valdes said. "Indeed, with time, we fully expect shipment volume to grow quite significantly."

Kevin swallowed hard; he felt giddy with the possibilities. "How quickly can we get started?"

"That is up to you, Mr. Matthew, provided it is within reason—but certainly within a month. As quickly as you can begin to make the necessary Trans-Texas shipments back to the United States, we can begin sending our … samples to your office in Maturin—and you can begin paying off your debt to Mr. Boutrand."

# 15

Kelley looked up the aisle. He could see Matthew standing by the door to the head, behind a middle-aged woman. The flight was nearing its conclusion. *It's now or never.* If Kelley were going to meet Matthew on this flight, as the plan hatched at Langley called for, it had to be done in the next few minutes.

The Langley plan was for Kelley to be seated next to Matthew, but a last-minute screw-up in his reservation by the airline when he got to Houston's Intercontinental Airport put Kelly several seats behind Matthew—with no empty seats near him.

The Agency had given Kelley three hot—so Langley believed— leads to try to check out in Houston or Venezuela, whichever could be done. Each man on the list was the CEO of a company fitting the Agency's profile for investigation—companies with a weak financial condition, owned largely by a small, close-knit group of people, rather than a conglomerate, trying to make a fast buck in the international oil business. Each regularly flew this Continental flight from Houston to Caracas, so Kelley had been booked on this particular flight to meet Matthew. It was better to make an innocent, informal initial contact with someone Kelley needed to investigate rather than trying to wiggle his way into the three companies as a damn oil services rep from off the street.

Kelley had already made his entrée to one of the other two men on his list at a business club luncheon in Houston prior week. During the meal, Kelley got an invitation to talk again with the man at his offices in Caracas.

The other man had been virtually leaving Houston for Caracas when Kelley got in to see him. He apologized for canceling his meeting but indicated an unscheduled business issue had come up in Venezuela that required his immediate and personal attention. He offered to meet Kelly in Caracas the next week, and Kelley had agreed to do so.

When Kelley found out Matthew was going to Caracas in a few days, he informed Langley, and their plan had been hatched.

Kelley's intuition about the two men he had already met, albeit based upon very short meetings, was that the two men played pretty much by the rules and were on the up and up. They did not seem to be the type that would get involved in the things that the Agency thought possible. But Kelley would still check them out once he got to Caracas.

On the other hand, the Agency put Matthew and his Trans-Texas oil company at the top of the Agency's list of small oil companies that had been targeted for Kelley to check out. Langley had nothing specific to go on, just rumors that Matthew was a wheeler and dealer—even more than most in a business that was replete with wheelers and dealers. If an American oil company were part of what Kelley was trying to figure out, a company like Matthew's would likely be it. Not only was it apparent that Trans-Texas was out to make a fast buck in the oil business, but Matthew was the sole owner of the company—and his company was on the ropes. A little wiggle of that rope might just flip him off—and into the hands of someone who could help him in return for big favors.

Kelley got up as if to stretch his legs, which in fact he was glad to do. The coffee he had been drinking was starting to take its toll, irrespective of whether he talked to Matthew or not. He walked up the aisle toward the head.

As Kelley reached the end of the aisle, Matthew gave a little laugh. "Popular spot near the end of flights like this."

"Your right about that," Kelley responded pleasantly. Then Kelley saw the small note that had been stuck on one of the two washrooms doors saying the washroom was out of order. Kelley frowned.

"Typical," the man said, noticing Kelley's frown. "I haven't been on one of these flights yet that at least one washroom wasn't out of order before we were over the Gulf. These Latin women, you know ...." The Hispanic-looking woman standing beside Matthew shot an unpleasant look at him but didn't say anything. Then the washroom door opened, and a young boy stepped out. The woman went into the washroom. Kelley heard the door lock snap.

There was a momentary pause. "You sound like you are a regular on these flights," Kelley said.

"Well, I am on this one to Caracas. I'm in the oil business—doing work in Venezuela. Trans-Texas Oil. Maybe you have heard of it?"

the man asked.

"Well, I'm not absolutely sure—you operate wells out in west Texas and in New Mexico, near Hobbs? Been operating out there for over a decade if my memory serves me right," Kelley said innocently, knowing full well that Trans-Texas had operations scattered all over central and west Texas, eastern New Mexico, and southern Oklahoma—as well as providing oilfield services in Venezuela.

"Sure do—a lot of wells all over the Southwest, across the Permian Basin. My name is Kevin Matthew. I head up Trans-Texas. You sound like you know the oil business."

Kelley stuck out his hand. Kevin shook it. "Kelley Castellano. I think I do. I'm with Consolidated Oil Services. Out of Colorado," Kelley answered, hoping the cover that the Langley people had set up was as good as it was supposed to be.

"Consolidated? I don't think I know the company," Kevin said.

"That's not surprising," Kelley said, going into his well-rehearsed cover story. "We're fairly new, at least under the Consolidated name. We were formed from several other smaller companies doing business in Colorado and other areas in the West. Some investors apparently saw an opportunity and put together the money to form Consolidated." Kelley ran off a list of names of several companies that were more or less defunct which were being used as part of Kelley's cover.

"I thought some of those companies went bust in the early '90s?" Kevin asked.

"They did—almost. But our investors gathered them together, picked up their best people, and formed Consolidated."

"Oh, so you're not really a big player now, so to speak," Kevin said not as a question but as an apparent matter of fact.

"Well, maybe not now, but our profits are going in the right direction. Just what does—"

At that moment the washroom door opened and the woman stepped out and pushed past Kelley.

"At last," Kevin said as he turned to the washroom and entered it, leaving Kelley alone.

*Great beginning*, Kelley thought. *Kevin Matthew is obviously more interested in taking a piss than learning about Consolidated*

*Oil Services.*

Kelley stood silently for a few more moments. Then the washroom door opened.

"All yours, Kelley," Kevin said as he stepped from the washroom. Then at that moment, an announcement came over the airplane's speaker, first in English and then in Spanish, saying that the aircraft was in its approach to the Simón Bolívar International Airport and requesting that all passengers take their seats.

"Better hurry," Kevin said with a slight laugh as he passed Kelley. As he did, he handed Kelley two business cards. "Maybe we can get together sometime," Kevin said.

Kelley looked at the two cards. One identified Kevin as President and CEO, Trans-Texas Petroleum Development and Field Services, Houston, Texas. The other identified Kevin as president also, but of *Tejas Petróleo de Venezuela*, with two addresses given, one in Caracas and one in Maturin. *That's interesting*, Kelley thought. *Langley hadn't said anything about a* Tejas Petróleo de Venezuela *subsidiary to Trans-Texas. How did they miss that? Maybe another reason for me to go to Maturin.*

"Yes, I would like that," Kelley said as he pulled a Consolidated business card from his shirt pocket and handed it to Kevin.

Kevin only glanced at the card as the shoved it into his shirt pocket. "Let's plan to do that—give me a ring," Kevin said as he turned and headed back to his seat.

With the bustling crowd coming off the airliner, Kelley didn't see Kevin Matthew again until the passengers began pulling their luggage off the carousel in the middle of the crowded customs area. As Kelley raised his hand to him, Kevin's luggage was picked up by a porter and carried rapidly out of the luggage area. Kelley saw Kevin wave his hand in recognition and then follow the porter out to a limousine, which took off quickly up the airport driveway.

# 16

The evening shadows were beginning to enshroud the city as the sun slid beneath the mountain tops to the west. Tony Luque sat in a chair by a window of a hotel room on the fifth floor of the Best Western Caracas, absentmindedly watching the small one and two engine planes land at the *Aeródromo Francisco de Miranda* as the Caracas business day came to an end. He took another sip from the bottle of beer in his hand.

Luque, ostensibly the local manager of an American-owned import-export company in Caracas, was a native Venezuelan who had spent many of his childhood years in the U.S. After his diplomat-father died, he had joined the U.S. Army, where he learned to fly helicopters, and then became a U.S. citizen. He was involved in the Granada invasion and then, shortly after that, had been recruited by the CIA. He was now the local station chief for the CIA operations in Venezuela.

Kelley came out of the bathroom, slipping on a clean shirt. Luque turned from the window and stubbed out his cigarette in the ashtray. Kelley reached into the small refrigerator and took out a beer. There was a loud pop as Kelley pulled the cap from the bottle with a church key hanging by a thin steel chain from the refrigerator door.

Kelley looked at Luque. "So, what's the lowdown on Carrillo? The admiral said you could fill in a lot of the details," Kelley said as he took a gulp from the bottle.

"Well, here's what I know about what he was doing the last few months," Luque began. "About five months ago, Carrillo, working with two DEA agents here in Venezuela, was investigating possible tie-ins of some mid-level Venezuelan custom agents in the Maracaibo area with some mules—in particular, some merchant marine officers moving drugs from Colombia through Venezuela to Mexico. Once it gets to Mexico, there are all sorts of ways to get into the U.S.—but I guess you know that."

Kelley nodded in agreement. Not much had changed from the times that he knew it—it seemed to be an ageless country when it came to politics and law enforcement. Bribery and police involvement in drug trafficking were still rampant in Mexico.

"Did the Federal police here in Venezuela know Carrillo was CIA?" Kelley asked, wondering whether a leak in the Venezuela police could have led to Carrillo's cover being blown.

"No—at least they weren't supposed to. The two DEA agents working with him didn't even know he was CIA. They thought he was DEA. I was the only one who was supposed to know he worked for the Agency," Luque answered.

"So, you figure that Carrillo being CIA didn't have anything to do with his murder?"

"No … not really. I think everyone thought he was just another DEA guy. Whoever murdered him probably still doesn't know he was CIA."

"Yeah—you're probably right. Okay, so what about these merchant marine officers Carrillo was checking out?" Kelley asked.

"Carrillo had uncovered some information that the officers on two different Venezuelan flag tankers were in cahoots with some customs agents in Venezuela and Mexico. The officers were carrying uncut cocaine into Mexico with the aid of these customs agents—the agents were turning their heads when these guys got onto the ships at Maracaibo and then later off the ships in Mexico, to visit, supposedly, the local nightspots. We nabbed several people—"

"We is who, Tony? You can't arrest anybody," Kelley said.

"Well, officially it was the *Cuerpo Tecnico de Policia Judicial*, the Venezuelan Federal police," Luque responded, "but the DEA guys were feeding them all the information. One of the guys that was caught—Carrillo got to question everybody since he was part of the DEA team, so far as the Federal police knew—this guy was a Venezuelan named Casares. Casares was a local ringleader for recruiting and managing the merchant marine officers—up to about five at a time—who were carrying the drugs on the ships, sort of coordinating the operations of the officers. The only reason that Casares was even in the group of people that was nabbed was because he was checking out the security on the routes being used— why he was doing that I'll get to in a moment. It was just coincidence that Casares was checking things out when the Venezuelan police locked down the ship and made their arrests."

"That was damn lucky," Kelley said.

"Yeah, your right, but once in a while things actually do go our way, rather than turning to shit, which I understand you know a lot about," Luque said with a small laugh.

"Oh, so you know about Nicaragua?" Kelley asked.

"Rumors only—the usual scuttlebutt around Langley," Luque said.

"Yeah, I know how that is," Kelley said with a grimace.

"Well, anyway, Carrillo pushed hard on this guy, and he broke, with a deal—protection of him and his family, and relocation to some South American country outside of Venezuela and a long way from Colombia—that type of thing."

Luque paused to light another cigarette and then continued. "It seems Casares had been coordinating these shipments for some time and gotten to hear or see a lot. He unloaded quite a bit for Carrillo, but the thing that really stuck out was some things he said about a Colombian guy name Huerta—Jose Huerta. We know Huerta is a pretty important player in the Colombian drug cartels. We think he is a pretty high-level member of the Metillo cartel."

"What was so important about Huerta?" Kelley asked.

"Huerta had come to Venezuela about two weeks before we nabbed Casares, something very unusual for important players in the cartels—they usually don't like getting away from the safety of their home territory. Huerta had met with various people, including Casares in Maracaibo."

"So, what was Huerta up to?" Kelley asked

"Gathering information for new routes, we think," Luque answered. "Huerta quizzed Casares about how to set up a deal like they have for the ships running through Lake Maracaibo—the in's and out's, so to speak, of running coca paste via oil tanker, like he was thinking about setting up another route similar to the one that Casares was already operating. With all the questions, Casares begins to wonder what's going on—that maybe the cartels are thinking about closing down his operation."

"That would seem like a reasonable assumption," Kelley said.

"Yes, but that wasn't it. But Casares didn't know that, at least at first. The more questions Huerta asked, the more worried Casares got. Casares didn't like much about the possibility of shutting down his routes—not only does he not get his cut anymore, but he's worrying that he might be viewed as a liability that needs to be permanently removed. So, Casares, to try to prevent what he thinks Huerta is maybe planning, volunteers to prove the safety of his routes by running some paste himself. Of course, that's what leads to his being on the ship at the Maracaibo docks when it was locked down. He named his own poison, so to speak."

"Well, so how does that tie into Carrillo?"

"Oh, yeah, I got a little sidetracked. In the discussion with Huerta, so Casares says, Huerta asked Cesares quite few questions: How difficult did Casares think it would be to set up some additional routes in eastern Venezuela; did Casares know much about the operations for oil coming out of the El Tigre fields; and how the oil got north to the tankers that fill up at Barcelona, the big resort town on the coast about three-hundred kilometers east of Caracas. Have you ever been there?" Luque asked.

"A hell of a long time ago—and it wasn't much of a place when I was there," Kelley said with a chuckle.

"Well, it is now—all the rich and famous, so to speak, go there. Well anyway, it's then that Casares realizes that Huerta is not trying to eliminate his operations, but just likely wanting to set up some similar operations in eastern Venezuela. He was just quizzing Casares to see what it would take to set things up in eastern Venezuela—whether eastern routes might really work. When Casares figures this out, he realizes that he didn't have to volunteer to run some drugs on his own routes thorough Maracaibo, but by then, he has already made his offer to Huerta, and he was stuck with it."

"So, Huerta and his cartel," Kelley interjected, "are out to set up some operation using tankers coming in and out of eastern Venezuela—through Barcelona," Kelley paused, thinking, and then continued. "And because oil shipments out of the eastern Venezuela fields are just going to be getting bigger, it would fit right in with the way the cartels built up their trade through Maracaibo years ago. It would be Maracaibo all over again—only in a different part of the country."

"That's the way we saw it," Luque said.

"But how does this tie into manipulation of the Venezuelan

government's management of the oil business here in Venezuela that the admiral is worried about—what makes it different than the usual bribery that goes on?" Kelley asked.

"That's what we weren't sure about until Huerta was murdered a week after we started interrogating Casares—and about a month before Carrillo washed up on that Texas beach of yours," Luque answered.

"Murdered? What the hell was going on?"

"It gets complicated, so bear with me," Luque answered. "Casares had given us enough information to go after Huerta—Casares had had a lot of contact with Huerta over the years—to make a case against him here in Venezuela, so the police started looking for him. They began a big sweep around the Caracas and Maracaibo area, checking hotel records and upping inspection on border roads and airports so he couldn't get out of the country—hoping that he was still in Venezuela. But he wasn't around either Caracas or Maracaibo—and maybe for Huerta's sake it would have been better if he had been."

"What do you mean?"

"Somebody tipped off the cartel that Casares was talking and that the Federal police were looking for Huerta, so the cartel apparently decided to cut its losses and kill Huerta before he could be picked up and spill the beans like Casares was doing."

"How did they get to him—how did he die?"

"It was played up in the papers as an accidental death. The Venezuelan police did not want an international incident occurring, as well as have it leak out that the cartel was tipped off by someone in their own Federal police," Luque explained.

"So, what really happened?"

"He supposedly died of a heart attack in some resort hotel in Barcelona," Luque answered with obvious skepticism. "We don't think Huerta was trying to hide in Barcelona; he was there doing what he was supposed to be doing: checking out the situation—and having a little fun on the side. He presumably died in the throes of passion with some lady of the evening—the hotel room had all the leftovers of a hot night, including the obvious arrival of a hooker at the hotel. The whole deal was made to look like his ticker couldn't stand the excitement."

"A pretty clumsy setup if you ask me," Kelly interjected.

"Right, and that's what Carrillo thought. He checked things out—got a look at the autopsy report. It was never made public, but he got a look at it on the sly. Huerta was loaded with atropine."

"Atropine!" Kelley said in surprise.

"Yeah—been around a long time, but it still works. Great for dilating your pupils—and speeding up your heart. Given enough of it, the heart takes off and works itself to death, so to speak. The initial reaction to it could be interpreted, like it probably was by the hooker, that Huerta was just really getting hot with her—having a real good time. But then, his heart never slowed down."

"What about the woman?" Kelley asked, wondering if he now knew who Bettina was.

"Huerta's body was found in the morning by a maid. The woman apparently hightailed it out sometime during the night, before the police arrived—they only got a description of her from the hotel clerk. She was never found, so we don't know exactly what part she played in the murder, whether she was in on the murder, or just brought in to provide the cover for the murder and kick in, unknowingly, the drug reaction," Luque said with a shrug of his shoulders.

"You're sure it was the cartel that was behind his murder—that they knew Casares was talking?"

"Damn sure," Luque answered emphatically. "The cartel killed Casares the same day that Huerta was killed."

"What! You gotta be kidding?"

"Don't I wish. We had Casares stashed in a safe house—or so we thought—in Maracaibo. One of our local guys got hurt bad—took two bullets but was able to drop the two thugs that had been sent in to kill Casares. Unfortunately, Casares got caught in the crossfire—took a bullet to the chest. The whole thing was treated as an attempted burglary gone sour as far as the police were concerned. We traced the two guys—they were Venezuelan but had Colombian connections, so there is no doubt the cartels were trying to shut Casares up—which they did."

"So, you have a bad leak somewhere," Kelley said with concern, understanding now the full magnitude of the admiral's concern. "The cartel not only got the news that you were going after Huerta but knew where you had stashed Casares."

"Yes, your damn right—and we're working on that," Luque said with conviction. "And that's why this is likely one of the few times you will see or talk to me—and why you won't be working with anybody but me. I want you to contact only me in this operation. You are going to be out of our usual line of communication on this operation. Let me know what the hell you are finding out—and if any emergency develops, contact me pronto. Got that?" Luque asked with finality.

"Sure, I got it," Kelley said, but wondered, *what is going on?* Before leaving Langley, the admiral had made it abundantly clear that Kelly was to report only directly to Langley. Kelley was to call a dummy Consolidated Oil Services number in Denver, despite the possibility of his phone being tapped. When Kelley gave the correct identification, he would be automatically transferred to Langley. *Reporting directly to Langley is the way the admiral wants it, at least until his fears about a leak are cleared up. But here is Luque telling me to keep him in the loop—something quite understandable given who Luque was, but ... not what the admiral told me to do. Well,* Kelley thought, *I'll just have to play it by ear.*

"So how do you think you are going to proceed—where do you want to start?" Luque asked.

"Well, I've got some small oil company names I want to check into—Langley thinks Carrillo might have stumbled onto some shady deals that some smaller oil company might be involved in," Kelley answered, not wanting to say too much. "Some leads might turn up there."

"What companies?" Luque asked.

Kelley reluctantly answered, giving the company names for the three men on Langley's list.

"Yeah, I think I have heard the names—except for the Trans-Texas outfit. Are they located here in Caracas?

"They have offices here in Caracas. The Trans-Texas outfit apparently has an office in Maturin too—I met the Trans-Texas president on the flight from Houston."

"What's his name?"

"Kevin Matthew," Kelley answered.

"I'll do some checking on him. If I find anything interesting about him, I will let you know," Luque said.

"Thanks."

"And here's how you contact me," Luque said as he handed Kelley a business card. It read, "Venezusa—Venezuela-United States Expedited Import and Export," and listed a Caracas address and telephone number. "My company—my cell phone and home phone are on the back."

Kelley turned the card over. He saw two handwritten phone numbers.

"I think my home phone is bugged, so use the office phone. We sweep the office regularly, so use it if possible. In an emergency, use the cell if you don't get an answer at the office. It just might be picked up by someone cruising the airwaves, so avoid it if possible. And too, cell coverage gets pretty spotty once you get away from the coast or the bigger cities—so don't rely on the cell. But, in any case, be damn careful what you say. If the cartel gets wind of you—that you are trying to find out what they are doing, you may be next on their list. You understand that?"

"Are you sure that no one knows that you are here now?" Kelley asked with concern.

"As far as anyone knows, I went shopping for a present for my mistress this afternoon. When I leave here, I will go down to the mall and get something—on Company money," Luque said with a grin.

Kelley nodded his head slowly, and then said, "You still haven't told me how Carrillo fits into all this."

"Well, Carrillo and I were pretty sure that Huerta was in Barcelona for some reason beyond trying to party with a hooker. It would be consistent with him looking into ways to set up an operation similar to what they do in Maracaibo. So, Carrillo went to Barcelona to see what he could find out. He reported in only two times before I lost contact with him and he washed up on your Texas beach. After Casares, we realized there was a leak, and we were trying to minimize out contact," Luque answered.

"Did he find out anything—did he say much when he checked in?" Kelley asked hopefully.

"Only two things: One, he had been able to trace some of Huerta's movements after Huerta arrived in Barcelona. It seems that Huerta met several times with a government official who was apparently in Barcelona on business, or so the story goes, attending some type of meetings. The official was staying in the same hotel as Huerta. He had dinner with Huerta at least once, and they may have gone to some nightclubs or high-priced whore houses together," Luque said.

"We think that Huerta was trying to get to the guy—bribe him or something like that. Apparently, they became real buddy-buddy for a while—then the official ups and leaves one morning, before his hotel reservation is up, and returns to Caracas. And guess what morning he left?" Luque said with a mischievous smile.

"The day Huerta was killed?" Kelley answered with a questioning look.

"Almost right. Huerta bought it the night after this official left."

"Sounds like the official suspected something and got scared—or just didn't want to get in involved with Huerta. Or maybe the deal was made with Huerta, and the guy was ready to go home."

"Who was he?" Kelley asked.

"Nicolas Bonilla, the head of the Ministry of Mines and Hydrocarbons," Luque said as he slowly exhaled a long line of smoke from his nostrils.

"Oooh! Now I see why you say there may be a tie-in to the Venezuelan government oil management," Kelley said excitedly. "But you said Carrillo had some other information?"

"Yes. Carrillo's second, and last, message," Luque answered. "A week after he had gotten to Barcelona, I get this message from Carrillo—real short, like there wasn't much time to give it, except I didn't get to take it directly. He left a message on my answering machine."

"What was the message?"

"He said, quote, I think I found the hooker who was with Huerta. She may work at a nightclub in Maturin. Going there to check, unquote," Luque said. "That's the last I heard from him."

"Nightclub," Kelley said with little surprise. *And I bet the club's name is Antonio's!*

"Did Carrillo mention any names?" Kelley asked, hoping to get some confirmation of Antonio's.

"No. Why?" Luque asked.

Kelley debated a moment about whether he should tell Luque about Carrillo's final message, the name he had written on Antonio's business card. But the less information that Luque knew, probably the better. There was no way of knowing who was privy to what Luque might know. "Nothing. I was just hoping," Kelley answered.

Kelley rubbed his chin in thought. "Have you checked out Bonilla—to see if Huerta made any deals with him before Huerta was killed?"

"That's going to be a little difficult," Luque said as he shook his index finger in the air.

Kelley's brow became furrowed as he wondered what Luque meant.

"About two weeks ago—guess who turns up dead in Caracas, as a result of—surprise, surprise—a heart attack while with a hooker, who, again, mysteriously disappeared before the police arrived?" Luque said with a wide grin.

"Bonilla!" Kelley almost shouted.

"Bingo!" Luque said as he wiggled his finger in the air again. "For some reason, the way I figure it, the cartel was afraid Bonilla might expose them. Maybe the cartel thought that Huerta's contact with Bonilla might lead to a bunch of unwanted questions. Maybe Bonilla wouldn't play along with Huerta, and they were going to send a message to some other people—I don't know. For some reason, they decided that Bonilla had become a liability. Who knows exactly why? But one thing for sure, the cartel—it had to be them—decided to eliminate Bonilla."

"Do the police suspect anything?" Kelley asked.

"We don't think so. We have been playing this pretty close to the vest after Casares was killed. Until we get it all sorted out, we don't think we better let the Venezuelan government know what we know—

it might shut down all the work we are doing down here and turn into a real international incident," Luque answered.

"But what about an autopsy—was it atropine again?"

"There was no autopsy, at least one that meant anything. Because Bonilla was a high government official with a wife from a very important, and wealthy, Caracas family, the whole thing was hushed up. The family did their best to cover up the whole incident as quickly as possible. The fact that Bonilla was with a hooker did not, apparently, surprise his family. And, in fact, Bonilla did have a heart condition. So, the thought of foul play just never entered their mind."

"You know, there is one thing. You say Bonilla was rich—how rich?" Kelley asked.

"Damn rich—he pretty well bought his way into the minister's job," Luque answered as he looked questioningly at Kelley.

"Maybe because he was already rich, Bonilla did turn Huerta down. Maybe Huerta didn't offer him enough money, or maybe Bonilla was just an honest politician. But, for whatever reason, Bonilla might have just turned Huerta down, and maybe the cartel knew it— and decided they wanted somebody in his office more amenable to their wishes," Kelley said slowly.

"That's interesting you should say that," Luque said.

"Why?" Kelley asked.

"Because a new minister was appointed by Chávez to replace Bonilla the week after Bonilla died, which is a pretty quick turnaround for a politically sensitive position like the oil minister," Luque answered.

"What do you know about him?"

"Not too much—his name is Eulogio Marulanda. He is a political confidant of one of the state governors and the treasurer for the governor's political party. It's his connection with the political party—the PHC I think they call it—that makes him important."

"PHC?" Kelley asked.

"Yeah—PHC—*Partido del Hombre Común*—the Party of the Common Man. Isn't that a hell of a name for a political party? With a name like that, you know there has to something rotten in Denmark."

Kelley smiled and nodded his head in agreement.

"Well, anyway, Marulanda probably has gotten to know a lot of the right people over the years, so when Chávez needed a new minister, he was the man."

Kelley pursed his lips in thought, then said, "I would think there was more to it than that—he would have had to have some pull in some way to get appointed so fast. Maybe Marulanda had some special in with Chávez."

"Maybe that could be it. The PHC party was a big part of Chávez getting elected. The PHC party is pretty strong in some parts of the country outside Caracas," Luque said.

"Like where?" Kelley asked.

"A little in the Maracaibo region, and a lot in the eastern part of the county—around Maturin and El Tigre."

"So, is Marulanda from Maturin or El Tigre?" Kelley asked.

"Maturin—until he moved to Caracas when he became the oil minister," Luque answered.

"Well, I guess that's where I start," Kelley said.

"Maturin?" Luque asked.

"Yes. I'll do some background work here in Caracas for a week or so on those oil companies I mentioned, and then maybe I'll do a little nightclubbing—in Maturin," Kelley said with a determined look.

# 17

Cinzia Maria Valentina y Cappadoro Beal looked at her husband as he sat on the couch in the bedroom of their Washington townhouse and began to pull off his shoes, talking as he did so.

"That was a hell of a fine dinner party, wasn't it? With the vice-president there, it really made things click didn't it, Cinzia," Roland Beal said.

Actually, Cinzia didn't like the vice-president—or, more precisely, his wife. The woman, in Cinzia's mind, ascribed more importance to herself than she really had a right to. She came from a poor family and her limited upbringing, despite her attempts to overcome it, was always apparent. Cinzia put up with her only because of the potential importance of the vice-president to Roland's aspirations.

"You know, the VP and I were taking alone there for a while—did you notice—and he said some pretty interesting things. He got pretty specific," Beal said.

"What did he say?"

"Well, he's talking about starting his run for the presidency next year—everybody knows that the party's going to nominate him. The President has been grooming him for the last two years now. Well, of course, if the VP gets the nod, then the question is: who gets the vice-presidential slot?"

"He didn't say he wanted you, did he?" Cinzia didn't think the VP would be so uncharacteristically daring or committal.

"No, no, nothing like that. But what he did say was that the party is watching how I do—that my name has come up a couple times in national committee talks with the President. Given where the VP is from, they will need some balance on the ticket. Texas might be just what's needed. It worked for Kennedy and Johnson, and it might work again," Beal said.

"Well, that's encouraging," Cinzia said, wondering how much of talk like that was just for show, just to keep people like Roland kowtowing to the party leaders.

"The thing, he said, that might be essential in the ultimate choice—damn important—is how effective the nominee might be in raising money for the election," Beal said.

Now Cinzia realized what the VP had been up to: more fundraising for the party coffers. "Roland, don't you see why he was talking like that—he wants you to get more money for the party."

"Well, of course, I know that. But the truth of the matter is, Cinzia, there is a real element of truth in what he was saying. If I can really make a solid contribution to the party's fundraising this coming year, it won't be forgotten. Combine that with the Kennedy-Johnson idea, and maybe it might all work out," Beal said enthusiastically.

"Well … perhaps. But I wouldn't get too wound up about it. You're still only in your first term as senator—the party may want you to prove yourself in the Senate before they really consider letting you take up the flag for the party."

"I know, I know. But, Cinzia, I need to think about where I'm headed—now, not later," Beal said.

Cinzia pulled off her dress, slowly, knowing that Kevin liked to see her do that—or at least used to, until he became so wrapped up in Washington politics. When Kevin didn't seem to take any notice, she slipped on her robe.

"You know, Cinzia, talking about raising election money, I need to really get focused on that. Forget about the VP possibilities. My re-election—for the Senate—is not that far away," Beal said.

"Isn't that what you always worry about?" Cinzia asked.

"Well, yes, but I had a discussion with Kevin Matthew just before we left Houston. Seems that he is going to start doing more work in Venezuela—already formed an oil drilling company down there called *Tejas Petróleo*," Beal said.

"Oil drilling in Venezuela!" Cinzia said with a laugh. "Does he really know what he is doing down there?"

"Well, he has been doing okay so far," Beal said defensively. "And he's got some good ideas. One thing—if he is successful he figures that the Coalition can raise a lot more money for my re-election. If I can help the independents, like Kevin, who want to work south of the border—give a little assistance with some legislation—then Kevin is sure that will be recognized—in a very dramatic way—by the Coalition."

"You didn't make a commitment to him, did you?" Cinzia demanded. Roland just didn't know how to say no when money was involved.

"Oh, no. I just said I would look into the possibilities. Maybe have a hearing to see what people like Kevin needed. You know, small businesses, like Kevin's, really have a tough time working in the international arena with the majors," Beal said.

*Hearing!* Cinzia thought. ¡Dios mio! *He's going to try to slip through some little hope-nobody-notices amendment to help Kevin Matthew make money in Venezuela.*

"What else did Kevin express an interest in—during your little talk?" Cinzia asked with suspicion.

"Not much. He did say that some governmental—Venezuelan, that is—understanding of his company's activities would be beneficial."

"What in particular?" Cinzia asked.

"My God, you know how it is down there, Cinzia," Beal said with exasperation. "You lived there half your life. All Kevin wants is for your sister-in-law to talk to her husband, Eulogio, and say a few good words about Tejas. Eulogio was an assistant to that Governor Uriarte down there in Maturin, but he heads the oil ministry now, doesn't he?" Beal asked.

"I think so," Cinzia responded. "Jorge did say something about that when I spoke to him last week over the phone."

"It wouldn't be so difficult, would it, to get your brother Jorge to tell her to talk to her husband about Tejas? In fact, your sister in-law might arrange for Jorge to spend some time himself with Eulogio, telling him about Tejas—maybe even introduce Kevin to him," Beal said rapidly as he blurted out his proposal.

"Roland, why would Jorge want to do all that?" Cinzia said, realizing now what the whole conversation had been leading up to, and wondering whether she wanted to get Jorge involved in whatever Kevin Matthew might have up his sleeve. She had never really trusted Matthew—and she could not understand how Roland did not see how Matthew used him. Hoping to impede Roland's onslaught, she said, "You know Jorge is not the political type—he's not much for that type of thing."

"But he likes to make money—and he could make a lot by working with Tejas."

"Working with Tejas? What do you mean?" Cinzia asked, wondering how deep into Matthew's morass Roland wanted Jorge to sink.

"Kevin wants Jorge to sit on the board of directors of Tejas to help keep a line of communication open, so to speak, between Tejas and Eulogio. Jorge could buy Tejas stock for almost nothing now. We could invite Kevin to your birthday party the week after next—he is always going to Venezuela, now. Jorge could arrange for an appropriate invitation to Eulogio. Then, maybe Jorge could get Kevin and Eulogio together at the party—let them get to know each other on a first name basis, so to speak. Anything that occurred between Kevin and Eulogio and Jorge after that would be their own business," Kevin blurted out in a final rush of words to get the whole story out.

Cinzia looked at Roland with hidden disgust. This man—so tall and slim—and such a little man inside. She wished she had never been so physically attracted to him when she had met him at the consulate those twelve years ago. But, sex, of any kind, was her weakness—and she knew it.

And, in the case of Roland, she had never met a man—never mind the women—who was so able to so physically fill her, to touch each and every nerve of her inner body. Well, she concluded, Roland had gotten her into another messy commitment. Perhaps he could do what he wanted—and maybe nothing of consequence would result from it. But, she warned herself, I have to control Roland more. One of these days he is going to do something *that will backfire, and I won't be able to prevent either of us from getting burned.*

# IV
# THE CHINESE
# CONNECTION

## 18

Wang Ling looked out the fifth-story window of the *Euro Edefico* at the streets below, his emotions momentarily seeking refuge in the seemingly haphazard passage of cars along the Caracas streets below. As usual, cars were constantly cutting in front of one another while other vehicles were coming to sharply braking halts only inches away. Venezuelan drivers never cease to amaze him—absolutely no sense of discipline in their driving.

Comrade Wang Ling was chief operating officer of *China y Venezuela de Petróleo Compañeros de Venezuela*—the name selected by the People's Republic of China's foreign ministry for its petroleum exploration and development company in Venezuela. The name had been chosen in an attempt to connote a bond of friendship between the People's Republic and Venezuela, an attempt whose ineffectiveness was evidenced by the casual name, China Petroleum, by which the company was referred to in virtually all Caracas business and government circles.

"Comrade Wang," Wang's aide said, bringing Wang's attention back to the present and Beijing's displeasure, a fact evidenced by the impending arrival of a new vice-chairman. "Should we not plan to send the limousine to the airport for our new vice-chairman and escort him through immigration?"

"No, the ambassador's instructions were quite clear. Our new vice-chairman wishes minimal notice to be attached to his arrival. He is quite able to deal with immigration upon his arrival—whenever that may be—and come here without assistance. Make room arrangements for him at the Santa Fe Suites. Tell them that his room must become available this afternoon and remain available even if he does not arrive today. Be sure they understand that the room is his whether he makes use of it or not until you personally tell the hotel management that he no longer has use for it. You are to check the room to see that it is fully prepared within the hour."

"Are there any other special arrangements that may be needed?"

"No ... at least none of which I am aware. See to his hotel arrangements immediately."

The aide departed, leaving Wang alone, with his thoughts.

Ambassador Jiang Shan had called Wang to his palatial office at the Chinese embassy earlier in the day, announcing to Wang that Jiang had received a priority message from Beijing. A special assistant, a new vice-chairman, would be arriving within only a few days with instructions for renewing efforts for securing development blocks in eastern Venezuela. Ambassador Jiang made it clear that the Chairman's Advisory Council was disappointed—at least that was the word the ambassador had used—at the lack of progress being made in securing service agreements from PDVSA. Jiang, in turn, had made it clear that Wang, as chief operating officer of China Petroleum, was responsible for the lack of progress. The failure to secure the agreement for the Guarapiche block was the particular event that had prompted the reprimand.

"Wang, you must understand," the ambassador had said in their morning meeting, "our leaders apparently attach extreme importance to securing a development block in eastern Venezuela with access to the Gulf of Paria. Obtaining the lease for the Guarapiche block was critical in their view."

Wang Ling had started to speak, "But—"

"Spare me, Wang Ling. I know as well as you the difficulties of dealing with these Venezuelans—and the unusual circumstances surrounding the bidding for the Guarapiche block service agreement," Jiang had said as he raised his hand to silence Wang.

"The British were lucky—and smarter than us. We focused our

attention only on the oil minister, at the expense of not paying attention to the local politics. Our strategy failed us because we did not plan effectively for contingencies. Bonilla is—or was—a different kind of Venezuelan, and you did not adequately recognize that he was not susceptible to a bribe—that, in fact, he would be insulted by it. We can't let British Petroleum—or anyone else—outsmart us again."

"Yes, our attempts to influence him—"

"No, Wang Ling, your attempts to influence, not our attempts," Jiang had interjected, as he looked harshly at Ling.

Wang's face had become rigid. He had been barely able to control his anger. It was not his fault that the Guarapiche service agreement was not won. *Why did Bonilla have to die now! Who would have expected him to die of a heart attack—he was only fifty years old—while in the throes of passion with some woman who happened not to be his wife?*

The minister's proclivity for young ladies was not unknown. Wang himself had arranged for such company for the minister on several occasions—though not in this particular instance—when the minister would visit cities well away from Caracas to tour, as the minister frequently managed to do, regional ministry offices unaccompanied by his wife; and there had been no hint of such weakness. All the efforts to gain influence with the oil minister would have to begin anew with this new minister, Eulogio Marulanda.

"But," Jiang had continued, "Bonilla is no longer an issue. His recent death removes him from our concern."

"Yes, perhaps we may be more successful with this new minister, Marulanda. I will attempt to call on him soon," Ling had responded hopefully, still stinging from Jiang's rebuke.

"No!" Jiang had responded in almost a shout. "The matter is now out of my—and your—hands," Jiang had continued with a sigh. "Beijing has decided to send a special assistant to lead further efforts in securing the desired blocks. He will be officially a vice-chairman of *China y Venezuela de Petróleo Compañeros de Venezuela*, with formal responsibility for managing China Petroleum government liaison activities. He will be responsible for establishing any arrangements with any government officials. My instructions are to give him my fullest and total support—and that means you are to provide him with any, I stress any, assistance he desires. His orders are to be obeyed without question."

Wang had lowered his head and nodded obediently, but inwardly had been seething.

"And one thing more, Wang Ling," Jiang had said, "the man who is coming is…Comrade Cui Shan."

*Admiral Cui* Shan! Wang had been shocked. Admiral Cui had been instrumental, as a young lieutenant, in the capture of a crew of Americans sailors and marines off the coast of China during the waning days of the Vietnam War of Liberation. The capture and subsequent release of the men, after considerable and very successful efforts by Cui to extract information from the captured men, had remained to the current day a secret tightly kept by both China and the United States, not only because of the capture of the men by Chinese naval forces, but also because of the significant concessions, also secret, that Kissinger and Nixon had made to secure the release of the captured Americans. Following that episode, Cui's rise to power and influence in strategic and often covert naval operations had been consistent and rapid.

"You do understand what I said, Wang—your fullest cooperation," Jiang had said, alluding with little subtlety to Wang's well known, at least to Jiang, dislike for Cui.

Wang had remained silent for a moment. Wang and Cui had crossed paths several times, and none had been pleasant. The last had been sufficient to create a deep hatred in Wang for Cui. Cui had ridiculed the plan that Wang, then stationed at the embassy in the United States, had proposed for securing Chinese navy docking facilities on the United States west coast at the Port of Long Beach only three years ago. Wang's plan had failed while Cui's untried alternative plan, in retrospect, appeared as if it might have worked. After that, Wang's influence had declined while Cui's had continued its almost meteoritic rise. "Yes, comrade—I understand," Wang had answered.

*Now*, Wang wondered with apprehension as he stared unseeingly out the window toward the cloud-topped mountains surrounding Caracas, *why is Cui coming to Venezuela—what is his real purpose? It has to be more than just obtaining an oil services agreement.*

# 19

Cui followed the rest of the passengers, a mixture of Venezuelans, Colombians, and American tourists and businessmen along with a smattering of English businessmen—Cui was the only Oriental on the flight—into the passenger-waiting area for TSCA Airlines at the Simon Bolivar International Airport. He turned left into the wide corridor, following the English and Spanish signs leading the way to customs and immigration. As he reached the immigration area, he purposely stood in the most crowded line, calmly waiting to reach the obviously busy immigration agent. His choice of airline on which to arrive in Caracas had been carefully chosen to maximize the number of arriving passengers passing through customs at the time of his arrival.

Cui moved to the head of the line, saw the agent nod his head, and stepped up to the agent's booth, passport in hand. Cui purposely assumed a look of bewilderment as he handed his passport to the agent. The agent, seeing it was a diplomatic passport, looked only briefly at the document. He looked at the picture and then Cui. Then, looking at the long line behind Cui, the agent quickly stamped Cui's passport and waived him on.

Picking up his two bags at the luggage carousel, Cui walked directly across the lobby, waving off the men offering to carry his luggage, and out to the taxi-lined street.

Cui said, "Caracas," as he slid into a waiting taxi.

The taxi driver quickly pulled into the lane of traffic curving away from the terminal, picking up speed as the taxi came around the curve and approached the now defunct airport toll booths. Ignoring the *despacio* sign, he zoomed through the narrow toll booth lane, as did other cars in the adjoining lanes.

Cui leaned toward the driver and said in Spanish, "I wish to go to the Santa Fe Suites in the El Rosal District. Do you know it?"

Cui saw the driver's eyes in the rearview mirror widened in apparent surprise at Cui's fluency. "But of course, *Señor.* We will be there in less than an hour—if the traffic is not too bad."

It was nearly two hours later, after a long wait in a massive traffic jam caused by a three-car pileup just beyond the short, third tunnel along the highway leading into Caracas, that the taxi reached the Santa Fe Suites. Cui looked at the taxi driver quizzically.

"80,000 Bs, *Señor,*" the driver said with a smile.

"Bs?"

"Bs, *Señor* ... Bs ... Venezuelan Bolivars."

"Oh ... I understand, 'Bs', like American dollars," Cui said as if he were just learning about Venezuelan currency.

"Do I not wish they were American dollars," the driver said with resignation.

"How many did you say?" Cui asked as he pulled a handful of 10,000 VEB notes from his wallet.

"80,000 Bs, *Señor* ... 80,000."

Cui smiled and gave the driver 80,000 Bs, which Cui knew to be about double the usual fare for the ride from the airport. "And, another 10,000 ... Bs, for your service," Cui said as he stepped from the taxi. As the taxi drove away, Cui could see the driver smirk, likely thinking that he had conned Cui.

An hour later, settled into his suite, Cui sipped a glass of wine, thinking through again his assignment—the sheer audacity of it—and how he was to accomplish it. Then he picked up the phone and asked for an outside line. He dialed Ambassador Jiang's personal number.

# 20

"I want to thank you, *Señor* Minister, for arranging your busy schedule to see me today," Cui said as he handed his business card to Eulogio Marulanda in Marulanda's Caracas office a week after Cui's arrival in Caracas.

"The pleasure is mine, *Señor* Cui. I am always pleased to talk to the representatives of those international companies that are bringing the fruits of petroleum development to our country—helping our country and its people as partners," Eulogio said in deference to the formal name of China Petroleum, wondering why Cui's meeting had created such a stir.

Two days ago, Eulogio had received a call from Uriarte telling him to be on the alert for a call from Chávez to discuss the arrival of a newly appointed government liaison officer from China Petroleum. Cui had met with Chávez and Munguia, so Uriarte said, to discuss possible cooperation between PDSVA and China Petroleum. Chávez wanted Uriarte to understand how important such cooperation was and that Uriarte should make sure that Eulogio knew that such collaboration would have the support of Uriarte and the PHC. Uriarte said he was in agreement with Chávez. When Eulogio asked for details, all Uriarte would say was that Chávez would speak directly to him.

When the call came, however, it was from Chávez's aide, Munguia. Munguia told Marulanda that he was to extend his full cooperation and assistance to Cui, repeating several times that Chávez considered cooperation with Cui to be of the utmost importance. But Chávez was also obviously distancing himself from Cui. It was as if Chávez was telling him to do Cui's bidding, except that Chávez wanted to be sure that nobody could accuse Chávez of exerting improper influence on PDSVA—it was all Munguia's doing should anyone accuse Chávez of exercising inappropriate pressure on PDSVA. Eulogio had no doubt Chávez would sacrifice Munguia if necessary to protect himself. Eulogio understood what was going on, knowing that he would have to step cautiously in his dealings with Cui. *But what I do not know is why—what does Cui want, whatever it is, and why is it so crucial to Chávez? Is oil development by the Chinese so much more important than the same development by the Americans, the British, or the Europeans?*

"Yes, *China y Venezuela de Petróleo Compañeros de Venezuela* considers the opportunity to work with the Republic of Venezuela of high importance. The leaders of the People's Republic of China wish me to extend to you their desire to cooperate with you to the fullest extent possible. We sincerely hope that our partnership would continue to be fruitful for both of us," Cui said with grand eloquence.

"*Gracias.* I am pleased to extend the cooperation of the Ministry of Mines and Hydrocarbons to China Petroleum in its endeavors— for the benefit of the people of Venezuela," Eulogio responded in kind, thinking, *now that that is over, we can talk about why you are really here.*

"I must compliment you, *Señor* Cui. You seem quite fluent in Spanish—a rather unusual talent for a gentleman of the Orient. How is it, *Señor* Cui, that you speak Spanish so well? Indeed, you arrived when—only a few days ago, I understand—to assume the position of vice-chairman in charge of governmental liaison, I am told. Indeed, is this not your first visit to Venezuela?" Eulogio asked politely, wondering, *just how is it that this man knows Spanish so well.*

"*Si,* I did arrive only a week ago—that makes me only more anxious to meet people such as you. I have an important charge from our company's leaders in China to foster the growth of our operations here in Venezuela. As to my limited capabilities in Spanish," Cui said self-deprecatingly, "I have a sharp ear, I suppose, for languages, and an uncle, of scandalous background I am told, who spent many years in South America as a young man. He taught me Spanish in his elder years when I was a boy in China."

"Perhaps if more of our international visitors were as fluent as you, more Venezuelans would appreciate their presence here in our county," Eulogio said, subtlety planting the seed, he hoped, that would make Cui aware that actions, not just words from Chávez, would be necessary to obtain the cooperation of the Ministry—and Eulogia's personal assistance.

"But how is it that I may help you, *Señor* Cui? Your ambassador— indeed even *Señor* Munguia, President Chávez's aide, from whom I received a call—seemed most anxious that we have an opportunity to meet each other."

"Yes, I was most anxious to speak to you. The Chinese Ambassador and I had the opportunity to spend a few moments with President Chávez and *Señor* Munguia yesterday and express China Petroleum's considerable desire to work here in Venezuela to the benefit of both China Petroleum and Venezuela. President Chávez expressed his considerable interest in encouraging China

Petroleum's success here in Venezuela."

"Yes, *Señor* Munguia made that clear in his brief remarks to me."

"Wonderful, *Señor* Minister. It is our eager hope to expand our operations here in Venezuela—for the benefit of both China Petroleum and Venezuela.

"Ah ... *si*, for the benefit of Venezuela. But is there some particular way in which I may help?" Marulanda asked.

"Perhaps, *Señor* Minister, perhaps. We understand that later in this year several new blocks in eastern Venezuela will be formally opened for bids for petroleum service agreements. As you most assuredly know, China Petroleum was not successful in its bid for the Guarapiche block in the last round of bidding, which, I understand, occurred before your appointment as minister."

"Yes, the previous bidding did occur before I was appointed by the president, so I am not intimately aware of the considerable efforts, shall we say, that various companies and consortiums expended in their attempts to be successful in their bids," Eulogio lied, remembering his stormy meeting with the previous minister Bonilla and several of his assistant ministers in the days before the successful bid was announced—a meeting in which it was made clear that the PHC's support of Chávez might wane if the British Petroleum consortium did not win the lease. The BP consortium's considerable contributions to the PHC party coffers in the months leading up to the announcement of the winning bidder for the lease could not go unrewarded by Eulogio and Uriarte.

"Yes, that is more to the point of why I am here, *Señor* Minister. You see, China Petroleum seeks to, shall I say, guarantee its success in the coming round of bidding. I am here to ask your advice as to how that might be accomplished—what I might especially do," Cui said as a smile came to his face.

*If you think I am going to openly say that I want a bribe*, Eulogio thought to himself, *you are rather naive*, Señor *Cui.*

But Eulogio did not want to incur the wrath of Chávez. And he certainly was not going to ignore the obvious opportunity to reap benefits from China Petroleum's largess.

"Well, you must understand *Señor* Cui, that we have very

rigorous procedures we follow in qualifying our bidders and evaluating their bids. It takes into many important considerations—factors that have been shown to be important to granting a lease which will lead to not only success for the bidder, but as time passes, benefits for our country."

"Oh, of course, I fully understand that," Cui responded. "But I am sure, within the limits of those procedures, there must be opportunities for enhancing the likelihood that one's bid is successful. I am only seeking your guidance in identifying those opportunities."

*It is time that we bring this dance to a close*, Eulogio thought to himself. "Well, I am appreciative that you fully understand our procedures—our attempt to be completely and extremely fair. One of those procedures of particular importance, though of course not the only one, is our new policy of certification of the benefit of the people in the state where the lease is located. Are you aware of it?" Eulogio asked.

"Certification of benefit? I ... do not believe I know its details," Cui said.

"Well, it is rather straightforward. It requires, for a bid to be accepted, that a certification be provided to the Ministry—which I would, of course, review—that the welfare of the people of the state in which the lease is located is adequately addressed in the operating agreement proposal."

"Could you explain how that certification is obtained? Just how is it issued?" Cui asked.

"The governor of the state appoints a committee of local citizens to review the terms of the proposed lease—particularly as it impacts the local population. If the committee feels the proposed lease terms are adequate, the certification is provided."

"So, to assure the adequacy of the benefits of the proposed bid terms, one must contact ...," Cui asked leadingly.

"The governor of the state in question handles the details of all that—it is a local matter for him with which to deal. Just where is China Petroleum potentially seeking a services agreement, might I ask?"

"Well, we are considering several locations, but we have a particular interest in what I believe is called the San Juan block on the Rio San Juan, in the state of Monagas. Is not the governor there *Señor* Juan Francesco Uriarte? Indeed, I understand that you are from there, that you were an associate of his before you became minister," Cui said, again with a smile.

"Ah ... that is correct. And, indeed, we maintain a close friendship," Eulogio answered with a bit of surprise. *This man apparently knows more than it first appeared. And he likely knows that if he hands over money to Uriarte that Uriarte will funnel some money back to me— if I set the deal up right.*

Eulogio knew he would have to speak to Uriarte to prepare him for Cui's visit—and carefully suggest how to handle Cui. "I encourage you to contact Governor Uriarte and speak with him about the detailed process for obtaining the necessary certification."

"I think that would be a wise thing to do, *Señor* Minister. Since you know Governor Uriarte well, perhaps I might ask a favor of you?" Cui said with dripping politeness.

Eulogio wondered what Cui might ask. He had to be careful not to become directly involved in any dealings that Cui might have with Uriarte. "Perhaps, perhaps not. How might I help you?"

"Perhaps you could facilitate a meeting between the Governor and me—merely encourage him to find a spot in his busy day to spend a few moments with me, in order that we might discuss how earnestly China Petroleum wishes to assure the welfare of the people of Monagas should China Petroleum be certified for bidding for an agreement in the State of Monagas," Cui said.

Eulogio pondered Cui's request a few moments. It was evident that China Petroleum was anxious to bid in Monagas. Eulogio wondered if China Petroleum's preliminary investigations had suggested that the San Juan Block, which was the only block in Monagas coming up in the next round of bidding, might be very lucrative, so lucrative that China Petroleum would be so willing to approach Chávez directly. If that were the case, so Eulogio reasoned, China Petroleum might be ready to make very sizable contributions to the PHC party— something that might be, along with what Eulogio was accumulating from the cartel, just what was needed to establish an appropriate

Swiss bank account—something for the rainy-day should it ever come.

"Perhaps I might be able to facilitate such a meeting," Eulogio said politely, thinking to himself, *It might be well to be more directly, but carefully, involved in helping this Cui, to be sure that everything goes well—such an* opportunity might not arise again. Eulogio wanted to be sure Uriarte didn't squander the opportunity presenting itself—nor possibly cut him out of the substantial amount of money that could most assuredly come out of any deal.

"You know ...," Eulogio paused as if remembering something, "I was planning to go to Maturin soon to speak to the governor on a variety of important matters. When I see him, I can ascertain if and when he might be available for a meeting. I think that perhaps the next week or so might be a very appropriate time for my visit. Perhaps I could contact you ... early next week sometime ... about specifics— and it might be useful if we met briefly before seeing the governor— to give you some insight into his views before you meet with him. Your card has a way I can contact you?" Eulogio asked.

"I think that is an excellent idea—my card has my number on it," Cui said as he handed Marulanda a card with only his name and a telephone number on it. "Someone will answer that number any time of the day and take a message in absolute confidence, even if I am not immediately available," Cui answered.

"Fine. I shall be looking forward to seeing you again, soon, in Maturin."

"Thank you, *Señor* Minister. I believe this visit has been most beneficial—and will continue to be, for both of us. I appreciate your considerable assistance today—and that which you may provide in the future. I am sure President Chávez will appreciate the assistance you have given me. And, China Petroleum does not forget its friends," Cui said as he rose and bowed politely.

# 21

Kelley sipped the Polar that the waiter had just put in front of him. The beer was cold and good. Driblets of condensing moisture ran down the side of the bottle, forming a pool on the black lacquered table. The humidity had soared after the rain that had flooded Maturin's streets—something easily done in Maturin—soon after his arrival on the midday flight from Caracas. Kelley felt drenched with smelly sweat, but the cold beer flowing down his throat began to make him feel better.

After finally making connections at the Maturin airport with Hermann Delgado—a local driver Luque had arranged for Kelley to shuttle him around Maturin, or where ever else he might want to go—Kelley had dropped his baggage off at the Green Parrot, a not-too-fancy hotel. In fact, it was a little on the sleazy side by American standards but appropriate for a businessman on a tight budget, as Kelley was trying to portray—in the downtown section of the city near the city's government offices. And for Kelley, it was also a low-profile hotel, one where he could do whatever he might have to do out of the eye of the Brits, Canadians, and Americans that overran Maturin.

Kelley hadn't felt like he particularly needed a driver; he would have preferred getting a rental car. But Luque said that rental cars—at least those that could be trusted not to break down after twenty miles—were few and far between in Maturin. The good rental cars were snapped up quickly by the oil companies for their managers' use when they visited their Maturin offices, so, Kelley had reluctantly said okay.

"Besides," Luque had said, "Hermann knows the area. I use him all the time to help out in Maturin—like checking with local people wanting to ship things into or out of Maturin."

"But does he know who you really are?" Kelley had asked with concern.

"All he knows about me is that I import and export things, usually in the time-tested way that works down here—by bribes. If some of what I ship is not quite on the up and up, that's not his concern. He gets paid well for being a good driver, irrespective of what is being carried or whom he talks to for me. All he's really concerned about is getting paid."

And when Kelley had expressed worry about Hermann knowing

too much about Kelley's reason for coming to Venezuelan, Luque had said not to worry. "The only thing he knows is that you work for an oil company that wants to make real sure that they can deal with the competition; and that you are trying to get the lowdown on how they operate in the Maturin area. He knows that you are going to do some digging around that may not be quite on the up and up, and that he needs to be sure to help you do the digging—as long as he doesn't have to work too hard," Luque had said with a laugh.

After checking in at the Green Parrot, Kelley had come to the Hotel Morichal Largo, where most of the "expats" involved in the oil business and on an expense account—if it wasn't watched too closely by an accountant—stayed while in Maturin. He wanted to meet Kevin Matthew and see what information Matthew might knowingly or unknowingly give him about petroleum development activities—or any other thing of interest—around Maturin.

Kelley had called Matthew before leaving Caracas at Matthew's Caracas office but was told he had departed for Maturin a day earlier. So, he called Matthew's Trans-Texas' office in Maturin and luckily found him in his office. After a few platitudes, along with Kelley dropping some comments about wanting to establish some business relations in Maturin, Matthew had suggested that they meet in the bar at the Morichal Largo at seven. Kelley had gotten to the hotel about 6:30, just to get a feel for the place before Matthew showed up—the last time Kelley had been in Maturin no hotel like the Morichal Largo had even existed.

— ~ —

Kelley sat casually at a corner table in the upscale, American-style barroom watching the evening crowd slowly build. Most people entering appeared to be businessmen and workmen—in a variety of outfits, from fine suits to work overalls—typical of the oil-patch mix that gathers at the end of a hard day in the oil business, whether it's setting up a new deal or a new rig.

A little after 7:00, Kelley saw Matthew walk in. Kelley waved his arm. When Matthew saw it, he walked over to Kelley, extending his hand.

"Well, howdy, Kelley. Glad we could get together," Kevin said.

"Same here. What'll you have?" Kelley asked as he waved his hand for the waiter and called, "*Señor, por favor.*"

"Make mine the same as yours," Kevin said as the waiter drifted by, never really coming to the table. Kelley pointed to his beer and held up two fingers. "And you can call me Kevin, Kelley."

Both men paused a moment as they looked at a strikingly pretty woman in a tight dress walk into the bar, greet two men, and sit beside them at a table.

"Damn. You know, Kelley, some of these women down here are fine-looking women. This is the umpteenth time I have been to Maturin, and I still swear that some of them have the best-looking tits I have ever seen—at least the younger gals that work in some decent job. And these gals don't mind letting you know about them, either. The first time over here in Maturin, I thought this town was a walking advertisement for women's bras. Every woman on the street, at least the ones less than thirty, had those titties just poking right out through their lace top blouses. But, I guess, maybe that's not why you called me."

"Well, your right—on both accounts," Kelley answered with a smile and a small laugh. Kelley finished the last of his beer as the waiter set two more bottles on the table.

"I'm down here looking into the possibility of doing some business with some oil exploration and development companies, providing some of the equipment and support services they may need. My boss sent me down here to sort of scout out the opportunities. As you probably already figured out from what I said on the plane, my company is only a smaller supplier—but it is big enough to meet the needs of our customers. A lot of them are independents—like you— rather than the big majors. But we plan to get bigger," Kelley said in a boastful tone

"Oh, so you're just a salesman," Matthew said condescendingly.

"Well, not really. I'm more like an advance man, seeing what type of deals might be possible, whether the type of companies we deal with are really a significant presence—and whether it makes sense for us to make a real commitment to do business here and possibly strike a deal with somebody. If we see good long-term possibilities, we might be willing to really bargain with someone—maybe even take an equity position in return for services, rather than cash."

Kelley paused a moment to take a sip of his beer, giving Kevin a moment to contemplate what Kelley had said—and the plum that Kelley had dangled.

"Most of our business has been in the U.S., and we have done only limited overseas work, at least where we are directly involved. Because we are willing to make a strong commitment, we are just a little cautious; we like to really check things out," Kelley said.

"Well, your company—what's it called again ... Consolidated? I don't seem to remember ever seeing the company's name in my operations," Kevin said.

"Consolidated Oil Field Supplies and Equipment," Kelley answered. "Like I said on the plane, we are fairly new, at least under that name. But we have people who know the business—and not just the U.S. business. In fact, I worked the fields over in Maracaibo—when I was a lot younger."

"Oh. Well, you are probably pretty smart doing what you are doing—scouting things out like you are. There's lots of development going on now, and there's going to be more—lots more probably. But doing business down here is real tricky—everybody has his hand out, so to speak. And if you're importing stuff—boy, my people tell me moving things through customs is a royal pain in the ass—unless you're willing to pay expediting fees," said Matthew as he raised two fingers on each of his two hands and put imaginary quotes around "expediting fees."

"Well, you're an independent—are there many like you here in Venezuela?" Kelley asked.

"Not many, to tell you the truth, from what I know. The majors, as usual, dominate everything. Lots of that goes back to, of course, the way the Venezuelan government has been opening up development to foreign investors in the last decade or so in central and eastern Venezuela—usually leasing only big blocks. That means, of course, big bucks are needed to bid on getting a concession—like that last big block that went up for bid, the Guarapiche Block northeast of here."

Kevin paused to take a long swallow of his beer. "That damn block covers about eight hundred square miles. That was snatched up by a consortium led by British Petroleum. The Pedernales block before that—it's east of the Guarapiche Block on the Gulf of Para—was almost as big," Kevin said as he took another swallow of beer.

"If that's so, how do the independents survive," Kelley asked.

"By being, unlike the majors, smart. We find areas that the majors don't think are worth much, or team up with a major who will give us a good deal because we know more than him. Most of the majors are bloated with people who don't know shit from Shinola—the government down here looks to the majors as a social program, to give people jobs. They have to fill up most of their ranks with locals left out in the cold when privatization really took off in the oil business down here in the early '90s. The independents, on the other hand, look too small to the government to worry about very much, at least for the time being."

"Well, you sound pretty optimistic—you must have some target area in mind, then?"

Kevin stopped talking for a moment, looking carefully at Kelley. Then Kevin continued, more slowly, more carefully. "Well, we have some ideas, but nothing for sure yet. We're just looking into the possibilities—like you."

Kelley was pretty sure that, with Kevin's sudden vagueness, Kevin had some specific targets in mind. "Well, if you happen to hear of anything specific, I would like to hear about it. One of the things we—Consolidated, that is—are interested in is possibly forming a joint venture, maybe taking a real equity position with some outfit down here, a smaller but aggressive one, sort of like yours," Kelley said.

"Really?"

"Sure. We have built up a lot of capital in the last couple of years—we have a large investment group backing our operation—and the company's board is looking to invest it ... if the situation is right."

Kevin looked intently at Kelley. "What would make the situation right?" Kevin asked.

"Well, you know I've heard, from the grapevine, that a lot of things go on down here in the oil business besides just exploration and development—things that might offer a lot of money for the right people," Kelley said as he tossed out a line to see just what might happen.

"Is that so? Well, I don't know anything about that. What have you heard?" Kevin asked.

"Oh, just talk, I suppose—how the oil business can help move things back into the U.S.—things that are hard to get into the U.S. otherwise."

"That's the first time I have heard about anything like that," Kevin responded with what seemed to Kelley too much innocence to be truthful.

"Well, perhaps things were being blown out of proportion—" Kelley stopped and looked intently at the two men who had just walked into the bar. One was apparently Venezuelan, but the other was clearly Oriental—and Kelley recognized him. *My God, it's Cui! What the hell is he doing here—and now?*

"See someone you know, Kelley?" Kevin asked as he turned to look at the two men at which Kelley was staring. Kelley stopped staring. "No, not really. I thought I did for a moment," Kelley lied. "Do you know them?" Kelley continued as the two men worked their way across the room toward some tables in the corner.

"The Chink—I don't know him. Probably some guy with CPP," Kevin offered.

Kelley brought a quizzical look to his face, pretending not to have heard of CPP.

"CPP—China Partners Petroleum." Kelley nodded in apparent understanding.

"I know the other guy, the Venezuelan," Kevin continued. "His name is Marulanda. He is an assistant to the governor of Monagas—or was an assistant when I met him this summer for the first time. I was attending some big government powwow sponsored by MARNE—that's the environmental agency down here, sort of like our EPA. It was recommended," Kevin said with a smirk as he put imaginary quotes, again, around "recommended," "by the Minister back then that all the oil companies have their top people at the meeting. They wanted to talk about some proposed new environmental regulation that bidders on various concessions would have to follow—you had to attend the shindig if you wanted to be able to bid. He was there—gave some goddamn stupid speech on protecting the environment during drilling. Somebody said he was the one really behind the writing of the law—the bill, that is, that became law a couple of months ago."

"You say he was an assistant to the governor? Did he lose his job?" asked Kelley as if he knew nothing about Marulanda.

"Lose? Hell, no. He was appointed the Minister of Mines and Hydrocarbons just a short time ago. His involvement in writing the new law was probably his way of trying to show how important he was—getting himself positioned to be appointed as minister."

Kevin laughed. "The goddamn minister, the one Marulanda replaced, had a heart attack while getting laid—boy, that was good timing for Marulanda."

Kelley mulled over in his mind what Kevin had just said, remembering what Luque had said in Caracas: The possibility that Marulanda had been grooming himself for a job that became available as a result of someone's heart attack. *Maybe it was more than a coincidence.*

"This whole environmental business is a bunch of crap," Kevin said with ridicule. "Like a drilling operation's going to have time to do all the shit he was talking about. Nobody's going to pay attention to those regulations, of course. It's too easy to do what you want, so long as you have the cash," Kevin concluded as he rubbed his fingers together in the international sign of payoffs. "About the only thing I got out of the meeting was that there is going to have to be another handout of money by potential bidders—only this time the hand is not in Caracas, but in the local governor's office."

"How so?" Kelley asked.

"This new regulation, when you throw away all the environmental shit, says that you have to get the approval of some local—the state, that is—government committee that is appointed by the governor. And guess how you get committee approval?" Kevin asked with a smirk. "More of the same, except they try to make it look like you are promoting the economic health of the local region—but it's still the same old thing.

"But all things considered, I better go over and say hello to him—congratulate him on his new position. I have been trying to meet him for some time; got some things I want to take to him about. It looks like a good time to say hello, maybe refresh his mind about the time I met him earlier this year," Kevin said as he started to rise from his chair. Then he asked, obviously as an afterthought, "Do you want to meet him, too? I'll introduce you."

"No ... no, I don't think so," Kelley said as he too rose from his chair. "But thanks, anyway," Kelley said casually. The last think Kelley wanted to do was to have Cui recognize him. It was time to get out of the bar—and try to figure out what Cui was doing in Venezuela.

Kevin looked at Kelley with a look of surprise.

"Really, thanks, but I think I'd better go. I have a dinner engagement, and she's very good looking—as you said, great tits," Kelley said with a smile as he put two $20 bills on the table.

"Oh, I see," Matthew said with a laugh. "Well, maybe we could talk some more—if Consolidated is really interested in possibly teaming?" Kevin asked tentatively.

"I'd like that," Kelley answered.

"Well, I will be at a big party here in town this Wednesday evening. A friend of mine, Senator Roland Beal—he's the junior senator from Texas—is the host. His wife was born here in Venezuela. It's her birthday. We can talk some more, then. Call my office tomorrow and get the particulars—I'll make sure you get on the invitation list. I let my secretary know that you will be calling—will that work out?" Kevin said as he extended his hand.

"Yeah, that would be good. I'll see you then," Kelley answered as he quickly shook Matthew's hand, turned, and exited the bar through the nearby side entrance, watching Kevin approach the table with Cui and Marulanda as he did.

Kelley made a circuitous path back to the hotel lobby. Picking up a house phone, he asked in Spanish for the room of a "*Señor* Cui," spelling it so the operator wouldn't make a mistake about the name. "We have no person registered here with that name, *Señor,*" the operator told him.

Kelley wondered what to do. *I have to find out why Cui is here in Maturin. Is he staying at the Hotel Morichal Largo under an assumed name, or is he staying somewhere else in town? The only way to know is to see if he leaves the hotel later that night.*

— ~ —

"I need to piss, *Señor* Kelley. Can I get out of the car?" Hermann asked. Kelley had been sitting with Hermann in the car in the corner of the dark parking lot of the Hotel Morichal Largo for nearly an hour—waiting, hoping to see Cui come out of the hotel.

"Okay, but don't go far. We might have to leave in a hurry," Kelley warned.

"Okay," Hermann said as he opened the car door. Hermann walked to the bushes at the side of the parking lot.

In a moment, Kelley could hear a stream of urine striking the ground. Then, as Hermann sighed, "Ahhhh," Kelley saw Cui come out the front of the hotel, along with Marulanda. The doorman raised his arm and waved to the first taxi in the line of taxis along the driveway. The taxi pulled quickly to the portico over the hotel doorway. Marulanda turned to Cui. They shook hands. The doorman opened the taxi door, but both men continued to talk for a moment.

"Hermann, get back here—quick," Kelley ordered.

"But, *Señor* Kelley, I am still—"

"I don't give a shit. We have to go—now," Kelley demanded.

Hermann stood still a moment a more, shifting this body slightly from one foot to the other as he zipped his pants, and then turned and ran back to the car.

The Venezuelan got into the waiting taxi. As the cab pulled away, the doorman waved his arm again, and another taxi moved forward to the portico. Cui got into the cab.

"See that taxi there with the doorman standing beside it, the one with the Chinese man getting into it. Follow it—but don't get too close. Don't let him know we're following," Kelley said, as Hermann cranked the engine of the car.

Cui's taxi moved quickly toward the street and turned left onto the parkway, heading toward the central portion of Maturin. Hermann pulled up to the street, slowing but not stopping, and then pulled rapidly onto the parkway.

Kelley looked back and saw the other taxi speeding away down the parkway in the opposite direction. Kelley soon lost the taxi in the dim street lights. He turned back to watch Cui's taxi, slowly weaving through the evening traffic. "Don't lose him, Hermann."

"No, *Señor* Kelley, I won't," Hermann said as he looked up in his mirror at Kelley in the back seat and smiled.

They rumbled down the parkway, passing through two traffic circles, and then, as they bounced along the southern side of the airport where the private helicopter operation buildings were located, they turned onto the broad, tree-lined Avenida Bolivar. A few blocks down the avenue, they passed a large Catholic Church and cemetery. Then Cui's taxi made a left turn onto a side street and stopped. At the corner of the intersection was a small hotel. The sign on the entrance read, "Hotel Colonial."

"Pull over down the street—in that parking lot by that restaurant over there," Kelley said as he pointed down the street and then twisted in his seat to watch Cui get out of the taxi, and, after paying the taxi driver, walk into the hotel. *I need to make certain that is where he's staying*, Kelley thought as Hermann bought the car to a stop.

"Hermann, go over to the hotel and talk to the clerk—when nobody else is in the lobby. Ask who the Chinese guy is that just came in—find out if he is registered there, and what his name is. Give him ... twenty bucks for the information and to keep his mouth shut," Kelley said as he reached into his pocket, pulled out a bill, and gave it to Hermann.

Hermann got out of the car, walked to the hotel entrance, and looked through the glass doorway. He turned away, looked at Kelley and shook his head. Then Hermann walked across the side street to a small food stand and said a few words to the man behind the counter. The man quickly prepared a hamburger and handed it to Hermann. Only a few minutes passed as Hermann wolfed down the hamburger. Hermann walked again to the hotel doorway, casually looked in, and then pulled the door open and walked into the hotel.

Kelley waited anxiously for Hermann to reappear. Several

minutes passed and then Hermann appeared and walked casually back to the taxi. As he opened the car door, Kelley asked, "Well, what did you find out?"

"Did I not handle that good, *Señor* Kelley. People were in the lobby, so I pretended to be hungry and bought the hamburger," Hermann said.

"*Si, si*, Hermann, great job. Now, what did you find out?" Kelley asked impatiently.

"The man's name is *Señor* Cui Shan. He represents the China Petroleum Company. He registered yesterday and is in room two-oh-two. He has reserved the room until the end of next week," Hermann said.

"Good job, Hermann," Kelley said, meaning it this time. A smile came to Hermann's face.

Kelley wondered what Cui was up to. Whatever it was, Kelley was sure it was no good. *Cui is not an oilman. He isn't in Venezuela to drill for oil—that is for damn sure. But just what is he here for? And why is he meeting with the Minister of Mines and Hydrocarbons? And what does that mean I should be doing next—bird dogging Cui or continue working on Carrillo's murder?*

As Kelley continued to ponder his options, Cui came out of the hotel. "*Señor* Kelley, there he is again—that is him, isn't it?" Hermann asked excitedly.

Kelley answered, "It sure is."

Cui was no longer in a dress coat. He wore a casual, American-style sports shirt. *Looks like he has finished his business for the day, but where is he going now?* Kelley wondered.

Kelley watched Cui walk up the street about half a block to a Chinese restaurant and bar—the House of Huan—squeezed between a stationery store and a dress shop and opposite the church. Cui entered the restaurant. *Of course, how dumb of me. Where else would he go for dinner if he were alone but to a Chinese restaurant.*

Kelley thought about what to do next. He could probably pick the lock on Cui's room if he had a lock pick with him. But that was not something Kelley usually carried with him. He could probably get one from Luque—but Luque was in Caracas. And Kelley didn't want to raise any suspicions by Cui by forcing the lock. If he got into Cui's room, it would have to be without any inkling by Cui that someone had been in his room—and it was unlikely that Cui would have any significant information hidden in his room. He was too smart for that. Kelley decided to just wait.

An hour passed before Cui exited the restaurant. As he did, one of several girls sitting on a bench in front of the church rose, quickly crossed the street, and approached him. Cui waved her away and continued walking back to the hotel. As he entered the hotel, Kelley said, "All right, Hermann, I think he's done for the night. I want you back here—right here—by five in the morning. I'll try to meet you here also, but just in case I don't, you follow him if he leaves the hotel. Watch where he goes. Try to keep tabs on him without him knowing you are following him," Kelley said.

"But *Señor* Kelley, where are you going—can I not pick you up at your hotel?" Hermann asked.

"I have got some other things to do—tonight. Take me to a place called Antonio's Night Club and House of Pleasure, on *Camino Capitán*. Do you know where it is?" Kelley asked.

"Oh, but of course I do," Hermann said with a broad smile. Kelley didn't try to correct Hermann's idea about why he wanted to go to Antonio's.

"But are you sure you want to go to Antonio's, *Señor* Kelley? I know a place closer to your hotel which is just as good," Hermann suggested. "The customers at Antonio's are sometimes a bit rough."

"No, I want to go to Antonio's," Kelley answered. "Get going."

Hermann turned the starter on the car. After a moment of grinding by the starter and Hermann pumping the accelerator with his foot, the engine roared to life. Hermann pulled out into the street, not bothering to look for other traffic. Some brakes squealed, but Hermann paid no attention as he picked up speed and drove north.

# V

# HOUSE OF PLEASURE

## 22

"There it is. See the sign," Hermann said as he pointed with his finger.

Kelley looked out the windshield. Perhaps a hundred yards ahead was a large sign under a dim street light. As the taxi got closer, Kelley could read the simple lettering on the sign. It read in Spanish, "Antonio's Club," and nothing else. A long, low building was set back behind the sign and away from the road. A few cars and numerous taxis were parked in the area of raw dirt between the building and the road. Hermann pulled into and then across the parking area, stopping in front of the door of the building.

A teenage boy stepped quickly from the shadows and opened the car door. He greeted Kelley in Spanish. "Welcome to Antonio's Night Club and House of Pleasure."

"Gracias," Kelley answered. "Are you open?"

"But of course, we are. Please come in."

Kelley turned to look at Hermann. As he got out of the car, Kelley said, "You be damn sure to be at that hotel by five in the morning."

"*Si*, I understand, *Señor* Kelley. And have an enjoyable evening, *Señor*," Hermann said as he made a silly grin, and then gunned the engine to drive off. The boy opened the door to Antonio's.

Kelley stepped into an entrance hallway. From beyond the hallway, from a darkened room, music emanated—a rhythmic, fast-paced Venezuelan melody. A man in a tuxedo emerged from under an archway and spoke. "*Buenos noches.*"

"*Buenos,*" Kelley responded.

"Ah, an American. It is a pleasure to have you at our club. My name is Freddie. I presume this is the first time you have been to our club—is that correct?" Freddie said in highly accented English.

"Yes, it is. Your club comes highly recommended, and I thought ... well ... maybe ... I could maybe ... spend a little time dancing. I understand you have young ladies here who ... will ... like to ... dance," Kelley stammered in what he hoped was tourist-sounding innocence.

Freddie gave a big smile. "Oh, yes, *Señor* ... *Señor?*" Freddie said leadingly.

"Oh ... Kelley, just call me Kelley," Kelley answered, seeing no reason why he shouldn't give his real name.

"Yes, *Señor* Kelley. We have many lovely ladies here who dance—and provide other pleasures. Let me introduce you to them. Follow me, please." Freddie turned and walked into the darkened room. Kelley followed.

The room was large, with a dance floor in the middle of it. A long bar and another doorway were along the wall opposite the one through which Kelley had entered. Booths with curtains lined the two walls on each side of the bar. Some of the booths were separated by doors in the back wall. A few of the booths had the curtains drawn closed. In some of the others, Kelley saw a man sitting beside a woman. Small tables, each with a burning candle inside a large frosted glass globe, ringed the dancing area.

Several couples were dancing, their bodies gyrating with the music, their sweat readily seen in the twinkling light provided by a large chandelier with blinking Christmas lights, slowly spinning first one direction, and then the other, as if on a gigantic hidden spring. Other couples sat at the tables, drinking beer. The music filling the room apparently emanated from a 1950s-style American jukebox in the corner by the bar.

As Kelley followed Freddie, a few of the people at the tables looked at Kelley. One man gave an ugly smirk as if to say that Kelley did not belong there. His apparent distaste for Kelley was reinforced by a low, "Go home, *gringo,*" said by someone from somewhere in the darkness of the room.

Freddie led Kelley to the wall to the right of the room's entry archway. The wall was lined with couches. And on the couches sat various ladies. All were young and fully, but exotically dressed, with low cut or virtually transparent blouses, or long slits up the side of their dresses revealing ample amounts of leg. As Freddie directed Kelley toward one of the couches, the young ladies there smiled expectantly.

"Ladies, may I introduce *Señor* Kelley, a Norte Americano," Freddie said. The smiles of the ladies became broader. "He wishes to enjoy the company of one of you." Freddie turned to Kelley. "Well, *Señor*, with which one would you like to ... dance?"

"Well, gee, I don't know. They all seem pretty ... nice. Maybe one who has been here a long time ... worked here a long time ... sort of knows the ropes, so to speak," Kelley said, hoping to latch onto somebody who might know who Bettina was.

Freddie looked at Kelley, wrinkles forming on his forehead, apparently surprised by Kelley's request. "Ah ... well then, I am sure you would enjoy ... Emma," Freddie said as he pointed to a woman on the couch near where he and Kelley were standing. "Emma, please come here and meet *Señor* Kelley."

Emma's face brightened as she turned to look at Kelley. She rose from the couch and straightened her dress. It was knee length, bright orange in color, and tight about her hips, but with a long slit up the side, extending to almost her waist, and a loose-fitting bodice of multiple folds of cloth. As she took the few steps toward Kelley, the slit opened wider, revealing most of her left thigh and a good portion of her hip. From what she showed of her hip, it appeared that she had nothing on beneath her dress.

She extended her hand to Kelley. He took it, not sure whether to shake it or kiss it—or merely hold it. He decided to hold it.

"Let me take you to a booth, *Señor* Kelley, where you and Emma can become acquainted," Freddie said as he began to walk toward an empty booth. "The cover fee for the booth is only twenty American dollars. A very reasonable charge, do you not think so, *Señor* Kelley?"

Kelley stopped, knowing that he should act surprised at the outlandish charge. "Well, gee ... I guess it's okay. Do I pay you now?"

Kelley asked.

"I would suggest, *Señor*, that you set up, as you Americans say, a tab?" Freddie suggested. "A tab would be more convenient, would it not, *Señor* Kelley?"

"Well ... I guess ... so ... if you think it would be a good idea, Mr. Freddie," Kelley answered, knowing he was going to get socked for a bunch of fake charges before he got out of the place.

"But, of course, a much better idea," Freddie answered with a smile. "I will send over the waiter to get your drink order immediately," Freddie said as he pulled the curtains of the booth open to let Emma and then Kelley slide onto the couch behind the small table in the booth. Freddie waved his hand, and a waiter emerged from behind the bar. "Have a pleasant evening, *Señor*," Freddie said as he pushed the curtains back to fully expose the booth and then walked away.

Kelley turned to look at the smiling Emma. He guessed she was probably about twenty-five or-six, clearly older than most women who worked places like this. Her complexion was light brown—her exposed hip and thigh were of the same hue as her arms and shoulders. Her body was thin, despite her ample bosom. Her dark green eyes were protected by heavily-coated eyelashes and eyeshadow and immersed in a wide face with a broad nose.

A dark-red coating of lipstick covered her lips, extending above her natural lip line to create an almost heart-shaped red lip-line. Her hair, pulled back tightly from her head and tied in a knot at the back, was as black as any Kelley had ever seen and seemed to radiate sparks in the light of the flickering candle on the table.

"Well, Emma, it's nice to know you," Kelley said innocently.

"It is a pleasure to meet you, *Señor* Kelley. I am sure we can have a wonderful time this evening," Emma said in English.

"Oh, you speak English," Kelley said.

"Enough, *Señor* Kelley, enough," Emma answered with a smile.

The waiter came to the booth, "May I get you and *Señorita* Emma a drink, *Señor* Kelley?" the waiter, an older gentleman, asked.

"I guess so. What would you like, Emma?"

"Champaign on ice," Emma said without a moment's hesitation. The waiter looked at Kelley for confirmation.

"That will be fine—but say, how much is that going to cost?" Kelley asked as part of his tourist act, knowing that that price quoted would be outrageous.

"Oh, *Señor*, it depends upon the quality. I could bring you a cheap champagne from Spain or a good quality, fine tasting one from France. The cheap one would be only thirty dollars, but the better one, the one I am sure that you would prefer, would be a very reasonable sixty American dollars," the waiter said as Emma placed her hand on Kelley's leg and began to slowly massage his thigh.

"Well, I don't know," Kelley responded, knowing what would happen next. Emma moved her hand higher, almost to Kelley's crotch. "Well, I guess the better one—yeah, the better one," Kelley said as he knew he should.

Emma smiled at Kelley, then leaned toward Kelley to kiss him on the check. "Thank you, *Señor* Kelley. I shall not disappoint you."

The music stopped for a moment, then started again. But now it was a slow and exotic love song, full of rich, baritone voices.

Emma looked at Kelley. "Would you care to dance, *Señor* Kelley. I love to dance. I want to dance with you—now," Bettina said in an enticing voice. "It is only ten dollars to dance with me."

Kelley looked at her and nodded yes.

Kelley led Emma onto the dance floor, putting his arm around Emma's waist as he did. She smiled at him and took his hand. She slid it down to her exposed hip. Her skin was delightfully warm to the touch.

Emma leaned against Kelley as they begin a slow shuffle along the edge of the dance floor. The twinkling Christmas tree lights of the chandelier created bursting shadows on Emma's black hair. Her eyes seem to move in and out as the lights blinked. As their dancing progressed, Emma pulled herself close to Kelley, pressing her body against his. Kelley could feel her two full globes pushing into his chest. Each time Kelley turned Emma to redirect their shuffle away from another dancing couple, Emma's body would separate slightly from Kelley, but each time Emma would return to mold herself against Kelley's tall frame.

The music stopped. Emma pulled herself away from Kelley.

"Wait—another song will start in a moment. We can dance some more," Emma said with a throaty voice. Driblets of sweat ran down Emma's neck and disappeared into the folds of her dress.

Kelley pulled a handkerchief from his coat pocket. Emma took it, but reached up to wipe Kelley's brow, and then his lips, with it. She put the wetted handkerchief to her lips and then slid it down between her breasts until it disappeared from view.

The music started. Another melodic, haunting sound of earthy, sensual tones emanated from the jukebox.

Emma again moved close to Kelley, and the two began to dance, again.

As they danced, Emma moved her legs so that Kelley's right leg would slide between her legs, pulling the slit of her dress open wider, until her entire left leg was fully exposed. Her movements made it impossible for Kelley not to be unaware of her bare skin beneath her dress.

As their slow, sometimes almost motionless dance continued, Emma would push herself against Kelley's leg each time it moved between her legs. Kelley began to respond. Emma pushed against him more, pushing against his growing hardness. They continued their slow, almost imperceptible movement around the dance floor, the twinkling, slowly spinning lights of the chandelier creating a surrealistic cloak under which Emma conducted her mating ritual.

Then, the music stopped again.

Emma stopped abruptly and pulled away from Kelley. Emma looked down at Kelley, seeing the obvious.

"Let us go back to the booth. I am thirsty," she said without fanfare. She walked back to the booth. Kelley followed, taking a few deep breaths as he did so.

The waiter stood at the table with the bottle of champagne, a small bottle—enough, perhaps, for four small glasses—immersed in a plastic bucket with a few ice cubes floating in water. As Emma and Kelley sat down, the waiter dutifully uncorked the bottle and poured out the bubbling liquid into two glasses.

Emma handed Kelley his glass as she turned toward him. She nodded her head as she raised her glass in a mock toast, crossing her legs as she did and exposing for a tantalizing moment a dark patch between them.

Emma sipped from her glass. Kelley did the same, using the time to cool his emotions. *Damn*, he thought, *I had better calm down and get down to business. If I don't, I soon may not be in good enough condition to ask any questions that make sense.*

"Have you worked here long, Emma," Kelley asked as he set his glass down.

"Longer than most, I suppose," Emma answered, as she emptied her glass. She picked up the champagne bottle and poured the sparkling liquid into her glass, filling it. Then she leaned over to fill Kelley's glass, letting the top of dress spill open, momentarily but fully exposing her breasts and the handkerchief lodged between them to Kelley's view. Her breasts were full and round and topped by pink nipples. She looked up at Kelley and smiled at him.

"Would you like me to close the curtain, *Señor* Kelley?" Emma asked in a sultry voice.

"Okay," Kelley answered, knowing he needed to get the curtain closed if he were to question Emma without interruption.

"Of course," Emma said as she rose from the couch. "But there will be a hundred-dollar charge for that—it is Freddie's rule. I like you and do not want to make you pay the charge, but I can do nothing about it." Emma looked at Kelley expectantly, her hand on the curtain. "You do not have to pay now. Freddie will know to put it on your tab."

Kelley nodded his head, and Bettina pulled the curtain across the booth entrance. They were now entirely out of sight of anyone else in the room. The booth was lighted only by the candle on the table and the faint glow at the top of curtain emanating from the chandelier above the dance floor.

Bettina sat down closely beside Kelley, the slit in the side of her dress allowing it fall to the side and fully exposing her left leg.

"So, if you have worked here a long time, you must be pretty familiar with most of the girls around here—or that might have worked here in the past?" Kelley asked in a nonchalant—so he hoped—voice.

Emma looked at him. "Why do you ask," she answered, a hint of suspicion apparent in her voice.

"Oh, no particular reason. The friend that recommended this place to me said there was one girl who would do almost anything he wanted—that she really knew her business, so to speak," Kelley answered.

"You don't think I know my business," Emma asked with visible irritation.

"Oh, I'm sure you do. But maybe this girl had some real tricks that you might ... well ... that you might do, without me telling you—it is sort of embarrassing for me to come right out and ask you if you can do what she does," Kelley said.

"You don't need to be embarrassed—what you say won't bother me."

"Aw, I don't know about that. I'd feel better if you just knew, without me telling you. You girls probably talk about things, so you probably know what she would do," Kelley said, thinking, *come on, Emma, ask me her name.*

Emma sighed. "What is her name?"

Kelley breathed a silent sigh of relief. "My friend said her name was Bettina," Kelley said as he watched Emma's face carefully.

Kelley saw Emma's face lose its color. Her smile disappeared. Then she spoke. "I do not know any Bettina—I never knew any Bettina—never," Emma said

Kelley knew it was now time to play hardball—with some inducement.

"Well, it's obvious that you do know her, Emma, so you're going to tell me about her, like it or not," Kelley said as he gripped her arm and twisted it behind her back as he put his free hand over her mouth. "Don't scream, Emma, or I'll bust your arm off before anyone pays attention to what's going on in here."

Emma turned frightened eyes toward Kelley. Kelley slowly released the pressure of his hand on Emma's mouth, ready to put it quickly back if necessary.

"Don't hurt me, please. I know nothing. Please let me go. I will say nothing to no one—just let me go, please," Emma whispered.

"Sorry, Emma, no dice. I'll make a bargain with you. Tell me who Bettina is—and if I believe what you say, I'll give you four-hundred dollars right now—you can give Freddie his two hundred and keep two hundred dollars for yourself—and I will tell him I gave you only two hundred. But if you don't tell me what you know right now, I'll walk out of this place without giving you a thing and say I gave you six hundred—and you can deal with Freddie. If the information you give me works out to be right, I'll get another thousand to you at some place where Freddie and his scum friends that run this place won't know about it. With a thousand dollars, you just might be able to quit this place and do what you want to do—before your body turns to shit and you end up selling yourself for a thousand Bs a customer. How about it, Emma?" Kelley asked.

Emma stared at Kelley for a long moment, then slowly nodded her head. Kelley slowly released his grip on Emma, ready to immediately tighten it if she made a wrong move.

"Okay, Emma, tell me about Bettina," Kelley demanded.

Emma began to slowly speak. "She worked here, until about a month ago. Then she was murdered—the police say it was an accident, but I know it was murder."

"Murder? Why do you think that?" Kelley asked.

"I do not think—I know it!" Emma spit back.

"How do you know?" Kelley demanded.

"Because of what she told me," Bettina said.

"What did she tell you—and why would she tell you?" Kelley asked.

Emma answered Kelley's second question first. "We were friends—she was my cousin."

"Okay—so what did she tell you?"

"She called me at my home—I live with my brother—only two days before she was killed. She wanted someplace to hide; she was very frightened. She came to my house, and she told me. She wanted to leave the country, and she wanted to stay with me until she could get away."

"What did Bettina tell you? What was it that got her murdered like you think?" Kelley asked impatiently.

"She had a customer one night—a man from Caracas. I was here the night the man came. He tried to get me to go with him, but I would not go. I did not trust him. His accent—he was not Venezuelan. But then he gave Freddie some money—lots of it—so he could take Bettina with him to his hotel for two days. I told Bettina not to go, but she felt safe since she knew the driver who was to take them to the hotel."

"The driver ... someone she knew?"

"Yes, I saw him when he drove them off, but I did not know him."

"So, what happened after they left?"

"Bettina said that after they left here, the man told Bettina he did not want her for himself. He wanted Bettina for another man—he wanted her to make love to a friend who was staying at a hotel in Barcelona. He said he would give Bettina a lot of money to ride with him to Barcelona," Emma said.

"Who was the man who hired her—what was his name?"

"The man said his name was Juan—but she did not think it was his real name," Emma answered.

"Who was the man that Bettina was to see in Barcelona," Kelley asked.

"She did not say—she did not know. Juan pointed him out in the hotel bar in Barcelona where he was staying."

"So why would that get her murdered? Husbands are always fooling around when they go on business trips," Kelley said suspiciously.

Emma turned her face from Kelley.

"Tell me, Emma. Stop screwing around with me," Kelley barked.

Bettina sighed. "Juan gave Bettina some pills to secretly put in the man's drink. He said the man—the other man, the man Bettina was to make love to—needed them to make love, but he was ashamed of it. She was to meet the man in the hotel bar and pretend she was attracted to him so he would take her to his room. Bettina was to secretly give the pills to the man so he would not feel ashamed. Juan said he would give her much money for doing this after she finished making love to him—if she made the man very satisfied."

"So, she went to his room and gave the man the pills—and what happened?" Kelley demanded.

"He became very sick, just as she began to make love to him.

Bettina became frightened. She was afraid the pills had made him sick—that he might die. She left right away—sneaked out the back of the hotel so Juan would not know she was gone. She didn't want the money if the man was sick."

*Something is missing here*, Kelly thought to himself. *That was still no reason for Bettina to be murdered.* "What happened after Bettina left, Emma—what happened?"

"Nothing—she caught a bus and came back to Maturin."

"You're lying. Why would she be murdered if she didn't do anything?"

Emma looked at Kelley with pleading eyes. Kelley gave her no quarter.

Emma sighed deeply. "The day after she got back to Maturin, in the paper, a small story about the man in Barcelona ... and his death. It said the man had died of a heart attack in the hotel, with a woman who had disappeared."

"Who was he, Emma?" Kelley demanded.

"Some businessman the papers said—from ... Colombia named Huerta."

# 23

*Bingo!* Kelley could barely contain his excitement. *Bettina was the girl that was with Huerta.* But it was apparent to Kelley that she was just a pawn—a pawn that knew too much. Huerta had to be silenced before he was picked up by the police like Luque had said. So, Bettina was brought from Maturin so she would not be recognized at the hotel in Barcelona and wouldn't be a threat to Huerta's death being discovered for what it actually was. But, Kelley figured, when Bettina bugged out, the cartel's local henchman, Juan or whatever his name was, probably got scared and decided he had better make sure Bettina couldn't become a liability.

*Couple Huerta's contact*, Kelley reasoned, *with Bonilla and then Bonilla's murder—and you have all makings of a perfect takeover of the oil ministry—if Bonilla's replacement is the right guy.* Kelley speculated—no, knew—that Marulanda being in the right place at the right time was no coincidence. Marulanda's appointment was not a simple twist of fate. He was the new minister because the cartel wanted him to be!

"How did Juan find Bettina—if she were hiding at your house?" Kelley asked, trying to fit all the pieces together.

"She left to go back to her apartment to get her passport the next night—and she fell off her apartment balcony on the fifth floor. The police said she was high on drugs. Juan must have forced her to take the drugs and pushed her off the balcony. Bettina did not use drugs— never! But the police did not believe me—once they found out that Bettina and I worked here," Emma said sarcastically.

"But how did Juan know where she lived?"

"Freddie probably told him. Juan came back here to Antonio's later the next night—the day after he took Bettina with him. I saw him. He and Freddie talked in the back room. He probably gave Freddie money."

"Didn't Freddie suspect something—like you—once Bettina was killed?"

"Freddie doesn't care; he cares only about money. And he was probably scared about what might happen to him if he said anything."

Suddenly, "*Señor* Kelley, may I come in. It is I, Freddie. I thought perhaps you would like some more refreshment," came from the other side of the curtain.

Kelley furrowed his brow and then spoke. "Ah ... ah ... just hold your horses ... just a minute." Kelley grabbed Emma's shoulders, pushed her back against the small couch on which they were sitting and pulled down the top of her dress so that one breast was almost fully exposed. He then pushed her dress up and over her thighs, high enough that it was apparent that she had no panties on. "Yeah, sure, come on in, Mr. Freddie. Sure, come on in."

The curtain was pulled aside. Freddie's smile became wide as he looked at Emma's disarray as she struggled to pull her dress down and cover herself. Then the smile went away as he looked at the champagne bottle, its contents still visible. "You do not like the champagne, *Señor* Kelley? Emma, do you want *Señor* Kelley not to enjoy the evening here?" Freddie said disapprovingly.

"Aw, don't blame Emma, Freddie. We just got busy ... talking," Kelley said as he let a silly smirk come to his lips.

"But I want to be sure you have adequate refreshment, *Señor* Kelley," Freddie said with a smile.

"Well, tell you what, Freddie. Why don't you have that waiter of yours bring over another bottle of champagne; this stuff is probably getting pretty stale by now—why don't you do that. Get another bottle brought in," Kelley said.

"Of course, immediately, *Señor* Kelley," Freddie said as he turned, looked at the bar, snapped his fingers, and pointed to the champagne bottle on the table in front of the couch.

Kelley could see the bartender immediately bend below the bar and reappear in a moment with two new glasses and a bottle in a bucket of ice. Reaching the table, he set the bucket down and, in a moment, had uncorked the bottle. He filled the two glasses under Freddie's watchful eye and departed, taking the other bottle with him.

Emma picked up the two glasses and handed one to Kelley. Kelley could see her hands shaking.

"I shall leave you along again, *Señor* Kelley. Emma, be sure *Señor* Kelley has adequate refreshment," he admonished as he stepped away from the table and pulled the curtain closed.

"He suspects! He suspects—"

Kelley quickly put his hand over Emma's mouth and put his finger to his lips. Kelley leaned over to look at the bottom edge of the closed curtain. He saw two feet.

"Aw, don't worry, Emma. It's all right he suspects you and me doing something. Shit, you do this type of thing all the time, don't you anyway? He understands what a man likes," Kelley said with a slightly drunken slur, as he motioned with his hand for Emma to say something.

"Ah ... ah ... well ... *Señor* Kelley, I did not want to ... ah ... embarrass you. I ... thought ... that ... that you would not want Freddie ... to know."

"No problem, little Emma, no problem. You forget all about Mr. Freddie and what he thinks. Let's have some more of that champagne— and pick up where we left off." Kelley motioned for

Emma to say something.

"Oh ... *Señor* Kelley, that is—so good ... so goo ... ood ... do ... it again," Emma responded.

Kelley looked down and watched the feet at the bottom of the curtain turn and move away.

Kelley let out a sigh. Emma's eyes were wide.

"You must leave—I can't tell you more. You must leave," Emma said in a whisper.

"Can't do that yet, Emma. Leaving now would only make Freddie suspicious," Kelley said in a low voice. "Besides, I have one more question."

"No! No more questions—no more answers. No."

"Yes, Emma—or you won't get the money I promised you," Kelley threatened.

Emma looked at Kelley with hate in her eyes. "Did Bettina know a Jose Carrillo?"

A surprised look came to Emma's face. "Jose—how do you know about him?" Then her surprised was replaced by fright. "Who are you?"

"I'm asking the questions, Emma. How did Bettina come to know Carrillo?"

"She met him at a PHC meeting about three months before she was murdered. He was very interested in politics—"

"The PHC party?" Kelley asked.

"*Si*," Emma said as she nodded her head.

"Why was Bettina involved in the PHC?"

"She wasn't, but her cousin—my brother Franklin—is. She would sometimes go to the party rallies to help him. He works for the party treasurer. She met Jose at one of the rallies."

*Hot damn! Carrillo suspected something was going on in the PHC and was using Bettina to worm his way into the party—and also probably getting to know Bettina as more than just a friend. Carrillo was always a ladies' man.*

"Bettina fell in love with Jose," Emma volunteered. "He said he would take her to the United States someday. But Jose left one day without her and did not return."

"Do you know what happened when he did?" Kelley asked hopefully.

"No. He was to meet Bettina at a rally one night, but he never came—I told her he would not stay with her if she told him she was going to have his baby."

"You mean Bettina was pregnant?" Kelley asked in surprised.

"*Si* and she knew it was Jose's baby—and he just left her. May he rot in hell. If he had kept his promise to take her to the United States, Bettina would be alive today. If he had come back like he said he would, she might not have gone with Juan that night."

Kelley looked at Emma but said nothing to dispel her hatred. It would only make Emma more reluctant to talk to him if he told her the reason why Carrillo was not able to keep his promise. Then something clicked in Kelley's mind.

"What do you mean, like he said he was going to? I thought you said he just walked out. When did he say he would be coming back?" Kelley asked

"His letter—his letter to Bettina said he was going to come back," Emma said in a matter of fact tone.

"Letter! Carrillo wrote a letter to Bettina after he left?" Kelley asked, wondering what leads might be buried in that letter.

"*Si*. That is why she was waiting for him. But the bastard never came back."

"What was in the letter?"

"I don't remember much about it, except that he said he was coming back to get her," Emma answered.

"Do you still have the letter?" Kelley asked hopefully.

"I gave it to my brother after Bettina's funeral. Why?" Emma asked suspiciously

"You mean Franklin has it?"

Emma spit out angrily, "I do not know what he did with it—and I do not care."

"I want to meet him—will you introduce him to me?"

"Why should I? I don't like you and your questions," Emma answered sullenly.

"Because, Emma, if you do, I will give you another four thousand

American dollars, in addition to the one thousand I already promised you if Franklin shows me that letter."

"Five thousand! And Freddie will not know?"

"That's right. When you introduce me to your brother, and he shows me the letter, I will give you five thousand dollars American," Kelley answered.

Emma was quiet for a long moment. "All right. There is a PHC rally Sunday afternoon in the Government Plaza near the governor's office. Meet me at the fountain in the center of the plaza—at three o'clock. You bring the money, and I will bring my brother."

"I'll be there—with the money. But don't try a fast one—no brother, no letter, no money." And then to sweeten the pot, the Kelley added, "And if your brother brings the letter with him and lets me read it right there, I'll give you another thousand," thinking he was going to have to contact Luque and get some money sent over from Caracas pretty damn quick.

Emma looked at Kelley and nodded her head.

"Okay—now listen," Kelley said. "You can't let anyone know that you told me what you did. And what I am going to do now will make sure of that."

Kelley pushed Emma back against the couch and again pulled down the top of her dress, revealing almost all of her two breasts. He again pushed her dress up and over her thighs, high enough to again reveal a dark wedge of pubic hair. He then took his wallet out and pulled four $100 bills from it. He stuffed the bills the top of Emma dress, between her two breasts, next to his handkerchief. Then he undid his belt buckle and pulled the zipper of his pants down. He turned away from Emma and threw back the curtains from the booth.

As Kelley pulled his zipper up and buckled his belt, he saw Freddie look toward the booth. Kelley put on a big smile, stepped from the booth, and walked toward the entrance hallway. Freddie came up to him.

"*Señor* Kelley, did you have a good time?" Freddie asked.

"The best," Kelley said with a grin. "But I got to be going now."

"So soon, *Señor* Kelley? The night is still young. A little relaxation and you will feel fresh—and vigorous again," Freddie said, obviously trying to eke as much money as possible out of Kelley.

"No, I've got to get up early in the morning—but you can be damn sure I'll be back soon if I get a chance—I want to ... dance with another one of your girls."

"Wonderful, *Señor* Kelley. Let me get your bill. Will you be paying with cash or credit card?"

Kelley removed his wallet from his pocket and gave Freddie his American Express card. "Use this—say, what is the bill?" Kelley asked innocently.

Freddie opened his waiter's pad, did some calculation with a pencil, and handed Kelley a bill. The number at the bottom was 900,000.

"Nine hundred thousand!" Kelley said in mock shock.

"Bs, *Señor* Kelley, bolivars. Not dollars," Freddie said in a calming voice.

"Oh. So, what is that in dollars?" Kelley asked.

"Ah ... at the current rate of exchange, only about four hundred dollars." Kelley knew that Freddie was using a wildly inflated exchange rate.

"And that includes, of course, a tip for the bartender and the doorman—and myself as well," Freddie said with a wide smile, as he swiped the credit card through the card reader on top of the bar.

In a moment, the credit card ticket was kicked out. Kelley leaned on the bar and signed it.

"Well, I guess I'll be going—hope to see you soon, Freddie," Kelley said as he walked toward the door.

"We would like that very much," Freddie said as he opened the door and pointed toward a taxi in the line of taxis near the building entrance. The driver leaning on the fender of the taxi straightened and got into driver's seat. Freddie motioned the car forward.

Kelley climbed into the taxi and leaned back in the seat. As he did, Freddie turned to the driver and said, "Please see that our American guest gets home safely, Fernando."

— ~ —

They had been traveling about five minutes when the taxi driver's cell phone rang. Fernando flipped back the phone cover and put the phone to his ear, saying, "*¿Si?*" as he did. A moment of silence passed after which Fernando said, "*Si,*" again and shut the phone cover. Fernando turned his head toward Kelley and spoke. "My wife—she wonders when I will be home."

Kelley smiled absent-mindedly, his thoughts focused on Cui and Marulanda. The taxi pulled to a stop at a red light. The dimly lighted intersection was empty. Kelley wondered why the cab was not moving—running red lights was common for most taxi drivers, particularly late at night.

Suddenly, the back door of the taxi was pulled open, and a man stuck a gun in, pointing it at Kelley. "Get out," the man yelled.

*Jesus,* Kelley thought, *I should have taken Hermann's advice.*

Kelley slowly exited the back seat. He stood beside the car. The taxi driver exited the car and stood behind Kelley. The man with the gun brought the gun up to Kelley's face. "Don't go back to Antonio's again," he growled.

The taxi driver raised his hand—there was something black and ugly in it—and swung it into Kelley's head. Kelley fell to the ground.

# 24

Kelley lay still for a moment, trying to get his bearings. As he did, he felt a throbbing pain in the back of his head. *Damn,* he thought, *I must be getting old. I didn't think Freddie would have me mugged.*

Kelly listened a moment more. He could hear birds chirping, then the sound of cars, a honk of a horn. He slowly opened his eyes, not moving his head. He could see he was lying face down in some tall grass. A short distance from his face a small lizard was looking curiously at him. Kelley moved his head slightly. The lizard scampered away. Kelley began to slowly move his limbs, cautiously, not knowing what to expect.

Nothing happened.

Kelley rolled onto his side and pushed himself to a sitting position. The throbbing in the back of his head exploded in pain. An uncontrolled "O-oo-ouch" came from Kelley's lips. Kelley moved his hand to the back of his head. He could feel flakes of dried, crusted blood, along with a large lump.

Steadying himself with his other hand, Kelley looked around. The sun was up. Looking over the top of the tall grass around him, he could see the tops of some cars moving along a road, and farther away, the upper stories of some buildings. *At least*, he thought, *I am somewhere near civilization.*

Kelley slowly lifted his himself to his feet. Yes, there was the highway, and beyond, what looked like the outskirts of what he hoped was Maturin. Kelley looked at his watch to see the time—but his watch was gone. He reached into his back pocket. His wallet was also gone. He felt in his coat pocket for his cell phone—it too was gone. *Shit.*

Kelley brushed himself off and began walking toward the road.

— ~ —

"Follow me," Kelley said as he got out of the taxi in front of the Green Parrot. The taxi driver walked with Kelley into the hotel lobby.

"Please pay the taxi driver—and add a twenty-thousand Bs tip," Kelley said to the desk clerk at the front desk.

When the desk clerk looked questioningly at Kelley, Kelley continued. "I lost my wallet last night. Please add the charge to my bill." When Kelley saw the desk clerk hesitate, Kelley continued, "And add another ten thousand Bs for yourself for your assistance— add another ten-thousand for me too."

The clerk looked at the taxi driver expectantly. The taxi driver responded with, "*Veinte mil.*"

The clerk wrote some numbers on a piece of paper and handed it to Kelley. "Your signature, please, *Señor*, for our records."

Kelley took the piece of paper and the pen the clerk held up for Kelley's grasp and then leaned forward over the counter to sign the paper.

"*Señor* Castellano!" the clerk said in surprise, apparently seeing the bruise on the back of Kelley's head. "You head, it has been bleeding. What happened? Do you want to see a doctor?"

"No, I don't need a doctor. I can take care of it myself—just have the bellboy go to the *pharmacia* across the street and get me some bandages—a bunch of different sizes—and adhesive tape, scissors, and antiseptic, if you don't mind," Kelley requested.

"Certainly," the clerk answered as he waved to the young boy sitting on a bench in the corner of the room. The clerk spoke to the boy, who then immediately exited through hotel's doorway.

Kelley handed the signed paper to the clerk.

The clerk took the paper and then turned to walk through a doorway into the office behind the front desk.

Kelley and the taxi driver waited in silence. In a few minutes, the clerk returned with a fist full of bills. He counted out some of them to the driver and pocketed the rest.

The taxi driver counted the bills again, said, *"Gracias,"* and left the lobby.

"Are there any messages for me?" Kelley asked.

"Ah, yes," the clerk replied, as he reached up to Kelley's mail slot and removed a piece of paper along with Kelley's room key.

Kelley looked at the paper the clerk handed him as the clerk placed the key on the counter. A message was written on the piece of paper; it was in Spanish. "What the hell is this—I am in jail, Hermann?"

"I do not know, *Señor. Señor* Hermann called this morning. He said to give you a message, and then said what is written there, and then hung up."

Kelley looked at the clock on the wall. It read ten after two. "Where is the jail?"

"It is next to the airport."

"Call me a taxi. Have it here in an hour," Kelley ordered as he picked up his key. I am going to clean up. Send those bandages to my room right away."

*"Si, Señor*, but are sure you do not want a doctor?" the clerk asked.

"No—it's not the first time I have gotten knocked in the head," Kelley answered caustically.

— ~ —

In his room, Kelley pulled his passport, a spare credit card and six hundred dollars in reserve cash from his combination-locked suitcase. He yanked off his clothes, letting them fall in a heap on the floor, and stepped into the shower. The water hitting the back of his head made his head throb again, but the dried blood began to break off and drain away. He continued to stand under the shower, slowly rejuvenating himself.

When he heard the knock on the door, he stepped out of the shower, grabbed a towel, and moved to the door. Opening the door, he said, "*Gracias,*" and took the bandages, dressings, scissors, and bottle of antiseptic from the boy standing there. The boy nodded his head and left.

Kelley sat on the edge of the bed, tore the wrapper off one of the gauze pads, and soaked with it antiseptic. He put the pad on the back of his head. "Aaa-hh—damnation!" Kelley howled in pain.

He continued dabbing the cut on the back of his head until the blood flow seemed to slow. He breathed a long sigh and then went into the bathroom. Looking in the mirror, he pulled his hair back and, as best he could see, cut off some of the hair around the cut. He applied some more antiseptic; it didn't sting nearly as much now. He then tore open another bandage, pulled his hair aside again, and taped a large bandage to the back of his head.

Kelley stepped back to the bed, sat down, and picked up the phone. He asked for an outside line and then dialed the U.S. international code followed by a number with a 303 area code. In a moment, a calm male voice said, "Consolidated Oil Services. May I help you?"

"Yes," Kelley said to the voice at the other end of the line.

"Your identification, please," the voice asked.

"Kelley Castellano, Vice President of Sales for Consolidated Oil Services of Denver," Kelley answered.

"And the address in Denver?" the voice asked.

Kelley gave the necessary sequence of numbers in the street address to complete the identification.

A moment of silence passed. Then the voice said, "Identification verified. Please hold a moment."

A new voice came on the line, one that Kelley knew was in Langley, Virginia.

"Please identify yourself," the new voice said sternly.

Kelley went through the same ritual he had just completed.

The new voice then said, in a friendly tone, "Your identification is confirmed. What's the purpose of your call?"

"I need some money."

"How much, when, and where?" the voice asked without hesitation.

"Wire fifteen thousand dollars to me at the *Banco Internacional de Caracas* branch in Maturin. Give specific instructions that identification will not be required, that only a code word will be required to pick it up—and make sure I can get the money in American dollars."

"What code word?" the voice asked.

Kelley paused, then continued. "The town of my immediately previous employment. You know where that is?" Kelley asked.

There was a long pause at the other end of the line. "Yes," finally came the reply.

"I want it available by noon tomorrow, local time. Can you do that?" Kelley asked.

"I believe that can be arranged," said the voice calmly.

"Oh … and arrange for a new American Express card and driver's license to be sent to me at the Green Parrot Hotel in Maturin. Have them delivered by noon tomorrow also."

"Will do. Is there any message you want to leave? Are you all right?" the voice asked without emotion.

"Reasonably well. I got mugged last night. I will have a headache for a day or two, but I don't think anything was really busted."

"Was the mugging a warning or—"

"No, I don't think so. I just got in with the wrong crowd … I think," Kelley answered.

— ~ —

Kelly looked with disgust at Hermann as they walked out of the jail. Arriving at the jail after leaving the hotel, Kelley had readily seen Hermann's car—its odd combination of color and style were unmistakable—in the impoundment area in front of the jail. Some questions of the people working the soft drink stand near the jail—they did a land office business from the people waiting to get police approval to recover their cars impounded by the police after auto accidents—soon made it clear what had happened. The police had arrested Hermann as he had been sitting in his car by the helicopter offices next to the jail for no apparent reason. Kelley had then gone into the station house and confirmed that Hermann was in fact in jail—and it did not look like he would get out unless a fine was paid.

After some haggling, two hundred dollars got Hermann out of his cell. "But I did not do anything, *Señor* Kelley. I was doing nothing," Hermann said in defense as they walked down the steps from the station toward the impoundment area to get Hermann's car.

Waiting at a street corner for cars to pass, Hermann suddenly looked at Kelley with a concerned, questioning look. "*¡Dios mio! Señor* Kelley, your head ... you have a bandage? What happened? Did you hurt yourself?"

"No, Hermann, I did not hurt myself—someone else hurt me. I was mugged on the way back to the hotel last night," Kelley said in a matter of fact voice.

"Mugged ... someone attacked you?"

"Yes, that's what mugging means, Hermann," Kelley answered in a disgusted voice.

"See! I told you the House of Pleasure was a dangerous place. Next time I will take you to a place near the hotel and bring you home myself. This must not happen again," Hermann said emphatically. "You must promise me that you will not go back to the House of Pleasure." Hermann paused a moment as the cars passed and then he and Kelley walked across the street.

Reaching the opposite sidewalk, Hermann continued with a tint of fear in his voice. "*Señor* Luque will be very angry if he finds out I let someone hurt you. He might not let me be your driver anymore. You will not tell him, will you?" Hermann asked, apparently now concerned that he might lose his job. "You do not blame me for your discomfort ... and the jail—that was not my fault either."

"Okay, okay, Hermann, none of it was your fault," Kelley said as they reached the guard both at the vehicle impoundment area. Kelley gave the impound attendant about two-thousand Bs to speed the process of getting the lock off Hermann's car. In a few minutes, they were driving out of the lot and down *Avenida Bolivar*.

"So, what happened to Cui?" Kelley asked.

"He came from the hotel in the morning and took a taxi downtown to a stationery store," Hermann answered. "I followed him in my car."

"Stationery store? What did he do in there?" Kelley asked in surprise.

"I do not know, but when he came out, he had a long roll of papers—at least that is what it looked like—under his arm."

"What do you mean—roll of papers?"

"A long package, about a meter long, in a roll about this big around," Hermann said as he held up his hand, forming a circle with his fingers.

Kelley thought about what Hermann had said for a moment, wondering what Cui had bought in the store that would be big enough to be rolled up like Hermann was describing. "What did he do next?"

"He came back to the hotel and stayed there about an hour. Then he came out again and took another taxi to the airfield, next to the jail," Hermann answered.

"You mean to the helicopter field next to the jail?"

"*Si*, the helicopter field. He went into the building where the offices are."

"And?" Kelley prompted.

"He was in the building a long time."

"Okay, so what happened when he finally came out?" Kelley asked in frustration.

"I do not know. After I had been parked in front of the building about an hour, near the jail, a policeman came to my car and arrested me."

"Do you know why?"

"He said I looked suspicious and wanted to know what I was doing sitting in my car by the jail. I tried to explain I was watching someone and—"

Kelley cut in, "You mean you actually told them that you were watching someone? Jesus, Hermann, no wonder they put you in jail. You couldn't think of a better answer than that?"

"I did not have time to make up a story. It all happened so fast,"

Hermann tried to explain.

"Okay, okay," Kelley said in resignation. "So, do you know what happened to Cui?"

"I am sorry, but I do not know," Hermann answered in a quiet voice as if waiting for Kelley's reprimand.

*Crap,* Kelley though. *What the hell do I do now? Wait a minute—*

"Hermann, you said he went to a stationery store."

"Si."

"Okay, let's go to the stationery store."

"*Si, Señor* Kelley."

— ~ —

Twenty minutes later, Hermann pulled to a stop in front of a stationery store sandwiched between a café and a woman's clothing store. The café was doing a booming business, but the clothing store—and the stationery store—were closed.

"Why didn't you tell me the damn store would be closed, Hermann?"

"I was not sure ... and you did not ask me if the store would be open," Hermann offered in defense.

Kelley shook his head, then looked again at the café, realizing that he had not eaten all day. Sighing, Kelley looked at Hermann. "Have you had lunch, Hermann?"

"No, *Señor* Kelley, but I am very hungry."

"So am I. Let's eat. Then I have to go to a birthday party."

# VI

# INSIDERS

---

## 25

After he gave his name to the doorman and was checked against the guest list, Kelley stepped from the foyer into a large living room with a high, two-story ceiling in the palatial Maturin home of Roland Beal's father-in-law, a former consul general for the Venezuelan consulate in Houston, at least so Kelley had been told by the taxi driver who had picked him up at the Green Parrot—Hermann had been directed back to the Hotel Colonial to see if Cui would show up there. A small band of guitarists, drummers, and trumpeters were in the corner of the room, playing a soft Venezuelan love song. Kelley sauntered across the living room, weaving between several small groups of guests and toward the patio where most of the people were congregating.

"Ah, there you are, Kelley," Kevin Matthew said.

Kelley turned.

"Good to see you, Kelley."

"Glad I could come," Kelley said as he shook Kevin's hand.

"Say, what's that on the back of your head—a bandage?" Kevin said with an inquisitive laugh. "Did that lady you were going to see get a little rough?"

"Don't I wish? No, nothing quite as exciting as that. Just had a little accident—slipped and fell in the shower."

Kevin wondered whether Kelley was telling the truth, but it made no difference to him. If Kelley played around with rough women, that was his business. He had done a little checking on Consolidated with his Denver contacts and found that Consolidated was, as Kelley had implied, apparently a reorganization of some oil equipment suppliers that were trying to move into the South American market. But, so his contacts said, Consolidated seemed to be somewhat of a mystery. Not too much was really known about their operations, except that they seemed to be well-backed financially—they seemed to have money to invest in whatever amount needed—if the investment looked worthwhile. That was music to Kevin's ears. Consolidated might be just the partner he needed to provide some up-front money for Tejas in return for some part of the action.

*Hell,* Kevin thought, *Kelley and Consolidated might even be duped into taking the risk of moving drugs back to the U.S. if I can use Consolidated as a subcontractor for handling some of the used equipment shipments going back to the states. Slip them into Consolidated's shipments and then pick them up after they pass customs.* Kevin surmised that if they didn't get by customs, he could easily claim innocence. It might be messy if that were to happen, but that would be far better than having any shipments discovered under *Tejas Petróleo's* name.

"Let me introduce you to some of my friends, Kelley," Kevin said as he began to steer Kelley toward a group of people on the other side of the patio. "And," Kevin continued as he grabbed two drinks from a passing tray and handed one to Kelley, "don't you run off tonight like you did at the hotel the other night. I have some serious business I want to talk to you about later this evening."

"I'll be sure to hang around," Kelley answered.

"Good, good," Kevin said as he propelled Kelley into a group of people. "Senator ... Senator Beal, I would you to meet a good friend of mine—Kelley ... uh ... Castellano."

— ~ —

Once Kevin had deposited Castellano with Beal, Kevin looked for Cinzia—he needed her to provide his introduction to Jorge.

After finding Cinzia among the 200 or so party guests and getting numerous introductions to Cinzia's family members, Kevin had been finally introduced to Jorge.

During dinner, Kevin was seated next to Jorge's wife, Cinzia's sister. Kevin tried to obtain as much information from her as he could about Jorge. He learned two important things: Jorge had a high opinion of himself—something that was not of particular concern to Kevin—and, more importantly in Kevin's mind, liked to make money.

And from what Kevin could tell—and hear—from where he was seated during the dinner hour, Roland, who was seated across from Marulanda, was getting along quite well with Marulanda. The two men were discussing international markets, business development and the role of oil in it, and relations between Venezuela and the U.S.—and how they could complement each other. And when Roland discovered Eulogio had spent two years in graduate studies at Baylor's business school while Roland had been working on his graduate business degree at Baylor's rival Southern Methodist, the discussion between Eulogio and Roland became even more affable, like two buddies sparing over who had the best football team—though in fact, neither school had a football team still worth a nickel.

Marulanda seemed well-informed and articulate—a man, so Kevin surmised, who could be trusted to understand the need for productive relationships to foster business development. Kevin smiled to himself. The idea of having Jorge and Roland be the bridge to enticing Marulanda into Kevin's plans for Tejas seem to be a better and better idea each passing minute.

As dinner neared its completion, the band shifted into high gear, and the music became more quick and hot, with a robust American beat. As some of the younger men and woman became enwrapped in the sensual sound of the music, the makeshift dance floor in the center of the patio began to fill. Cinzia, who loved to dance but seldom could because of Roland's knee, approached Roland and Eulogio, breaking into their conversation, and suggested that she and Eulogio dance, saying, "Eulogio, my brother-in-law, do you still remember how we used to dance? Are you still young enough to dance as we once did?"

"Of course—anything for the birthday girl," Eulogio answered as he looked at Roland, "if it is acceptable to Senator Beal."

"But of course, Eulogio ... of course," Roland answered, glancing across the table towards Kevin, knowing Kevin wanted to speak to Jorge before the evening got too late.

Eulogio rose from his chair, took Cinzia's outstretched hand, and led her to the dance floor. Roland watched them only a moment before turning to look at Kevin.

Kevin nodded his head toward Jorge, who was still sitting at the main dinner table.

Roland rose and approached Jorge. Roland leaned toward Jorge and whispered something in his ear.

Jorge nodded his head and rose from his chair, excusing himself from the nearby guests. He followed Roland towards a hallway.

Kevin rose and followed them both.

Roland led Jorge and Kevin to a closed door. Roland opened the door and invited Jorge and Kevin into the room with a wave of his hand. The muted sounds of the music could still be heard as Roland closed the door.

"Jorge, Kevin," Roland nodded his head toward Kevin, "and I wanted a moment to speak to you about some important business opportunities in which we think you might be interested—something we needed to discuss with you in private," Roland said with a smile.

"Yes," Kevin chimed in. "As I told your wife during dinner, Jorge, I have a successful oil exploration and development company in the U.S."

Jorge nodded his head in agreement. "Yes, I heard you tell her that. You also said you were doing business here in Venezuela. Cinzia also said something about that this morning at breakfast."

Kevin smiled to himself. *Apparently, Roland had been able to convince Cinzia to grease the ways for the meeting.*

"Yes. My company, Trans-Texas, has been providing some subcontracting support to some of the major oil companies for several years through Trans-Texas. But here's what I didn't tell her. I have started a new company under the name *Tejas Petróleo*. Tejas is ready to branch out on its own—to do our own exploration and development here in Venezuela. Trans-Texas has been doing it for years in the U.S. We have the know-how. From a technical standpoint, we are ready to do the same here in Venezuela. But until now the timing—the conditions—have not been just right."

"But you think they are now?" Jorge asked with a smile.

"Yes—with the help of the right people," Kevin said as he smiled in return.

Beal, apparently not wanting to be left out of the conversation, said, "Yes, Jorge, Kevin and I have been talking quite a bit about the current opportunities here in Venezuela—for everyone involved. I suggested that having someone—someone like you—who understands the political scene here in Venezuela would be a worthwhile addition to the Tejas team. Kevin here believes that your participation as a member of the board of Tejas would be highly beneficial to the ventures Tejas wishes to undertake."

"Member of the board of this ... Tejas company," Jorge said hesitatingly.

"Yes," Kevin said with enthusiasm. "A full voting member of the board, with a full three percent of the company stock—a not insignificant sum when considered in light of potential revenues we expect to receive once our development activities begin to pay off."

"But how much would the company stock cost. I might not have enough money to make the required investment," Jorge asked skeptically.

"Oh, you don't understand, Jorge," Kevin responded. "You see, Jorge, your three percent wouldn't really cost you anything. The purchase money would come from your compensation for serving on the board—and assisting in some key responsibilities. You would only formally be buying the stock, just to keep the paperwork straight. It would be like taking Tejas money from one account and merely putting it in another account—with you getting some money in the transfer process. Kevin and I have used this transfer process in other business arrangements we have developed in the past—works quite well; keeps old Uncle Sam—the IRS, that is—happy and doesn't really cost me anything to become a successful partner in a joint venture."

"Isn't that like, I believe the saying is, robbing Peter to pay Paul?" Jorge asked as he looked at Kevin with a tight-lipped smile.

"Yes—except it's not robbing. It's more like taking money from your left pants pocket and putting it in your right pants pocket but getting a brand-new pair of pants as you do it."

"I see ... I see. So, what is the nature of this assistance you would want me to do—what would be my responsibilities?" Jorge asked slowly.

Sensing the caution in Jorge's voice, Kevin spoke quickly. "Yes, some minor, but important things, some loose ends so to speak—some things that you can help us with."

"And what would those loose ends be, *Señor* Matthew?" Jorge asked with dripping politeness.

Roland spoke before Kevin could answer. "Kevin's use of the term 'loose ends' is not to say it is unimportant—your role would be very important, Jorge, crucial in fact."

Apparently mollified, Jorge asked, "Just what matters are we speaking of?"

"Yes, Kevin, why don't you explain it to Jorge, our Tejas board member-to-be," Roland said with an attempted infectious lilt.

"As you may or may not know, Jorge," Kevin began, "there has been recently a new policy issued by your government—the Policy for Equitable Lease and Use of Mineral and Petroleum Resources of Venezuela for the Benefit of the People of Venezuela. Among its various elements is a requirement for certification by the government of a bid for any exploration and development block."

"A certification?" Jorge asked.

"Yes, a certification of benefit that the bid being made not only is financially appropriate but also adequately recognizes the welfare of the people in the state where the block for which the bid is made is located."

"That seems reasonable—and appropriate," Jorge said.

"Of course, highly appropriate and very reasonable—very much so," Roland said in agreement.

"Of course, it is," Kevin said. "But obtaining the certification is not entirely, shall we say, straightforward."

"Why would that be?" Jorge asked.

"The certification must be provided by the governor of the state in which the lease is sought. And, in the opportunity we see at the present time, that lease would be located in Monagas."

"Monagas ... the governor ... you mean Governor Uriarte?" Jorge asked.

"Yes," Kevin answered.

"But, I do not know Uriarte—I have only briefly met him one time," Jorge responded.

"But your brother-in-law—your sister's husband Eulogio—is he not only the new Minister of Mines and Hydrocarbons but also a long-time confidant of Uriarte as well? Would not Eulogio be able to assist us in perhaps making a fruitful arrangement for the certification—indeed, perhaps provide an endorsement himself—of Tejas's bid for the Rio San Juan block?" Kevin asked with measured words.

"Rio San Juan block?"

"Yes," answered Kevin. "That is the area for which Tejas wants to make the bid. It is a small block located at the mouth of the Rio San Juan on the *Gulfo de Paria*. What do you think about getting Eulogio to help us—to provide his personal endorsement, to be our flag bearer so to speak, for our bid?"

Jorge sat quietly for a few moments, apparently thinking. "It is a possibility, but family ties can do only so much. And of course, Eulogio could not, as head of the ministry, openly show favoritism."

"But," Kevin said, "an inducement might prove valuable, indeed useful and necessary, to obtain his ... shall I say ... informal support at key times during the bidding process."

"From where would that ... inducement come?" Jorge asked.

"Well, I think Kevin here could do what might be necessary, in that regard. Couldn't you, Kevin?" Roland said as he looked at Kevin.

Kevin nodded without saying anything.

"What do you think might be appropriate, Jorge? Eulogio appears to be a very knowledgeable man, quite aware of the realities of the world—quite reasonable it seems to me," Roland asked, not questioning whether Kevin had the resources needed for whatever would be required.

"I am not sure. It would be something that I would have to explore with Eulogio," Jorge said.

"Would you be able to do that—perhaps in a fairly short time? We want to move forward rather rapidly. It should not be too long before bid requests are formally released, and we would want to be clear about our ... relationships before the formal bid submission process gets too far along," Kevin said with obvious urgency in his voice.

"Umm ... I would have to see when I might be able to meet with him—to discuss the situation," Jorge said, as he stroked his chin.

"Well, why don't you introduce Kevin to Eulogio before the evening is over? Then you two can plan to meet him for an extended, private discussion in the next few days?" Roland asked.

"Actually, I have already met the guy—sort of," Kevin injected. "I ran into him a couple of weeks ago here in Maturin at the Morichal Largo, but I got to speak to him only a few minutes—to tell him I remembered him from an oil minister meeting last summer when he gave a speech about new regulations, the same regulations that require this damn certification of benefit. He was meeting with another guy—some Chink from China Petroleum. About the only thing I got to do was puff up Marulanda's ego about his speech—it was clear Marulanda was there to talk to this guy, not me. He may not even remember me, now."

"Oh, I am sure he remembers you, Kevin," Jorge said, his sarcasm not fully disguised.

An uncomfortable moment of silence followed. Then Roland asked, "Kevin, what do you think he was talking about with this person from China Petroleum—whoever they are?"

"China Petroleum is one of newer players in the oil business down here—a midsize outfit, quite a bit larger than Trans-Texas but a lot smaller than BP or Exxon," Kevin answered. "They're run by the Chinese Communist government—no matter what they claim."

"So, this man might have really been a Chinese government official?" Roland asked.

"Possibly. I don't know, but whatever he was, it can't be good. I don't know whether China Petroleum is interested in the Rio San Juan block, but if it is, we need to be sure to knock them out of the competition. Just one more reason we need to be sure to get Marulanda in our corner," Kevin said.

"You are quite correct, Kevin," Jorge said with authority. "So, it is absolutely essential that Marulanda get to know you better in a relaxed setting—perhaps we should arrange to have an extended lunch with him ... at some location quite away from the hustle and bustle of his office."

"I like that idea, Jorge," Kevin said.

Jorge looked at Kevin, then turned his head to smile at Beal. "Before the evening is over, I'll mention to Eulogio that Kevin and I would like to meet with him in Caracas, somewhere more conducive to complex business matters—to discuss some oil leasing issues ... just to explore some issues, of course ... just seek his advice and discuss some opportunities."

"Certainly, Jorge, understanding the opportunities—that's what needed, a full understanding of ... the opportunities," Roland said with a satisfied tone.

"Yeah, opportunities—lots of opportunities," Kevin said with a smile, and thinking, *all that is needed to close the deal are appropriate ... inducements for Marulanda and Uriarte. And as to how it might be handled, I can get the necessary money to them using some arrangement that will just look like a contribution to the PHC party—just like the support I arrange with the PACs for Roland's campaign needs.*

# VII
# BUILDING THE WEB

## 26

Kelly saw Kevin wave his hand—a condescending wave—from across the patio as if to tell Kelley to come over to him. Kelley raised his hand in acknowledgment, gave a nod, and began working his way through the gyrating dancers. He wondered whether the evening's efforts were finally going to yield some fruit, although he had already gotten quite a bit of useful information from Senator Beal's wife, Cinzia Beal, who now appeared to be having quite a good time dancing with various men at the party.

Kelley had talked for some considerable length of time to Cinzia Beal in the hour before dinner had started. Apparently, being able to speak to an American in Spanish was something she enjoyed. Kelley had learned not only quite a bit about her family ties but also the significant involvement her husband had on a subcommittee on Latin American commerce and trade and his connections with U.S. oil companies. Kelley also sensed the considerable strength she had in influencing, perhaps what might even be said to be controlling, her husband and his political life, something particularly interesting given his Senate responsibilities and the involvement of many of her family in Venezuelan politics.

Kevin spoke as Kelley neared him. "Sorry I haven't been able to talk to you more, but I have been getting a little business done—had to speak to some people before they left for the evening."

"Did you get it done," Kelley asked.

"I think so, but more important, Kelley, do you have some time to talk—now?" Kevin asked with apparent urgency. Kelley hoped that

*157*

Kevin was finally going to open up to him—and take the bait that Kelley had thrown out to him at the hotel.

"Sure."

"Good," Kevin said, as he turned toward the hallway leading to the room in which he, Roland, and Jorge had made their plans only minutes ago. Kevin motioned for Kelley to follow.

Entering the study, Kevin pointed to a sofa. As Kelley settled himself on the sofa, Kevin closed the study door.

"I wanted to explore in a little more depth, Kelley, what you had mentioned in the hotel—about possibly teaming in some fashion," Kevin said as he sat down in a chair opposite Kelly.

"I'm all ears, Kevin," Kelley responded.

"Well, here's what I'm talking about," Kevin said enthusiastically. "My company here in Venezuela, *Tejas Petróleo,* could use a sort of silent partner, a partner who is not a competitor, but who could help Tejas grow and benefit itself as well—a company, I think, like yours."

"Why us, and what do you mean by silent partner?"

"You, because you do have something Tejas could use—equipment and people we need."

"But a lot of companies have that," Kelley said, wondering what made Kevin apparently so interested in Consolidated—was it just the fact that Consolidated was available, or was it something more? Kelley hoped it was something more.

"You have something that a lot of the companies I know don't have, Kelley. I did a little checking on your outfit. You have some backers who have considerable money to invest, and do something more than just lease drilling equipment," Kevin said in a conspiratorial tone.

*Well,* Kelley thought, *maybe the cover story for Consolidated is paying off.* "Invest? What kind of investment?" Kelley asked with a hint of innocence.

"I, Tejas that is, have a sure shot at getting a new lease block that will be opening up soon. But to make it happen, we need investors now, some people who can ante up pretty quickly in both Venezuela and the U.S.—in return for some big rewards down the road."

"Well, my guys are pretty sharp—they have been around a long time in the oil business. They have gotten a lot of empty promises over the years," Kelley said, trying to get more details out of Kevin.

"This is virtually a sure thing," Kevin said in a reassuring tone.

"I have heard that before," Kelley said mockingly.

"No, Kelley, this is the real thing—let me explain it to you," Kevin said. "You met that Marulanda guy tonight—the head of the Mines and Hydrocarbon Ministry, the same guy we saw at the hotel the other night?"

"Yeah—but I only got to talk to him for a few minutes."

"Well, he's a relative of Senator Beal—a relative of his wife, Cinzia, that is. And I am a very good friend, in case you haven't figured it out yet, of the senator. A group of us on the board of Tejas, including the senator, are in the process of speaking with Marulanda, to gain his ... support ... for our bid for the block that Tejas is going to bid on."

"Gain support?" Kelley asked leadingly.

"Endorse our bid—to put his support behind our bid. With his support, Tejas is a shoe-in," Kevin said with finality.

Kelley knew there had to be more than just the ties of family that would make Marulanda put his weight behind the Tejas bid, but he wanted Kevin to spell it out. "I didn't realize family ties were so strong down here."

"They aren't—there will have to be some additional inducements," Kevin said in a matter-of-fact tone.

"What kind of inducements? Are they what I think they are?"

"Of course," Kevin answered. "If you know anything about the oil business here in Venezuela, you know that's the way it is."

"That would be pretty risky, wouldn't it—bribing the head of the Ministry of Mines and Hydrocarbons?"

"Well, first of all, it wouldn't be a bribe—not the way we would work it," Kevin said with assurance.

"How so?" Kelley asked, his interest rising.

"Marulanda is buddy-buddy with Uriarte, the governor here in Monagas. Having Marulanda and Uriarte in our pocket will assure us of winning the bid. We are going to work it so the money goes to Uriarte, in the form of a political contribution to Uriarte's party.

Uriarte heads up the local political party here, something called the PHC party. Political contributions are made all the time down here; it's no big deal. How Uriarte and Marulanda get their cut is up to them—I'm sure they have some way of getting the money from the party coffers and divvying it up between themselves. You and I both know how politics runs down here," Kevin said smugly.

"Well, how much are we talking about?" Kelley asked.

"We are not exactly sure yet, but maybe ... in total ... about a million," Kevin said softly, as he started biting his lip.

"Jesus Christ!" Kelley said in astonishment. "That's a hell of a lot of money for some damn bribe for a lease you don't even know that's going to produce."

"But it doesn't make any difference—that's the beauty of it," Kevin responded with narrowing eyes. "Every bit of it will be a tax write-off—right off the bottom line, even if the lease doesn't produce a damn thing—and I'm betting it will. Every dollar you invest will be recouped in a reduced tax or tax credits to be used in later years."

"Off the bottom line—how are you going to manage that?"

"Senator Beal is going to get a little amendment tacked onto a trade bill next month—get a little set-aside, what we call a rainy-day fund, for smaller companies like us who want to promote international business cooperation," Kevin responded with a wide grin.

"And what does Beal get for his little effort?" Kelley asked.

"Nothing directly, but we have some PACs back in the states that are very appreciative of his support for the oil industry, particularly independents like Trans-Texas, and maybe, now, Consolidated," Kevin said with a smile. "About a half million of your million would actually go into PACs in support of Senator Beal's re-election campaign fund."

"Aren't PAC contributions that large ... illegal?" Kelley wasn't really sure what was legal and what was illegal so far as political contributions were concerned.

"Not the way we will handle it," Kevin said self-assuredly. "We take money from the accounts down here and purchase services—at least that's the way it looks on the books—from the U.S. oil companies providing the services. We have a network of companies we regularly work with. The execs of these companies get a bonus for supposedly bringing in new business, but they turn around and donate the bonus money ... as individuals to the senator or through their company by giving company donations to a PAC. They get a ten percent cut for their ... assistance. We use a bunch of PACs and spread the wealth around so to speak—we've done it before, and no one is the wiser."

"You said a million—where is the other half-million going to?"

"The other half-million would go into Marulanda's PHC party for Marulanda and Uriarte to split up. They would get two-fifty up front, to get their initial support for our lease bid, and another two-fifty when our winning bid is announced. And Trans-Texas would add another two-fifty to that when the lease contract is signed—so all together we make a three-quarter million contribution to the ... Venezuelan people."

"Damn—you have it all figured out, don't you," Kelley said, thinking, *this guy is a real operator. Bribes here in Venezuela and political contributions to a friend in the U.S. Senate that, if not illegal, surely skirt the law.*

"You're damn right, Kelley," Kevin said boastfully. "Are you in?"

"In the final analysis, it's not up to me, but I think I can tell you that Consolidated's investors will be very receptive to the deal," Kelley answered, wondering how the Admiral would deal with this mess: not just under-the-table bribery in a foreign country, but the U.S. Senate as well. "Where is this lease," Kelley asked.

"Northeast of here, on the coast near the mouth of a big river— the Rio San Juan. The block is about a hundred square miles of swampland running from the river mouth inland along the river about ten miles or so."

"Rio San Juan?" Kelley said in surprise. He knew the Rio San Juan as a transitway into the inland oil port of Caripito.

"Yeah. It connects the *Gulf of Paria* to Caripito. Caripito—it's about eighty miles inland—was big in the forties and fifties when oil was first being developed north of Maturin. But only smaller, older tankers can get upstream now, and only when the tide is high. The big tankers like we use now can move up the San Juan only a few miles—

but that's where the lease block is located, near the mouth of the river, so access is no problem," Kevin explained.

Kelley mulled over what to do next. *Just handing over a million bucks is not going to go over too well with the admiral and the Agency. But that damn senator—I sure would like to put a kink in his action.*

"Tell you what I can do. I will talk to my people and get back to you. We will see what we can do," Kelley finally said, an idea beginning to take shape in his mind.

"When will you know? Things are beginning to move pretty fast."

"By tomorrow, I would think. But there is one thing I am sure my people will want."

"What's that?" Kevin asked.

"Some type of solid assurance that Beal will come through on that 'rainy-day' amendment."

Kevin was silent for a few moments as if pondering Kelley's demand.

"How about this?" Kevin said tentatively as he began to bit his lip. "Sometime in the next four weeks, when Beal gets back to Washington, he formally announces a date for subcommittee hearings—he's chairman of the subcommittee that's going to sponsor the amendment we want. The hearings will be on new initiatives for greater economic cooperation between the U.S. and South America. Consolidated shows its good intentions by putting up a quarter-million for your first contribution—to Beal. The money goes into the PACs for Beal—in escrow. If Beal doesn't make the announcement, you're off the hook. You get your money back out of escrow and Beal doesn't get anything."

"How the hell are they going to do that? A contribution like that won't go unnoticed," Kelley said in real surprise.

"Shit, like I said, I have some PACs already set up. We just sprinkle it around the PACs, and they give it to Beal—contributions for his next election. But, I will also need two-hundred-fifty-thousand here by the end of next week for the first installment to Marulanda—or to his PHC party, that is—to keep him on the hook, so to speak. And then no later than the date of final bid submissions, we will have to get another two-fifty. When the bids are closed, we come up with the other two-fifty to make sure we win the bid. The last money for Beal's re-election fund will be given to his campaign when the trade bill with his amendment passes the Senate."

"So, what you're saying is a quarter million by the end of next week for Marulanda and this PHC party, another quarter, in escrow, for Beal when he announces his hearings—by four weeks from now—and then another half-million in two installments by the time we win the bidding. So, what are you putting up for Marulanda—or is it just going to be Consolidated?" Kelley asked, trying to make his voice as cynical as possible.

"Like I said, when the contract is signed, we give Marulanda another two-fifty. I will cover that. And I have already personally put a hundred thousand into the PACs for Beal," lied Kevin.

"So, what you are telling me is that Marulanda is Consolidated's responsibility up to the point that we know that Marulanda has come through on the deal. I don't know if my people will buy that," Kelley said, thinking, I need to get Matthew directly involved in handing own money over to Marulanda before the bidding was done.

"You drive a hard bargain, Kelley. Tell you what. I'll pitch in a hundred thousand to Marulanda's pocket for his first payment," Kevin said as he bit his lip. "Consolidated puts up only one-fifty for Marulanda's first payment—making it only nine-hundred by Consolidated before we sign the lease contract. But for Marulanda's last payment, you kick in another hundred, and I provide a hundred," Kevin said with a benevolent tone, but still biting his lip. "You still don't go over a million."

"That sounds good," Kelley said softly, now knowing that if the contributions to Marulanda were made, some Trans-Texas or Tejas money would be part of that money and could be used to trace the bribery path.

Kevin smiled. "Are you in?"

"I think so. I'll confirm, one way or another, by tomorrow evening and give you a call. If my people say yes, you will need to tell me where and how the four-fifty is to be sent to this PHC party and Beal's political re-election fund," Kelley answered, thinking, *now all I have to do is sell this plan to the admiral.*

# 27

Kelley was standing at the front desk of the Green Parrot, opening the Federal Express package with his new credit card and driver's license when Hermann arrived. Kelley figured he had several hours before he would be able to get the fifteen thousand he had requested from the bank—and getting the money, considering its amount, would not be easy, even if the bank followed the instructions they were supposed to. And changing the money to American dollars would be no easy feat, even with the exchange fee that would be charged. But Kelley figured he still had enough time to find out what Cui had been doing at the stationery shop yesterday before needing to get to the bank.

As Kelley turned from the desk to leave, the desk clerk emerged from a back room and said, "*Señor* Kelley, a fax has just come in for you." He handed the fax sheet to Kelley, asking, "Do you wish to pay the fax fee now or should we put the charge on your bill?"

"Put it on the bill," Kelley looked at the fax. A Consolidated Oil Services letterhead, complete with a Denver address and phone number, was at the top of the page.

Kelley read the message, knowing it was from the admiral: "Have considered investment proposals you outlined your call of yesterday. Members of Board consider investment recommendations worthwhile in light of possible returns. Arrangements being made for initiating investments per your directions."

*Well, that meant the money for each of the quarter million payments would be delivered to Matthew's office for distribution to the PACs in the U.S. and the PHC party in Venezuela.* After that, Kelley knew, it would be up to the Agency to track what happened to the money.

Kelley turned to the desk clerk. "I need to make a phone call from my room. Please get me an outside line."

"Certainly. The line will be open when you get to your room."

— ~ —

Picking up the phone in his room, Kelley heard the dial tone. Kelley took the piece of paper with Matthew's number on it from his pocket and dialed the number.

For a few seconds, there were several clicks and hisses. Then, "Matthew."

"This is Castellano. I have your answer for you—yes."

"Great—great," Kevin responded, with a sigh that Kelley could hear over the phone.

Kelley told Matthew the name of the accountant, or so Matthew was led to believe, at Consolidated's Denver office to whom instructions should be sent for the delivery of Consolidated's "San Juan Project Investment Funds" to Trans-Texas for subsequent dispersal. "My people will ID the money as the San Juan Investment. You be damn sure that the transfer is identified as the San Juan Investment at your end—I don't want this transfer to be confused with something else and just cause a delay in getting it to you or getting lost in your accounting system. I have had problems with Consolidated's accounting office before, and I don't want anything screwed up ... at your end or mine."

"Right—right, I will make sure there is no confusion," Matthew responded.

"I mean it—you have to be sure there is no screw-up. If there is, the whole deal will be fucked up—and my people don't like screw-ups. They can get mean—very mean—when there are." Kelley hoped he had scared Matthew enough to be sure the funds would be identified with the San Juan lease—making it that much easier to secure an indictment in the future.

"I will, Kelley. I want this thing to work as much as you."

"Okay. I will be in contact about the other ... funds later," Kelley said.

"Good, but, remember that we are on a tight schedule here—we have some deadlines we need to meet," Matthew said anxiously.

"Oh, we will, we will. Don't you worry. You just make sure the right people get that money."

Hanging up the phone, Kelley thought about the telephone call he had had with the case officer last night, trying with carefully guarded words to justify the need for the money. The officer had finally asked, "Is this arrangement critical to your assignment, Mr. Castellano?"

When Kelley answered absolutely, the officer answered, "Well, then, I'll be sure to convey that thought to the chairman of the board."

But Kelley had not said anything about Cui. He had not really had the time or the ability with his necessarily guarded words—or so Kelley tried to justify to himself—to talk about Cui.

But Kelley really knew that he did not want to raise the issue of Cui to the admiral. The admiral might consider Cui just a diversion from Kelley's real purpose: Finding out what had happened to Carrillo, and how it happened—and had there been a leak which may have led to Carrillo's death.

# VIII
# WIDE AND DEEP

## 27

With the call out of the way, Kelley returned to the hotel entrance to look for Hermann. Exiting the hotel door, he saw Hermann's car parked at the curb.

"So, Hermann, what happened last night?" Kelley asked as he got in Hermann's car.

"Nothing. The Chinese man had dinner at the same restaurant as the last time and returned to his room at the hotel."

"That's it?"

"*Si*," Hermann answered.

"Where is Cui now? Did he leave the hotel this morning?"

"*Si*. He went to the helicopter field. I think he went for a helicopter ride," Hermann answered hesitatingly.

"Why do you think that?" Kelley asked.

"He did not come out of the building before I left. I did not stay at the helicopter field—I did not want to be put in jail again."

Kelley paused. He needed to figure out where Cui went—if he went anywhere, which he likely did. But if Kelley got to the airfield right now, he might run into Cui, and he didn't want that to happen. *I better wait until late in the day, when it is more likely that Cui will have returned from wherever he had gone and then, hopefully, gone back to the hotel. Besides, he had to pick up the money at the bank— I can't meet Emma without it.*

"Okay, Hermann. Let's get back to that stationery store—it is open isn't it?"

"*Si, Señor*, it opens ...," Hermann paused as he looked at his watch, "in five minutes."

— ~ —

Entering the stationery store, Kelley saw it was more than a simple stationery store. It appeared to handle not only stationery but a combination of engineering drafting supplies and surveyor equipment, as well.

Kelley's eyes swung across the room, looking for something that would resemble what Cui had taken from the store. Then he saw it: maps: large and small maps of Venezuela stapled to a wall, and on a shelf beneath them, rolls of maps for sale.

Kelley walked to the shelf with the maps. A clerk walked toward him and greeted him in Spanish. Kelley responded, also in Spanish. "And how may I help you, *Señor*," the young clerk asked.

"Do you sell many of these maps?" Kelley asked as he pointed his hand at the maps on the walls.

"No, not too many anymore. There are much more detailed maps that the oil company people bring. We sell these to people who only want to know more about Venezuela," the friendly clerk responded.

"Oh, then you may remember a friend of mine. He suggested I come here to get a map to know more about Venezuela—as you can tell, I am not from Venezuela."

"What map do you want? We have very excellent maps," the clerk said, realizing that perhaps a sale might be consummated.

"Well, I am not sure, but I think I would like to get one like he did—perhaps you remember him ... an Oriental gentleman. He bought the map yesterday, I believe," Kelley said innocently.

"Yesterday ... ah ... oh, yes, I remember. He wanted a map of the northeastern part of the country, in the delta region of Monagas, along the coast near the Rio San Juan. But most of that area is very undeveloped, except for Pedernales on the coast," the clerk said as he looked up at the map on the wall and pointed to a black dot on the southern edge of the Gulf of Paria. "There are no really good maps of the area along the Rio San Juan—until you get close to Caripito, where the inland oil terminals are."

"Did he say he was interested in visiting Caripito or Pedernales," Kelley asked, hoping to get some specifics of the area in which Cui was interested.

"No, but he did buy a map. Would you like to buy the map he did?" the clerk asked expectantly.

"Yes, I think I would. What map did he buy?"

"Actually, he bought two—this one here," the clerk said as he pointed to a regional map of the states of Monagas and Sucre, which extended from west of Maturin to Trinidad on the east, "and this hydrographic map of the Gulf of Paria."

The clerk unrolled another map showing the Gulf of Paria with nautical information, including depth soundings spread across the gulf.

"Did he say why he wanted this map?" Kelley asked.

"No, except that he seemed very pleased when I found it for him," the clerk responded. "Would you like both of them?"

"Yes, I would," Kelley answered, wondering, *what is Cui up to?*

— ~ —

Getting into the car, Kelley looked at his watch—the bank would be opening soon. Kelley told Hermann to drive him to the bank. Kelley spent the next several hours getting the money that had been wired to him. He had expected it would take about that long, but it was still a hassle. There was no way around it. He needed the money for Emma, or whatever else might pop up.

Kelley checked his watch—one-thirty, still a little too early to go to the airfield.

Kelley asked for Hermann's suggestion about where to go for lunch. Hermann's named a small restaurant, *Restaurante de Medina*, only a few blocks from the bank. Medina's was small, like its bar, but it had a reputation, so Hermann assured Kelley, for excellent steaks. At Hermann's suggestion, Kelley had *Chuleta de res* in a pepper-laden tomato sauce. After an hour and a half of mouthwatering flavors, Kelley finished his second bottle of beer and Hermann gave a large belch, signifying the completion of the midday meal.

"All right, Hermann, I think it's time we get to the helicopter field,"

Kelley said as he looked at the large circular clock on the wall.

Hermann gave another belch and nodded in agreement as he rose from his chair.

About a half an hour later, Hermann turned into the heliport driveway beside the jail. As he did, a rain shower started—showers were frequent this time of year. Getting out of the car and holding a newspaper over his head, Kelley looked at the sign above the doorway into the office building. It read "Escobar's Air Services. Helicopters for rent, by day and hour," in Spanish.

"You had better come with me, Hermann," Kelley said as he looked at the jail a short distance away. "I don't want you to be hauled off again."

Hermann, surprisingly, shook his head. "No, I will wait for you. I would like to get a fruit drink from the vendor on the corner when the rain stops. If someone comes, I will tell them I am waiting for you."

Kelley paused, then answered, "Okay, whatever you say. I'll be back in a few minutes."

Once inside, Kelley approached a young, attractive woman sitting beside a desk with a large radio transmitter and receiver on it.

"*Buenos tarde, Señorita.* My name is Castellano. I wish to speak to the station manager. Is he here?"

The woman looked up. "*Buenos tarde, Señor* ... Castellano. *Si*, the station manager is here, but he is with the pilots for a moment. What do you want with him?"

"I wish to inquire about renting a helicopter," Kelley answered.

"I will get him," she answered as she rose from her chair and walked into a narrow hallway leading off the side of the room.

In a moment, a man appeared from the hallway.

"I am Captain Cabrella, the station manager. I understand you want to hire a helicopter?"

"Yes, that is correct," Kelley answered in Spanish

"Ah, an American. Well, we have excellent helicopters and the best pilots in Venezuela—all American trained. Where do you want to go?" Cabrella asked.

"I want to go the same place as a friend of mine wanted to go," Kelley answered.

"Well, where is that?"

"I do not know—but I believe he used your services this morning ... a Chinese gentleman." Kelley was betting that Cui had actually taken a flight, and not just talked to Cabrella. "I want to go the same place he went."

The station master looked at Kelley with suspicion. "Why don't you ask this Chinese gentleman—your friend, as you say?"

"I would rather not, but let's just say that I will pay double the price he paid if you tell me where he went and you take me to the same place," Kelley said.

"Three thousand dollars, cash American, now, before we leave?" Cabrella said quickly.

Kelley paused. He figured Cabrella had probably upped the price quite a bit. Cui had paid probably only about a thousand dollars, at most. But, he needed to know where Cui went. "I'll pay you a thousand now and two thousand before we take off. When can we go—and where will we be going?"

"All right, one thousand now. But it is too late in the day to fly now. You can go tomorrow—leave at eight in the morning. The same pilot, Captain Mendez, and his copilot can fly you—they will know exactly where the Chinese man went. Is that acceptable?"

"That sounds good," Kelley answered in an agreeable voice, not wanting to lose the cooperation of Cabrella. "But what can you tell me about where he did go?"

Cabrella paused. "The one-thousand-dollars, *Señor?*"

Kelley sighed. "*Si*, sorry."

Kelley pulled out his wallet and counted out ten one-hundred-dollar bills, leaving another ten in the wallet. The rest of the wired-money was in the hotel safe.

"*Gracias, Señor*," Cabrella said with a smile as he pocketed the money. "Will you need a receipt?"

Kelley shook his head. "Well, where did he go?"

"Margarita, pull the flight record for that flight we had this morning," Cabllare said to the secretary at the table.

"*Si*," Margarita said as she opened a log book on the corner of the table beside the radio. She handed it to Cabrella.

Cabrella took the book and studied it for a moment. "The total flight took about five hours—and it looks like they flew up toward Pedernales, on the coast—on the Gulf of Paria."

Kelley remembered Pedernales as a small, isolated fishing village, but because of its strategic location, it had a one-strip airfield which provided initial access into the oil-rich Orinoco Delta area. And between Pedernales and Maturin—nothing but jungle forests and the wild, almost impenetrable coastal *pantano,* a thousand square miles of tall swamp grass, occasional Moriche-covered hummocks, and river-hugging mangrove forests. Kelley did a mental check of the time that Hermann had said Cui had probably left. Guessing that Cui probably landed a couple of hours ago, the timeline seems to check.

"Five hours! Is there anything I need to bring?" Kelley asked as if flying on a helicopter were new to him.

"Perhaps a couple of candy bars or a sandwich to eat—I will make sure there are some bottles of water on board," Cabrella answered.

Kelley smiled. "I will see you on Monday then, by eight—with the rest of the money,"

"*Si,* with the money."

Kelley shook Gabriella's hand, turned as if to leave, but then stopped. "Oh, by the way, Captain, what type of helicopter will we be flying?"

"A Bell Ranger four-seater. Don't worry. It is a very safe helicopter."

"Oh, I am sure it is, Captain," Kelley said, as he did another quick mental calculation. Most Bell rangers could go about three hours or so, maybe four at the very best, without refueling, so he had to have set down somewhere. Pedernales seemed to be a logical place to do that.

"Will we be refueling along the way, Captain?"

"Yes, you will have to. The log says they set down at Pedernales to do that."

*Well, that seems to check out, too, so maybe Cabrella is playing straight with me.* Kelley walked out the door.

As Kelley got into Hermann's car, Hermann asked "Where do we go now, *Señor* Kelley?" as he threw his empty paper drink cup out the open window of the car.

"To the Colonial Hotel to see if we can catch up with Cui."

Thirty minutes and another twenty American dollars later, Hermann came out of the Hotel Colonial door. As he opened the car door, Hermann said, "He left about an hour ago—in a taxi. The hotel clerk gave me the name of the taxi driver."

"Do you think we can find the taxi driver?" Kelley asked.

Hermann grinned. "*Si*, I am sure of it."

"Why are you so sure?"

Hermann grinned widely. "Because I know him, *Señor* Kelley—he is my cousin."

# 28

They sat in a small bar across the street from the Green Parrot Hotel. The sweat from their bottles of beer made little pools of water on the small table in front of them.

"So, Alberto, where did you take this man?" Kelley asked.

"He had me take him to Geologist Dolanyi's office."

"Geologist?" Kelley asked in surprise.

"*Si*, geologist. *Señor* Dolanyi is a much-respected geologist in Maturin."

"What did he do there?"

"I do not know—he told me to wait in the car. He just took his papers into Geologist Dolanyi's office. He was in the office about an hour—but he paid me for all of my waiting time."

"His papers? What do you mean his papers?"

"The big rolls of paper he had under his arm," Alberto answered.

*The maps!* "Where did go after he left the geologist's office?"

"I took him to the clothing store near the main square—near the government center. You know where I mean, don't you, Hermann."

Hermann nodded in agreement. "*Si*, I know it."

"What did he do in the store?" Kelley asked.

"Buy clothes," Alberto answered.

"Of course, what else," Kelley answered sarcastically. Kelley thought for a moment, and then asked, "What kind of clothes?"

"Clothes ... what you Americans call khakis, I think ... and boots. Like he was going into the field to work."

Kelly was dumbfounded. *To work in the field—that doesn't make sense ... unless ... unless that is precisely what he is going to do. That's it! He is going somewhere where street clothes wouldn't be suitable. But where? Maybe somewhere near where the helicopter went.*

"Where did you go after he finished buying the clothes?"

"Nowhere. I mean we came back to the hotel—Hotel Colonial."

"You mean he is there now?" Kelley asked.

"*Si*, at least I think so," Alberto answered.

"Damn, all this running around and he's back where he started from. So that's it ... you didn't go anywhere else?" Kelley asked, trying to make sure nothing had been overlooked.

"No, that is all," Alberto answered.

"Do you have any idea where he might be going to wear his new clothes?"

"No—unless it is tomorrow when we go to Azagua."

"What do you mean when we go to Azagua?" Kelley said in surprise. He knew where Azagua was—about fifty miles north of Maturin, on a small tributary to the Rio San Juan, and about the same distance from the Gulf of Paria.

"*Si*, he hired me to take him to Azagua—to the docks there. We leave before dawn. He said he must be in Azagua by six—before the tide becomes highest. He said we will return before late night."

Kelley said nothing for a few moments, pursing his lips. Then he took a long, satisfying swallow of his beer and looked at Alberto. "Alberto, you are going to get very sick tonight."

"I am not sick, *Señor* Kelley. And I cannot get sick. I must take *Señor* Cui to Azagua tomorrow," Alberto said in protest.

"Oh, yes you are—very, very sick. But don't worry. Your cousin Hermann here will be able to fill in for you tomorrow."

# 29

The wap, wap, wapping noise of the chopper's whirling blades and whining hum of the engine filled the small plastic bubble-enclosed compartment in which Kelley sat behind the pilot and co-pilot of the Bell Ranger. Kelley looked out the side of the copter and saw row after row of neatly aligned palm trees—a palm plantation—over which they had been flying for the last several minutes. Maturin was behind them, to the west. In the distance beyond, he could see the beginnings of the tropical forest—a biological menagerie of tall and short trees with a dense undergrowth of vegetation, natural and uncultivated but with a strange sense of order: circles of small trees surrounding one or two tall trees, like bodyguards, with the undergrowth forming a regal green carpet about both.

"How much farther to the San Juan, Captain," Kelley asked in Spanish, speaking into the microphone attached to the earphones he wore on his head.

Mendez shrugged his shoulders. "Maybe twenty minutes," he replied into the microphone.

His co-pilot, the Haitian, nodded his head and said in English, "Twenty—that about right," into his microphone.

Kelley nodded, as he continued to stare at the rainforest beginning to pass below them, thinking, wondering—*what was Cui up to?*

Clearly, he had been getting the lay of the land along the coast. And this morning he apparently was returning to the same area, but this time by boat—apparently to be able to do a ground level inspection, to be able to walk the land rather than just fly over it. But, again, why? Well, maybe Hermann would provide some answers when he got back tonight.

Kelley had waited down the street from the Hotel Colonial, standing in the morning shadows, when Hermann had arrived to pick up Cui at the hotel, making sure that Cui went with Hermann—that Cui believed Hermann's story that Alberto had gotten sick during the night. And apparently, Cui did. Cui came out of the hotel dressed in his new khakis and work boots, looking like a New Yorker at a western dude ranch, with his maps under one arm. Hermann's car had already been loaded with two ice chests filled with ice, bottled water, and sandwiches, in accord with the instructions that Cui had given to Alberto. The two had piled into Hermann's car and taken off down the street. Everything seemed to be going according to plan.

Kelley returned his thoughts to the present. "Are you sure we are following the same route as you took yesterday, Captain," Kelley asked, trying to reassure himself that he was not missing anything.

"*Si*, exactly," Mendez answered.

Kelley continued to scan his eyes across the fast-moving landscape some six hundred feet below him, wondering, wondering ....

— ~ —

Kelley's concentration was broken by the Haitian saying, "There, see it coming," as he pointed outward in the direction of the helicopter's flight.

Kelley looked up. There it was, the *pantano*, its beginning marked by a sharp ending in the rainforest, almost like God had said, "I am tired of the forest, and I want to make a swampland—here, at this line." And that was what the *Guarapichie pantano* was—a coastal marsh of tall swamp grasses sliced by winding, twisting rivers—the canos—lined by dense fringes of mangroves swamps, with island hummocks of trees and dense undergrowth, all invaded by saline waters from the Gulf of Paria to the east. And in the middle, slicing through it like a massive, winding, black snake was the Rio San Juan. No one lived there, except the coastal Indians of Venezuela—Warao and Karinas—in isolated villages along the tributaries beneath the dense undergrowth that encased the canos like a tight glove covering a hand with a hundred fingers.

The helicopter flew straight and level across the wilds of the *pantano*. Except for occasional hummocks of Morichal palm trees and a cano, each bit of land was without difference from another.

"How big did you say this swamp was," Kelley asked.

The Haitian answered, "About two-hundred-thousand hectares."

They continued to fly on, in silence now, except for the whine of the engine and overhead rotor, as Kelley continued to look at the lush, unending landscape unfolding beneath him.

Perhaps fifteen minutes had passed when Kelley felt the helicopter tilt in a turn.

"Why are we turning," Kelley asked.

"This is the path we followed yesterday—we turn toward the Rio San Juan," Kelley heard Captain Mendez say through the earphones.

— ~ —

They had been flying along the Rio San Juan for about forty minutes when, suddenly, as they turned to follow a bend in the river, he saw them: A boat about twenty feet long with two outboard motors pushing it along slowly at an angle against the current with the net result, Kelley soon realized, that was close to a straight line across the half-mile width of the Rio San Juan. The boat had a low cabin and various pieces of loose gear, life preservers, and ropes thrown haphazardly on the top of the cabin roof. And there, among the loose equipment scattered about the stern of the boat, Kelley saw what he was looking for: the large, orange-colored ice chest that he and Hermann had selected to help identify the boat on which Cui was expected to be.

"Drop a little lower so I can get a closer look at that boat, Captain," Kelley said into his microphone. The helicopter dipped lower and began to track the boat from about three hundred feet. Kelley could see two dark-skinned men on the aft part of the deck; one was sitting beneath an awning at the wheel, guiding the boat. The other hovered near the outboard motors hanging over the stern of the boat. And at the bow of the boat, two other men. One was a light-skinned man with a white goatee, and the other was Cui, in his new khakis, now wet and dark.

Cui and his companion were busily turning a crank on a pulley suspended by an A-frame projecting out from the bow of the boat. As they continued to turn the crank, a torpedo-shaped, metal-looking object, about two feet long, rose out of the water. Cui's companion reached over to the object and pulled it, with obvious difficulty— apparently, the object was quite heavy—on to a small platform at the base of the A-frame. As it settled on the platform, both men seemed to relax. As they relaxed, they both turned to look upward toward the helicopter, as if realizing for the first time that the helicopter was overhead. Cui's companion waved. Cui did not move.

"Take her back up to our normal altitude, Captain. I have seen all I want for now." Kelley didn't want Cui to become unduly suspicious about a hovering helicopter.

As the helicopter rose upward, it began to also turn away from the river. "We need to refuel at Pedernales, like yesterday," came the words of the Haitian through Kelley's earphones.

"Fine—just do everything like yesterday," Kelley answered back.

Kelley looked back toward the river as helicopter continued its banking turn. He could see the boat had moved closer to shore and that Cui and his companion were apparently lowering the torpedo-shaped object back into the water.

Kelley pondered for a few moments about what he had seen—and then it dawned on him as he recalled a long-ago lecture in oceanography he had heard as a young officer-to-be. The torpedo-like object was a ballast bomb, a lead weight that is dropped into the water and which, because of its shape, aligns with the current. It could be used to provide a stable subsurface platform for instruments, and by measuring the length of line that played out until the weight sank to the bottom, determine the depth of the water.

*That's what Cui was doing! He was measuring the depth of the river. And the only reason an old navy man like Cui would want to measure the depth of the Rio San Juan would be to determine if the water were deep enough to handle sea-going ships.*

*But small oil tankers have been sailing up and down the Rio San Juan on a regular basis for decades; that's no secret. So, why did Cui need to know more than that, unless—damn!—unless they aren't ships, at least not regular ships, but larger ships—like warships!*

Kelley knew that had to be it. Cui wanted to know if Chinese warships could enter and move safely up the Rio San Juan! And if that were true, those warships might need a place to dock ... a safe place to dock and refuel. And where better to dock than a dock under Chinese control!

*My God! This has to be the same area where Matthew is trying to get his oil lease block. That's what Cui is trying to do: get the Rio San Juan Block—but not for oil. He wants the shoreline to construct a docking facility—and create a naval base for Red Chinese warships in the Caribbean!*

# 30

"I picked up *Señor* Cui as we planned," Hermann said as he shoved a fork full of morning *huevos con jamón* into his month, "with the ice chest that we bought filled with ice and bottles of water. I explained to *Señor* Cui that I was coming for my cousin, who was very, very sick. *Señor* Cui told me to drive to Azagua. I did. We did not stop along the way, and he said almost nothing. In Azagua, we went down to the river. Two boatmen, and another man, an older man with a goatee, were there already."

*The man he had seen from the helicopter*, Kelley thought. "Did Cui have anything with him that he took on the boat?"

Hermann thought silently for a moment. "*Si*, a roll of papers and a little notebook with some pencils."

Maps again, and apparently a notebook for recording the sounding data he was going to collect, Kelley thought. "Go on. What happened when you got there?"

"They were loading the boat—and bolting down a funny looking apparatus on the bow of the boat, a metal frame with a wench with a thick, strong rope. When they finished bolting down the frame, they finished loading the food and water and then left—left the dock, I mean, and started down the river. I watched them until they passed a bend in the river and I could not see them anymore," Hermann finished with a smile.

"So, what happened the rest of the day?" Kelley asked.

"Nothing. I just waited for them to return, as *Señor* Cui told me to," Hermann answered.

"You mean you just sat at the dock all day?" Kelley asked in disbelief.

"Well, not exactly. I have two cousins and an uncle in Azagua. I visited with them most of the day."

*More cousins*, Kelley said to himself. "So, what happened after you visited your cousins?"

"I went back to the dock and waited. The boat with *Señor* Cui returned about eight o'clock. *Señor* Cui wanted to leave right away; he looked very tired. He left the other men to finish unloading the boat."

"And what did Cui bring back with him?" Kelley asked.

"Just the same roll of papers, except that they were folded and not in a roll, and the notebook—but I did not see any pencils," Hermann answered meticulously.

*Well, that all fits,* Kelley thought.

"Do you want to go anywhere now, *Señor* Kelley," Hermann asked.

"Take me to the office of Geologist Dolanyi," Kelley answered. "I have a few questions I want to ask him."

— ~ —

Kelley got out of the car, looking at the sign on the front of the two-story building as he did so. It read, "Juan Dolanyi, *Geológico y Hidrológico Servicios.*" A taxi was parked on the street near the building; the driver seemed to be sleeping.

"Park down the street, beyond that hamburger stand, and wait there, Hermann. If *Señor* Dolanyi is who I think he is, I don't want him to see you."

"*Si, Señor* Kelley, I will wait over ... there," Hermann said as he pointed up the street to an empty curb space beneath the shade of a tree, a short distance beyond the hamburger stand.

"That should be okay—just stay with the car," Kelley ordered.

"*Si.*"

Kelley got out of the car and walked up a sidewalk to the large entry door of the two-story building. Hermann gunned the car motor as it pulled away from the curb. Stepping inside the doorway, Kelley found himself in a small reception area. At one side of the room, a young woman sat behind a desk, busily writing on some papers in front of her.

The woman stopped her writing and looked up, smiling. "*Buenos tarde.*"

"*Buenos tarde, Señora,*" Kelley responded. "I wonder if I might speak to *Señor* Dolanyi? Is he in? I am interested in possibly hiring his services."

"It is *Señorita* Dolanyi, *Señor* ...?"

"Castellano ... *Señor* Kelley Castellano."

"*Señor* Castellano, thank you. And my grandfather is in, but he is with someone at the moment, but I expect him to be free soon. Can you wait a short time?"

Kelley answered without thinking, "*Si*, I can wait."

As Kelley waited, he looked at the pictures on the wall. Many were pictures of groups of men in work clothes. As he studied them, Kelley realized that one man was always in the photos—first as a young man, then middle-aged, then as an older man—with a goatee. It was clear that the man was the same man whom Kelley had seen in the boat on the Rio San Juan.

"Those are pictures of exploration or study groups my grandfather has led into the jungle or the *pantano* over the years," *Señorita* Dolanyi volunteered. "He is often sought after to lead such groups because of his knowledge of eastern Venezuela."

"Really," Kelley answered politely, thinking, *I can see why Cui would hire him.*

"Oh, yes. In fact, you see that framed map near the door?" *Señorita* Dolanyi asked as she turned to point toward the door behind her desk.

Kelley turned to look at the map; he recognized it as the hydrographic map he had purchased at the stationery store.

"My grandfather prepared it some years ago when oil development began to expand along the Orinoco—it is recognized as the most authoritative early map of the Gulf of Paria. And—"

The door beside the framed map opened. A man with a white goatee came through it. And following him was a man with a large brown mailing envelope in his hand—and the man was Cui!

Kelley tried to turn away, but it was too late. Cui had seen him. But did he recognize Kelley? Kelley continued to look the other way as if studying the pictures on the wall.

Dolanyi spoke, in Spanish, to Cui. "It has been a pleasure to be of assistance to you, *Señor* Cui. I am sure all the information you have requested is in my report."

Cui spoke, also in Spanish, directly to Dolanyi, as if Kelley were not even there. "I am sure it is. Thank you again, *Señor* Dolanyi" Cui turned and walked quickly to the front door, opened it, and left.

*Damn,* Kelley thought, *I hope Hermann stayed in the car. If Cui sees him, Cui will know something is going on even if he didn't recognize me.*

"Grandfather, this is *Señor* Castellano. He wishes to speak to you," *Señorita* Dolanyi said as she pointed with her hand toward Kelley.

"*Señor* Castellano," Dolanyi said in English as he turned toward Kelley. "I am Juan Dolanyi. May I help you?" the man said as he extended his hand.

Kelley shook the extended hand and spoke. "Perhaps. I am interested in possibly obtaining some hydrographic data on the rivers in the area. Would you be able to help me to obtain such data?"

"*Si,* that is one of the services I provide—making hydrographic surveys. I am often hired by oil companies to help in gaining access into inland areas where they wish to take exploration equipment. Is that why you wish to make a hydrographic survey?"

"Sort of. You see, I do represent an oil company, actually an oil services company—Consolidated Oil Services, out of Denver, in the United States. We supply equipment for use in oil exploration and drilling work. We don't actually do the work—we just supply equipment."

Dolanyi nodded his head in understanding. "So what type of assistance do you need?"

"We—my company, that is—are trying to get a handle on how difficult it will be to bring in equipment into coastal regions along the Gulf of Paria—just how easy some of our supply ships could move up the rivers draining into the gulf. We figure they could be an inexpensive point of access into interior regions if the rivers are deep enough. Do you know much about them—the rivers, that is?" Kelley asked leadingly.

"Well, it depends a great deal upon the river you are talking about. And many of the rivers, particularly the larger ones, are strongly influenced by the tides. In some places, because of the geometry of the river as you move upstream, the tide may be three meters in range. So, as I say, it depends upon where you are talking about," Dolanyi answered with obvious authority.

"Well, I have been looking at a lot of maps, and it seems the San

Juan River might be a pretty good way to go inland—maybe then use a tributary off of it to go farther inland. You know anything about that river?" Kelley asked innocently.

"Well, in fact, I do. It is a major river draining to the *Gulfo de Paria*. It is quite deep, at least near the more downstream portions, nearer the coast. As you move upstream, it is strongly influenced by tides—upstream it is sometimes very deep and sometimes very shallow."

"How can you be so sure? Have you ever measured how deep it is?" Kelley asked, hoping to get Dolanyi to talk about his work with Cui.

"Yes, indeed, I have, several times. In fact, only yesterday," answered Dolanyi, as if insulted that someone would question his knowledge.

"Yesterday? What do you mean, yesterday?" Kelley baited Dolanyi.

"Yes, yesterday. I took a gentleman to the San Juan yesterday—the man who left moments ago, in fact. We made several traverses across the Rio San Juan a few kilometers upstream from the river mouth. We measured depths greater than thirty meters in the central portion of the river. The river is really quite deep in the reach below the confluence with the Cano Frances tributary."

"Really ... that deep?" Kelley answered with true surprise. "How far upstream is this Cano Francis confluence?"

"Here, let me show you. Come back to my office. I have a map of the area."

Kelley followed Dolanyi into his office, where a map of the eastern coast of Monagas was hanging from the wall in a picture frame.

Dolanyi pointed to the map, with apparent pride. "I prepared that map many years ago, as part of my doctoral research. It is still recognized as the definitive hydrographic map, before satellite photography, of the rivers in eastern Monagas. And, you see here," Dolanyi said as he put his finger on the map, "is where the Cano Francis joins the Rio San Juan, about ten kilometers upstream of the mouth of the Rio San Juan. Between the Cano Francis and the mouth of the Rio San Juan, depths of twenty to thirty meters are typical of the mid-channel portions of the Rio San Juan."

"That is hard to believe," Kelley responded.

"Hard to believe, but true. The gentleman for whom I made the soundings yesterday—he didn't want to believe me either when I told him of such depths, until he saw for himself," Dolanyi answered with satisfaction.

"So," Dolanyi continued, "do you want to go with me to the Rio San Juan—do I need to show you, too, the depths in the Rio San Juan?"

"No, *Señor* Dolanyi, no, you do not. You have convinced me. What about upstream of the Cano Francis confluence?" Kelly asked, trying to pin down where Cui would want his docks to be built.

"Upstream of the confluence, tidal influences are much greater. There is much more variability and uncertainty about depths. Ships attempting to move upstream of the Cano Francis must be more cautious—shoals are common. Steaming above the Cano Francis confluence poses many hazards, particularly for those unfamiliar with the river and its tides." Dolanyi answered.

*Well, that's it,* Kelley said to himself. *Cui will build his docks on the Rio San Juan below the Cano Francis confluence—along the shoreline where he plans to get the San Juan block.* Kelley knew Cui would do anything to get it—bribe or kill anyone necessary. No wonder he was cozying up to Marulanda at the Morichal Largo.

"Well, I think you have provided me more information than I ever expected to obtain, *Señor* Dolanyi. I am indeed indebted to you," Kelley said with real thanks. "How can I pay you for your advice— you are, of course, in business to make money providing your services."

Dolanyi hesitated.

*Señorita* Dolanyi, who had entered the office, spoke. "My grandfather is bashful when it comes to money—he has too much scientist in him. He regularly charges one-hundred-thousand Bs per hour for consultation. An hour of his time seems appropriate."

"I quite agree, *Señorita*. Will one-hundred dollars, American, be sufficient, *Señor* Dolanyi?"

Dolanyi smiled. "You will have to excuse my granddaughter—she is very much the businesswoman, and perhaps at times a little too assertive. Yes, one-hundred dollars will be more than sufficient," Dolanyi answered.

Kelley took out his wallet and gave Dolanyi the money. "And now, *Señor* Dolanyi, I must take my leave of you. I have other business to which I must attend. Thank you for your assistance," Kelley said as he turned to leave Dolanyi's office. Dolanyi followed Kelley out of his office and into the reception room.

Kelley walked across the room to the front door. Dolanyi followed as a matter of common courtesy. As Dolanyi opened the door for Kelley, Kelley could see Hermann's car up the street, beyond the hamburger stand—and standing beside the stand was Hermann, gulping down a hamburger. Kelley attempted to block Dolanyi's view, but it was to no avail. As Dolanyi extended his hand for a farewell handshake, he eyes suddenly widened, and a questioning look came over his face.

"Well, thank you again, *Señor* Dolanyi. Perhaps we shall meet again," Kelley said as he turned to walk to the sidewalk paralleling the street. Turning onto the sidewalk next to the street and away from the direction to the car, Kelley looked back at Dolanyi, who was still standing in the doorway. Kelley gave a small wave of the hand. Dolanyi nodded his head in acknowledgment. Kelley kept walking, hoping that Hermann had not seen him come out of the office.

But then Kelley heard the car start, followed by a squeal of tires as Hermann made a U-turn in the street and started toward Kelley.

In a moment, Hermann was beside Kelley. Hermann leaned toward the open window and spoke, "*Señor* Kelley, why are you walking the wrong direction? Did you forget where I parked?"

"Damn you, Hermann, why didn't you stay in the car," Kelley growled as he got into the car.

"I am sorry, *Señor* Kelley. I only wanted something to eat."

"Did you see Cui come out of the office? What did he do when he came out of the office?" Kelley asked, hoping against hope that Cui had not seen Hermann or the car.

"Oh, yes, I saw him," Hermann answered with a smile.

"Well, did he see you?" Kelley asked with an irritated voice.

"I do not know, but he did stare at my car—I could see him in the rearview mirror before he got in the taxi by the building."

*Damn, fucking, damn,* Kelley though in disgust. *Cui knows now something is going on.* Kelley knew that Cui would eventually remember Kelley, even if he had not immediately recognized Kelley. And seeing Herman would only make Cui more suspicious.

"So, he just drove away, after he got into the taxi?" Kelley asked, hoping that no further damage had been done.

"Yes, he left. I know, because the taxi turned around and drove right past me. He went straight down the street to the boulevard," Hermann answered innocently.

*Jesus! That tears it.*

# IX

# BUG OUT

## 31

Kelly told Hermann to find a parking space on a side street and wait. Kelley watched Hermann slide into one of the few open spaces along the side street.

Then Kelley turned to look at the crowd gathering in the plaza in front of the governor's offices. It was already large but still growing. Many people held PHC posters in their hands. Young men, students from the look of them, were working their way along the sidewalk surrounding the plaza, handing out leaflets, and when people would take them, posters for people to carry. The leaflets and posters proclaimed the power of the people—the common man—and the PHC as the party of the common man.

In the middle of the plaza on a covered podium was a small band with two guitarists, several trumpet players, and two competing drummers, trying to keep the crowd occupied until the real show started. But few paid any attention; they milled about, laughing and talking in small groups, waiting for their leader—the governor—to arrive. But they were not growing impatient.

The gathering was a party as much as a political rally. The candy and soda hawkers were having a field day. Ice cones with colored sugar water were in almost everyone's hand—today they were free, compliments of the PHC. Take a leaflet and get an ice cone. Want another ice cone, take another leaflet. And for anyone willing to carry a poster proclaiming the support of the PHC, there was the promise of twenty-thousand Bs if the numbered poster he was holding was selected as the winning poster by the governor at the end of his speech. The PHC knew how to get and keep a good turnout as well as anyone.

Kelley worked his way through the milling, increasingly dense crowd toward the fountain at the center of the plaza. As he got close to the fountain, his eyes scanned the crowd, looking for Emma. He did not see her. He continued to expand his field of view, searching for Emma.

Then shouts began to come from the people in the crowd as the governor and his entourage emerged from the governor's offices across the street and moved toward the podium upon which the still-playing band sat. The more than a few policemen surrounding the governor and his entourage pushed by the people as they surged toward the governor with outstretched hands, crying, "*¡Viva Uriarte! ¡Viva Uriarte!*"

The first two people to climb the steps to the stage were people Kelley did not know, but the third he recognized as Marulanda, who waved and turned with a flourish to invite Uriarte to the stage. As Uriarte began to ascend to the stage with a broad smile on his face, the band switched to a ceremonial song, vaguely reminiscent of the American *Hail to the Chief.* Reaching the center of the stage, he shook hands with Marulanda and the other men standing there. Then Uriarte and Marulanda stepped to the rear of the stage and sat down in canvasback chairs in front of the band as one of the other two men stepped to the podium, clapping and smiling toward Uriarte. Uriarte nodded his head in appreciation, smiling widely and beginning to clap, in response. The crowd joined in, and the clapping became infectious. Everyone was clapping. Including Kelley.

Uriarte rose from his chair, continuing his clapping, then bowed, slightly, as if in thanks to his supporters, and turned his hand to give a small flourish to the man still standing at the podium.

"*Gracias*, most honored governor, *gracias*," the man said, speaking into the microphone, as he returned Uriarte's welcome with a motion of his own arm and hand. The man turned back to the crowd, and began to speak, "My fellow citizens, the great and wonderful people of Monagas—"

Kelley felt a hand on his shoulder. Kelley turned quickly, ready to strike out. But what he saw made him stop. It was Emma, except it was not Emma. It was a man whose face was as close to the face of Emma that a man's face could be. Kelley knew it had to be Emma's brother—her twin brother. There was no doubt.

"Are you Kelley?" the man asked in strongly accented English.

"Yes—and you ... you are Emma's brother, Franklin," Kelley said with certainty. Then, still not seeing Emma, Kelley asked, "Where is Emma?"

"She is not here. She was afraid to come. She sent me to get you. She described what you looked like. Finding you was easy. You stand out, as they say in the *Estados Unidos,* like a sore thumb."

"Why was Emma afraid to come?" Kelley asked with concern.

"She was beaten by Freddie—"

"Beaten—how badly?"

"Bad enough. She has a broken nose—and she is afraid to talk to you where someone might see her. Freddie said she talked too much to Americans; that she had better keep quiet about Bettina."

"Damn!" Kelley said. So, Freddie did hear something at the House of Pleasure—and his mugging was not just an ordinary mugging. It was Freddie's message to Kelley to stop asking questions. Freddie was probably as scared as chicken shit that questions were being asked about Bettina, and he didn't want *Señor* Juan—or whatever his name was—or any of his friends to find out. If they did, what happened to Bettina might happen to him.

"Emma said you would give her something if I were to give you ... something? Is that still true?" Franklin asked.

"Yes, now more than ever."

"Good. We will both need to use it now. Come, we go to Emma now," Franklin said as he turned from Kelley to lead the way out of the crowd.

But at that moment applause began again. The man at the podium was finishing his introduction of Uriarte. Uriarte rose from his chair, and the applause grew in intensity. Even the people who had been sitting in the few chairs around the podium began to rise and join in the applause. And, suddenly, Kelley could see him, standing there, clapping with all the others—Cui, acting like an ardent supporter of Uriarte and his PHC party.

*What the hell is Cui doing here?* Kelley thought and then answered himself. *Shit, he's working on getting some big payoff money to Marulanda—and maybe Marulanda's buddy Uriarte as well—to be sure China Petroleum is awarded the San Juan block.* And, Kelley knew, somehow guaranteeing that neither Marulanda or Uriarte would renege on the deal. Cui's grand scheme had been set up; all he was doing now was working out the details.

"*Señor* Kelley, come, we must go," Franklin said as he called to Kelley and waved his hand.

Kelley hesitated. He wanted to see what Cui was going to do next. Franklin spoke again. "If you are going to come, come now, or I leave without you."

Kelley turned toward Franklin and nodded his head.

— ~ —

It was an hour later that Hermann pulled his car to a stop beside a rundown apartment building. Up the street a block away, another car slowed and then pulled silently to the curb.

Franklin, who had refused to talk with Hermann present, got out of the taxi. Kelley followed. "Wait here, Hermann—and relax. This may take a while. And, oh," Kelley said as he leaned his head in the open window of the taxi and handed Hermann a thick, filled but unsealed letter-sized envelope with a wide rubber band wrapped around it. "Take care of this for me while I am gone."

"What is it?" Hermann asked as he took the envelope.

"Never mind. Just hang on to it while I am gone," Kelley said sternly.

"*Si, Señor* Kelly," Hermann said as he leaned back and closed his eyes.

Franklin went to the stairway along the wall of the building and climbed to the third floor.

Kelley followed.

Franklin went to a door and knocked. "Emma, it is I, Franklin. Open the door."

A moment of silence followed. Then Kelley could hear the latch being turned. In a moment the door opened slightly. A bruised face appeared. An audible sigh followed as the door opened wider. Franklin and then Kelley entered.

Kelley looked at Emma. Her arms and upper shoulders, as well as her face, were badly bruised. Her lips were swollen, and one blackened eye was in sharp contrast to the white of the bandage across her nose. "Damn, Emma, I'm sorry this happened to you—Freddie did this?" Kelley asked.

Emma answered with an obviously painful voice, "*Si*—he did it while one of the bartenders held me."

"Before this is over, I'll make sure Freddie pays for what he did to you, Emma," Kelley said with conviction.

"No. No. I don't want to be hurt again. Just give me the money so Franklin and I can leave Maturin and go someplace where we can be left alone. Whatever you are doing, I do not want to be a part of it."

Kelley could tell that Emma's mind was made up. All she wanted was to get out, away from Freddie and with whatever he was connected. And what he was connected with was somehow part of what was in the letter that Carrillo had written. No matter how much Kelley wanted to deal with Freddie now, it would have to wait.

"Do you have the money?" Emma asked.

"Yes, I have the money—two-thousand American."

"You said five thousand," Emma said quickly.

"The rest is with my driver—I get it when I see the letter."

Emma looked at Kelley, then Franklin. "I believe him," Franklin said. "He gave his driver an envelope when we got out of the car."

"Give me the two thousand," Emma barked.

Kelley reached into his coat pocket, withdrew an envelope, and handed it to Emma.

Emma took the envelope and pulled it open; the envelope was filled with money. She handed the envelope to Franklin and said, "Count it while I get the letter."

As Emma turned toward the bedroom, Franklin took the money out of the envelope and began counting it. As he finished his counting, Emma returned to the room with a thin envelope in her hand. She opened the envelope and withdrew several folded sheets of paper. As she did, a flower petal fell from between the folded sheets. Emma picked up the flower petal from the floor, put it in the envelope, and placed the envelope on a table next to the lone sofa in the room. She looked at Franklin with questioning eyes.

"It is all there—two-thousand," Franklin said

Emma separated one sheet from the several she held. She handed the one sheet to Kelley. "The rest when you give us the rest of the money."

Kelley took the one sheet of paper and looked at it. It appeared to be the first page of a letter addressed to Bettina, dated August 11, just two weeks before Carrillo washed up on the beach in Spanish Palms, and, as best Kelley could remember what Carrillo's handwriting looked like, a letter from Carrillo. It had been some time since Kelley had had to read Spanish, but he was able to get the gist of the words. Carrillo's initial words were amorous, asking Bettina's forgiveness for suddenly leaving Maturin because of business, saying, in the last lines at the bottom of the page, he had to meet with an operator of a marine services company in Barcelona.

Kelley looked up from his reading. "Can I have the other pages?" Kelley asked, hoping the remaining pages would give the name of the company in Barcelona.

"The money—the money first!" Emma said as she pulled the remaining sheets of the letter close to her breast.

Kelley stared at Emma for a moment. "Okay, let me get my driver up here. He's got the money."

"Go onto the balcony and call him up here," Franklin ordered.

Kelley nodded his head, turned and stepped toward the sliding glass door leading to a small balcony. Both Franklin and Emma followed. There was a gritty scraping sound as Kelley pulled the glass door open. Kelley stepped onto the balcony. Franklin followed and then stood beside Kelley. Emma stood in the shadow of the balcony from the floor above.

Kelley put his hands on the balcony railing and leaned outward to better look at the car in the street below. He hoped Hermann could hear him. Kelley yelled out, "Hermann! Hermann!"

There was no motion in the car.

Kelley yelled again, but louder this time, "Hermann, wake up! Herman, answer me, dammit! Wake up!"

Nothing happened for a moment. Then Kelley saw some movement in the car. "Hermann, get out of the car. It's me, Kelley. Get out of the car!"

The car door opened. Hermann slowly looked around.

"Up here, dammit. Look up, Hermann!" Kelley shouted again.

Hermann looked up. A smile came to his face. "*Si, Señor* Kelley. What is it?" Hermann shouted.

Emma suddenly said, "Oh ... oh."

Kelley turned to look at Emma. She looked pale, even in the shadow of the balcony above.

"Don't worry," Kelley said, trying to ease her apparent fright. "He's got the money. He'll bring it up to me." Kelley turned back toward Hermann. "Bring that envelope up to me," Kelley shouted.

A frown came to Hermann's face. "Are you sure you want me to do that, *Señor* Kelley?" Hermann shouted suspiciously.

Emma stepped from the shadow and close to Franklin. She whispered something in his ear.

"Yes, goddamn it—bring it up to me, right now,"

Franklin moved close to Kelley, placing his hand on Kelley's shoulder, and spoke angrily into Kelley's ear. "You will get nothing—you are trying to trick us. You're just one of them."

"Don't be a fool, Franklin. I'm want to help you if you will just help me," Kelley said in exasperation as he looked momentarily at Franklin and Emma; Emma had now shrunken away from the balcony and back into the apartment.

"Are you really sure," Hermann yelled back to Kelley.

Kelley, his frustration rising, shouted, "Yes, damn it. Get your ass up here. I'm all right. I just want the damn envelope!"

"*Si, Señor* Kelley, I understand. I understand," Hermann said as he waved his hand.

Hermann got into the car, started the motor, and, gunning the engine, sped off down the street.

Kelley shouted, "What the—"

"You lied to us ... you are just one of them. It has been all a trick," Franklin said as he turned and ran back into the apartment.

"No, I didn't. That stupid driver of mine ... he must have thought something was wrong—"

"I don't care what he thought," Franklin said as he grabbed Emma's arm and pushed her into the bedroom, and then, following her, slammed the bedroom door. The click of a turning lock followed, and then came a scraping noise as if furniture were being pulled across the floor. A loud bump followed as something hit the door.

"What do you think you're doing?" Kelley shouted.

"Staying behind this door until you get out of here," came the muffled response.

"But we have a deal," Kelley shouted back.

"Yes. And you have not kept your end of it! We stay in here until you leave."

"But our deal—you're going to get your money," Kelley pleaded. A long silence followed—punctuated with sharp, muffled, inaudible words between Franklin and Emma. Then from behind the door came the words, "You come back with the money, and we will go on with our deal."

Kelley thought about what Franklin had said, and the consequences if he tried to break down the door. If he did, any cooperation, any other help he might get from Franklin and Emma would be lost. And getting whatever else was in the envelope would be difficult, if not impossible, without some serious arm twisting—literally. No, he couldn't do that. He would have to get the money and come back.

"All right, all right. I will get the money and come back. Just wait for me ... probably take about two hours to catch up with my driver and get back here. Just wait for me—just two hours," Kelley said, hoping they would wait.

A long moment of silence followed; then Franklin replied, "We will wait two hours—no more."

— ~ —

Forty-five minutes later, Kelley's taxi pulled up to the Green Parrot. Hermann's car was parked at the curb. Kelley paid the taxi driver and went quickly into the hotel lobby. Hermann was sitting in a chair beside a table with a telephone in his hand—talking.

"What the hell were you doing—driving off like that?" Kelley yelled as he walked toward Hermann.

Hermann quickly stopped talking and turned to look at Kelley, a surprised look coming to this face. *"Señor* Kelley! You are okay. I was so worried," Hermann said as he rose from the chair, the phone still in his hand.

"What do you mean?" Kelley asked angrily.

"The man, Franklin, standing beside you—did he not have a gun on you?" Hermann asked.

"Gun—where the hell did you get that idea?"

"Well, with all that money in the envelope ... and ... well ... I could not see his hands ... and he was standing beside you, like a guard ... so I—"

"Did I tell you to look inside the envelope?" Kelley said angrily.

"But you did not say not to look inside," Hermann said in defense. Kelley shook his head in disbelief. "Jesus—so you assumed he had a gun on me?"

"It seemed that might be so ...." Hermann said sheepishly.

"Hermann, don't try to second-guess me. I can take care of myself," Kelley said authoritatively.

"Like after what happened to you when you left the House of Pleasure?"

Kelley sighed and looked with disgust at Hermann.

A loud squawk came from the phone. Hermann put the phone to his ear again and listened for a moment. "He is here now," Hermann finally said, as he offered the phone to Kelley.

"Who's on the phone?" Kelley asked Hermann.

*"Señor* Luque. I called him to find out what to do," Hermann said in explanation.

Kelley put the phone to his ear. "Is that you, Miguel?"

Muffled sounds came from the phone handset.

"Everything is okay. Hermann jumped to conclusions," Kelley said as he looked at Hermann with a scowl.

More muffled sounds came from the phone handset.

"I was trying to get some information—that's what the money was for. I had given it to Hermann for temporary safekeeping. His imagination got the best of him. He thought I was being robbed."

More muffled sounds.

"It was information about Carrillo. Apparently, he was in Barcelona just before he ... got to Texas." Kelley was hesitant to use the word "murdered" with Hermann standing nearby. "He was checking out some marine services company ... No, I don't. Just some company .... Yeah, I know there are lots of marine services companies in Barcelona .... Well, there was more information—that's what the money was for. I have to go back with the money to get the rest of the info .... From a girl that worked with Carrillo's girlfriend.... No, I can take care of it. No need for you come over here, at least yet ... but maybe you can start doing some checking on the marine services companies in Barcelona—see if any of them look dirty, beyond the usual level of payoffs that go on .... Yeah, that's right. I know, I know. But things are getting confused—I don't have time to explain it all to you now. I gotta go .... Yeah .... Okay, maybe then. Bye."

Kelley returned the phone handset to its cradle. "All right, Hermann, let's go."

"Where are we going, *Señor* Kelley?"

"Back to the apartment building—and give me that envelope back."

— ~ —

Kelley knocked on the door. There was no answer. He knocked again. No answer. He put his hand forward and twisted the doorknob. To his surprise, it turned easily, and the door opened.

Kelley entered the small living room of the apartment. No one was there. Kelley looked at this watch. Only ninety minutes had passed since he had left Emma and Franklin, but they were apparently just too frightened to wait.

Kelley surveyed the room. A closet in the corner of the room had its door open. There were empty hangers, in tangled disarray, on the pitted metal bar spanning the small closet opening. A pair of bright red high-heeled woman shoes lay on the closet floor, looking lonely and forlorn. The bedroom door was open. Kelley walked into the bedroom and surveyed the room. Both of the twin beds were along one wall and unmade. The dresser was pulled away from the wall and to the side of the door. Its drawers were pulled open. A few clothes, for both a man and a woman, were scattered about on the beds and floor. Kelley walked to the dresser and looked in the drawers. Except for some remnants of a woman's face power case, two torn black stockings, a single pair of men's underwear, and several unmatched men's socks, the drawers were empty.

Kelley stepped into the bathroom. It too looked like there had been a rapid departure; some bottles of makeup were overturned on a shelf above the sink. Other bottles lay broken on the floor, their contents intermixed with the broken glass spread across the bathroom floor. And in the corner of the room, next to the toilet, lay a small electric clock, it plastic face cracked and the prongs on its electric plug bent as if it had been yanked from the wall socket in the rush of gathering things together.

"Damn," Kelley said in anger, looking at the time on the stopped clock. Emma and Franklin had taken off after only twenty minutes.

Then Kelley glanced at the toilet. Floating in the water were remnants of burned sheets of paper. He could tell from some small unburned pieces that the ashes were from Carrillo's letter. Emma and Franklin were apparently so frightened they didn't want anything to do with the letter—nor the money they could get for it. Kelley could not understand why they were so frightened. *Fucking damn! Emma and Franklin are gone for good—and whatever was in Carrillo's letter is gone, too.*

But as Kelley stepped back into the living room he remembered the envelope—the envelope from which Emma had withdrawn Carrillo's letter. Emma had placed it on a table as she stood near the bedroom door. Kelley turned to look at the table, and there, on the floor beside the table, was an envelope. Kelley quickly picked it up. It was empty except for the beautiful dark pink petal of an orchid that Emma had returned to it earlier. It was just like Carrillo to include a flower petal in his love letter. He was always the romantic, even when it was just trying to get into a woman's pants—only this time he had apparently gotten more than he bargained for with Bettina.

The envelope offered little else. It was addressed to Bettina Mendoza Ayala at a Maturin address and had a Barcelona postmark with the date of August 11, the same date as the letter.

Kelley now had only two choices: to deal with Cui or go to Barcelona and continue his search for Carrillo's murderer.

"Get me back to the hotel, Hermann. I need to pack," Kelley said decisively.

— ~ —

As Hermann came around a sharp corner along the narrow street several blocks from the now-vacant apartment, the car was brought to a squealing stop by a long line of stopped vehicles.

"Damn, Hermann, be careful. What going on?" Kelley asked.

"I am not sure," Hermann said as he strained to look beyond the cars in front of his own. "It looks like it might be a police roadblock."

"Shit—see if you can turn around. I don't want to get bogged down here ... I've got things to do."

"*Si, Señor* Kelley," Hermann said as he tried to turn the steering wheel to extricate the car from the trap that the car in front and, now, the truck in the back had made. Hermann started moving slowly backward and forward, twisting the steering wheel slightly on each forward roll, slowly getting the fender of his car clear of the car in front. Finally, when he was about able to get out of the line of cars and make a sharp U-turn in the narrow street, a policeman walked toward the car and wiggled his finger, clearly indicating his desire that the car, and its passengers, not go any farther.

The policeman leaned toward Hermann's window and said in Spanish, "Why are you so anxious to leave? Everyone else is willing to wait."

"*Señor* Kelley wants to go to his hotel," Hermann answered.

"*Señor* Kelley ... would that be you?" the policeman asked as he turned his head slightly and looked at Kelley.

"*Si, Señor*. I am Kelley Castellano. My driver and I were returning to my hotel, the Green Parrot. I have some business matters to attend to," Kelley answered pleasantly.

"You are from *Unidos Estados*? Do all Americans work on a Sunday afternoon?" the policeman asked suspiciously.

"They do if they are in the oil business," Kelley responded, getting a little irritated with the officer's questioning.

"Well, you will have to wait—until we are sure that no terrorist is trying to sneak through our roadblock—and no one can go back. You must move forward and be inspected," the officer said in an authoritative tone.

"Terrorist—what happened?" Kelley asked.

"Four innocent people were murdered," the policeman answered.

"Murdered!" Kelley said in surprise.

"Yes, about an hour ago. A man in a car sped down the street and shot four people on the sidewalk—two children and a man and woman. They were just walking down the street. The man and woman were apparently going to the bus station on the next block—they were carrying several bags of luggage. It is a wonder more were not hurt. The murderers got away, but not for long. We will get them for their cowardly act."

"Were the man and woman the poor children's parents?" Hermann asked solicitously.

"We do not think so—the man and women looked like they were related—but not man and wife."

"Why do you say that," Kelley asked out of curiosity.

"The man and woman—they looked like twin brother and sister."

Kelley's shoulders slumped. "Jesus—Emma and Franklin ... how in the hell—"

"You know them?" the policeman asked.

"I think so ... I think ... so," Kelley said sorrowfully.

"Then come with me—to see if it is the people you know," the policeman demanded.

Kelley slowly opened the car door, stepped out, and began to follow the policeman.

# X
# BEAUTIFUL FLOWERS

## 32

Cui smiled to himself with satisfaction, thinking, *except for Castellano, all is going well.* He had dropped the money into one of the donation buckets as they were passed through the crowd, something that was always done at these rallies—particularly in the front rows of the crowd where the more affluent members of the party sat—to see who the real supporters of the party were. And the party faithful never forgot to show their loyalty—generously—to be sure, that when the PHC handed out its favors, they would be among those to receive them.

But it was not just one of the many buckets in which Cui had deposited the money. It was the bucket that Marulanda himself had held out for donations as Uriarte called for support of his party at the end of his speech. Marulanda had nodded his head in acknowledgment when Cui had put into the bucket a significant but appropriate amount of money for a donation to the PHC coffers before the bucket was passed onto the next person in the line of the PHC's ardent supporters.

But what was more important than the stack of bills that Cui had placed in the bucket was the blue-edged envelope that he had also put into the bucket under Marulanda's watchful eyes. Within the blue-edged envelop were two smaller envelopes, one for Marulanda and one for Uriarte, each with similar contents.

Marulanda's envelope contained the name of a bank in the Cayman Islands and, handwritten on the back of Cui's business card, an account number. Also included was a photocopy of the signature card complete with Marulanda's signature that Cui had used to open Marulanda's account.

Marulanda, as could Uriarte if he wished, could take a short vacation to the Cayman Islands and be able to confirm that his money, two-hundred-fifty-thousand dollars—American—was there, but in escrow awaiting to be automatically deposited the day after the already-scheduled closing date for submittal of letters of certification of benefit from Uriarte.

Uriarte, who would receive his envelope from Marulanda, would soon after its receipt announce with a formal letter of certification of benefit to the Oil Ministry in Caracas that China Petroleum had not only met but considerably exceeded all the conditions of the Equitable Lease Policy and was qualified—no, not only qualified, but indeed highly recommended—to bid on the service agreement for the San Juan block when the Ministry received and opened bids before the end of the year.

And Marulanda would, for his part, find that China Petroleum had provided an exceptionally competitive bid, which of course China Petroleum would provide, and certify that it should be accepted. And to assure that the letter of certification accomplished its goal, along with the support of Marulanda, another two-hundred fifty thousand dollars currently held in escrow would be placed in each of the bank accounts a day after the formal announcement of China Petroleum's success in winning the San Juan Block Service Agreement.

And the bid, at least in its amount, would be sufficiently competitive, though perhaps not the highest, with the other bids to demonstrate to those who might be concerned that the new oil ministry was objective in its evaluation of bids for the lease.

With the service agreement obtained, China Petroleum could hatch the next component of Cui's plan: Completion of the contractual arrangements with PDVSA that would follow the announcement of the service agreement to China Petroleum. The contracts would allow construction of docking facilities for ships with oil drilling equipment—and, for that matter, as the contracts would say, any other Chinese ships—to service or otherwise support and protect China Petroleum's exploration and development activities. And to be sure that PDVSA would allow the contractual agreements to move quickly forward and be sufficiently flexible to provide perhaps unusually large docking facilities—large enough, should someone think about it, for major ships of any type—Marulanda would take an active hand in the contract negotiations. And for his assistance in bringing the contract negotiations to a successful conclusion, Marulanda would receive in his Cayman Islands account on the day after PDVSA and China Petroleum signed their contract another quarter million dollars.

*But, to be sure that the plan would move forward, I have to find out what Castellano is doing in Maturin. And whatever it is, it is going to have to be stopped.* Seeing him at Dolanyi's office, after all those years, had been a quite a shock, and then, outside, the taxi and its driver—certainly not a coincidence. Cui realized that Castellano explained the helicopter that took so much interest in Dolanyi's boat when the sounding measurements were being made on the San Juan; Castellano was probably in the helicopter. Whatever Castellano was doing in Maturin, Cui was sure that Castellano knew too much, or might soon deduce it. Castellano was a pinprick that could not be allowed to fester.

Cui picked up the phone and dialed a number for the China Petroleum offices in Caracas. After a few moments, he spoke in rapid Chinese. "Wang Ling, do you recognize my voice .... Good. Listen carefully. I have need of your assistance. Come to Maturin tomorrow so that I can explain what I need. Meet me at the Hotel Morichal Largo at three in the afternoon."

# 33

Kelley scanned the names of the various businesses that lined Paseo de Costa, the highway hugging the Caribbean coast between the two cities—Puerto la Pirtu to the west and Cumana to the east— guarding the hundred kilometer stretch of Venezuelan coastline that with Barcelona and Puerto la Cruz at its center and Margarita Island in the *Bahia de Barcelona* to the north was the equivalent of the Florida Gold Coast and Las Vegas rolled into one tiny, brilliant but slightly flawed jewel: warm sun and white beaches, historic buildings with the tales to go with them, the chic vacation homes of the rich and those aspiring to be, and a hidden decadence where the desires of the flesh could be fulfilled with abandon.

By this time, about three in the afternoon on Thursday—Kelley had started his search early in the morning—Kelley was on the highway west of Barcelona. Oil tankers were lined up along the piers jutting into the *Bahia de Barcelona* to receive the raw petroleum piped from the El Tigre and Anaco oil fields a hundred kilometers to the south. Where Kelley was now riding in a slowly moving taxi, the businesses were dominated by boatyards and docks used by industry and commerce, machine repair shops, salvage yards, fish processing and packaging plants, and marine services and repair operations—the industrial base of the Barcelonan coast.

*Servicios Maritimo de Barcelona*—Marine Services of Barcelona—was the next to the last name on the list that Luque had provided him and was, according to the taxi driver, only about half a kilometer farther. This would be the fifteenth, and from the way it was going, Kelley figured, maybe his last, marine services company he would visit since his arrival in Barcelona three days ago, trying to turn up some connection to Carrillo. He was beginning to wonder whether he had made the wrong decision to come to Barcelona. But he was here, and he did not want to miss anything, so he had ordered the driver to proceed slowly, even at the risk of the frequent angry shouts from drivers who would speed around the taxi.

As he looked at the names on the various offices, warehouse, and shops lining the seaward side of the roadway, Kelley suddenly saw a name that was not on Luque's list, and that perhaps should have been: "*Cumaraima Servicios Maritimo y Excursións*." The name was printed on a sign above a doorway of a large warehouse. Painted on the wide window next to the doorway, written in both Spanish and English, were the words, "Complete marine supplies, rental and excursion services - commercial and tourist." And in a brilliant array of colors in the sandy lot in front of the building, like an island in a vast sea, was a massive cornucopia of flowering plants, including a large collection of orchids, all surrounded by a chain-link fence.

"Stop here!" Kelley shouted.

The taxi driver slammed on his brakes; a honking horn and a loud shout came from behind the taxi. In a moment, a car zoomed around the taxi.

Kelley got out of the taxi and stepped across the sidewalk to its edge where one of the beautiful orchids drooped over the chain link fence. He pulled the envelope with the one page of Carrillo's letter from his coat pocket, turned the envelope so the flower petal in it dropped into his hand, and put his hand next to the drooping flowers. Except for the color, the petals were the same. Yes, Carrillo's flower petal was from an orchid, with a deep purple color like some of the vibrant colors on the flowers inside the fence.

"Wait here until I return," Kelley ordered.

The driver nodded his head, saying, "*Si, Señor,*" and pulled the taxi closer to the curb. He turned off the engine. In a moment music flowed from the open window of the car.

Kelley surveyed the building and its surroundings. The front face of the building had been painted numerous times, as evidenced by the different colors under various layers of flaking paint. And next to the building, about fifty yards away, marked with a large white cross guarded by a painted warning circle, was a sun-bleached asphalt helicopter landing pad, apparently ready and eager to receive a wealthy fisherman about to embark upon his rented fishing boat.

The back side of the warehouse, as best as Kelley could see, was jammed against a narrow canal funneling in from the bay to end in a small turning basin at the back of the warehouse. Along the edge of the canal was a long dock with two large yachts tied up to it; both boats were outfitted with lines and rigging for deep sea fishing. Several workers moved about the boats, apparently getting them ready for new customers.

Kelley went along the walkway next to the fence that led to the front door. Reaching the door, Kelley adjusted his tie, put on his wealthy businessman's face, and entered the building.

Inside the building, Kelley found himself in a sales room lined with glass display cases filled with fishing equipment and gear. The walls above the showcases were covered with photos of proud fisherman displaying their catch. In the corner of the room an elderly, heavyset woman sat on a stool behind a counter with a cash register on it; behind the counter was a radio receiver-transmitter. The woman was arranging several vases of flowers, drawing flowers from different piles of cut flowers lying on the counter. Several of the piles were orchids similar in color to those growing in the front of the building.

The woman looked up briefly as Kelley entered the room and then returned her attention to the flowers, smiling. As Kelley reached the counter at which she was working, she paused in her work, and asked, "May I help you, *Señor?*"

"Perhaps, *Señora...?*" Kelley asked with a smile.

"*Señora* Cumaraima. And you, *Señor?*"

"*Señor* Castellano."

"Ah, an American. *Si*, what can I do for you?" said *Señora* Cumaraima as she switched to English and stopped arranging the flowers.

"I wish to hire a boat, a fishing boat for an extended period of time—do you rent boats?" Kelley responded in Spanish.

With a thankful smile, *Señora* Cumaraima, returning to her more comfortable Spanish, answered, "We rent boats with crews; we do not rent boats by themselves. We will take you where you want to go. My husband knows the very best fishing areas, and our daily rental rates are very reasonable."

"I wish to rent a boat and its crew for several days, not just one day," Kelley said, hoping that his idea, which he had been using without success thus far, of asking about a multi-day rental might draw out the type of people he was looking for.

"Several days—without return to port?" *Señora* Cumaraima asked.

"Yes, several days, at least without returning to a Venezuelan port."

*Señora* Cumaraima eyes narrowed as she looked at Kelley. "You will have to ask my husband about that," she said as she rose from her stool and pointed to a door at the back of the room.

"*Gracias*," Kelley said as he turned and took one step toward the doorway. Then he stopped and turned to look at *Señora* Cumaraima, who was already busy again arranging flowers. He stepped to the counter and reached out to touch an orchid, with petals similar to Carrillo's flower.

"These are lovely flowers. Do you grow them yourself?" Kelley asked politely as he bent his head forward to smell the flowers' aroma.

"*Si, si.* They come from my orchids in the front yard as well as my home a short distance from here. The one you smell is a *cleistes moritzii*—it is very rare here along the coast; many people come to me to ask for them to be used at weddings and funerals. I am one of the few people here in the Barcelona area that can provide them."

"How interesting," Kelley said, attempting to control his growing excitement. Kelley turned back toward the doorway. "You said *Señor* Cumaraima is in the back," Kelley said to calm his emotions.

"*Si, si.* He is in the workshop. That is what I said."

Kelley pushed open the door and stepped into the next room. He found himself in a large workshop area making up most of the warehouse space he had seen from the outside of the building. The workshop was in general chaos—from chains, large and small hand tools, cable cutters, and rope of all sorts hanging on wall hooks, to fishing rods, paint cans and rolls of sail canvas stacked on shelves, to oil and gasoline cans, old bollards, cranking rods, and even several ship propellers among the pumps and motors, some new and some old and rusty, scattered apparently randomly about the workshop floor.

The far end of the building was open to the canal, with wooden skids and two rusted steel rails angling out from the canal waters for bringing boats into dry dock for refit and repair. A small yacht, perhaps fifteen feet in length, undergoing repair was perched on the rails between large wooden chock blocks and braces. A young boy, standing on a ladder, was scraping the hull near the boat's stern.

Sitting at a table in perhaps the only open area between the dry-docked yacht and the doorway Kelley had entered was a dark-skinned, thin man in well-worn, greasy coveralls with a screwdriver in one hand and a large fishing reel, only partially assembled, in the other. Kelley recognized the reel as a Penn seawater reel, a top of the line reel from Penn's international series favored by deep-sea fishermen. A side-assembly plate, several springs, numerous screws, and a cam lay on the table along with a rusted pinion gear.

"Piece of junk," the man said in Spanish, with obvious disgust. Throwing down the screwdriver, he looked up at Kelley. "What do you want?" he asked gruffly as he put the reel on the table, picked up a nearby oily rag, and wiped his hands. Then examining Kelley more closely, apparently impressed by Kelley's expensive clothes and sensing that Kelley might be a customer, he said in a now-polite tone, "May I help you?"

Kelley answered, also in Spanish. "Perhaps. My name is Castellano, and you *Señor*, are...?"

"Juan Cumaraima. My brother-in-law, Henry, and I own this business," Cumaraima answered.

"A friend recommended your services to me. I am interested in doing some extended deep-sea fishing. My friend said you have the type of vessel that would be needed."

"Yes. We have several ships for rental. Our daily rates are very fair. We can provide all the gear that will be needed."

"I want to fish for more than a day—several days at least. Do you have vessels that could be at sea for several days without return to port—at least to a Venezuelan port?" Kelley said, again dangling his hook, hoping the man would bite.

The man looked carefully at Kelley for a few moments. "We have a trawler. It can stay at sea for quite a few days, but we do not normally rent it. We use it ourselves to catch the fish we sell for packaging. And it is not really suitable for deep-sea game fishing. And it would be very expensive to rent—so why would you need such a ship?"

"Let us say that I am not concerned about the type of fishing. I just have a need to be at sea for several days—quite a distance from the Venezuelan coast—in international waters, in fact, and be, shall we say, inconspicuous."

Cumaraima tilted his head and looked carefully at Kelley for a few moments, pursing his lips. "In that case, the price would be quite high, particularly if we have to dock at some port not in Venezuela."

"I don't really want to dock—I just want to meet someone—

another boat—at sea," Kelley answered. "You could return without me once the meeting occurs."

"Then you would have to pay before we left port," Cumaraima said in a conspiratorial voice.

"That could be arranged," Kelley said encouragingly.

"Let me call my brother-in-law and see when he expects to return to port—he is at sea with the ship we would want to use," Cumaraima said as he rose from his chair and begin winding his way through the mess on the floor toward the shop door through which Kelley had entered.

"When would you want to do this—and would you have any ... luggage?" Cumaraima asked as he reached the door.

"Within a few days, and as for ... the luggage, I would have only a few travel bags and several boxes, nothing that could not be easily carried by hand," Kelley answered, trying to weave a web that Cumaraima would recognize as a drug transfer.

Cumaraima looked at Kelley with pursed lips and then yelled out at the boy working on the boat, "Fidel, stop slacking off. I did not hire you to waste my money. You work faster, or I will fire you." Turning to Kelley, Cumaraima said, "Come with me. We will call Henry."

Kelley followed Cumaraima back into the sales room. "Maria, raise Henry on the radio. I must talk to him."

*Señora* Cumaraima turned from her flowers, lifted the radio switch to the send position, picked up the microphone, and began to speak into it, putting out a call to the Cumaraima boat. As she did so, her husband watched Kelley intently. Kelley turned to look at the pictures on the wall, trying to look and act relaxed. As he scanned several of the photos, he saw the same face in many of the photographs, a face that seemed vaguely familiar.

Then Kelley came to a picture that made him stop and stare. The picture was of four smiling men standing by a very large marlin, perhaps three to four feet longer than the tallest of the four standing men, hanging from a sturdy, tall tripod frame. Of the four men, two Kelley did not recognize, and one was the man who had appeared in the other pictures. The remaining man was a noticeably younger man whose face favored the man who appeared in the other pictures. It was the man who had been with Goldie the night Carrillo washed up on the shores of Spanish Palms: Victor Valdez!

Kelley took a deep, satisfying breath and then turned to face Cumaraima. "That is an enormous marlin—quite a catch. I see this gentleman here—the second on the right," Kelley said in what he hoped was a nonchalant voice as he pointed to the picture of the four men, "is in many of the pictures. Is he a friend of yours?"

"Him? That is Henry, my brother-in-law, the one we are trying to call right now," Cumaraima answered.

"Oh," Kelley responded innocently. "And the other man, the man who favors Henry—who is he?"

"That is Victor, Henry's younger brother."

— ~ —

"... and here's the kicker, Tony. The guy in the picture, the guy who was the brother of one of the owners of the shop, is the same guy that was on the beach the night when Carrillo washed ashore. That's the connection I have been looking for—and probably the lead we need to figure out who murdered Carrillo. I figure it was their fishing boat that the brother-in-law is supposed to bring into port tomorrow afternoon that carried Carrillo into the Gulf in its hole. I think we can go in and—"

"Wait, wait, Kelley," Tony Luque interrupted over the phone. "We have got to get this more tied down before we start shoving our weight around here in Venezuela. Just because you say you recognized a guy in a picture won't be good enough for the Venezuelan Federal police. And besides, you don't think that boat runs all the way up to Texas, do you?"

"Well, I don't know ... they may make a transfer out in the Gulf somewhere," Kelley answered with a bit of indecision creeping into his voice.

"Right! We need to get more info, without you getting killed in the process. And, there's that Matthew guy you said you need to check out. I've been doing a little digging on him. He may be real dirty. Some of his dealings with customs people look pretty shady. Do you know where he is now?" Luque asked.

"He's in Maturin," Kelley answered.

"That guy needs to be checked out—to see if he fits into any of this. You need to get back to Maturin and do some more digging," Luque said authoritatively.

"So, what do you propose?" Kelley asked with little enthusiasm.

"Let me contact Langley and see about maybe getting some satellite tracking started on that fishing boat—as soon as it leaves port the next time we will start tracking it and see where it goes. You contact the Cumaraima outfit and tell them the deal is off—that some unexpected difficulties came up. Drop the hint that your drug shipment got delayed. You head back to Maturin and figure out what Matthew may be up to."

Kelley sighed, concluding Luque was probably right about going back to Maturin, although he already knew a great deal more about Matthew than Luque could even begin to suspect. "Okay, I will get a flight back to Maturin tomorrow."

"Why don't I have a helo from Maturin come up to Barcelona to pick you up and ferry you back to Maturin. I can have the chopper at the heliport station at the Barcelona airport ... better yet, I will have the helo pick you up at the pad at Cumaraima's place—say ... ten in the morning. You'll be back in Maturin before lunch," Luque said reassuringly.

"Well, I guess that would be okay. I'll be at the helo pad by nine-thirty," Kelley said.

"Yeah, you do that," Luque answered. "I'll take care of everything."

Kelley returned the telephone receiver to its cradle beside the bed, stood, and began to take off his shirt and tie, thinking about a shower. Then it hit him. *How did Luque know about the helo pad at the Cumaraima warehouse?*

# XI
# COLLISIONS

## 34

Eulogio put the phone down in its cradle, shaken by what he had been told—no, not told, ordered to do. Alexis had called on behalf of Benavides. While cordial, Alexis had made his message clear. Benavides wanted a particular American oil exploration and development company to prosper in its activities in Monagas state.

Why Benavides wanted this to occur was not spelled out by Alexis, but it was obvious that Benavides wanted to use the company for some purpose. And that purpose would be, so Alexis implied, considerably enhanced if this company were to have the support of the Ministry of Mines and Hydrocarbons, and, in particular, its minister.

When Eulogio asked what particular form of support might be required, Alexis said to assist in whatever way that might become apparent, but certainly to lend his full support to awarding the bid to the company for an operating service agreement the company was pursuing on the Rio San Juan, near Maturin.

When Alexis had asked, "Are you aware of a block to be soon awarded along the San Juan," Eulogio had answered, "I believe I have received some information on it, but I am not fully aware of the status of PDVSA activities in receiving bids on the block."

"Well, find out what's going on—and make sure the American firm wins the contract for that block," Alexis ordered. "Remember our discussion of your last visit here; this company is part of our plan."

Eulogio had broken out in a cold sweat. The only block on the San

Juan was the same block that China Petroleum wanted—and for which Eulogio had already received one-quarter million dollars from Cui to assure that China Petroleum would be the forerunner in winning the bid for the block.

"But Alexis," Eulogio had protested, "I cannot guarantee what the bidding results will be ... PDSVA makes the evaluation ... the recommendation—"

"Do not argue with me, Eulogio. This is what Benavidez wants. He did not arrange for you to become the Minister of Mines and Hydrocarbons to say you cannot do what is needed. You have the power, even if you have to override PDVSA's recommendation. Do what is needed to assure the American firm wins. Benavides will have it no other way."

Not knowing what else to say, Eulogio concluded by asking, "What is the American company's name?" But Eulogio already knew the name: *Tejas Petróleo*. It could be no other. Cinzia's brother, Jorge Rodriquez, had introduced Matthew, the Tejas president, to Eulogio at Cinzia's birthday party. Eulogio had then realized that he had spoken to Matthew very briefly only a few days ago when the man had interrupted his meeting with Cui at the Morichal Largo. He, Matthew, and Jorge had spoken only a few minutes at the party, but were able to convince Eulogio, despite the fact that Eulogio rapidly took a disliking to the American, to meet with Jorge and Matthew the following week in Caracas—for a private lunch to talk about some bidding on a block northeast of Maturin, a block which Eulogio now knew had to be the San Juan block.

"*Tejas Petróleo de Venezuela*," came the reply.

*So now he was beholden to both Benavidez and Cui. What am I going to do? Benavides might well kill me if* Tejas Petróleo de Venezuela *does not win the San Juan bid. And what will China Petroleum—Cui—do if China Petroleum does not win?*

And it was not just what Cui might do; it was also what Chávez and Munguia might do. Munguia had called him only a week ago, a courtesy call so Munguia had said, to ask how the bidding process for the San Juan block was proceeding.

*I, like a fool, said that not only were things progressing smoothly but that I felt confident that China Petroleum would do well in the selection process. Munguia would have relayed that message—likely embellished with considerable optimism—to Chávez. Now Chávez would be expecting China Petroleum to win; I practically guaranteed it.*

True, Cui had not yet delivered all the money he had promised. Marulanda had only, at this point, pledged to agree with a positive recommendation for the *Certificate de Beneficencia* to be formally provided by Uriarte. Uriarte was supposed to officially provide the certification in less than two weeks—*perhaps I can stop Uriarte before it is announced! But I have to be sure what I will say ... what I should do. But if I can make it look as if Uriarte had broken the deal with Cui, I might escape Chávez's retaliation.*

Without very good reason, Uriarte was certainly going to object, if not refuse, to not issuing the certification. The certificate had to be issued if Uriarte was to get all the money that Cui had promised him—and not invoke the dangerous ire of Chávez.

How could he stop Uriarte—but wait, should he? Maybe he could blame Uriarte, make Benavidez believe it wasn't Eulogio's fault—that Uriarte was responsible. Let Cui have his certification and tell Benavidez that Uriarte had double-crossed Eulogio.

Eulogio's intercom buzzed; his secretary's voice followed. "Your luncheon meeting at one—you wanted me to remind you, Minister Marulanda."

"*Si, gracias.*" Eulogio rose from his chair and began putting on his coat, thinking, *Maybe Jorge and this president of Tejas can shed some light on what is going on—and maybe show me how to get out of this mess.*

— ~ —

"I am so pleased we could meet today, Eulogio. I know how busy your schedule must be. We really did not get to talk much at Cinzia's party—and I wanted to let you spend a little more time with *Señor* Matthew, President of *Tejas Petróleo*," Jorge Rodriquez said as he extended his hand to Eulogio.

"*Si,* Jorge, it was a pleasant party—but one that did not allow for much discussion of business matters. And, I would assume, *Señor*

Matthew, that would be the purpose of your meeting today?"

"Well, in a way, certainly," responded Kevin, "but my real purpose is to have you understand how much Tejas wants to work with the Venezuelan people in developing the petroleum resources of your country—for the benefit of both my company and your country. And to assure you of our considerable qualifications for successfully doing that."

"Well, perhaps then *Señor* Matthew, you might tell me more about your company, both here and in the United States," Eulogio asked graciously.

"Certainly," Kevin answered. Kevin paused a moment and then began. "My company in the United States operates under the name of Trans-Texas. We do oil exploration and development over much of the southwest U.S.—have been in business since the late '70s ...."

As Kevin continued talking, Eulogio quickly sorted out fact from Kevin's fiction. Eulogio already knew a great deal about Trans-Texas and *Tejas Petróleo* from the information he had developed for Benavidez in preparing the list of smaller, struggling American oil companies doing business in Venezuela. The one thing that Matthew's discourse revealed to Eulogio's surprise was the close connection that Matthew had to the American senator, Roland Beal. That connection, Eulogio concluded, might somehow become useful.

Sensing that Matthew was coming to the end of his discourse, Eulogio interrupted, politely but firmly. "Have you had any opportunities to work jointly with other ... parties here in South America outside Venezuela—Colombia or Ecuador perhaps?" Eulogio asked, hoping Matthew might reveal some connection to Benavides.

A long pause followed. "No, we have been dealing only with Venezuela ... companies and contractors that provide us services or to whom we provide services here in Venezuela. Is that important to the work we might do here in Venezuela?" Kevin answered, the surprise in his voice evident.

"Not critically, of course," Eulogio answered disarmingly, "but every bit of experience south of the border, so to speak, is useful I would think. Contacts from different countries can be quite useful, do you not think so, *Señor* Matthew?"

"Perhaps, but—," Kevin began to answer when Jorge cut in.

"Perhaps, Eulogio, we should focus our attention on Venezuela, the country about which we are most concerned."

"*Si*, you right," Eulogio answered, still not sure how Tejas was connected with Benavides. "*Si*, let us do that, Jorge. And, in that regard, *Señor* Matthew, do you have any particular ... operations ... ventures ... in which you are engaged? You and Jorge indicated at the party that you wished to talk about some bid opportunities in the Maturin area."

"I'm glad you asked, *Señor* Minister. We, in fact, do," Kevin responded confidently. "We will be making a bid—a successful one I believe—for the San Juan block. Are you aware of the block, *Señor* Minister?"

"*Si*, I am. I believe it is along the Rio San Juan northeast of Maturin. I understand the block encompasses much of the land near the mouth of the San Juan."

"I must say to you, in confidence, *Señor* Minister, that we have very optimistic projections for what can be developed from that block. Combined with its location with direct access to the Gulf of Paria, we think it provides an excellent opportunity for generation, in the long term, of sizeable revenue, a significant portion of which, of course, will go to your country."

"Well, I hope you are correct. I wish you well," Eulogio answered, wondering whether Jorge and Matthew would ever get to the real point of their meeting.

"Yes, in that regard, Eulogio," Jorge asked in brotherly tone, "we are seeking your advice and assistance."

Eulogio looked at Jorge in an innocent, but inquisitive way.

"Yes, there is the issue of the *Certificadi de Beneficencia,*" Jorge continued. "We would think that Governor Uriarte's support would be essential for a positive recommendation in regard to the *Certificadi de Beneficencia*. We know that you and he are long-time friends. We would like your assistance in meeting with him—convincing him that we would fully meet, even go beyond, the purposes of the *Certificadi de Beneficencia.*"

"I am sure you would do just that, but in my official capacity I cannot be an advocate for a particular bidder," Eulogio said with an imperial voice.

"Well, perhaps," Jorge began to say, "in an unofficial capacity—"

"Yeah," Kevin broke in. "Tejas has a Board of Directors that need people, like Jorge here, who are familiar with the situation down here and can pull some weight—in the political sense. I think I can be frank here, given that you and Jorge are relatives. You would be an ideal candidate for the Board. With some stock ownership because you're a member of the Board—board members automatically get stock as remuneration—the financial returns can be expected to be pretty sizeable down the road. And, for especially important Board members, there can be a sizeable upfront payment—like a signing bonus—for becoming a Board member."

*Well*, though Eulogio, *that certainly makes it plain—and maybe gives me a way out. This American is so without sophistication, so blunt as to be offensive—a perfect tool.* Eulogio wondered how he could get Matthew to make some major public blunder that would, of necessity and without Eulogio's overt intervention, make the Tejas application for the *Certificadi de Beneficencia* invalid. *If I could do that, Benavides could not blame me that Tejas did not win the bid for the San Juan block.*

"Well, Señor Matthew. I cannot participate, at this time—before the bidding takes place—in such arrangement." Eulogio said, intentionally implying but not committing to any involvement with Tejas after the award of bids. "My impartiality must be maintained during the bidding and selection process.

Kevin turned his eyes momentarily toward Jorge. Eulogio could see an ever so slight nod of Jorge's head.

"And, too, I would certainly," Kevin continued with some, what appeared to Eulogio, apparent unease, "want to be supportive of Governor Uriarte's efforts to continue in his office in the coming elections. Tejas would be able to make a sizeable contribution within a short time to the PHC for the benefit of ... the functions of the party."

Eulogio waited a moment, then asked, "How short of time ... and how sizeable?"

Kevin responded quickly, and now, confidently, "Before the decision on the *Certificadi de Beneficeancia* must be made—by the first of this coming week. And I would think two-hundred-thousand dollars, U.S.—almost a quarter of a million—would be very supportive of Governor Uriarte's re-election bid—and after we win the bid, another two-hundred-thousand for your ... party."

"That is quite a significant amount of money ... you have that available?" Eulogio asked, to see just how far Matthew was really prepared to go.

"The first payment is available now—my investors wired the money to my account here in Caracas yesterday," Kevin answered.

"Investors?" Eulogio asked slowly.

"Yes, investors—investors in *Tejas Petróleo*. There are many important people participating in this bid. They too are quite confident of the return that the San Juan block can bring," Kevin said in a reassuring tone.

"So many people ... are you sure that is wise?" Eulogio asked, worried that too many people might know what was going on.

"No problem. Full power is invested in me. I ... and Jorge here are the only ones who know of the ... arrangements that I may make. The investors just provide some of the ... resources needed to make our bid successful ... in whatever way that may be necessary," Kevin said with a knowing smile.

"I understand fully, *Señor* Matthew," Eulogio smiled in return, thinking, *just what I needed him to know; Matthew is responsible for it all—whatever might be necessary. All I have to do is work out the details. As for Jorge ... he will just have to take whatever might befall him.*

"I will certainly contact my close friend Governor Uriarte and arrange for you to spend some considerable time with him. I will maintain contact with him just to see how your discussions with him are developing. I will recommend to him that he give you his fullest attention for potential cooperation with you—all within the realm, of course, of appropriate propriety," Eulogio said as his smile joined the smiles of the other two men.

# 35

The sky was bright with the morning sun, but ominous darkness was beginning to fill the horizon to the far south. Kelley could see the helicopter approaching from the east, tracking the coast road, as he stood near the helo landing pad a short distance from the *Cumaraima Servicios Maritimo y Excursións* warehouse. Kelley had already told Juan Cumaraima that the trawler-hiring deal was off, at least for a while—that certain things had just not worked out on time. After that, Cumaraima seemed to rapidly lose interest in Kelley and his now-canceled request for use of the trawler. And he seemed to have no concern or question about Kelley being picked up by helicopter at Cumaraima's landing pad. But Kelley ... he was still wondering how Luque knew about the landing pad.

The copter was close now, beginning to hover above the slightly deteriorating square of asphalt that formed the landing pad, then slowly settling down onto the pad surface, rotating as it did so that the left side of the helicopter fronted toward Kelly. The copter had Escobar's Air Service painted in white on the blue-colored tail of the copter. Kelley saw that the side doors had been removed from the chopper; somewhat unusual but certainly not uncommon for working directly from a helicopter.

Luque sat in the pilot's seat, smiling. *What the hell is going on? Luque was supposed to be in Caracas, not Maturin.* Had Luque been in Caracas or Maturin when Kelley had spoken to him? Thinking back, Kelley wasn't really sure since he had talked to Luque on his cell phone.

And Kelley could see that Luque was not alone. Someone else was in the right front seat of the copter. Luque had apparently brought a copilot, though the reflecting sunlight off the windshield of the helicopter prevented Kelley from seeing little more than a dark outline of the man in the copilot's seat. As Luque slowed the rotor speed, Luque first waved and then motioned for Kelley to come to the copter. Kelley picked up his travel bag and went toward the copter, ducking his head to stay well below the slowly whirling blades. As he neared the copter, the co-pilot slipped out of the copter seat, momentarily dropping out of Kelley's view as the man started walking quickly around the blue-colored nose of the helicopter. When the man reappeared, Kelley recognized him. It was Valdes! And he had a gun in his hand.

Kelley stared at Valdes, seeing the silencer on the end of the pistol in his hand. Then Kelley refocused his attention on Luque, who was still smiling—no, now sneering more than smiling.

*Damn, how could I be so blind! It's all so fucking obvious—why hadn't I seen it before! They are all in it together—Luque and Valdes, Cumaraima, and likely others I don't know about.* It all made sense to Kelley now.

*Luque had to be the leak that the admiral was so worried about. Who would know more about what Carrillo was up to than Luque? And when Carrillo got too close to the truth, Luque, somehow, made sure Carrillo was murdered and taken out of the picture, at least until he inconveniently washed up on Goldie's beach. And Valdes—he had to be part of Carrillo's murder too.* But it still didn't all quite jive to Kelley. Why was Valdes in Spanish Palms that night when Carrillo washed ashore? How could anyone have planned for Carrillo to wash up on that beach?

Luque twisted in his seat and pointed with his thumb to the rear seat of the helicopter. "Climb on in, old buddy. We all need to take a ride."

Valdes motioned with his pistol. "Like the man says, get in. And if you don't, I'll shoot you right here—and nobody will hear a thing." And as if to reinforce what Valdes was saying, Luque reached down to the collector by his left side and revved up the engine of the helicopter so that its noise was loud enough to hurt Kelley's ears— and loud enough to cover any shots from a gun, silenced or not.

Kelley had no choice. He climbed into the rear seat of the helicopter, putting his travel bag on the floor by his feet. Luque then turned in this seat and pointed a small revolver at him while Valdes climbed into the rear seat beside Kelley.

"Give me that seat belt," Valdes demanded.

Kelley reached beside his leg and pulled up the unbuckled seat belt. Valdes grabbed it from his hand, dropped it in Kelley's lap, and ordered, "Put your arms down, against your side."

Kelley did as ordered. Valdes took a piece of rope from the floor and tied Kelley's arms from the back so that his elbows were pulled nearly against the small of his back. Then he took the two loose ends of the seatbelt and hooked them together with the seatbelt buckle, capturing Kelley's forearms beneath the seatbelt straps. He pulled the seatbelt tight, tugged at the cloth of the belt to make sure it was tight, and then said, "As snug as a bug under a rug. He's not going anywhere. Let's get out of here. We can talk to Cumaraima later."

"Right," answered Luque, as he pulled back on the cyclic stick and the helicopter began to rise.

Kelley looked at the receding ground and wondered what was going to happen next—though he had a pretty good idea that whatever it was it would probably mean that he wouldn't be seeing Texas again—unless he could come up with some really smart idea to get out of this fix.

Kelley turned his eyes to the front and the direction in which the helicopter was moving—toward the southeast, and the darkening clouds on the horizon.

— ~ —

They had been flying to the southeast for about an hour, reaching a point well inland from the coast and its mountains, and away from the dense coastal population. Even the small farm huts had been long left behind. The tropical forest landscape was giving away to the savannah with its tall plume grass punctuated by patches of broadleaf forests with mixtures of tall trees, slender palms, dense understory, and small ponds fed by rainfall.

"Don't you think we better get rid of him pretty soon?" Luque said into the microphone of his headset. "I don't like the looks of those clouds coming up. They could really hold some bad weather."

Valdes answered back through his headset. "Still too many people out here. We need to get farther into the interior—that's why we picked the spot we did. We don't want any loose ends this time. No bodies, nothing left to find, nothing to connect us to anything. Keep going."

"I don't like this," Luque said, as he turned his head for a quick look at Kelley. A sudden lightning bolt dropped out of the now menacing, two-thousand-foot-tall clouds a few miles away, turning the sky beneath the clouds bright for a split second, reflecting off the bottom of the water-filled black clouds.

"Keep going," Valdes shouted into the microphone, as he undid his seatbelt to allow himself to reach across Kelley to check again the seatbelt holding Kelley in place.

Luque shook his head, shouting, "No, it's too dangerous."

Valdes lifted his hand and put his gun to the back of Luque's head. "You keep going. Just a little farther, where we picked out. It's not that far—is it?" Valdes asked, seeking confirmation.

Luque turned to look at Valdes in disgust. "That's not going to help. I want him dead, too, but not at the expense of my life. Put that goddamn thing down before you shoot me. You don't know how to fly this thing. You shoot me and we all die."

"Can't you just fly over the clouds?" Valdes yelled as he lowered his pistol.

"No, they're too damn high," Luque shouted back as another lightning bolt, this time less than a mile away, lashed out as if to confirm what Luque said. "But maybe we can fly under them. I am going to get lower; maybe we can get beneath the really bad stuff," Luque said as he dipped the nose of the helicopter lower.

Suddenly, a torrent of rainfall began. Sheets of water began cascading down the helicopter's windshield. Luque flipped on the wipers. Rain poured in through the open doorways of the copter and swirled about in the turbulence of the interior of the copter. Soon all three men were soaked.

Valdes swiveled his head to look at what was surrounding, almost overpowering the helicopter, and then turned to look again at Kelley, as if seeking some refuge from Kelley's forced immobility.

Kelley could see the fright in Valdes' eyes, understanding why it was there. Storms over the Venezuelan plains could be sudden, treacherous, and deadly. And from what he could see swirling around them, Kelley was getting damn scared himself. Black clouds were now completely surrounding the helicopter. The once clear sky behind them had disappeared.

Then came another lightning bolt along with an ear-splitting clap of thunder, this time so close as to rock the copter as the thunder's shock wave rolled past the helicopter.

Luque pushed the cyclic hard, dropping the copter toward treetop level. "We can't go on; we have to land! Look for an open spot that's got some hard ground—we land in that sawgrass out there, and we'll sink in mud up to our eyeballs. Maybe a hummock with some open space between the trees," he yelled to Valdes.

Valdes began to stare out his open doorway of the helicopter, waving his hands as if they were windshield wipers sweeping back and forth furiously across the wall of water that the rain was creating.

Then suddenly, "There! There!" Valdes yelled as he excitedly leaned toward Luque and pointed his arm to the right toward what appeared to be a sizeable tree-covered hummock rising high out of the savannah grass, but with a large break in the middle of the trees forming the hummock.

Luque violently nodded his head and immediately began to turn the copter toward the landing spot at which Valdes was pointing. "I see—"

Lightning struck the copter. For an instant, the inside of the helicopter turned an eerie, iridescent green with streaks of burning white tinged with red slashing across the instrument panel. Valdes screamed, his arms flaying, as a red streak attacked his arm. The pistol in his hand fell to the deck of the helicopter. The copter tilted sharply upward and to the right, throwing Valdes and Kelley's travel bag toward the open side door. Kelley realized in the short instant before Valdes fell from the helicopter that Valdes had never refastened his seatbelt, and only Kelley's tightly binding seatbelt prevented him from following Valdes into the sky below. An instant later Kelley heard the beginnings of a blood-curdling scream and then felt the copter bump as Valdes body hit the still spinning tail rotor.

Luque was struggling with the cyclic and collector, trying to keep the chopper flying. But as a loud cough came from the engine, the engine quit. The turning helicopter blades rapidly slowed as the copter plummeted toward the trees.

Kelley's body was pulled and shoved back and forth, straining against the binding seatbelt, as the copter begin to fall and crash through the tall trees and toward the ground. Valdes' dropped-gun flew toward Kelley; Kelley tried to move his head out of the trajectory of the flying gun but did not fully succeed. The gun struck Kelley on the side of his head and then continued on its path, careening out of the helicopter doorway. The last thing Kelley remembered before losing consciousness was Luque's cry, "What the fuck! It's a damn lake."

— ~ —

Kelley could feel warm wetness surrounding him, and for a moment thought he might be back in his mother's womb. Then awareness slowly began to seep into his mind. He wasn't in his mother's womb; he was chest deep in water.

He opened his eyes. He could see he was still inside the now-wrecked helicopter, with its tail and fuselage cocked upward toward the sky at a forty-five-degree angle and its nose wedged beneath a dead tree partially submerged in the water. The wrecked chopper was on the edge of a swampy lake surrounded by deep undergrowth, scrub trees, and Moriche palms. And in the pilot's seat with slumped shoulders and head just barely above a wide pool of pale red water was a dead Tony Luque, a thick tree limb and a large triangle of broken windshield Plexiglas protruding from his neck and chest.

Kelley took stock. He wondered how long he had been unconscious ... probably quite a while. The forest was quiet; the chaos of the copter falling through the trees and the frightened pandemonium of bird shrills, cackles, and screeches had subsided. And looking up, Kelley could see an almost clear sky with a sun nearly vertically above. There was no rising water, so apparently, the copter was sitting on the bottom of the lake; Kelley had time to figure out what the situation was.

His head hurt like hell, and so did his side—probably some cracked ribs. He had had them before, and he knew the feeling already. But could he move? He began to shift his weight, trying to move his arms and legs. His legs seemed okay, but his arms were still bound by the rope and seatbelt, though the belt seemed looser than it had before, perhaps stretching as it became wet. *The damn seatbelt probably saved my life*, Kelley said to himself, *but how the hell do I get loose. But if I wait awhile longer, maybe it will stretch enough that I can wiggle out of it.*

So, Kelley decided to wait, until he began to see something moving in the sandy mud at the edge of the lake a few yards from the copter: a slithering grayish black and brown mud-covered form, maybe four or five feet in length. As it continued to stir, Kelley realized what it was: a caiman, an alligator-like creature found in the South American tropics, cousin to the North American alligator. Caiman could be aggressive, and Kelley didn't want to tangle with a possibly highly-disturbed one when evening feeding time came around while he was held down by a seat belt.

Kelley began to strain against the seatbelt but soon came to the conclusion that the only way to get out was to try to break the belt end loose from the belt lock. He wiggled and moved his forearms to a position under the clamp-like lock. The rope holding his arms cut into his flesh, but he began to push against the lock with all his strength. It didn't want to budge, but he kept pushing with his arms, knowing that at some level of force either he would break the lock— or his arms.

With a sudden snap, the lock broke, and so did Kelley's left arm. With a yell that frightened the now snoozing birds into a howling frenzy, Kelley broke free. His arm was afire with pain, and another pain was thrusting through his chest; he had to fight to keep from passing out. He quickly but gingerly slid down from the seat and out of the partially flooded door opening. Kelley's feet touched the muddy bottom of the lake. *Thank God, I don't have to swim.*

Kelley looked at the copter for a moment and then saw a sharp piece of ragged metal hanging from what had once been the frame for the copter door. Kelley turned his back to the copter and began to saw the rope holding his arms against the ragged edge of the metal. In a few moments, the rope parted, freeing his arms. A few moments more and Kelley was ashore, and at a safe distance from the caiman.

Kelley looked around—assessing what to do next. Peering through and beyond the mass of trees around the small lake, he saw nothing but clusters, large and small, of forested hummocks amid tall grass, spreading out in all directions across a broad plain. Far in the distance, to the north as best he could see, was a low line of mountains into which the savannah grass merged. He guessed he was a long way from civilization, based upon what he remembered seeing, or, more correctly, not seeing, in the last few minutes before the rain started and the copter had gone down. But he figured the most likely direction to find something or someone would be to go north, toward the coast and the mountains.

But before he did, he needed to immobilize his arm and chest as best he could. The most likely place to find some type of sling would be in the wrecked copter; so, he started to wade back out to the helicopter. Then it hit him—his luggage bag! He had put his bag in the copter when he was ordered into the back seat by Valdes. And in his bag was a cell phone! *I must really be groggy not to remember the bag. I hope to God it didn't fall out of the chopper with Valdes. And maybe, just maybe, the helo radio might still work.* But if the radio were going to work, he would have to get to it before the copter's batteries were ruined by the water.

Kelley splashed back into the water but quickly slowed when his fast steps sent rays of pain up his arm and across this chest. But in a few moments, he was back at the copter. The first thing he did was reach toward the radio, which was now several inches under water and flip the on-off switch. He pulled the earphones from Luque's sagging head and put them on. He flipped the on-off switch again—and again. Nothing, no red on-light, no noise, no anything. He flipped the switch several more times, hoping against hope that something might happen, but nothing did. *Damn.*

Kelley began feeling around the floor of the helicopter cabin, ducking his head under the water several times so he could reach the deck and run his hands across it. Nothing, absolutely nothing. Kelley's travel bag had apparently gone the way of Valdez. *Damn, damn, damn!*

Well, the only thing left in the cabin seemed to be the lightweight jacket that Luque had worn. Kelley didn't like doing what he had to do, but he did it. He ducked his head under the water and with his one good arm—and a lot of pain across his chest—slowly worked the jacket off Luque's body. After several submergences, he finally got the now blood-soaked jacket free. He also made another useful discovery: Luque's gun in a deep pocket of the jacket.

He got out of the helicopter and then remembered that these helicopters had small storage compartments in the fuselage just back of the passenger compartment. Kelley moved through the water toward the upended tail of the copter. He reached up and turned a small handle. The storage compartment door fell open, and four life preserves and a large canvas bag fell out. Kelley used the life preserver straps to sling the life preservers over his right shoulder and then grabbed the canvas bag with his right hand before it sank fully under water. He looked in the compartment and saw nothing else.

Kelley trudged back to the shore, dropped the canvas bag, life preservers, and Luque's jacket on the ground, and put Luque's gun in his waistband under his belt. He then turned back toward the copter to check the storage compartment on the other side of the copter fuselage.

Back at the other side of the copter, the side of the copter closest to where the caiman was, he reached up and turned the handle to the storage compartment and pulled the door open. Nothing fell out, and because of the height of the compartment, he was barely able to see inside the compartment. Kelley, with pain screaming across this chest, stretched his right arm and stuck it into the compartment, hoping to find something. In a moment he felt something—a box, a metal box, with a handle. Kelley struggled to pull it from the storage compartment. Finally, with one last heave, the box came free. It was a toolbox. Its weight surprised Kelley, and it slipped from his hand and fell like a rock into the water with a loud splash. Kelley felt it land on his foot, fortunately not with great force due to the several feet of water through which it had plunged.

*Shit—another dunking session*, Kelley said to himself as he began to duck his head under the water to retrieve the toolbox. But just as he put his head in the water and grabbed the handle of the toolbox, Kelley saw a dark black mass slithering toward him. The caiman!

Kelley grabbed the toolbox, jerked it upward, and stepped back toward the side of the helicopter. The caiman started his plunge toward Kelley. Kelley pushed the toolbox in front of himself, into the path of the caiman. The caiman hit it, bounced off to the side, and slide by only inches from Kelley. The box dropped from Kelley's hand, and again the box fell to the bottom, but this time not on his foot. Kelley did not know where the toolbox might be and he did not have time to find it. Kelley could see the caiman beginning to turn, about to make another pass.

*He's not going to miss this time!*

Kelley pulled Luque's pistol from under his belt, hoping to God the gun would still fire. It was, of all things, a .38 Smith and Weston Special snub nose—easy to fire, reliable, but with lousy accuracy except at short range. But the short range was just how it was going to have to be used!

Kelley aimed the pistol toward the barely visible head and nose of the approaching caiman, trying to adjust for its speed and depth as the caiman sped toward Kelley. Kelley fired ... and fired again ... and again. The caiman lurched sideways and slowed. Blood began to boil upward around the caiman as it rolled on its side. The momentum of the caiman's charge carried the now almost lifeless body into Kelley, knocking him down. Kelley's head slipped beneath the murky water. The caiman's head, only inches from Kelley's face, moved and its jaws twitched open. Kelley didn't know whether the animal was alive or dead, but he was not going to wait to see. He brought the pistol to within inches of the submerged head of the caiman and fired directly into it between its two open eyes.

A mass of exploding water and caiman hide, muscle, and blood filled the water in front of Kelley's face. Kelley pulled his head from the water, screamed, and began to run, as best he could, through the chest deep water toward the shore as birds screeched and cawed, taking flight. The caiman did not follow.

Kelley fell to the ground, into the mud, sucking in deep breaths, his eyes turned toward the water to see what might be following him. He saw nothing, except a dead caiman floating near the tail of the helicopter. Kelley lay on the ground, in the mud, for several more minutes, trying to recover his sanity. Finally, he slowly rose, still breathing hard, but no longer too frightened to think.

"Jesus, what a way to start the day," Kelley said to no one. He stepped to the canvas bag and pulled open its wide-teeth zipper. He found clothes, along with some shirts which were embroidered with the words, *Aero Servicios de Escobar. Interesting,* Kelley thought. *Apparently, Luque used Escobar's helo services in Maturin, one way or another, fairly regularly.*

And, much to his delight, wrapped in one of the shirts was a plastic bottle of water, about half full—maybe fifteen ounces of water left. *Thank God for small favors,* Kelley said to himself. Kelley put the bottle aside, deciding he had better not drink any water until he knew more about the fix he was in.

Kelley dug a little deeper into the bag, finding a map of Venezuela. Looking at the map, he saw an area southeast of Barcelona circled. The circled area contained no apparent landmarks or human habitats—it was just open savannah and marshlands as best he could tell. Estimating how far the distance of the circled area was from Barcelona, the locations of the mountains in the distant, and thinking over how long the flight out of Barcelona had been before the crash, Kelley came to the conclusion that the circled area was probably where Luque and Valdes had planned to dump him. And if that were the case, Kelley at least knew the general line of flight along which they had traveled. So, in rough terms—very rough terms—Kelley knew where he was.

Looking at where he figured about where he might be, Kelley knew it was not going to be easy to get back to civilization, but it could be done. To the north offered his greatest hope of reaching some sort of civilization—a farm, a small village ... something.

Kelley finally turned the bag upside down to empty its remaining contents. He found one treasure: A box of .38 Special ammunition, full except for six cartridges.

Kelley knew he had one remaining thing to do, as much as he did not want to do it. He had to find the toolbox; there just might be something useful in it. Kelly reloaded the gun and put it under his belt. He waded out to the helicopter, carefully watching for movement in the water. Reaching the side of the helicopter where the toolbox had fallen, he began systematically moving his feet across the muddy bottom around the copter. It took about two minutes of searching to locate the toolbox. Kelley pulled it from the mud and returned to the shore.

Kelley undid the latches on the toolbox, pulled open the lid, and carefully poured out the rusty red water in the box. He then set the box down on the mud and started to search. He found some screwdrivers, a collection of screws of various sizes in several clear plastic containers, a small roll of 16-gauge steel wire, a pair of wire cutters, a hammer, an old log book, a well-worn book of instructions on how to fly and maintain a Bell-Ranger helicopter, and much to his delight, a small machete with about a foot-long blade and four unused flares wrapped in plastic along with a flare gun. And at the bottom of everything, wrapped in an oil-stained Yankee's baseball cap, a smashed package of cellophane-wrapped cheese and crackers, in which there had been—at one time—six mini-cracker sandwiches.

Kelley took the machete and cut some of the straps off the life preservers to fashion a long strap-like bandage to go around his chest. After quite of bit of painful twisting, he was able to get the makeshift bandage twice around his chest and make a knot to pull it reasonably tight. Kelley immediately began to feel a lessening of the pain in his chest as his ribs were restrained from free motion. He next fashioned a sling from two long-sleeve shirts and a pair of dirty socks.

Thus bandaged, Kelley moved to the edge of the muddy beach surrounding the lake and sat down on a dead tree trunk to rest and think. Kelley sighed heavily, knowing it was a thousand-to-one chance that anybody would be looking for the helo—at least where it might actually be. Knowing what Luque and Valdes planned to do, it was doubtful that they had even filed any type of flight plan, or if they had, it wouldn't have said where they were really going. No, waiting for a rescue would only delay his possible demise. If he were going to get out alive, he would have to walk out.

His decision made, Kelley made an assessment of what to take with him on his trek. He needed essentials, but any excess weight, while not much now, would feel ten times heavier a day later.

What to take? The gun, ammunition, machete, and, of course, the water. He contemplated filling the bottle with lake water, but if the water wasn't good enough to drink—something he wouldn't really know unless he drank it and got sick—he might just ruin what water he had. He decided not to put lake water into the bottle.

The wire and wire cutters could come in handy, too. And certainly, the smashed crackers; he probably could make them last three days. And the flares, yes, the flares. If anybody happened to be flying nearby, he needed to be able to signal them. And, who knows, the map might be useful, even though he really only had a very rough idea of where he was. And finally, one of the shirts, to use as a wet rag to wrap around his neck, and the baseball cap; without the cap, the sun would be merciless.

Kelley dumped out the remaining clothes in the canvas bag, and put the ammunition, wire, bottle of water, wire cutters, flares, map, and crackers in the bag. He slung the bag over his back using the strap on the bag. He put the gun under his belt, the cap on his head, the machete in his hand, and looked at the sun to get his bearings. He set off to the north.

— ~ —

Kelley had been struggling for about half an hour through the tall plume grass and the hot, humid, sticky air which blanketed the grassy savannah. He was maybe a mile from the downed helo; working his way through the tall grass was slow, even with the help of the machete to cut a pathway. The sun was now on its downward swing toward the horizon, and he was beginning to wonder what he was going to do for the night; he didn't relish trying to push on into the night—too many creatures liked the cool of the night. But ahead he could see a hummock thick in Moriche palms. He could rest there, at least for a while, before moving on.

As he got closer to the patch of palms, he saw something strange hanging from a palm tree near the edge of a collection of palms. Kelley pulled the pistol from his waistband, not knowing what to expect. But as he got closer, he realized what it was: Valdes, hanging upside down with one foot and a portion of his left leg caught in the base of the palm fronds. His right leg below the knee and virtually his entire right arm were gone; only bloody stumps remained. Blood had drained from his leg down across his body to cover the side of his face. He was already beginning to become bloated, and several King Vultures were already circling above.

Kelley moved to the base of the palm, reached up and grabbed Valdes by his remaining downward hanging arm, and gave a solid yank, wincing as he did because of the stress it put on his rib cage. Valdes came tumbling down, hitting Kelley's left arm as he did. Kelley winced again.

Kelley took a deep breath to steady himself and then bent down to search Valdes. He began going through Valdes pockets, one by one. In his wallet, he found several credit cards, two of which were American, and, not surprisingly, an American driver license giving a Houston address. He also found a small notebook with three phone numbers. One number he recognized: Goldie's place in Spanish Palms. The other number he recognized as a Houston number because of the 713 area code. The third he didn't recognize at all, except it was American, possibly Chicago if Kelley remembered the area code correctly. Kelley also found two keys, one a rental car key and one a room key for a hotel in Caracas—something to check out—if he ever got out of this mess. The remainder of what he found appeared to be of no importance—some meal receipts from Caracas restaurants, several American hundred-dollar bills, and a handful of Bs, maybe 200,000 or so.

Then, finished with his search and as he was about to let the body roll away from him, Kelley saw it: an empty cell phone holder on the side of Valdes' belt. Kelley felt a ray of hope. Maybe, just maybe, the phone was nearby. Kelley began scanning the ground beneath where Valdes had been hanging, forcing himself to look slowly and methodically so as not to miss anything. Then he saw it: the shiny black plastic, almost too deep to see in the thick grass mat at the base of the palm. He reached down and picked it up, remembering what Luque had said in Caracas—that cell coverage was spotty away from the coast. Would there be coverage here?

Kelley pushed the power button and watched the small screen light up—then search for a connection. It continued to search. Finally, a message popped up: "No connection."

"Damn!" Kelley said in disgust as he powered off the phone and threw it into the canvas bag.

Kelley picked up his few treasures, got his bearings, adjusted his baseball cap, and started walking.

— ~ —

It was fast approaching sundown when Kelley pushed aside the tall grass and saw just ahead a small hummock of palms intermixed with low-lying vegetation around a small pond. In a few more minutes he was at the edge of the hummock. Kelley dropped to the edge of the pond, drew his pistol, and looked around for other possible visitors. Seeing none, he fell back in the water with a splash. He lay there for several minutes, trying to soak up the coolness of the water, thinking about what to do next.

He permitted himself to taste the pond water, but it was so acidic it burned his tongue. He had heard before about the acidity of some of the savannah waters; it was created by the organic acids formed from biological decay, but this was the first time he had actually experienced it. Kelly did not dare drink such waters, so he allowed himself one mouth-full of water from his bottle of water. It was now down to a quarter full—or three-quarters empty, Kelley mused to himself, depending upon your point of view. Right now, he preferred to consider it one-quarter full.

He was beat—dead tired. But he knew what he had to do before he could rest—and before the sunset.

Kelley moved to an open space on the side of the hummock away from the pond. With the machete—and a lot of pain—he cleared a large circle of all brush and tall grass, trying to create a quasi-dead zone to which animals would not be attracted. Kelley then gathered up the life preservers and some dead tree limbs and set fire to them, using one flare to get the fire started. The odor from the slowly burning life preservers was pungent and nauseating, just what Kelley wanted to keep animals away. Kelley allowed himself a short hour of sleep before it became too late in the night—the remainder of the night he sat awake, listening and watching for intruders. Only once did he have to fire the pistol to keep away something with two eyes in the night.

As the morning sun came up, Kelley allowed himself to eat one, or at least the crumbs of one, of his cracker sandwiches. He wet his clothes, the extra shirt to wrap around his neck, and his cap in the pond, and then started off again to the north.

Midday came, and Kelley found another small island-like forest in which to rest for about twenty minutes. He allowed himself one swallow of water, then started out again.

Two hours later, storm clouds began to form. Shortly thereafter, rain started, slowly, but soon became a torrent. Kelley opened his bottle of water and let the rain fall into it as he turned his face skyward and opened his mouth, capturing what water he could. By the time the rain stopped a half an hour later, the bottle was nearly full, and he almost felt like a new man as rainwater evaporated from his wet clothes, bringing a soothing coolness to his skin.

Refreshed, he started off again—still to the north.

— ~ —

Sunset came, and Kelley did as he had done the night before. He found a relatively large open space near the edge of a small forested area, again with a pond of acidic water, and with his machete cleared a large circle of all brush and tall grass to create his surrounding protection zone.

He couldn't use the life preservers again; all of them had been burned the first night. But Kelley found a small oil seep—not uncommon in the open lands between Barcelona and Maturin—near the edge of the pond. He cut off several large chunks of the hardened, tar-like substance that had formed at the seep. He brought them into his protective circle and foraged almost an hour in the area to collect dead branches and rotting tree trunks for his nighttime fire. He used the second of his four fares to start the fire. Once it was burning well, he put the hardened chunks of petroleum on the fire. In about twenty minutes, they began to melt and burn, giving off not only an oily smell but also a black cloud of smoke.

Kelley sat down near the fire, just out of the reach of the smoke, and rested his back against one of the logs to be put on the fire later in the night. He reached into the canvas bag and withdrew the crackers and water. He ate one cracker, as best he could estimate, and had several measured sips of water. The bottle was now down to half full. Kelley wondered how long he could go on. He was not sure how far he had come, but he was sure he still had a long way to go, and he was beginning to doubt whether he could make it. He continued to stare at the fire.

— ~ —

Kelley woke with a start. He shook himself to get his mind alert. It was dark now, and the fire was almost out. Kelley had not wanted to sleep like this, but he was not surprised that his exhaustion had overtaken his plan to stay awake. But what had awakened him? Something had disturbed his sleep. Then Kelley heard it, a low growl, something he had never heard before. And in the direction of the sound, he saw two pairs of red-looking eyes, about six inches off the ground. Kelley didn't know what they were, but he surely didn't want to find out.

Kelley pulled his gun and quickly shot twice in the direction of the eyes. The eyes jumped and then sped away. He had missed, but the danger was gone—provided he stayed awake the rest of the night.

Kelley stood and picked up several large branches and carefully put them on the fire, holding them in the flames until he was sure they had caught fire. He added another chunk of dried petroleum. In a few minutes, it began to melt near its edges. A few minutes later, the petroleum was giving off its oily smoke.

Kelley turned from the fire and oily smoke emanating from it. He blinked his eyes to remove the irritation—and then he saw it. He blinked again to be sure what he saw was real. Yes, it was! A light, like a light from a distant house window!

Kelley knew he could not get to the light in the night, but he needed to know what direction he would have to go when morning came. Kelley got two of the larger yet unburned dead tree limbs and set one on one edge of his circle and the other on the other edge. He carefully adjusted their locations, and once he was sure, he pushed the limbs into the ground. He made a final check; the line of sight from one limb to the other extended into the night and intersected the light in the distance. And just as Kelley finished his check, the light went out. Whoever was there at the light had extinguished it for the night.

— ~ —

Morning came, and an excited Kelley prepared for the march to the light—or at least to where he hoped the light would be if he followed the guide poles he had set out the night before. Kelley spent the first moments of the new day tearing and cutting, with the wire cutters, the shirt he had been wearing around his neck into two flag-like pieces of cloth. He used his wire to attach the pieces of cloth to the ends of two long branches. He then attached, with the last of his wire, the branches to the guide poles he had set up the night before. He now had two guide poles, maybe fifteen feet high, that he could see from a far distance and use to guide him toward the location of the nighttime light.

Looking at his guide poles, and seeing the direction he needed to go, Kelley set out on his trek. Every fifteen or so minutes, he would look back over the tall grass at the poles and realignment himself. But, by midday, the flagged poles were becoming more and more difficult to see. By midafternoon, Kelly gave what he figured would likely be his last look at the poles and tried to do his best to set his direction for the remainder of the day.

— ~ —

Kelley had been working his way through the tall grass about an hour after his last look at the poles; he had tried to see them one more time, but they could not be seen. He was on his own now, and the sun was getting low. Kelley took a swipe with the machete at the tall grass in front of him, stumbling as he did so, something he had been doing often since midday as exhaustion began to settle into his entire body. He put his hands down to pick himself up ... then realized that the grass was no longer surrounding him and the ground under him was hard, not soft and mushy like what he had been walking through. He looked more closely at the ground through the sweat pouring over his eyes. *By God, it was a road! A fucking, damn road!*

Kelley slowly pulled himself up and looked around him. It was a narrow, dirt road, with ruts that looked to have been formed by wagon wheels, going east and west, if Kelley had his directions right. It had to be going somewhere, but which direction should he go? But wait ... there appeared to be something in the distance to the west. Something ... Kelley took his now torn shirt and wiped his eyes, trying to focus. He blinked several times, then wiped his eyes again. And then he saw it. It was a building—a building!

Kelley began to run, then stumbled, got up, and tried to run again; he went a few more strides and then stumbled once again. The building looked so far in the distance. *Would he ever get there?* he asked himself as he slowly struggled to his feet. He tried only to walk, not run, but he stumbled again. He got up again, only to take a few steps and fall to the ground again. One more time he struggled to his feet, took two steps, and one more time he fell to the ground. And this time he was not sure he could get up. He began to crawl on his hands and knees.

Then he heard it—a bell, some type of bell. He looked down the road toward the building. He saw nothing but the building in the distance. Kelley knew he was becoming delirious. He heard the bell again. Yes, he had to be delirious. Kelley fell and lay prostrate on his stomach, unable to go farther. He knew it was over. He could go no farther.

He heard the bell again. Then a big, wet, sloppy ... tongue brushed across this ear. "What ... is," Kelly mumbled as he slowly rolled over on his back, as the bell rang again. Kelley looked into the face of a mule! And around the mule's neck was a cowbell. And behind the mule was a wagon. And in the wagon seat, an old man, his head bent toward this chest as if asleep, with a straw hat covering his head. He wore an aging black coat and pants and, beneath his bent head, a white collar around his neck.

Kelley began shouting in a cracked voice, "*¡Holó! ¡Holó! ¡Sococorro!* Help me! *Por favor. ¡Sococorro! Por favor. ¡Sococorro!*"

The old man's head jerked up. He looked at Kelley lying on the ground.

A look of fear, then concern came to the man's face. Then the man got down from the wagon. He cautiously approached Kelley lying on the road, looking down at Kelley. Kelley did not move; he was unable to move.

Then the man bent down, picked up Kelley's shoulders, and looked into his eyes. "My son, what is wrong? Are you hurt? What has happened to you?"

Kelley looked at man's face and saw the crown-like corona formed by the light of the setting sun coming from behind the priest's head. Tears came from Kelley's eyes and streamed down his burnt, mosquito-bitten checks. Kelley closed his eyes.

— ~ —

When Kelley next opened his eyes, he realized he was gulping down water, with a man saying, "*Despacio ... despacio.*"

The water gushed down his throat—it was the most wonderful thing he had ever tasted. The priest smiled. Kelley looked at him and then closed his eyes again, aware only that someone, a priest, was there to take care of him. Kelley felt an inner peace clothe his body. He closed his eyes again.

— ~ —

Kelley felt weak and groggy, but alive. He opened his eyes and looked about, slowly turning his head. He realized he was lying in a bed in a small room with one tiny window. He could see it was nighttime. A woman and the old priest sat beside the bed, with solicitous-looking faces.

Kelley struggled to speak. "Where ... am ... I?" he asked first in English, and then in Spanish.

"At the home of my good and faithful parishioners Juan and Maria Urias, to whom I have come to minister," the priest answered.

"Where is ... that?"

"About twenty kilometers from Santa Barbara," the priest answered.

Kelley vaguely remembered Santa Barbara was about fifty kilometers west of Maturin.

"We have sent for help from Santa Barbara. Maria's husband has taken his horse and gone to Santa Barbara to tell the police you are here and need a doctor."

Kelley thought for a moment, trying to organize his thoughts. "Father, I had a canvas bag—strapped over my shoulder. Do you have the bag?"

"*Si*. Do you want it?"

"Yes, please," Kelley answered.

The priest turned to the woman and told her to bring Kelley's shoulder bag.

In a few moments, the woman returned.

"Would you see if there is a cell phone in that bag, Father?" Kelley asked.

After a moment of searching, the priest withdrew a cell phone from the bag. He handed it to Kelley.

"Thank you," Kelley said, hoping that Valdes phone would have international access, which it just might, given Valdes' travels in Venezuela and the U.S.

Kelley pushed the power switch and watched for a few moments as the screen when through some gyrations, and then lit up ready to accept a call. "Hallelujah," Kelley said under this breath.

"What did you say, my son," the priest asked.

"Nothing, Father, nothing. Just giving a little thanks to where it's deserved."

With shaking fingers, Kelley punched in the +1 international access code for the U.S. and then the dummy number for Consolidated Oil Services in Denver. Some clicks, followed by a short buzz, then a short period of silence, and then a ring, immediately followed by, "Consolidate Oil Services. May I help you?"

An American voice had never sounded so sweet.

— ~ —

It took about seven hours for two Maturin policemen, a doctor, and the American Consul in Maturin to arrive at the Urias' home. They had flown in by helicopter, apparently under direct orders from the Federal police in Caracas, who seemed to have taken a particular interest in the wayward traveler found by a priest in the wild Venezuelan grasslands west of Maturin. Kelley was immediately airlifted to a Maturin hospital.

By late the next day, the Federal police, based upon information Kelley gave them, had found the crashed helicopter, and brought back Luque's body, at least what was left of it. Kelley did not tell them about Valdes. As best as Kelley could figure, there was nothing to indicate that Valdes had even been on the flight. But, just in case, Kelley acted delirious on the flight back to Maturin until it was apparent that no one seemed to be missing Valdes.

# 36

It was the second day after arriving at the hospital. His arm had been set and put in a cast. Then Kelly had been loaded up with antibiotics. And his ribs, after numerous x-rays, had been tightly bandaged. Now Kelley was dressed and ready to leave the hospital—the doctors, with some urging from the American consul, had given Kelley a clean bill of health—at least one sufficiently clean for Kelley to leave. Kelley wanted to leave as soon as possible, as did the American consul who had been told by the American ambassador in Caracas to get Kelley out the hospital as quickly and quietly as possible—to minimize police questioning. The consul was doing his best but had not been very successful. A Federal police captain and his lieutenant were still questioning Kelley.

"So, *Señor* Kelley, it is your contention that Luque died because of the crash."

"What the hell else could have happened, *Capitán*. We were flying to Maturin. The damn lighting struck us, and we went down. When I recovered consciousness, Luque was dead. Your police must have told you the condition of his body when they found it." Kelley said nothing about Valdes.

"*Si*, they did. His wounds were very apparent, at least from what could be determined from the remains of his body."

"Well, maybe if you had gotten there sooner, his 'remains' would have been in better shape, *Capitán,*" Kelley said with apparent anger, trying to play the innocent bystander.

"But *Señor* Kelley, why did *Señor* Luque fly into such stormy weather—he should have known better."

"Well, that's easy for you to say, *Capitán*. It came up fast, and I guess Luque made a bad decision. He said he had a hot date waiting in Maturin, and he didn't want to disappoint her."

"Do you know her name?"

"No, he never did say it—but she must have been a really hot one, from the way he talked."

"Why did your flight not follow the flight plan that *Señor* Luque filed in Maturin," the captain asked.

"Shit if I know. He was flying that damn bird, not me. About the only thing I can figure, if you really have to know, is that maybe he didn't officially plan for me. Maybe he was breaking some rules by picking me up, and he didn't want anybody to know. I had called him the night before we left Barcelona and he volunteered to pick me up and bring me back to Maturin—I'm working on some oil deals here for my company, Consolidated Oil Services."

"Yes, *Capitán*, just what did his flight plan say?" the consul asked.

A pained expression came to the captain's face. "You may be correct. His flight plan said he was he was flying to Anaco and then returning to Maturin. No mention of Barcelona was made. In fact, there is no record of him even landing in Barcelona or Anaco."

"He picked me up at a private field outside Barcelona," Kelley quickly said, hoping that no one had seen Valdes in the copter with Luque when the two landed.

"If *Señor* Luque was supposed to fly to Anaco, why wasn't there a search formed when Luque failed to land there?" the consul asked.

A guilty look came to the captain's face. "We do not know. Some mistake was made, and his absence was not noted. We are investigating why the helicopter services in Maturin did not file a missing plane report when he did not return in the afternoon as his flight plan indicated."

"Really, *Capitán?* And *you* are questioning why *Señor* Luque made an error in judgment that led to his unfortunate death? Perhaps if other errors had not been made, *Señor* Kelley would have been found earlier—and his painful suffering could have been avoided, and my report to the Ambassador on your lack of search would have been unnecessary," the consul said in an authoritative voice.

"Perhaps," the captain replied apologetically.

"And now, Captain, if you will, *Señor* Kelley wishes to return to his hotel room," the consul said without a bit of hesitation as to what Kelley could do.

"*Si*, he is free to go," the captain said without objection.

— ~ —

It was nearly eight o'clock in the evening as Kelley got out of the car at the front door of the Green Parrot Hotel, telling Hermann to go home and return tomorrow afternoon. Hermann glumly agreed, seemingly lost as to what to do, now that his sometime boss, Luque, was dead, but not knowing that Luque had tried to kill Kelley, something Kelley thought Hermann did not need to know, at least for the present.

All Kelley wanted to do now was go to bed, rest, and rethink all that had happened, to see if he could begin to fit together all the pieces of the puzzle that were finally being placed before him. Luque, Valdes, and Cumaraima—but who else? Valdes had been awfully friendly with Goldie; and he found her number, along with the others, in Valdes' pocket—did that mean anything?

Kelley continued to think again about that dark night—about what had happened on the beach—as he limped back to his room after telling the desk clerk that he was okay, that the doctor at the hospital had given him a clean bill of health, so to speak. All he had were three cracked ribs, which were now well-taped, and a broken arm, which he now carried in a cast.

He had briefed the admiral via a patch through the dummy Consolidated Oil Services number as best he could over a line from the hospital, but since neither he nor the admiral was sure how secure the line might be, he could not say too much. But he did get the point across that Luque was dead and with his death, the admiral's "plumbing" was probably fixed. With that said, the admiral said not to talk any more, and that he would be in Maturin within 24 hours. In the meantime, he ordered Kelley to get to his hotel, rest, and wait for him.

Kelley thought back over the night that Carrillo's body washed ashore. Was Kelley missing something from that night? Everybody's story seemed to check, even though he knew now that Valdes had to have been lying somehow. Those kids couldn't have been in on anything, particularly since the Weedens seemed to corroborate their story—wait a minute! The Weedens—they said they had been walking along in the moonlight—but there had been almost no moonlight! The moon was about to set and was shrouded in clouds by the time Carrillo was found. The Weedens had to be lying, and the only reason they might have been lying was because they were working with Valdes. *Jesus, who else was involved?*

Kelley turned the last corner in the hallway before his room, took a step, and was suddenly grabbed. Kelley started to struggle, but whoever it was—there had to be at least two of them—threw a cloth bag over his head and begin to drag him down the hallway toward the back exit of the hotel. As Kelley tried to fight back, a wasted effort given his condition, he heard coarse whispers from his attackers as they struggled with him; and what they said wasn't in English—or Spanish. Then he felt something hit his head, and, as he began to lose consciousness, he realized what he was hearing was Chinese.

# 37

Out of the frying pan and into the fire was about all Kelley could think about his current fix. He knew that Cui was responsible for his being wherever this windowless room was. The few words in Chinese that his captors would sometimes say in his presence were proof of that. Cui had pegged him the moment he had walked out of Dolanyi's office, or within a few minutes after the taxicab fiasco had unfolded. And if Kelley were right about what Cui was trying to do, it was damn sure that Cui was planning to get rid of him, discretely and without suspicion, but definitely completely get rid of him.

Kelley didn't even know how long it would be before the admiral was to arrive in Maturin; Kelley's watch had been taken from him and he had lost all track of time. The admiral would not find Kelley at the hotel and would know something was wrong but not what. The admiral and everyone else, for that matter, did not know about Cui.

Under the light of a single bulb hanging from a cord wrapped around one of the several steel beams holding up a tin roof over the room, Kelley begin to look at the walls that formed his small prison, trying to find a small opening, something he could pry away, something he could pull open, something he could kick out, something which could be a path to freedom; but the only opening was the steel door on the one side of the room. With no furniture, not even a chair, he couldn't reach, even by jumping, the light bulb hanging from the ceiling to possibly cause a short circuit and maybe blow a fuse that might cause some commotion, something that he could use to start a fight that might get him out of this place. But it was useless, just like it had been useless in Nam when Cui had been his interrogator before.

*But why haven't they killed me by now? What is delaying Cui? I know Cui is going to kill me, so what's the wait.*

Then Kelley began to slowly realize why—why Cui was not ready to kill him yet. It was the same as in Nam. Cui wanted information, information about who else knew what Kelley knew. If no one else knew, then Cui's plan could go forward. But if someone else knew what Kelley knew, then Cui had a whole different set of problems with which to deal, problems that might bring his plan tumbling down.

Now Kelley realized what might save him, or at least give him some hope. *As long as Cui believes I told someone about the Chinese plan to use the San Juan block for a Chinese naval base, Cui will continue to try to get me to tell him who else knows. And as long as I can say no one else knows, Cui will not kill me. It might be true that no one else actually knows, but Cui will remain unconvinced of that as long as I can say that no else knows. Cui will not believe the truth unless he is convinced nothing else can be true.*

Kelley began to mentally gear himself for the torture he knew would soon start.

# 38

The car stopped at the front door of the Green Parrot. Two men in business suits, Admiral Francis Marian and his aide, Brad Samuelson, got out of the car and entered the doorway. Samuelson passed the man sitting on the overstuffed sofa by the door and approached the clerk at the front desk, and, speaking in Spanish, said the two men were there to see Mr. Castellano. Would the clerk please ring Mr. Castellano's room, Samuelson asked.

"*Si, Señor*," the clerk responded as he glanced at his guest list and then dialed a number on the phone on the counter. Both Samuelson and the admiral silently noted the number the clerk dialed.

The admiral couldn't hear the ringing through the phone set, but his aide could. He turned to the admiral and spoke in English. "It's ringing ... still ringing ... still ringing. Kelley isn't picking up."

The clerk pulled the phone from his ear. "He is not answering."

"I don't like it, Brad. I told Kelley to stay in his room. He should be there."

The admiral turned to the clerk. "Do you speak English," he demanded.

"*Si, Señor*, I do," the clerk replied.

"Has Mr. Castellano gone out today?"

"No, *Señor*, he has not. He came in yesterday evening and went straight to his room. He looked very tired and hurt."

"What do you mean ... hurt?"

"He had his arm in a sling, and he had a bandage on his forehead—and he was very sunburned, and there were small cuts on his face."

The admiral turned to his aid. "Come on, Brad, we are going to check his room. And you," the admiral demanded as he turned back to the clerk, "get a passkey and take us to his room."

"I cannot do that, *Señor*. That is against the rules," the clerk said without conviction.

"Fuck the rules," the admiral said as he motioned for Samuelson to take the passkey from the counter in front of the clerk.

Samuelson grabbed the key and started off, with the admiral following at a somewhat slower pace.

In a moment, the man sitting on the overstuffed sofa by the door rose and followed them.

— ~ —

"One-eighteen. That's it over there," Samuelson said as he moved to the side of the door and drew a pistol from under his coat.

The admiral stood back a short distance. "See if it's unlocked."

At the end of the hall, the man from the overstuffed sofa peaked around the corner of the wall, intently watching what was going on.

Samuelson gently put his hand on the doorknob and slowly tried to turn it. It did not move.

"It's locked," Samuelson whispered.

"Use the key, but be careful," the admiral said.

Samuelson slowly slid the key into the lock and turned it. A loud click followed. Samuelson looked at the admiral, the admiral nodded, and Samuelson burst through the door.

A moment of silence followed, then from inside the room came, "It's clear ... no one is here."

The admiral stepped into the room and looked about. What he saw really worried him. Clothes were hanging in the closet, neatly arranged, as were the T-shirts and underwear in the chest of drawers by the closet. On the table beside the bed were some sheets of hotel stationery, a couple of cheap pens, and, surprisingly, a stack of folded maps and several business cards. But the bed ... the bed was neatly made.

"Brad, go check with the clerk and find out when the maid was here last," the admiral ordered.

"She has not made her rounds yet."

Both the admiral and his aide turned quickly to face the doorway, with Samuelson bringing his pistol up.

"No ... no, *Señor*, I do not want to hurt you," the man in the doorway said as he raised his hands as if to surrender. "I am your friend ... I think."

"Who are you and what are you doing here," Samuelson asked brusquely, not lowering his pistol.

"My name is Hermann Delgado. I am *Señor* Kelley's driver."

"Well, where is he?" the admiral demanded.

"I do not know ... exactly. I brought *Señor* Kelley here to the hotel yesterday after he left the hospital. He said I was to return this afternoon, that he had some things to do—after he met someone coming from the United States. I think you are the man from the United States."

"Yes, I am. Kelley was to meet with me," the admiral responded.

Brad lowered his pistol, satisfied the man was not a threat.

"I am so glad. I did not know what to do ... without *Señor* Luque or *Señor* Kelley to tell me what to do, I am not sure what to do."

"Luque—you know him?"

"*Señor* Luque was my boss—*Señor* Kelley told me *Señor* Luque died in the helicopter crash when *Señor* Kelley broke his arm," Hermann said as he made the sign of the cross.

Samuelson raised his pistol again. "What do you mean ... your boss?"

"I did errands, made deliveries for him here in Maturin—I live only fifteen kilometers from here. He sometimes made me a driver for his guests, like *Señor* Kelley."

"You mean you have been chauffeuring Kelley around for the last month?" the admiral asked in a surprised voice.

"*Si* ... and sometimes doing errands for him."

"Like what?"

"Taking him to stores and business offices, getting information about people at the Hotel Colonial... sometimes following people—"

"Following people!" the admiral said in surprise as he looked at his Samuelson, who just shook his head in disbelief. "Who did you follow?"

"A man that stayed at the Hotel Colonial."

"Well, who the hell was that?" the admiral said angrily.

"A Chinese man named *Señor* Cui Shan."

The admiral furrowed his brow as if in deep thought. Then a look of alarm came to his face as if he had remembered something from long ago. "Jesus Christ. What the hell has Kelley gotten into?"

Samuelson looked at the admiral and then said, "Admiral, we better not stay here much longer. That clerk might have called the police."

"Your right, Brad. Grab those cards and maps on the table. Hermann, you're coming with us, back to the consulate office."

"*Si*, but why not go after *Señor* Kelley?"

"What do you mean ... go after Kelley? We don't know where he is," the admiral said with a quizzical look.

"That is what I wanted to tell you—but you keep asking me questions."

"All right, goddammit, what do you want to tell me?"

"*Señor* Kelley ... two Chinese men—they looked Chinese—took him away after I brought him to the hotel. They took him out the back door of the hotel—I saw them as I was starting to drive away."

"Damn," the admiral said.

Samuelson then spoke, "You said that you didn't know where *Señor* Kelley was ... exactly. How exact is exactly?"

"I followed their car to the industrial district on the other side of the city but was unable to enter into the place they went, so, I came back to here to wait for *Señor* Kelley's visitor—you."

"What do you mean—unable to enter?" the admiral asked.

"They drove through the gate going into the equipment yard at an oil company—many oil companies have equipment yards here in Maturin. The gate had a guard; he would not let me in."

"What company?" the admiral demanded.

"It is a company many call China Partners Petroleum."

The admiral looked at his Samuelson, slowly shaking his head.

"Admiral, time's running out," Samuelson said, as a siren wailed in the distance.

"You're right. Let's get out of here. Hermann, show us the back way out of here," the admiral said, not knowing for sure whose time was running out.

— ~ —

Kelley was hanging from a chain slung around one of the steel beam rafters. His feet were a few inches above the floor, and his arm sling was lying in the corner of the room. Kelley's full weight was supported only by his arms, including his broken arm. The pain was excruciating. He had already fallen into unconsciousness several times, only to be awakened by icy water being tossed onto his face. Then questions would begin by his three tormentors; the same questions, over and over. What did he know about the San Juan project; when did he learn about it; who told him about it; who else knew—whom did he tell about the plans for the San Juan project?

At first, Kelley tried to play dumb, saying he didn't know anything about any such project. He was rewarded by burning cigarettes being pushed between his toes, and then later, when the burning cigarettes did not work, electricity became the messenger of Kelley's agony. Electric wires were affixed to his toes, and jolts of electricity were given to Kelley to send bursts of pain through his feet. The technique was painful—oh, so painful—but not enough to kill him or render him incoherent. They wanted Kelley to be aware so he would answer their questions—and they could gauge whether he was telling the truth. The questions were repeated over and over, with Kelley finally succumbing, saying between his screams that he had told no one. The questions and the electric jolts were repeated until Kelley lapsed into unconsciousness—and then aroused again, to begin the questioning again.

How long this had been going on Kelley was not sure; he had lost track of time and space. He only wanted to die, to end the pain. But then, when he was almost ready to say a name, any name, just to make them stop, his torture stopped. Now limp as a wet rag, Kelley dangled from his chains, his head sagging onto his chest. His left arm was fiery red and swollen to the size of his thigh; it probably would never be able to function properly again, even if he were to live.

Then the steel door opened. Cui entered the room.

Cui spoke, "Ah, Lieutenant Castellano—or is it perhaps commander by now—we meet again. Are you ready to tell me to whom you have spoken about the San Juan project?"

Kelley opened his eyes only barely, just enough to let Cui know that he had heard Cui's question, that Kelley knew what he was saying

"Who?" demanded Cui. "Who did you tell about the San Juan base?"

Kelley looked at Cui and said nothing.

Cui made a smirk and then turned to the three men who had been questioning Kelley. He said something to them in Chinese.

The three men stepped close to Kelley and yanked down his pants, and then his underwear. They removed two wire clips from Kelley's toes and affixed them to each of his testicles.

Kelley's eyes widened in terror.

The three men looked at Cui, who nodded his head.

One of the three men picked up the switch on the wires and briefly punched the switch.

Kelley screamed.

"Who?" demanded Cui.

Kelley said nothing, but his eyes showed his fright, the horror that Kelley knew would come again. Kelley looked at Cui, and almost unnoticeably shook his head.

Cui looked at the man holding the switch and nodded his head again.

Kelley's cried out in agony—a horrifying scream. "Stop! Stop!" Kelley begged.

Cui looked at Kelley and smiled.

Kelley looked at Cui with barely open eyes, knowing now was the time to end it—now that Cui had been there to see Kelley's torture and now to hear his answer.

"Are you ready to tell me?" Cui said with confidence.

Kelley mumbled, "Yes ... yes."

Knowing his life would be coming to an end shortly, Kelley summoned his last bit of remaining strength, giving an answer that he hoped—no, knew—would confound Cui. "Marian ... Francis Marian—I work for him ... China Blue Sailor—he knows."

A look of doubt, then consternation came to Cui's face. Kelley knew Cui knew, as did only a few of the old Chinese guard did, about what a young American naval officer with the code name China Blue Sailor had almost accomplished in the final years of the Vietnam War when the Chinese were lending their full support to the North Vietnamese. Kelley knew the name was so preposterous, the thought so dangerous, that Cui wouldn't know whether to believe Kelley or not.

Kelley knew what had to be going through Cui's mind. Cui could not believe that Kelley could be lying. How could Kelley be doubted; he had to be telling the truth if he knew about China Blue Sailor. Only a very few like Cui would know that the codename China Blue Sailor was for Francis Marian. Kelley would not speak of China Blue Sailor and Marian in the same breath unless he had succumbed to the torture and were telling the truth. What Kelley was saying had to be true. Cui could not believe Kelley was lying ... but Cui could not believe Kelley was telling the truth—how could Marian know about everything—about this?

And because of that, Kelley knew he had won. If Cui didn't know what to believe, then Cui's plan was worthless—his whole plan was possibly entirely compromised, just as the Chinese plan for the takeover of Long Beach Harbor had been compromised—and would thus ultimately fail. Kelley smiled weakly at Cui and then lapsed into unconsciousness.

Cui stood silently for a long, long moment. He finally turned to the other three men in the room. "Get him down. Get rid of him—I don't care where—just somewhere along the road to Barcelona. Load his asshole and stomach up with cocaine, and make it look like he was just another dumb *Yanqui* who died trying to smuggle drugs out of the country. You ... yes, you," Cui said as he pointed to one of the men, "come with me. I have some final things in my car to dispose of along with that piece of meat hanging up there."

Cui turned and walked from the room; he did not look back.

— ~ —

"There he is—do we follow him?" the CIA agent asked of the admiral as the four of them—the admiral, his aide Brad, Hermann, and the CIA undercover agent from the Caracas consulate—hid in the back of an old gray-colored Volkswagen van, a common sight on the streets of Maturin.

"No. We can always find Cui," the admiral said as he saw Cui get into a car and turn right as he exited the equipment yard gate and drove unknowingly passed two other vans, each filled with four other agents. "We need to know where they're holding Kelley. He's got to be inside that place, but once we go in, we won't have much time to search before all hell breaks loose. We have to avoid that—if we can."

"Look," said Hermann, as he pointed excitedly toward a building near the equipment yard fence and a large sign with the words, *"China y Venezuela de Petróleo Compañeros de Venezuela,"* painted in red. "That man, that man going up the stairs to that doorway—he is one of the men that took *Señor* Kelley from the hotel."

"That has to be it," the admiral said excitedly.

"But what's that he is carrying up the stairs," Samuelson asked.

"I don't give a damn. Get our people in the other vans ready. They're going in there, now."

The agent clicked his microphone twice and spoke. "On my order, van one will crash the gate and head to the building by the big sign. Hold the bottom of the stairs. The second van will follow and storm the stairs on the side of the building. Get whoever is in there out damn fast, and then get out the place as fast as possible. Split up, van one go south, and van two go west. Meet back at base. Over."

"Roger that. Van one ready to go on your command," a voice from the first van said

"Team two, ready on your command," the second van responded. The agent looked at the admiral. The admiral nodded his head. The agent double clicked his mike, broad it close to his lips, and said, "Go."

One van roared forward, its power and speed surprisingly great for an old van. It crashed forward through the wire gate, leaving a wide opening. In a moment, the other van leaped forward, surging through the now open gate. The guard in the shack by the gate threw himself on the floor of the little building, not knowing what was going on, but not wanting to get killed by the terrorists who must be attacking the equipment yard.

The first van streaked toward the stairs, then braked to a halt. Three men jumped from the rear of the van and took positions around the stairway, assault rifles at the ready. The second was only a moment behind. It also disgorged three men who dashed up the stairway two steps at a time. A short burst of fire opened the door, and the men were inside. Loud shouting in Spanish, English, and Chinese followed. Another short burst of gunfire, and then the microphone clicked. "We got him. He doesn't look good, but he looks alive."

In a few minutes, the three agents exited the bullet-riddled doorway at the top of the stairway; the second agent carried a man wrapped in canvas over his shoulder. The three Chinese that had been in the room interrogating Kelley were left tied in the chains from which Kelley had hung only a few minutes ago. The last man to exit the doorway carried a canvas travel bag under his arm.

Across the street, the agent said to the admiral, "I think we had better get out of here, now. This place will be crawling with police in a few minutes."

As the gray van did a U-turn and started up the street, the two other vans came through the mangled gate, one turning right and the other left. A total of five minutes had passed. Another five minutes passed before the guard rose from the floor of the guard shack and reached for the phone.

# 39

"Yes, Armando, you wish to see me?" Marulanda said to his assistant as the young man entered Marulanda's office, finding it difficult to put the morning newspaper down. The headline covered the full width of the top of the front page: "Terrorist Attack on Oil Company Properties in Maturin."

"Yes, Minister, I have some important ... results," the young assistant said.

"Yes? You have found something?" Eulogio asked hopefully ... and anxiously. The San Juan bidders were down to four; only four certificates of benefit had been approved and forwarded from Maturin by Uriarte before the deadline. Only two, the *Tejas Petróleo* and the China Petroleum bids, had any chance of winning, but he needed the cover of the other two to make the competition look honest and aboveboard.

Eulogio had been unable to convince Uriarte to disallow a certificate of benefit for China Petroleum. Uriarte could not understand why Eulogio would even suggest such an idea.

Indeed, Uriarte had been more inclined to disallow a certificate for *Tejas Petróleo*. He argued that because *Tejas Petróleo* was such a small company, in comparison to China Petroleum, it could be claimed that Tejas did not have the financial resources to meet its obligations under the certificate of benefit.

When Eulogio had realized that Uriarte could not be swayed, Eulogio knew he would have to find some problem in China Petroleum's bid documents that would require that they be disqualified.

Eulogio had to make a decision by this afternoon; he had had his people reviewing the bid documents and certificates all last night and into the morning to find some reason why the Tejas bid was the best. Eulogio had decided in the early morning hours after his unsuccessful attempt to change Uriarte's mind that the winning bidder had to be *Tejas Petróleo*. It was not a matter of money now. Both Matthew and Cui had already paid some money, and more money would come irrespective of who won. But if Tejas did not win, Benavidez would almost certainly kill him. Chávez, at worse, would only remove him as minister, or so Eulogio wanted to believe.

*As for Cui, if the Chinese lost—well, they would just have to accept it. The money they had already paid—that was just part of the game, just the down payment to get in the game, just to be considered. And they were considered. Uriarte returned a favorable endorsement for them, but everyone knows,* Marulanda reasoned to himself, *that would not be the only reason for selecting a winner. Everyone ... everyone knows nothing could be guaranteed.*

"Yes, we found an error in the bid documents of the El Largo group."

"An error?" Eulogio asked in surprise.

"Yes—it was in their financial bonding sheet. They failed to show that all members of the consortium could provide the necessary bond. One of the smaller suppliers' bond did not have a sufficient bond size. Their bid is ... invalid."

"Invalid ... remarkable. How could they not meet the requirement?" Eulogio asked solicitously, but with a silent sigh of relief.

"I do not know; just a stupid mistake I think," the young man said.

"Well, just document your findings. Tell the others we can stop our review now; I am ready to validate our three remaining bidders," Eulogio directed.

"Do you not to want to finish the review of the other three

remaining bids?" the assistant asked.

"No, absolutely no. We are done, and I am ready to formally validate the three remaining bidders. Bring me the validation letters; I wish to discuss them with our president before I sign them and we make our final decision," Eulogio ordered, knowing that the last thing he wanted was another bid to be invalid. The bidding regulations required that there be at least three valid bids; if there were not three valid bids, then the bidding had to be voided.

"As you wish, Minister Marulanda. I will inform the others," the young assistance said with chagrin after being chastised by the minister. The young man turned and left the office.

*Yes, this was the way it has to be*—Tejas *has to win.* Marulanda knew he had no other option. In the long run, it was just as well. He never did really like the Chinese anyway—they had made their play and lost. All was as it should be. Benavidez would be happy, and the money from Matthew that was delivered last week as a contribution to the PHC party was already in the PHC treasurer's account—ready to be split with Uriarte.

Marulanda's intercom buzzed, disturbing his thoughts. "Yes?"

"*Señor* Wang of China y Venezuela de Petróleo Compañeros de Venezuela is on the line. He wishes to speak to you," the young female voice said.

*Wang, the CEO of China Partners! What could he want now? There is no way he could know of my decision*—*maybe he will try to make some last-minute offer to make sure China Petroleum wins the bid. This is perfect,* Marulanda thought with glee. It was just the reason he needed to downgrade the evaluation of China Petroleum's bid package: improper contact with the Ministry during the bid review period. It was another reason he could give to Chávez and Munguia for not accepting the Chinese bid.

Marulanda picked up the phone. "*Señor* Wang. What a surprise— a pleasant surprise."

Wang answered, "*Buenos dias.* I hope I am not disturbing you."

"Well, we are rather busy this morning, but it is always a pleasure to speak to you. You know we are in the very process of evaluating the bids for the San Juan block, including your bid."

"*Si*, I thought that might be the case. That is why I felt I must call you as soon as possible."

*Here it comes*, Marulanda thought to himself. "And why would that be, *Señor* Wang?"

"Are you aware of what happened in Maturin yesterday?"

"You mean the terrorist attack—yes, I was reading about it. Quite shocking, but I am sure our Federal police will get to the bottom of it shortly. There is nothing to be worried about—no one was hurt, were they?" Marulanda asked.

"Fortunately, no. But my government has decided to withdraw from the San Juan bid. We will be sending you our formal letter of withdrawal by messenger. It should be reaching your office within the hour."

"Withdrawing! No ... no. You cannot do that ... you must not ... you are in an excellent position to win," Marulanda was in shock. *There have to be three bidders! If there are only two, the bidding will be declared null and void. China Petroleum cannot withdraw ... they just cannot do that!*

"I am sorry, but we—my government—has made its decision ... and as I am sure you are aware, the bidding rules do allow it."

"Is there not something we ... I ... could do ... something," Marulanda pleaded.

"I am so sorry, Minister Marulanda, there is nothing you ... nor I ... can do. *Buenos dias*."

Marulanda did not say goodbye. He just put the phone down with a shaking hand. *If the bidding is declared null and void, Tejas will not win. And if Tejas does not win—there is no way that Benavides will accept that result.*

Marulanda mind raced, wondering what he could do ... what could he do? *But wait ... the president. Yes, that was it. Chávez could do what he wanted. All he had to do was to convince Chávez that the bidding should be allowed to continue.*

He picked up the telephone and dialed President Chávez's office.

— ~ —

".... But *Señor* Munguia, the two remaining bids are very good. Just because the China Petroleum bid was withdrawn at the last minute is no reason to not consider it to show just how good all three bids really are. Please, if you will allow me to speak to the president directly—"

"I told you, the president is unavailable! He is attending very important meetings with some industry leaders in the south at Ciudad Guayana and Barrancas," Munguia snapped.

Marulanda had known it was a losing battle with Munguia as soon as he told Munguia that China Petroleum had withdrawn from the bidding. But he had continued to try—to grovel—to convince Munguia to put in him direct contact with Chávez. Marulanda had to talk to Chávez if the bidding process were to be able to continue— before word got out that China Petroleum had withdrawn its bid.

But Munguia would have none of it. Marulanda knew that Munguia was now doing what he had to do to protect himself. Munguia was going to be sure that Marulanda could not have a chance to defend himself in front of Chávez. Munguia's final words to Marulanda were, "How could you be so stupid as to allow the China Petroleum bid to be withdrawn? You have ruined the San Juan project."

As he heard the slam of the Munguia's telephone, Marulanda began wondering how long he could survive Chávez's anger. But what puzzled Marulanda were Munguia final words—that Marulanda had ruined the San Juan project. *What was the San Juan project?*

# 40

Kelley began to feel the pain as he slowly opened his eyes.

A voice said, "How do you feel, Kelley?"

Kelley shifted his head slightly; he could see the admiral standing by the bed. "Absolutely like fucking shit, Admiral."

Marian smiled. "Then I guess you're going to be okay."

Swirling his eyes, Kelley could see he was in a hospital room, with a bunch of hanging bottles and tubes running to both his arms; he could feel the bandages around his testicles. One arm, his left, still looked like, except for its color, a watermelon. Slanting his eyes down toward his feet, he could see that his feet, even though they were under the sheet, were heavily bandaged.

"Where are we?" Kelley asked.

"In a hospital. Where do you think?"

"I damn well know that, but what hospital?"

"Brooke Army Medical—in San Antonio. It was the closest U.S. military hospital we could evacuate you to that looked like it had the specialists you might need. You certainly needed more treatment than you could get in a Maturin hospital—and we didn't want to raise flags by sending you to a Caracas hospital. Our ambassador told the Venezuelan immigration people you were a U.S. diplomat who had gotten a contagious disease, so they didn't give us much of a hassle getting you out of the country. In fact, I don't think they really cared much; they seemed to be more concerned about some terrorist raid that occurred a day before at a China Petroleum equipment yard in Maturin."

"Is that where they had me?"

"Yes."

"How did you get me out?"

"Seems the terrorists attacked the place—created quite a stir for a few minutes. But nobody seems to know who the terrorists really were or went—they seemed to have disappeared into thin air."

Kelley gave a weak smile.

"Sorry we didn't get to you sooner, but, I have to tell you, we wouldn't have found you at all if it hadn't been for that driver of yours, Hermann."

"Hermann, that dumb ass? What the hell did he do?"

"He saw you taken from your hotel and followed the guys that took you."

"Damn. I guess I really owe him. Is he okay?"

"Yes, he's fine, though he is apparently out of work since the demise of Luque. But a company I know very well might find some part-time work for him."

Kelley nodded his head in understanding.

A nurse entered the room. "Admiral, it's time for this man to have a sedative; he needs his rest." She helped Kelley take a sip of water to down a pill.

Kelley sighed, and, turning his face away from the admiral, he said, "Well, things really got screwed up, didn't they?" Kelley said with resignation.

"Maybe ... maybe not. You didn't tell me that Cui was in town, but I guess you had your reasons—which I expect you to fully explain later. But, whatever Cui was up to seems to have fallen apart. He left Venezuela the day after the ... terrorist raid—flew straight back to China. He had a pretty somber welcoming party—including an armed escort—in Beijing."

"Are you sure ... how do you know?"

"We have our sources," the admiral said with a smile.

"Any idea why they his welcoming party was there to take Cui in tow when Cui got off his plane?" the admiral asked.

Kelley turned his head to look directly at the admiral. "Cui was after an oil lease on the east coast of Venezuela—apparently Cui didn't get it."

"That apparently explains it."

"What do you mean," Kelley asked.

"A couple of days after we got you out Maturin, there was a big newspaper story about PDSVA shutting down an oil lease bid program for some lands near the Venezuelan cost."

"Why ... was ... that," Kelley asked slowly.

"Something about not enough bidders."

"Not ... enough ... bidders?"

"Let's take about the details...later," the admiral said as he saw Kelley's eyes begin to flutter as the sedative began to take effect.

"I think it's time I left, let you get back to sleep. I'll be back tomorrow, and you can give me more details—a lot more details."

"Good ... idea. I can ... you the whole ... lowdown ... later."

Kelley's eyes closed.

# XII

# UNRAVELING

## 41

Kevin had his secretary translate the article, for the second time. It was from the *El Universal*—Caracas' business daily. Because it was in Spanish, he was not sure of all the things it said, but when he had first seen the headline on the stack of papers at the street vendor's stand, the little Spanish he could read made him shudder. "PDVSA Denies All Bids for San Juan Lease." *How could that be ... how could that be!*

Kevin's secretary continued her translation while Kevin felt himself sinking lower and lower into a quagmire of drugs, bankruptcy, and ... God knows what else. "... A spokesman for the *Ministro de Minas y Hidrocarburos* announced yesterday that the Ministry had ... stopped ... no, no ... declined to award a lease for the San Juan Block located on the Rio San Juan in northeastern Monagas, telling ... saying, no ... speaking ... no ... citing—that is the better word—the lack of ... not much ... not enough ... an inadequate number of bidders," his secretary said with a smile, happy that she had been able to put the correct nuance into her translation.

"Under the new Policy for Equitable Lease and Use of Mineral and Petroleum Resources of Venezuela for the Benefit of the People of Venezuela ... made ... no ... put into place ... *si,* that is better ... put into place by national regulations passed in August of this year, a minimum of three acceptable bids must be made before a bid can be awarded. President Chávez ... required ... required, no ... made sure ... the regulations had added the inclusion of the minimum bidder number to assure that bad ... no ... unfair ... bids, no ... no ... that bids would be competitive ... and provide assurance that the ... winning bid would be in best interests of the people of Venezuela."

The secretary stopped for a moment, looked at Kevin, and asked, "Go on?"

"Yes ... go on," came the words in a weak, panicky voice, as Kevin continued to bite his lip.

"According to unnamed sources, the lease had generated a great deal of interest, but a requirement for a certification of benefit, a requirement of the new regulations ... made up ... no ... promul ... gated ... promulgated—that is the American word I think—at the request of President Chávez, had narrowed the list of bidders to three only a week ago. Then, according to the source, one of the three bidders, *China y Venezuela de Petróleo Compañeros de Venezuela*, withdrew its bid, only a day before the bids were to be ... told ... announced. It is widely speculated that the recent terrorist attack on the Maturin warehouses of *China y Venezuela de Petróleo Compañeros de Venezuela* was largely the cause of the Chinese company's decision to ... remove ... withdraw its bid."

The secretary looked again at Kevin. Kevin nodded his head. He had to hear it all.

"President Chávez made a statement to the press that the political terrorists that were responsible for the attack would be caught and punished most ... bad ... severely. The President further stated, most firmly, that, 'It is time to think about how petroleum development can be conducted without harm to the Venezuelan people from such things as this terrorist raid. The government must recognize it has an important role of authority in petroleum development operations and in the protection of its friends such as the People's Republic of China.'"

"*Gracias*, Maria, ... you can stop ... now. Please return ... to your desk."

The secretary left the office, her steps in her high heel shoes accenting, as they always did, the swing of firm buttocks.

Kevin did not watch; helplessness and despair overwhelmed him.

Then Kevin paused in his self-misery. *Maybe—maybe there is something I can do—maybe I can salvage this. I'll get a hold of that goddamn double-crossing Marulanda and find what the hell happened—what really happened—and by God get him to straighten it out.*

"Maria," Kevin said as he rose from his chair and strode quickly to the open doorway of his office, "get Minister Marulanda at the *Ministro de Minas y Hidrocarburos.* Tell him I must speak to him—today."

Some forty minutes later, Maria knocked gently on Kevin's office door.

"Yes, Maria, come in," Kevin responded. "Is the minister on the line?"

"*Señor* Matthew, I tried ... numerous times," Maria said in a timid voice.

"Well, is he on the line or not?" Kevin asked with growing concern.

"His office, his secretary, said he could not be reached—that he had gone on vacation ... that the last few weeks had been very stressful for the minister."

"Does she know where the hell he went?" Kevin exploded.

"She said he has gone to Barcelona, but she does not know where he is staying ...."

Kevin rolled his eyes and tilted his head back, his body slumping in his chair.

Maria backed out of Kevin's office.

# 42

Eulogio walked through the glass doors to the Cayman International Commercial Bank. In his pocket written on the back of Cui's business card was the number of Eulogio's account. In that account was enough money to get to the United States, out of the reach of Benavidez ... and Chávez—enough money to start over—and to stay alive.

Marulanda strode confidently to the desk where there sat, according to the nameplate on the desk, an assistant vice-president for deposits and withdrawals.

"*Buenos dias, Señor,*" Eulogio said with a smile.

"*Buenos, Señor,*" the assistant vice-president said, speaking without hesitation in the language of the man before him. "May I help you?" the man asked politely.

"*Si.* My name is Marulanda. I wish to withdraw money from my account."

"Certainly, *Señor* Marulanda. And what would be your account number?" the assistant vice-president asked as he turned to the desktop computer on the side of his desk.

Eulogio removed Cui's card from his pocket and looked at the number. "Five-four-two ... three-three ... seven-zero-nine-two." The assistant vice president typed in the numbers on the keyboard of his computer as Eulogio spoke.

"Five-four-two-three-three-seven-zero-nine-two," the man said as he looked at his computer screen. "Is that correct?"

Eulogio paused as he looked again at the card in his hand. "*Si*, that is correct."

The assistant vice president nodded his head and hit the return key on his keyboard. The screen before the man flashed and blinked, creating a new view. The man nimbly tabbed over two spaces and then asked, looking to see that no one was near, "And what would be the access code—would you please tell me or write it down on this piece of paper?" The man placed a pen and a small pad of white paper before Eulogio. A shaded watermark on the pad said: DESTROY AFTER USE.

"I do not mind telling you. The access code is 'San Juan'," Eulogio said with confidence.

The assistant vice-president looked at his computer screen, typed in S-a-n J-u-a-n, hit the return key, and waited an instant for the computer to respond. A message flashed across the screen. Then the man frowned. "That does not seem to be correct, *Señor.*"

A scowl came to Eulogio's face. "It is correct! It has to be correct!"

"I am sorry, *Señor*, the computer says that is not correct."

"What are you trying to do here; I know that is correct ... oh, wait. San Juan—it is one word, not two. Did you type it in as one or two words?"

The assistant vice-president smiled. "Ah, that must be it." The young man typed in S-a-n-j-u-a-n and tapped the return key. A smile came to his face. "*Si, correcto.*"

Eulogio smiled in return, the tension beginning to ease as he realized he was about to get to his money—the two-hundred-fifty-thousand dollars that Cui had placed in the escrow to be transferred to Eulogio's account once the certificate of benefit had been provided by Uriarte. *If there had only been more time to get to Maturin and the money Matthew gave me as "donations" to the PHC—it would have doubled the money I will have once I walk out of here. But—my life depended on getting out of Venezuela as quickly as possible.*

"Would you please sign this signature card," the assistant vice-president said as he wrote the box number and date on a red-bordered card beneath a blank signature line and then slide the card across the shiny desk to Eulogio. Eulogio signed the signature card and pushed it back across the desk.

The assistant vice-president then took a key from his pocket and turned to the cabinet beside his desk. Unlocking the glass door of the cabinet, he scanned the several labeled file boxes there and then withdrew one file box and placed it on his desk. He thumbed through the cards in the file box and, after a moment, found the divider tab with the number 7-0-9-2 at its top.

The assistant vice-president withdrew a card from behind the divider tab and compared it to the card Eulogio had signed. A moment passed as the man carefully scrutinized both cards. "All seems to be in order," the assistant vice-president said as he started to return both cards to the file box. Looking casually at the other cards already in the box, the assistant vice-president said in a friendly voice, now that the formalities of accessing the account had been completed, "I see that you are here again—and so soon. You must like our islands very much."

"Oh, yes I do ... what do you mean—again so soon?" Eulogio asked, his voice suddenly filling with apprehension.

"Why, you were here less than a week ago—according to the last signature card. Is that not correct?" the vice-president asked, his voice becoming suspicious.

"Oh ... yes, of course ... just slipped my mind ... I have been extremely busy of late ... very busy. Can we proceed?" Eulogio said confidently. ¡Madre de Dios! *What's going on? Has someone gotten into my account? Did Uriarte take my money somehow? That double-crossing prick! Or maybe ... Cui had deposited some more money without telling me. That's it—that has to be it!*

The assistant vice-president paused as if debating with himself, then asked, "How much money do you wish to withdraw?"

"Two-hundred-forty-five thousand dollars," Eulogio responded, thinking it wise he leave some money in the account to keep it active just in case some additional money needed to be deposited.

"Certainly," the assistant vice-president said without pause; cash withdrawals and deposits of such magnitude were not infrequent at the Cayman International Commercial Bank. The man turned back to his computer and punched some keys. The man stared at the flickering computer screen. A frown came to his face. He typed in some numbers again. The monitor screen flickered again and threw up a list of numbers and a paragraph of text. He slowly shook his head. "But, *Señor* Marulanda ... you do not have that amount."

"What do you mean—not have that amount?" Eulogio said sharply.

"You do not have two-hundred-forty-five-thousand dollars in your account—our records show that you withdrew two-hundred-forty-nine thousand dollars four days ago. Do you not remember doing that?" the assistant vice-president asked, an anxious look coming to his face.

"But ... but the money was in escrow; you held it in escrow—it was to be deposited to my account two weeks ago."

The assistant vice-president looked at the numbers on the screen before him. "Ah, *si*, the money in escrow was indeed deposited just ... two weeks ago, as you say it was to be. *Si*, the transfer to your account was made—two-hundred-fifty-thousand dollars. But the withdrawal—it was also made. Perhaps, I should get our senior vice-president. Perhaps he can explain—"

"No ... no," Eulogio said, not wanting to draw attention to what had happened. "I remember now—as I said a moment ago, I have been under much stress ... much stress."

"You are sure?" the man across the table asked.

"*Si*, I am sure," Eulogio answered with a shallow voice as his mind screamed: *What do I do now? I have almost no money with me. I do not dare go back to Venezuela—now.*

"As you wish, *Señor*." The assistant vice-president hesitated, but then added, "Your computer record also says that a message is being held for you. Do you want me to get it?"

*That's it ... that must be it. Cui must have transferred the money to another account for security purposes—yes, for security purposes.* "*Si* ... the message, please, the message," Eulogio said anxiously.

The assistant vice-president picked up the phone on the desk and spoke to someone. Eulogio sat silently while they talked.

The assistant vice-president hung up the phone. "It will be just a moment, *Señor* Marulanda."

Eulogio said nothing; he just sat motionlessly, staring out the window behind the desk. The window fronted on the bay. Eulogio looked at the water with blank eyes, not seeing the waves cascading onto the shore.

In a few minutes, a young woman approached the desk with a brown business envelope in her hand; it had the 7-0-9-2 account number neatly typed on its front. She gave it to the assistant vice-president. The assistant vice-president handed it to Marulanda.

Marulanda undid the metal clasp on the envelope, looked inside, and, then, withdrew another envelope, an ordinary white business letter envelope. "Eulogio Marulanda" was typed on its front side.

"*¿Señor?*" the assistant vice-president asked as he offered Marulanda a small chrome-coated steel letter opener.

Eulogio took the letter opener. He slit the envelope open and removed a folded piece of white paper. *Ah, the new number—si, it has to be the new account number.* Marulanda unfolded the piece of paper. It had one sentence typed on it: "Without fulfillment of obligation, the down payment is withdrawn."

Marulanda stared at the paper. Beads of frightened sweat began to fall from his contorted face and stain the paper.

# 43

Cinzia looked out the window of the Washington townhouse at the heavy rain coming down. It was getting to be that time of year—repeated days of biting wind and chilling rain or snow, interspersed by days of crisp, icy coldness. Soon, there would be the snow—it was always so pretty, the first day. After that, as the snow turned to mush under the pressure of car tires and the feet of people, it would emote its underlying ugliness. By the New Year, Cinzia would be longing to return to the warmth and beauty of Venezuela.

It was the same every year. After the excitement and rush of the Christmas holidays, the days would become dreary, unless she returned for a few weeks to Venezuela for the Carnival holidays, or, as she often did now, find a sexually satisfying distraction. She thought again about Castellano—a little old, but still quite handsome, and certain to have exquisite capabilities in bed.

Cinzia contemplated what Castellano might be like—allowing fantasies to fill her mind. As she often did, she transplanted herself to that first time after her marriage to Roland, when Roland had been off politicking on one of his reelection campaigns. The man at the door had introduced himself as working for Roland—one of his many minions—and said that Roland had asked him to take Cinzia to the airport where she would fly by private jet to Dallas for an important campaign dinner the next day.

When Cinzia, who was already packed, had asked how long did they have before they had to leave from Hobby Airport, the young man—who looked more and more attractive to Cinzia as he stood in the entryway, tall and slim, with a self-conscious smile coming from beneath his blue eyes and blond hair—answered that no specific time had been set. The plane was ready to leave whenever she arrived at the airport.

Cinzia had then suggested the young man come to her bedroom to help with her luggage. Once there, the rest followed rather naturally when Cinzia had announced she had decided to change into different travel clothes and invited the man to remain in her bedroom while she changed. The hour that had been spent in her bedroom became quite extraordinary, particularly when the young man had revealed his unusually large physical endowments.

Cinzia sighed, wondering how she could turn her fantasies about Castellano into reality. Roland said Castellano, without Kevin in tow, had come to his office once since their return from Venezuela. Roland had made a point of telling Cinzia that Castellano was still recovering from an auto accident and still had an arm in a cast. Roland did not provide any further details, other than to say it would only be a matter of time before recovery.

And strange, too, was the fact that she had not seen or heard from Kevin Matthew since her return from Venezuela—Kevin would usually send his regards to Cinzia when he spoke to Roland, who would dutifully pass them on to her. Kevin usually visited with Roland, at least on the phone, quite regularly, but since their return from Venezuela just before Thanksgiving, Kevin, as best she could determine, had not been in contact with Roland. As for Castellano, perhaps Roland might know how to contact him. Correctly asked, Roland would think nothing of it, especially if she put her inquiry in the guise of concern about Castellano's well-being.

Just thinking about Castellano and the possibilities with him began to excite her. In a moment her hands had lifted her dress and were sliding between her legs. But her stroking was interrupted when she saw a taxi stop in front of the townhouse. Then, as a man got out, she realized that it was Roland, which was strange. Roland never came home in the middle of the afternoon—especially in a taxi.

She saw Roland walk slowly—despite the rain—to the townhouse steps, and in a few moments heard him enter the front door. Cinzia turned from the window and saw Roland standing in the doorway of the sitting room. Rainwater rolled steadily from his coat, forming puddles of water about his feet on the polished wood floor. He was slumped, and his face was ashen.

"What is it, Roland? Why are you home so early?"

Roland just stood there, his coat still on, as if in a daze. Dripping water continued to puddle about his feet.

"What's wrong ... Roland, what's happened?"

"They're going to investigate me, maybe bring me up on charges,"

Roland said in a shallow voice.

"What ... who is going to investigate you? What are you talking about!" Cinzia asked in shock.

"The majority leader—he said allegations have been made about political contributions coming from Venezuela—to influence legislation. Political contributions from another country are illegal— you know that."

"But you didn't take contributions from anybody in Venezuela ... did you?" Cinzia asked incredulously.

"Well, no ... no, I didn't ... at least I didn't know I was," Beal answered.

"What do you mean 'didn't know'—was Kevin Matthew behind this?" Cinzia asked angrily.

"That Castellano—his company was trying to do work in Venezuela—it made some contributions, somehow, related to an oil lease block—his company made the contributions to the Coalition— through Kevin's Trans-Texas and that Tejas subsidiary he set up in Venezuela. Kevin apparently arranged to have Tejas send the contributions to the Coalition—the Coalition put the money in my reelection campaign fund—".

"Kevin arranged! I knew it—how could you let Kevin do this to you? How!"

"But Cinzia—it was supposed to be only for contributions to political parties of local people ... in Venezuela, not here, not in the U.S. ... to make sure that the right people won some leases—"

"Right people ... you mean Kevin, don't you? That explains it!"

"Explains what?" Roland asked.

"Why Marulanda is missing."

Beal straightened in surprise. "What are you talking about?"

"Daniella, Jorge's sister-in-law—her husband, Eulogio, the Venezuelan oil minister—I had a call from Jorge this morning. Eulogio is missing. Jorge said Daniella is distraught. Jorge said he had arranged for Kevin and Marulanda to meet."

"Well, what's that got to do with me—with us?" Beal asked in a defensive tone.

"Got to do with us! How could you be so blind, Roland? We are all family—and a prominent member of the family is missing under suspicious circumstances—and you are a member of that family, even if only remotely," Cinzia explained as if chastising a little boy. "Who knows where questions might lead?"

Beal's eyes widened as he realized how explosive—how damaging—a Congressional investigation could be if missing Venezuelan nationals were brought into the picture. "I have to speak to Kevin—I have to find out more ... what's going on ... find out what I can do to get out of this mess."

Cinzia looked at Beal for a long moment, apparently contemplating what Beal wanted to do. Finally, she spoke. "You must be very careful; everything you say must be very circumspect—as if you know nothing. Can you do that, Roland ... can you do that?"

Beal took a deep breath. "I think so," he finally said.

"You must. You call him." Cinzia looked at her watch. "He is probably in his office. You call there. I will get on the extension, just to listen, unless you start to say too much."

Beal nodded as Cinzia went to the phone near the window. Beal picked up the extension phone from the table in the entry hall and dialed the long-distance number he knew by heart.

In a moment the connection was made, and a voice, a shaking voice, answered, "Trans-Texas Oil Company."

"This is Senator Beal. I would like to speak to Kevin. Is he in?" There was a long silence. "I said I would like to speak to Kevin." Another pause, and then, "Yes sir, I heard you. But ... but ...."

The voice on the other end of the line began to cry.

Cinzia broke in. "What is wrong, young lady?" Cinzia demanded.

"Mr. Matthew ... Mr. Matthew ... a burglar ... last night ... Mr. Mathew was murdered!"

Cinzia put the phone down, knowing nothing but disaster lie ahead.

# 44

"Looks like the late-night crowd has gone," Kelley said, as he sat in the right front seat of the nondescript Buick.

The DEA agent beside Kelley put down his binoculars. "As best I can tell, the person that just came out was the last person in the bar—except this Goldie woman. I think we can go in now before she closes."

"I think you're right," Kelley answered.

The DEA agent started the car, moved it slowly down the street, and parked it in front of Goldie's place, next to the Volkswagen van.

Kelley, the driver, and the two DEA agents in the back seat got out. They walked toward the door of the bar, with Kelley leading the way. As Kelley pulled the squeaky screen door open, Kelley saw the "open" sign on the window turn dark.

"Hang on, Goldie, I want to get a beer," Kelley said in a loud voice.

"Who the hell is that ... by God, is that you, Kelley ... Jesus, Kelley Castellano. What the hell are you doing here? You haven't been around here for ... what ... maybe three, four months—where the hell did you go after you quit as chief?"

"Well, been traveling around. But I am back now. Can I get that beer?"

"Sure, anything you want. Come on in."

As Kelley entered, he held the door open, and the three DEA agents followed him into the barroom.

"Who's that with you? I'm not open for business. I thought it was just you that wanted a beer—maybe talk about old times."

"Don't worry; these people don't want anything. They are just friends of mine. And that's just what I want to do—talk about old times, so to speak."

Goldie stood in the light of a neon "Schlitz Lite" sign over the back of the bar. Kelley could see the questioning look on her face. "What's going on, Kelley? And why is that arm of yours in a sling?"

Kelley sat down on a stool by the side of the bar. The three DEA agents remained standing.

"Had a run-in with a guy a few weeks ago, but the doc says everything should be fine in a month or so," lied Kelley. His physical therapist had said it was likely that Kelley would never again have full function of his left arm. The therapists at Walter Reed said his ability to lift his arm above shoulder height just wouldn't be there—he would do good to be able to lift a few pounds with the arm. "Why

Unraveling

don't you just give me a beer, and then we can talk," Kelley said politely but firmly.

Goldie looked with narrowing eyes at Kelley, then reached down into the ice cooler behind the bar, pulled out a Budweiser, popped off the cap, and set the bottle in front of Kelley. "You remembered," Kelley said.

"Damn straight I do. I don't forget what my customers like."

"Well, let's see what else you remember, Goldie. Come out here so we can talk," Kelley said as he pointed to a stool next to his.

Goldie went to the end of the bar and walked slowly toward the stool to which Kelley had pointed. One of the DEA agents, a woman, quickly approached Goldie, pushed her toward the bar, and began to frisk her. "What the fucking hell you doing, lady?" Goldie said in surprise.

"You know what she's doing, Goldie, so just be quiet and let her finish her job," Kelley said.

The DEA agent said nothing until she finished her checking. "She's clean."

"Good. Now we can have a nice pleasant talk," Kelley said, pointing to the bar stool again. Goldie lifted her short frame onto the stool using the crossbar near the bottom of the stool. She stared at Kelley.

"Now, just so you know, Goldie, these people are DEA agents—"

"DEA!" Goldie interrupted. "What the hell is going—"

"I know you know what the DEA is Goldie," Kelley said with a slight wave of his hand.

"Sure, I do—I read the papers. But why are they here?"

"Well, I think you know, but first things first, Goldie," Kelley said as he raised his index finger. "These agents are going to listen to everything you and I talk about, and they may and probably will use what you say in a court of law against you."

An innocent smile came to Goldie's face. "Fire away, Kelley, I ain't got nothing to hide."

"Good, Goldie. Let's talk about the night about four months ago when that body washed up on shore and was found by those kids— you remember that night?"

"Sure, I do, and like I told you then, I didn't have nothin' to do with that body—I never touched it," Goldie said.

"Interesting. Well, you remember who was there—you, Claudio, and that Valdes guy ... the kids, of course ... oh, and the Weedens, out for their walk in the moonlight."

"I don't know nothin' about them Weedens—they never come in here," Goldie said with certainty.

"Is that right? Well, let's talk first about Vic Valdes—that was his first name, Vic, wasn't it?" Kelley asked.

"Best I can remember. He ain't been around here for some time."

"Well, that's probably true. He was killed in a helicopter crash a few weeks ago—in Venezuela," Kelley said nonchalantly.

A look of surprise came over Goldie's face.

"Yeah, he was with me when the accident occurred. Not many people know about it yet, but now you do, Goldie. So, he's out of your operation—permanently."

"I don't know what operation you're talking about, Kelley."

"Well, we'll see. Let's talk about Claudio. He said he had been here all afternoon, got here before that late afternoon shower, and stayed the rest of the day—that the weather was still too bad to go out in his boat after the hurricane."

"I don't remember what he said," Goldie responded.

"Well, I do. And I remember you not contradicting him. Funny thing, though. The Coast Guard reported one of its cutters from Corpus stopped Claudio's boat just about forty miles down the coast a little after sundown the day before that body washed ashore—had to tell him to get back to shore because of the bad weather. Strange that Claudio wasn't afraid to get out into the Gulf only a day after the hurricane but was afraid to go a day later."

Goldie just looked at Kelley, but wrinkles came to her forehead.

"And then the Weedens—"

"I told you they don't come here," Goldie broke in.

"Well, then, tell me why they were out walking around in the moonlight when the moon was about to set—and the clouds covered up what moon there was. They may have been walking in the moonlight when they came into your place, but not when they left here when that body was found."

"You don't know what you are talking about, Kelley," Goldie protested. "Shit, I barely know them—they was always too highfalutin to come into my place."

"Really? Then how is it that two of the restaurants you ship your shrimp to are owned by the Weedens. And, by the way, a search warrant was executed today at their restaurants, and it seems that two of the raw shrimp crates that arrived at their restaurants this morning from here had some things other than shrimp in them—cakes of coke worth about six-hundred thousand street value.

"So, I want to know only one thing, Goldie. That man that washed up on the beach—his name was Jose Carrillo, by the way—when did you find out he was a DEA agent?"

Goldie looked at Kelley a long time, saying nothing. Then she let out a big sigh, and a slight smile came to her face. She leaned close to Kelley and whispered, "I'll tell you what I know, but you give me your word, Kelley—you, Kelley—your word—that you will tell ... whoever ... that I cooperated."

Kelley looked at Goldie for a long moment. "I'll do what I can, Goldie."

"Fair enough," Goldie said as she straightened her small body.

"Okay, Goldie, from the beginning," Kelley said. "And speak up so these two gentlemen and the lady can hear you."

"We—me and Vic—Vic Valdes—was waiting for a shipment going to Chicago that Claudio was supposed to be bringing in, but he was late. Claudio had picked up the shipment several days ahead of the hurricane—got it from some big fishing boat out in the Gulf way east of here. He had to dodge around the edges of the hurricane that was coming in—that was why he was a few days late—he came into shore just in front of the hurricane.

"While we was waiting for him, Vic got a call from Venezuela, on the morning when Claudio was supposed to come in, about a guy on Claudio's boat—the same guy that washed up on the beach. Claudio said, when he did finally arrive, that everybody in the boat they met had vouched for the guy. Claudio didn't want to bring the guy back with him, but the instructions down in Venezuela had been real clear—that Vic would be expecting him to be on the boat.

"What about the phone call?"

"That's the deal, Kelley. When Claudio finally got here, Vic acted real friendly with this guy, like they was old buddies. Then when the guy went to the john, Vic got a baseball bat from the rack over there," Goldie said as she paused and pointed to the wall where several souvenir bats from local high school tournaments hung on the wall.

"It's the bat at the bottom. Vic cleaned it up after he used it."

"So, what happened?"

"After he got the bat, Vic put it in the back storage room. We asked what he was doing, but Vic just said to shut up. Then when the guy got back from the john, Vic took him into the back room to talk, so he says, but he goes in back and closes the door and then whacks the guy on the head with the bat—really hard. Damn blood was all over the place. It was a mess cleaning it up," Goldie said.

Kelley cringed at the thought of what had happened to Carrillo. Then Kelley thought a bit about what Goldie had said. *It was likely that Carrillo became suspicious when Valdes acted so friendly toward him. Carrillo, sensing his cover was maybe blown, probably went to the john to hide the one bit of information that Valdes would not know Carrillo had and would not be looking for if Valdes searched him—Antonio's card with Bettina's name on it. And to be sure Valdes did not find anything, Carrillo rolled up the card and hid it in his underpants. And apparently Valdes didn't search Carrillo body well enough; Valdes never even thought about checking in Carrillo's underwear.*

"Go on," Kelley said.

"When I asked Vic what the hell was going on, he said the call had been from Venezuela—that his contact down there said this guy was dirty, that he worked for the DEA. And Vic said we would have to get rid of the body—dump him way out in the Gulf off of Mexico."

"So, Claudio, I guess, was elected to dispose of the body," Kelley asked.

"Sure. He didn't like it, but he agreed to do it, except he said he wasn't going to go out until the weather got better. The hurricane was hitting the coast just about the time Vic killed the guy. And he said he wasn't going alone. Vic had to go with him."

"So, what did you do?" Kelley asked.

"We wrapped the guy in canvas and put him in the walk-in cooler overnight—didn't want him to start smelling. By next evening things was getting better, so we got the guy out of the cooler and dropped him out the back into Claudio's boat—there was nobody around because of the weather—and threw the body into the ice locker on the boat.

"So, you see, I didn't have anything to do with the killing—it was Vic and Claudio, not me."

"Yeah, you're just as innocent as a babe in the woods," Kelly said sourly.

"So, maybe you got no case against me for his death—"

"Don't push it, Goldie. You just keep talking."

"Okay ... okay. So, Vic and Claudio took him out to sea to dump him off the Mexican coast, way south. But, it didn't work out that way. They almost ran into a Coast Guard cutter. They thought the damn Coast Guard people might board and search the boat. So, they had to dump the body real quick before the cutter got too close to them. But the Coast Guard just hailed them and told them to get back to shore—they never did come aboard. But the body was already dumped, and it was only a short way down the coast. They didn't even get a chance to weigh him down. They just let him roll out of the canvas and into the water. But they didn't think the body would float back here."

"Yeah, everyone seems to have a bad day once in a while," Kelley said sarcastically.

Goldie looked at Kelley.

Kelley returned her look, the disgust on his face evident.

"So, what was everybody doing here the night Carrillo washed up on shore if you thought Carrillo had been taken care of?" asked Kelley

"Well, all of us was pretty scared that maybe this guy—cause he was, like Vic said, a DEA agent—that maybe he had spilled the beans to a bunch of people. The Weedens had come in to bring the money for the shipment; they didn't know what was going on until they got here on the same day that the guy washed up on shore later that night. None of us didn't know for sure what to do. A guy, a DEA agent no less, had been killed, and we was all pretty jumpy. We was talking about it in the back when those damn kids pounded on the door. As soon as we got close to the body, Vic could see it was the guy he killed. Since those kids was standing nearby, we couldn't do anything but pretend we didn't know anything—we came back to the bar and called the station."

Kelley pondered what Goldie had said. Then he asked, "Who called Valdes and where was the call from?"

"Like I said, it was from someplace in Venezuela."

"Was it Caracas?"

"Nah—some place named Mattery, or something like that. Vic only said the place only once—that the guy he worked with was calling from this place."

"Did he say who was calling?"

"He mentioned the guy's name twice, I think. He called the guy Hermann."

# XIII

# SACRIFICE

## 45

As he settled into the couch in the admiral's office, Kelley thought through again about what had happened with Hermann, still trying not to believe what Goldie had said two days ago. Was it really true? Likely it was.

The admiral looked up from the papers he had been signing. "Well, that should take care of the official accounting for Valdes. He can stay out there and rot—nobody's going to want to look for him," the admiral said as he pushed the papers across the desk. "Brad, you need to sign this as witness."

Samuelson nodded and picked up a pen from the desk.

"I doubt there is even enough to rot now," Kelley said in a matter of fact voice.

The admiral nodded his head in agreement. Then raising his eyebrows and looking inquiringly at Kelley, he said, "So you want to tell me all about Cui now?"

"Well, there is really not too much to tell," Kelley said in an offhand voice.

The admiral rolled his eyes, looking at Kelley in obvious disbelief.

"I just ran across him in a hotel in Maturin—just out of the blue. He was apparently meeting with Marulanda, the Venezuelan oil minister. I knew he had to be up to something—though I didn't think it had anything to do with Carrillo. And I was sort of right about that. It didn't have anything to do with Carrillo but was all mixed up in the oil business."

Kelley raised and shook his forefinger. "You know that Cui was officially a representative of China Petroleum Partners, Beijing's front in Venezuela?"

"We didn't know at first," the admiral said, "but once we found out that he was involved in your disappearance, we started checking on things pretty fast. Then we found out he was there—in Venezuela—and up to apparently no good."

"Yeah, the way I figure it," Kelley said, "Cui was sent to Venezuela to get a site for establishing a naval base for the Chinese navy—"

"I couldn't believe you when you first told me that in San Antonio. I thought you were still delirious from your trek across Venezuela after the helo crash—until I started thinking about Long Beach and what the Chinese tried to do there," the admiral said.

"It took me awhile to catch on, too," Kelley said as he nodded his head. "But the longer I thought about it, the more working out a deal with the head of the oil ministry, Marulanda that is, made sense. Cui needed the cover of the government, not a government investigating something they didn't know about. An oil services contract, with the right contract terms—terms that Marulanda could assure—was all they needed—except for one thing."

"One thing? What's that?" Samuelson interjected.

"The Chinese had to be sure that the San Juan block area would really be suitable for the docking facilities they wanted to construct—that explains why Cui had his little expedition to the mouth of the San Juan back a few weeks ago—just to verify that the San Juan channel was deep enough for the Chinese ships they might want to station in Venezuela."

"What are you talking about—a little expedition?" the admiral asked.

"A couple of days after I ran into Cui at a hotel in Maturin—he rented a boat with a local hydrologic expert on the coastal areas of Venezuelan east of Maturin and did soundings in the area near the mouth of the Rio San Juan. I had tracked Cui down and watched him from a helicopter. And, guess what? The mouth of the San Juan, from what the local expert told me, would be a great place for an unobtrusive naval base," Kelley stated in a matter-of-fact voice.

"A base like that in Venezuela would have changed the whole complexion of our relationship with the countries around the Caribbean—and most of South America, too, for that matter," the admiral said in a professorial tone.

Samuelson then said what was on the minds of the three of them. "You know that the whole deal couldn't have been done without one particular person at least giving his blessing—"

"Of course," Kelley broke in, "but you'll never prove that—"

"I'm not even sure we would want to try—it is enough that we just know," the admiral said with finality.

"So, am I forgiven for following Cui, rather than staying on top of Carrillo's case?"

"What do you think? That's why I sent you down there—to do whatever had to be done. And you did it—though you almost got yourself killed doing it."

"You're right—if it hadn't been for Hermann, you would have never found out about Cui ... or me, for that matter."

"This guy Herman is an enigma—" Samuelson started to say.

"Well, not really," interpreted Kelley. "I have been giving quite a bit of thought to him. He may have been in cahoots with Valdes and Luque; but telling you where Cui had taken me—and all the work he did with me tailing Cui—makes sense if you think about it, at least in hindsight, if Hermann was working with Luque and some Colombian drug cartel."

"How do you figure that?" Samuelson asked.

"Luque and Hermann didn't know who Cui was. He probably looked just like more competition, just another person to get in the cartel's way. Cui was obviously trying to wiggle his way into getting the lease block on the San Juan—and if the cartel is trying to control the oil business to move more drugs through eastern Venezuela, then Cui is a fly in their ointment. Helping me follow Cui just made it more likely that Cui and the Chinese would be cut out of the picture. The cartel—and Luque as their inside guy in Venezuela—would figure that Cui and China Petroleum were just getting in the way of the things they wanted to do in controlling the oil business."

"That makes sense to me, Kelley," the admiral said, "but how did

Hermann find out about Carrillo—unless Luque told him."

"Luque likely did tell Hermann—when he decided that Carrillo had to be eliminated. That's why Hermann called Valdes at Goldie's. But Luque probably never told Hermann or Valdes that Carrillo was CIA to better keep things under his control. The less Hermann or Valdes knew about Carrillo, the better it was, Luque figured."

"But why didn't Luque tell Hermann or Valdes about Carrillo early on so they could get rid of Carrillo right way? And why kill him the way they did?"

"Two reasons, I think," Kelley answered. "First, as long as Carrillo was not digging up too much information, Luque could contain the situation. Better to contain the situation than raise a flag with you here at Langley by killing Carrillo. It was a matter of risk: the risk of Carrillo finding out too much or the risk of too much Langley interest in Maturin and Puerto La Cruz if Carrillo were killed.

"You said two reasons," Samuelson interjected.

"Yes, two. Apparently, Carrillo found out about Cumaraima in La Cruz, either by just snooping around—which Carrillo was damn good at—or something that Casares had said before Casares was killed that alerted Carrillo to Cumaraima. If Casares had said anything about Cumaraima's trawler operation, Luque probably picked up on it, too, but didn't say anything about it—not to Carrillo—or me when Luque gave me his briefing at the Best Western in Caracas. When Carrillo did find out about Cumaraima and his operation, Luque decided that Carrillo was learning too much, and the scales tipped in favor of Carrillo's elimination," Kelley said with finality.

There was quiet in the room for a long moment.

Then the admiral spoke, "That makes sense—in so far as it goes. But why was Carrillo killed like he was?"

Kelley looked at the ceiling for a few seconds and then turned to look at the admiral. "Luque knew that the routes that the Metillo cartel was using—and probably still is for all we know—had to be protected. Maturin and Barcelona are two of the centers for those routes. Any elimination of Carrillo had to be done so as minimize the connection of Carrillo to Maturin and Barcelona if Cumaraima's deliveries north for the cartel through whatever transfers that were used to reach Claudio's boat were not to be compromised. And what better way to do that than have him killed anywhere but in Venezuela, like along the Mexican Gulf Coast where his body would be found—if it was ever found after being dumped into the Gulf."

"But then the next question—how to get him out of Venezuela!" Samuelson said with growing excitement.

"Right. How could that be done without creating suspicion? Luque probably figured that Carrillo would jump at the chance to get on Cumaraima's trawler and learn the whole set of transfers that went on between Barcelona and the American coast. Luque could tell Cumaraima that Carrillo was okay—that he could be trusted—and that he was to handle the drugs on the trip across the Gulf from La Cruz to Spanish Palms. Luque probably said that Carrillo needed to know the setup because he was going to start similar operations; so, it was important that Carrillo got all the way to the Gulf Coast."

"So Luque told Cumaraima who Carrillo really was?" Samuelson asked.

"No, I don't think so. Luque couldn't tell Cumaraima himself; Luque could not let Carrillo get any hint that he was involved with Cumaraima. If Carrillo ever figured out that Luque was involved in the operation, Carrillo would know he was being set up. So Luque needed an intermediary—and the intermediary was Hermann," Kelly said with finality.

"So, once he was on Cumaraima's trawler, Cumaraima treated him like one of the gang, because that's exactly what Cumaraima thought he was—Hermann had told him so. Carrillo just played along with all the necessary transfers along the way, eventually getting him to Claudio's shrimp boat and into Spanish Palms. But Hermann called Valdes at Goldie's to let him know that Luque wanted Carrillo killed when he got to Goldie's. But the damn hurricane just generally screwed up everything."

"How so?" Samuelson asked.

"Claudio was behind schedule because of the hurricane—Goldie there in Spanish Palms told me that. Valdes, waiting in Spanish Palms and wondering where Claudio was, probably got more and more nervous, now knowing that Carrillo was, so Hermann said, DEA and that he, Valdes, would, on Luque's orders, have to kill him. So, when Claudio finally got into port, Valdes was really anxious to kill Carrillo and get him dumped at sea. But Claudio wouldn't go right away because of the hurricane. That delay led to their running into the Coast Guard cutter—and their hurried dumping of Carrillo's body. And the only reason that Carrillo was still in one piece when he floated ashore was that he was dumped fairly close to shore, and likely because he was so damn cold, he just wasn't an attractive piece of meat to hungry sea scavengers," Kelley explained.

"What a damn comedy of errors," the admiral said.

"Valdes was probably so damn spooked by the way things were turning out he probably never thought about what might happen if Carrillo was dumped like he was," Samuelson speculated.

"Running into the Coast Guard probably scared the crap out of Valdes," Samuelson added with a smile.

Kelley smiled.

"So, Kelley, what do you think we need to do to wrap this up?" the admiral asked.

"Well, things seem to be wrapping themselves up. Goldie is pleading out and spilling all she knows to the DEA lawyers. And that Houston wheeler and dealer Matthew got himself murdered." Kelley paused, and then continued, "Do you think the same thing I am thinking about him, Admiral," Kelley asked.

"Well, we know that Matthew was trying to cook up a real shady deal for that San Juan block with the bribes he was handing out, with your help. We were going to get the SEC and Justice Department to pounce on him for that, provided we could keep information about our involvement secret. Of course, that is not a problem now," the admiral said.

"That's for damn sure," Kelley exclaimed.

"And for that matter," the admiral said, "Matthew's behind-the-scenes dealings have given us the information, and the proof we needed, to alert both Justice and the ethics committee people in Congress to Beal's money-raising schemes—and some of his shady connections with Venezuelan politicians. I have heard from the grapevine that Beal may decide to resign from his Senate seat because of health problems, but we will have to see about that," the admiral said with a slight smile as he put imaginary quotes around "health problems".

"I'm sure glad the shady dealings of that crook Beal are coming to light," Kelley said a satisfied grin.

"So, Admiral, what are your thoughts about Matthew's murder?" Kelley asked.

"Well, in this business you can't put too much stock in coincidence. Matthew's murder was just too convenient—it cut a lot of loose ends about where and how Matthew was getting money here in the U.S. He apparently either knew too much about something or his murder was a payoff for losing the San Juan block."

"But," Kelley asked, "if it was payoff, why was the loss of the San Juan block so important to anyone but Matthew? We know it couldn't be the Chinese—they wanted to get the block, not Matthew to get it. So, I just don't think we really know what all Matthew was into."

"It may take some time to sort it out. But we are alerting the Houston police to some things that we know about Matthew that might help them find his murderer," the admiral finished.

"So, all that is left is ... Hermann?" Kelley asked.

"Well, of all the people we have the potential for dealing with—it looks like only him. But he is only one small cog in the wheel. We may have disrupted what the Metillo cartel was up to, but we still can't touch them ...."

The admiral paused, as if thinking of something, then continued, "unless ... unless Hermann ... that's it!"

Kelley and Samuelson looked at the admiral.

"Kelley, get your things together—you too, Brad—and get to Maturin right away," the admiral said with a look of conviction. "I think we may have a way to get at the Metillo cartel."

# 46

A smiling Hermann greeted Kelley as he entered the Maturin airport terminal. Kelley smiled in return and shook Hermann's hand. "You look good, *Señor* Kelley. Much better than the last time I saw you."

"Damn straight. I guess I looked pretty much like a dead fish."

"Dead fish? Oh, yes, a dead fish ... *Si*, you did."

"I want to thank you, Hermann, for what you did—no matter what happens, you saved my life, and I am grateful."

"It was ... nothing," Hermann answered.

"Well, nothing or not, I owe you a lot."

A long moment passed as Kelley and Hermann looked at each other. Then the spell was broken as Brad walked up.

This," Kelley said, "is your new boss, so to speak—Brad Samuelson. You remember him, I guess?"

"But of course—the hotel and the Chinese company maintenance yard where you was a prisoner."

"He is temporarily taking over Luque's position at Venzeusa in Caracas," Kelley said.

Brad pushed his hand toward Hermann.

"*Buenos dias, Señor* Samuelson," Hermann said as he shook Brad's hand.

"*Buenos dias.* A pleasure to see you again, Hermann," Brad responded.

"Thought I would bring him here to meet you—he might want to use your services like Luque did," Kelley said.

"*Si Señor* Kelley, I hope he can," Hermann paused and then spoke again. "It is such a sad thing about *Señor* Luque, so sad."

"Yeah, I guess so—but we can talk about that later," Kelley said brusquely. "Let's get our bags and then go for some dinner—maybe at *Restaurante de Medina.* A lot of things we need to talk about, Hermann."

Hermann looked at Kelley, smiled, and spoke, "*Si*, as you wish, *Señor* Kelley."

— ~ —

Kelley pulled the plate of *chuleta de res* toward himself and cut a piece of meat. He put the meat in his mouth and savored the taste. Then he looked at Hermann.

"Well, Hermann, what have you been up to since I last saw you—

when was it, when I went up to Barcelona," Kelley asked as he put another piece of steak in his mouth.

"Si, *Señor* Kelley, it was then. But where did you go? When they took you from the maintenance yard, I did not what was going to happen? It has been more than a month since I saw you. *Señor* Samuelson and the other men that rescued you told me that you would be taken back to the United States to a hospital. But it was only two days ago that I received your call that you would be coming back to Maturin. Are you well, now?" Hermann asked.

"I spent most of the time in a U.S. hospital—but everything is okay now," Kelley answered. "But, like I said, Hermann, what have you been doing?"

"Oh, just driving a taxi—my car is a really a taxi—you remember that don't you, *Señor* Kelley?"

Kelley nodded yes.

"My cousin and I— you remember him, Alberto—Alberto and I have joined together to make a taxi company. Of course, it is not as exciting as driving you around, *Señor* Kelley, but we make good money. When I drive, he sleeps; when I sleep, he drives. Did *Señor* Kelley tell you about all the things we did together, *Señor* Samuelson? Maybe Alberto and I can both work for you like I did *Señor* Luque?"

"Maybe, Hermann, maybe, like Kelley said earlier, maybe. But we need to talk about some things," Brad answered.

"Yes, Hermann, about your taxi business—have you ever considered providing service between major cities, like ... maybe Maturin and Barcelona?"

Hermann looked at Kelley. "That is too far—my license does not allow me to carry passengers to Barcelona."

"Funny, I would have thought you could make a lot of money taking someone to Barcelona—and who would know that you didn't have a license to operate outside of Monagas," Kelley said slowly. "Are you sure you never drove someone to Barcelona—maybe a man and woman back in early July?"

"I do not know what you are talking about, *Señor* Kelley."

"Well then, did you do it and not get paid for it—or were you getting paid some other way, Hermann?"

"I do not understand what you are asking, *Señor* Kelley."

"Well, let me explain it to you, Hermann. Then maybe you will understand."

"*Si, Señor* Kelley, please explain," Hermann said.

"A man named Juan—maybe you know his real name—needed a woman, a prostitute, to go with him to Barcelona. Juan came to you because you are both working for the same people—a Colombian drug cartel."

Hermann straightened in his chair, but said nothing, his lips tightening.

"You took him to Antonio's and got Bettina to go with you. Bettina knew you and trusted you, so she thought everything would be okay. But when she ducked out on you and Juan, Juan knew a loose end had to be taken care of—Bettina couldn't be allowed to talk about what had happened in Barcelona. So, you and Juan either killed Bettina or had someone do it for you. Was it your cousin, Alberto?

"Alberto would not do such a thing—or me. I do not understand why you think I would do such a thing, *Señor* Kelley."

"Let me go on, Hermann, so you get the whole picture. You tried to make it look like an ordinary accident, but Bettina had already talked to her cousin, Emma. She had seen you at Antonio's, and now she knew that you were involved in killing Bettina. That was what made Emma so frightened up on the balcony when we went with Franklin to his apartment—Emma recognized you. I should have realized something was wrong then, but I didn't. When you realized that Emma was going to talk to me at Franklin's apartment, you knew something had to be done. That's why you bugged out, not because of some gun that Franklin was holding on me—you wanted to stall whatever was happening and get someone to kill them both—was it Alberto again? I just made it easier for you by leaving them alone and following you back to the Green Parrot. Would I have been killed, too, if I had stayed at the apartment with Emma and Franklin?"

Hermann's face had turned ashen. "I called *Señor* Luque when you went upstairs to the apartment and told him what was happening. He said I had to get you away from the apartment; if I did not, there would be no other choice but to kill you along with Emma and Franklin. So, when you called me from the apartment balcony, I drove away, hoping you would follow me. I did not want you to be hurt."

Kelley looked at Hermann, not knowing whether to believe him, not knowing whether Hermann had saved his life or not.

"Emma and Franklin were killed by the man you call Juan—his real name is Alexis. He comes from Colombia. Believe me, Alberto and I did not kill anyone—it was always Alexis or someone else that Alexis hired. He did all the killing. I only did what *Señor* Luque told me to do ... and he never told me to kill anyone. He only told me to tell him what you were doing. I called him almost every day and told him what you did. When Emma and her brother left the apartment, it just made things easier for Alexis."

"Where is Alexis, now?" Kelley asked.

Hermann hesitated, then answered, "I am not sure."

Kelley looked intently at Hermann for a long moment, thinking over what Hermann had said, and the way he said it. Then Kelley said, "He's here in Maturin, isn't he, Hermann?"

"I do not know—he could be, but if he is here, I do not know where. Believe me, I do not know."

"Why would he be here?" Kelley said.

"I called him after I learned you would be coming here," Hermann said with tears coming to his eyes. "I did not know what else to do."

"So, you know who I am—who I work for—you knew who Luque worked for, what he did in Caracas?"

Hermann looked at Kelley with confusion. "*Si*. He used his import-export business to cover the shipment of drugs for the cartel. They would be delivered to me. Sometimes I would pick up the package from Escobar's Air Services—"

"So that's why you didn't want to go inside the helicopter offices with me the day after you got put in jail; you knew they would recognize you—and maybe say something they shouldn't," Kelley interrupted.

"*Si*. So, when I picked up the packages—sometimes there was many—I would take them to the boat in La Cruz—to *Señor* Cumaraima or the two men that worked with him—the two brothers,

Victor and Henry. I would give the packages to any one of them."

"So, you knew Cumaraima and both of the Valdes men."

"*Si*, but only a little. *Señor* Luque went with me one time so I would know who they were—after that, I knew who they were, and I would give the packages to whoever was there when I arrived at the boatyard in La Cruz. Then I would leave."

"You didn't know Luque also worked for ... the U.S. DEA?"

"The American DEA!" Hermann asked in shock. "How could he work for them ... and ship drugs from Colombia?"

"Because he tried to burn the candle at both ends ... and got burned. Luque was killed trying to kill me—and Victor Valdes was also killed doing trying to do the same thing."

"Valdes—you know Valdes," Hermann asked.

"Yeah—Victor and his brother Henry too ... and Cumaraima."

Hermann just looked at Kelley, shaking his head in disbelief.

"So, did Luque tell you I was DEA?" Kelley asked.

"Yes, he told me over the phone, the Sunday morning before you met Franklin at the political rally. But he did not say he was working for the American DEA—only that you were. And I guess that means *Señor* Samuelson is also working for the American DEA."

"Sure does," Brad answered.

"And to tie up one other piece of information—you phoned Victor in Texas and gave him the order that he was to kill a man named Carrillo that you had introduced to Cumaraima—that you had vouched for him so Cumaraima would take him on his boat."

"You know about that—about Carrillo?" Hermann said in disbelief.

"I damn sure do. That's why I came to Maturin in the first place—to find out who killed Carrillo."

Hermann's shock was evident. "You did not come because of the drugs?"

"Not really—I knew drugs were involved, but I came because I wanted to find Carrillo's killer. Carrillo was a friend of mine."

Sweat began to bead on Hermann's face. "I did not order Victor to kill Carrillo—I just told him that Luque had said he was to be killed. I just said what Luque told me to say—only what he told me to say."

The beads of sweat rolled off Hermann's chin.

"Well, you got yourself in a real bind now, Hermann—right in the middle of a murder. We can have you sent back to the U.S. where you will be thrown in jail—or worse."

Kelley looked at Hermann and shook his head in resignation. Then he turned to Brad and said, "He's all yours, Brad."

Brad nodded his head. "There is one thing, Hermann," Brad said slowly.

Hermann turned to look at Brad; Hermann's eyes were wide and glazed.

"You and I know you are in a real mess, but maybe there is a way out of this for you."

The look of despair on Hermann's face softened slightly. "What do you mean?"

"Maybe we can work out a deal. You work for us and help us go after Alexis and his bosses, and we don't turn you into the police—so long as you continue to help us," Brad offered.

"Help you—but how?"

"You know Alexis. You help me meet him and get the line of contact between us and Alexis' bosses going again so that we can start dealing with them and eventually get them all in jail. You work for us while pretending to work for Alexis and his Colombian friends."

"That would be very dangerous, *Señor* Brad," Hermann protested. "Can I help you for just a little time? I can tell you what I know, but I know only a little. Then can I quit and work with my cousin in our taxi business?"

Kelley smiled to himself as he realized that Hermann had called Samuelson "*Señor* Brad." Hermann had bought into the offer without even saying so; he was only bargaining now to get the best deal possible.

"No way. You work for us as long as we need you, in the way we want you to. But we would want you to run your taxi business like you say you want to. It will provide cover for you, just like it did when you worked for Luque—and we will protect you from Alexis."

Hermann looked at Kelley, "Is there nothing you can do, *Señor*

Kelley?"

Kelley looked at Hermann, realizing that he probably owed his life to Hermann—but then so did he owe his life to Carrillo.

"Take the deal offered, Hermann—it's only open for now. Close the deal now. It won't be on the table after we walk out of here."

Hermann nodded his bowed head in acceptance.

— ~ —

The sun was bright when the three men exited the dimly lighted *Restaurante de Medina* and stepped onto the cobblestone walkway leading to the street. Hermann's car was parked only a short distance down the street. Kelley squinted against the bright sunlight to see better, as did Hermann. Brad brought his hand to his forehead to shade his eyes.

As his eyes adjusted, Hermann raised his hand to point at a black BMW parked at the curb, its motor running. He yelled, "The car—the car." The yell quickly turned to a scream, "That's him—Alexis, in the—"

Hermann had no time to say more. The grim but smiling face Hermann had seen in the fleeting moment as he had raised his pointing finger was now replaced with the short barrel of a machine gun poking its ugly snout from the rear window of the car. Hermann pushed Brad away and stepped in front of Kelley as a staccato of bullets erupted from the vehicle and sprayed across the walkway area and the men standing there.

The first burst of bullets tore into Hermann's upper torso. One bullet continued its trajectory through Hermann and into Kelley's side. Another hit Herman in the chest and stayed there. The next bullet missed Hermann and found Kelley's thigh. The force of the bullets slammed Hermann's body back into Kelley. Both men fell in a heap, with Hermann's body covering much of Kelley. Blood poured from Hermann's chest onto Kelley. Another burst of fire followed, its bullets pummeling the prostrate Hermann.

The remaining bullets continued their dance across the front of the restaurant, forming a line of pockmarks in the restaurant's stucco walls. The last three rounds found Brad's chest and neck as he was raising his pistol to aim at the car. Brad fell backward, dead before his body touched the now blood-red cobblestones at his feet. The rattle of the machine gun stopped momentarily as its operator assessed its results.

But then the firing began again, continuing for a short but seemingly eternally long moment as bullets now sprayed across the street in front of the restaurant, the face behind the gun wanting to be sure the job was complete. A ricochet tore into Kelley's calf. People on the sidewalk screamed and fell to the ground, shielding their heads with their hands and arms. Two bystanders fell to the ground, not covering their heads because they had no life left to do so.

Kelley pushed Hermann away, rose to his knees, his body weaving on his one sound leg, and pulled his pistol from his holster as the firing stopped and the car began to speed away. Kelley emptied his gun at the fleeing vehicle, but it seemed not to slow at all.

As people began to run away, screaming and shouting, Kelley turned to look first at Brad and the two bystanders. None of the three moved; Kelley instinctively knew they were dead.

Kelly, still on his knees, turned to Hermann. Hermann's shirt was blood-soaked; his chest was pumping up and down as blood spurted from it.

"Hermann, can you hear me? You saved my life again—you know that," Kelley said as tears came to his eyes. Kelley lifted Hermann's head and shoulders and cradled Hermann in his arms.

"*Si* ... *Señor* ... Kelley. Did I ... not ... do ... do ... good?" Hermann asked in a weak voice. Kelley nodded his head. Then Hermann's head slumped. Kelley gently lowered Hermann back to the ground as Kelley's tears fell on Hermann's cheek.

# 47

Admiral Marian, from his office in Langley, and the American ambassador in Caracas listened to Kelley's report on the secure line from the Maturin consulate. "Where is Brad now—where did the police take his body?" the admiral asked.

"We have it—him—at the consulate clinic here in Maturin. He is under the guard of two of our Marines here at the consulate," the American consul answered.

"I will make arrangements for the body to be flown back to the U.S. as soon as possible," the American ambassador added. "I will let you know more details as we get them figured out."

"Good—he will be buried at Arlington. His military service more than qualifies him to be buried there," the admiral said.

"And what about you, Kelley—how bad are you?" the admiral asked

"I took three hits—one in the calf, one in the thigh, and one in my side. But they were not much more than flesh wounds. They are already bandaged up," Kelley responded.

"Is that an accurate assessment, Mr. Counsel?" asked the admiral.

"Well, it's a little more than Kelley has described. The one in the side also fractured a rib. The bullet in the calf has put Kelley on crutches, at least for a while. And, so the doctor tells me, if the bullet in the thigh had been two inches higher and an inch to the left it would have punctured Kelley's aorta artery, and Kelley wouldn't be talking to you now."

"Well, hell, I am here now talking to you now, so it's no big thing. In a month I will be okay—no problems," Kelley interjected. "But there is one thing you need to know, Admiral. I wouldn't be here if it weren't for Hermann—he shielded me from Alexis' bullets."

"Too bad there weren't two of him—maybe Brad might have come out of this, too," the admiral said with a heavy voice.

"You can blame me for some of what happened today. If I had been more alert, maybe nobody would have been shot. If I hadn't been so damn sure of what I was doing, I might have been more careful about what we were doing in talking to Hermann."

"You're wrong about that, Kelley," the admiral quickly said. "We all planned out what we wanted to do—and I was part of that planning. It's those damn cartels—they are the ones to blame for this mess—and, by God, we are not going to let them get away with it. We will have our revenge."

There was a long moment of silence.

Then the admiral spoke again. "What about the political

consequences—what are the police and government saying?"

"The Venezuelan government is in an uproar about this—three Venezuelans killed in what looks to be a drug deal involving two Americans," the ambassador said.

"Well, the damn thing wasn't our fault. It was drug related, all right, but it was that damn Metillo cartel trying to cut their losses by wiping out the last connection to themselves."

"What do you mean ... last connection?" the ambassador asked.

"Hermann, the third Venezuelan—the man we had come to see. He knew some of the people in the cartel and the people working for the cartel. He was our only remaining source who really knew any details," Kelley answered with a disgusted voice.

"So, Mr. Ambassador, what can we do to placate the Venezuelan government?" the admiral asked.

"I have already told the Venezuelan government—I spoke directly to President Chávez's foreign minister—that the American government will provide full monetary restitution to the families of the three Venezuelan people who died—and that's including this Hermann fellow you are speaking about. That will probably come to a pretty tidy sum when all is over and done with."

"Anything else?" the admiral asked.

"Yes. Chávez wants his pound of flesh too. I was told by his office—through an aide of his named Munguia; Chávez will not speak to me directly—that he wants us to tell him what this whole thing is all about."

"What the goddamn hell does that mean—all about?" Kelley retorted.

"Yes, Mr. Ambassador. While Kelley may put it slightly more graphically than I might, I have the same sentiment—what does that mean?" the admiral said, the anger in his voice unmistakable.

"Well, I need to know enough to provide a reasonably believable explanation of why what happened did happen, or at least what we want to say why it happened—enough that Chávez, whatever he really believes or knows, will be able to say over Venezuelan TV that Americans are responsible in some way for what happened, and that they will pay for what happened, and that it will not happen again."

"I think we can manage to do that, Mr. Ambassador. We can tell him just enough to appease him: About how two DEA agents, without, unfortunately, properly informing the Venezuelan government, were working with a brave Venezuelan to expose criminal drug activity in eastern Venezuela; and how they were attacked by the very criminals the agents were attempting to bring to Venezuelan justice," the admiral said. "The agent who was not killed will be properly reprimanded, and be reassigned to the U.S. How does that sound, Mr. Ambassador?"

"I think that sounds like a pretty good start, but I will need more details to embellish it—to give it more substance."

"I will be meeting with the Director in an hour—and we will flesh out the details. We should be able to get everything figured out in a fairly short time and get back to you before the night is out."

"That, Admiral, is exactly what you are going to have to do. I'm scheduled to meet with Chávez tomorrow morning."

"I guess I am the guy who is going to be reprimanded," Kelley said, the sarcasm evident in his voice.

"Yes, Kelley, my boy, you will have to pay the piper, so to speak. You are no longer welcome in Venezuela. I will expect you to get on the next plane out, under diplomatic passport, and get here to Langley as soon as possible."

# 48

Kelley sat beside the admiral across the table from the Director of Central Intelligence, ready to receive his tongue lashing or whatever else the admiral and the director had in mind for him.

"Admiral, you and your people really created quite a stir—a real hornet's nest."

"Yes, sir, but, as I briefed you yesterday, we found out who killed Carrillo, and we think we put a real crimp in the Metillo cartel operations—at least for a while. And, just as important in my mind, we are pretty sure we upset the Chinese government's plan for getting a naval base established in Venezuela."

"I hope you're right. The President understands that someone who happened to see Cui—and knew who he was—began to wonder what was going on—and put the kibosh on the thing. If we stopped a Chinese plan for a Caribbean naval base, all the trouble this whole situation has created has been well worth it. Anything you want to add to that, Mr. Castellano?" the Director said as he looked Kelley in the eye.

Kelley paused. "Not much, other than it really was pure, damn luck."

A slight smile came to the Director's face. "If you say so, Kelley, if you say so. As for our relations with Chávez—they weren't helped much, for sure, but, to tell you the truth, I don't think he is very interested in good relations with the U.S."

"I think you right about that, sir," the admiral said as he nodded his head. "All our analyses point to some tough years ahead in dealing with Chávez, at least as long as he is in power. And from the way he has been taking more and more control of things so far, I think he is going to be in power a long time. And unfortunately, what we will have to say to cover ourselves is going to do nothing but help him further cement his power."

"Yes, Admiral, you're probably right. All the more reason we need somebody that can keep close tabs on him. Are you up to that, Admiral?" the Director asked.

"Well, as you pointed out yesterday, my age is creeping up on me. I really could use some help—from somebody who knows the territory and the way things are down there," the admiral said as he turned to look at Kelley.

"Have you anybody in mind," the Director asked, also turning to pointedly look at Kelley.

"Shit ... now wait a minute. I got out of the Agency once. This last thing in Venezuela was only a temporary assignment—a special deal," Kelley said as he shook his head.

Both men smiled.

# EPILOGUE

Hugo Chávez is reelected president in 2000. Relations with the United States continue to deteriorate, to the point that Chavez blames the United States for an attempted military coup d'état against him in 2002. The attempted coup fails to remove him from office.

A PDVSA management-organized strike also fails to dislodge Chávez from power, as also does a 2004 Venezuela recall referendum.

In August 2005, still-President Chávez charges the U.S. DEA with conducting espionage in Venezuelan and operating outside of Venezuelan law. Venezuela breaks off relations with the DEA.

Chávez wins reelection again in 2006. Despite a certification of the election by the Carter Center and its head, former U.S. President Jimmy Carter, doubts about the validity of the election are widespread.

On September 1, 2008, the *New York Times* reports that the U.S. Ambassador to Venezuela has charged that cocaine smuggling through Venezuela has risen dramatically in recent years, and that drug traffickers are taking advantage of poor relations between the United States and Venezuela to facilitate drug shipments. Chávez threatens to break already-strained diplomatic ties with the U.S.

The Council on Hemispheric Affairs reports on October 23, 2008, that China and Venezuela have signed energy agreements providing for the export of half a million barrels of oil a day from Venezuela to China in 2009. The agreements include construction of a refinery to process crude oil from the oil-rich Orinoco Belt in eastern Venezuela. It becomes increasingly apparent to knowledgeable observers that Chávez, a self-proclaimed Maoist, is using Venezuelan oil to promote a policy of confrontation with the U.S. and strengthen economic ties with China to complement already existing political ties.

Cooperation between China and Venezuela expands in many economic areas—infrastructure, electric power, education, agricultural, rail transportation—not just energy. With expanding Chinese investment in not only Venezuela but also other countries of Latin America, the influence of China in Latin America—not only Venezuela—continues to grow.

And Chávez remains in power and continues to resist efforts to bridle the narcotics trafficking through his country, becoming more and more outspoken and critical of the United States.

Chávez forms oil-driven alliances with other nations, many not considered friends of the United States, including China, Cuba, Iran, and various African countries.

But in June 2011, Chavez is diagnosed with cancer and undergoes several operations in Cuba—none of which are fully successful.

After Chávez's conspiracy-surrounded death in March of 2013, interim-president Nicolás Maduro wins election to the Venezuelan presidency.

By 2015, the policies of Maduro are driving the Venezuelan economy downward in a free fall toward disaster.

# NOVELS BY

# M ALBERT COLLINS

**PRELUDE TO PEARL** (2014) ISBN 9781500627355
A tale about intrigue and murder in the Orient in the decade leading up to the Japanese attack on Pearl Harbor. Naval intelligence officer Francis Marian grapples with a German spy and an ambitious Japanese naval officer to thwart growing Japanese superiority in the Pacific.

**BRAZORIA SUNRISE** (2015) ISBN 9781512009255
Texas sheriff Josh McCall, CIA agent **Kelley Castellano**, and a college professor pursue the murderer of a federal agent in Brazoria County, Texas. Their pursuit uncovers a ruthless international drug smuggling operation spanning from Venezuela to Texas—and even into the White House.

**RACE TO WAR'S END** (2017) ISBN 9781542328142
In the final months of World War II, a US naval intelligence officer surreptitiously enters Manchuria and then Korea to prevent Japan from exploding an atomic bomb on American soil and winning the Pacific War.